CW01666733

The Tapestry of Life

Celine O'Donovan

Celine O'Donovan

Tribes Press

All rights reserved; no part of this publication may be reproduced, stored in a retrieval system, or transmitted in any form or by any means, electronic, mechanical, photocopying, recording, or otherwise, without the prior written permission of the publisher.

This paperback edition first published in Ireland in 2019 by Tribes Press.

Copyright © Celine O'Donovan 2019

Copyright: art © 2018 Béibhínn McCarthy

Cover Design by Béibhínn McCarthy

You must not circulate this book in any other binding or cover and you must impose the same condition on any acquirer. The moral right of the author has been asserted.

All characters in this publication are fictitious and any resemblance to real persons, living or dead, is purely coincidental.

Tribes Press policy is to use papers that are sustainably sourced from manufacturers with EU Ecolabel certification and FSC® and PEFC™ chain of custody certification.

ISBN 978-1-9124411-13-6

www.tribespress.com

To Mum and Dad,

For being there every step of the way

ONE

"Abbie, rise and shine!" shouted Frank Hughes, Abbie's Dad.

He was full of his usual bon viveur, even at this hour of the morning. Abbie rubbed her sleep-filled eyes and squinted to make out the time on her bedside clock before three loud knocks sounded on the bedroom wall.

"*Alright, Dad!* I'm coming," Abbie shouted.

Abbie loved school, but this was a cruel way of marking its return. She sensed the house waking up and shuddering like its inhabitants. Doors banged, showers ran, and she heard some racket coming from the kitchen at this ungodly hour of the morning.

"It's only half seven!" Abbie cried out, knowing nobody was listening.

It was a big day today, starting secondary school. It was the beginning of a whole new phase of her life and it had the potential to be the most amazing day ever or the worst. She lazily stretched in the bed and threw back the blankets.

"Are ya *up* yet?" Frank shouted.

"I heard you *the first time,* Dad, and *yes I'm up!*"

Satisfied she was making a move, Frank went back to the en-suite to shave.

"Oh, what a beautiful *morning...*" he sang, as off key as ever. Frank turned to admire himself in the bathroom mirror, running his fingers through his thick, black hair.

"Not bad for an auld fella pushing sixty," Frank said, as he lightly ran his hand over the dark shadow on his jaw and smiled. Frank hitched up his trousers, tucking in the greying vest that had seen better days and pulled his belt in tight over his sagging belly. "Time to sort you out once and for all, my Amigo."

Just then, Frank's wife, Joan, stuck her head in the door.

"Come on, Frank, please. I'm making a special breakfast for their first day back," Joan said.

"Alright, love, I'm on my way," Frank said, affectionately. He watched Joan pick up one of his wayward socks from the bedroom floor and then leave. "*Jaysus*, if *that* woman doesn't go easy on the cookin', I'll be the size of a house."

Frank had recognised the slight agitation in Joan's voice as the routine of a new year started all over again. He shook his head, walked across the bedroom floor to the wardrobe and pulled out one of his many stripy shirts. As he buttoned it up, Frank took an admiring glance in the bedroom mirror. However, his expression changed to a frown at the sound of the neighbour's crazy spaniel howling his head off in their front garden. This was a customary habit every morning as the giddy canine waited for his walk. Frank flicked back the net curtains to see Toby, the little terrier almost having a conniption.

"*Bloody* mad dog. I'll give him something to howl about if he doesn't shut up," Frank said and flicked the curtain back to its original position. He turned his attention back to inside the house. "From the sounds of it, he's not the only mad one around here. The water of that shower must be running for a half an hour," he said, now becoming agitated by every single sound he heard. Frank opened the bedroom door and let out a roar.

"*Cyril, go easy will ya?* And *make sure* you turn off the immersion when you're finished!" Frank shouted.

Cyril, however, took little heed to his Dad's words and was instead lost in his own world, enjoying the tingling feel of hot water on his body. Cyril was the eldest child. He was at least six foot tall and 'a string of misery', his teacher Mr O'Shea liked to joke. It was so far from the truth, Cyril thought it very funny.

Contrary to Mr O'Shea's views, Cyril had a very easy disposition with a ready smile. As he washed the shampoo out of his blonde floppy hair, Cyril was deep in thought. This was his final year of school and a year of exams and expectations, not that there were very high expectations for him. Cyril wasn't the academic type and couldn't wait to be free of the constraints of school and books.

Cyril reached for the soap and it catapulted out of his hands.

"Damn it!" Cyril shouted, watching the soap sloshing around in the pool of water that had gathered at his feet.

With one easy movement, his long arms reached down, grabbed a firm hold and resumed his scrubbing. Inspecting his calloused hands that were still deeply engrained with car engine oil, he smiled at the visible signs of his hard work.

What a summer it has been, he thought. Two months working with his father's friend, Bill, as a mechanic's assistant. Heaven. Cyril was more of a hands-on type of guy, and he liked the physicality of moving and doing. Sitting still, reading a book was his idea of hell. Stick him under the bonnet of a car or in a shed full of tools and he was at his best.

"Oh Danny boy, the pipes, the pipes are calling…" Frank sang.

"*Dad*, a towel!" Cyril shouted from the bathroom.

"*God almighty,* I can't get *a minute's peace* around here," Frank snapped.

Frank banged the bottle of aftershave down on the dressing table and went out to the landing.

"*Dad*, did you hear me? *A towel.*"

"Hold your horses. I've only one set of hands."

Frank opened the hot press, pulling out a towel from under the messy pile of clothes. He stuck his head in the bathroom door.

"*Get a move on*, Cyril," Frank said. "Johnny will be looking for the shower next and you know what he's like first thing in the morning."

"Dad, I'm not bloody deaf, you know!" Johnny shouted out from his room next door to the bathroom.

Johnny was the middle child and looked nothing like Cyril. He was stocky, red-haired and had a rosy complexion to match.

"Name *one person* who wouldn't be pissed off living in a madhouse like this," Johnny muttered under his breath.

Johnny flung back the duvet and slowly sat up in the bed, rubbing his hands through his tousled thick hair. He surveyed the room, where clothes of all description were strewn on the floor. Lazily stretching over the side of the bed, Johnny found the remnants of his late night snack and took a bite out of it.

"Not bad," he said, devouring the remains of the stale cheese sandwich.

Sitting back against the headboard, Johnny wondered how he had ended up with a mother he could never figure out and a father who was on cloud nine most of the time.

Down in the kitchen, Joan Hughes put the final touches to a breakfast that was fit for a king. It was a rare occurrence, but today was a special occasion. Grapefruit, porridge, a full Irish fry-up and a pot of tea. Joan knew she had forgotten something. She stood back from the table, pushed her blonde, wispy curls back from her small, heart-shaped face, which was now red from all her efforts and thought.

"Oh, the milk and the sugar," Joan said, and rushed to the fridge to fill up the empty jug.

It wouldn't do to have the carton on the table. She also resurrected the sugar bowl from the back of the press. It hadn't seen the light of day all summer. Joan had given up correcting them all as they had shovelled directly from the bag. It was her mother's sugar bowl, a dainty decorative ornament that brought a tear to her eye as she filled it up.

"That's more like it," Joan said. Joan then shoved all the place settings closer together on the cramped table and accidentally sent the cutlery flying. "*Damn it*, get it together, Joan! And where did I put those napkins?" she asked.

Joan made a beeline for the press, and as she bent down to retrieve the napkins, the door burst open. Frank barged in, knocking her sideways.

"*For God's sake*, Frank!" she shouted. Joan's nerves were now in tatters.

"Ah Joan, *relax*," Frank said in a tone that wouldn't make anyone feel at ease.

Frank picked Joan up off the floor and gave her a peck on the cheek. "Sit down there and take it easy," he said, helping Joan to the chair. "Are we expecting the queen for breakfast?" he laughed, glancing at the table that looked more suited to Christmas Day dinner than breakfast on the run. Joan jumped out of the chair.

"Enough of that, Frank. I've too much to do. This kitchen really isn't good enough. *You can't swing a cat in here. I told you* we needed an extension."

"Darling, it was always going to be the kitchen or an en-suite. I didn't win the lotto you know."

It was true she had been torn between the two, but the idea of an en-suite had won the day as Joan had imagined herself impressing the neighbours with tales of his and hers sinks and a Swedish style walk-in shower. It hadn't exactly materialised like that and she now regretted her decision.

"Oh, I know, but they've all become so big. Two adults and three growing ones just don't fit anymore."

"Well I'm afraid there's not much more we can do about it unless you want me to take a hammer to that *wall* again," Frank said, exasperated.

They had bought an old council house on the edge of town when they were first married and the cosy little two-up two-down had made a comfortable home for them as newlyweds. They loved every inch of it and had wonderful neighbours whose families went back generations. Although Joan was a blow-in from Cork, Frank was a born and bred Galwegian, and a native of the area, so they had felt at home straight away. Frank had always called the neighbours 'salt of the earth types'.

As the years passed, the family expanded, tempers frayed, and it wasn't long before the house bulged at the seams. With each new child, Frank took on a new building project with the help of a few friends. It started with a playroom for the children at the back of the house, a bedroom eventually on top of it for Abbie, and then a porch at the front that now housed everything from bikes and shoes to coats and toys. The en-suite was a bonus that Joan had begged for and Frank couldn't resist a little shed for himself in the garden. Only for his redundancy money, they couldn't have afforded it all. After spending thirty years working in a local factory, it had been a big shock when they suddenly closed their doors three years ago. However, the blow had been eased by a generous severance payment.

"Every cloud, love, I'm telling you," Frank kept reminding Joan, who just raised her eyes to heaven.

Now in a world of open plan living, their home was almost claustrophobic in its layout. Despite everything, however, Joan was secretly delighted with how it had all turned out. But she would never admit that to Frank.

"They'll be late for school. Will you go hurry them up?" Joan asked. She nervously eyed the clock on the wall. Frank grabbed a sausage and taking a mouthful he walked to the bottom of the stairs. "*Get a move on,* guys. Breakfast now, I mean it."

Frank proudly walked back into the kitchen having fulfilled his role as head of the house.

"Now love, they're on their way," he said, and sat down.

"Frank, there's no need *to shout* at them. You're not setting a very good example, you know," Joan said, and busily filled his plate and then poured him a cup of tea. Frank looked at her and raised his eyes to heaven.

"Well, I'd like to see another way of getting them down here. If that was my father, they'd have a clip around the ear and more by now," he grumbled through a mouthful of food.

"Frank, *please* don't say that… I don't want the children hearing things like that. You're nothing like him Frank, thank God," Joan whispered.

Joan then turned and vigorously stirred the porridge, putting all thoughts of Frank's father out of her mind.

Upstairs, Cyril passed by Abbie's door and then checked himself in the landing mirror. He slicked back his hair and straightened the hated tie on his school uniform.

"One more year to go, and then I'm rid of this shirt and tie for good," Cyril remarked.

Never had a pair of overalls seemed so appealing as today.

"Will you get a move on before *Mam gets herself in a heap?*" Cyril asked, pounding on Abbie's door on his way downstairs.

"Okay, *I'm coming,*" Abbie insisted.

Abbie took her new uniform out of the wardrobe and paused to look at it. This is it. A whole new life. She prayed that she would be in the same class as her friends from primary school. It hadn't occurred to her until now that they might be split up, and that was more than she could contemplate. Abbie walked over to the sink and splashed cold water on her face, washing away the residue of sleep. Glancing at the mirror, Abbie frowned.

"Why couldn't I have blonde hair like Mam or Cyril? I look like a *monkey*," Abbie chastised.

Despite her parents telling her that she had inherited the best of both of them, Abbie couldn't see it. Thick dark curls fell to her shoulders and a light smattering of freckles ran across her face. Otherwise, Abbie's complexion was clear and in stark contrast to the deep-set olive green eyes that stared back at her disapprovingly. Abbie quickly pulled on her dressing gown and clattered downstairs to join the others.

Cyril was the first one to make his way down to the kitchen to his Dad's delight, but finding it hard to resist having another look in the mirror downstairs, Abbie wasn't long catching up with him. On seeing Abbie, Cyril moved on quickly.

"An early bird like myself, son, that's what you are," Frank said proudly, when Cyril entered the kitchen.

"Aw, there you are, finally," Joan said, on seeing Abbie rush in behind Cyril. "Now sit down and I'll get you some porridge first." Joan filled the bowl until it was precariously close to spilling over.

"Mam, I'll never eat *all that*," Abbie argued.

"You're in secondary school now. You'll need your energy for that long day. And Cyril, you'll have another sausage," Joan insisted.

Joan topped up Cyril's plate, which he had already cleared in a matter of minutes, and placed another plate of toast on the table.

"Eat up now, Abbie. Is it too hot for you?" Joan asked.

"Mam, *I'm not a baby*," Abbie snapped.

"I'm *only* trying to help, love," Joan said, disappointed.

"Joan, *will you sit down for God's sake* and have something *to eat. We're all fine*," Frank snapped, and clumsily placed his cup down on the saucer.

"*Okay, okay!*" Joan said, and sat down.

Joan nervously nibbled on a slice of toast, but couldn't help herself and had to scan the table to see if anything was missing.

"I'm telling you in my day…" Frank started.

They all raised their eyes to heaven, not remotely interested in hearing for the umpteenth time what it had been like in his day.

"As I said, in my day..." Frank said, sensing their discontent. "In my day, we had to fend for ourselves. I was out working at Johnny's age, you know," he said, and puffed out his chest proudly. "Look how well I turned out. Hard work never harmed anyone. We all have to find our own way in the world, you know?"

Abbie giggled as Cyril made a 'not again' face at her across the table.

Slowly slurping on each spoonful of porridge, Abbie looked around the table. Her Dad was still expounding. Cyril hardly came up for air as he cleared his plate. She squinted her eyes at him enviously. She couldn't figure out how he could eat all round him and still resemble a famine victim. He was definitely model material when you added in his gorgeous blonde hair and blue eyes.

"Now, where is Johnny?" Joan asked.

"Relax, love. You know what he's like in the mornings," Frank said to Joan, and then winked at Abbie.

"What he's like, full stop," Abbie said, under her breath.

A pain in the arse as her friend Saoirse would say. He was definitely that. Johnny only grunted at her at the best of times. In Abbie's eyes, Johnny always received special treatment while she and Cyril had to play by the rules. She was sick of tiptoeing around him and his moods. Life wasn't a bed of roses for her either.

Abbie had been so excited about school when she woke up, but now she felt sick with anxiety. Abbie didn't know what was happening to her. It didn't feel like she had any control over her emotions anymore.

"Eat up, Abbie. You'll fade away if you don't eat something."

"I'm *eating it,* Mam," Abbie snapped, gulping down a large spoonful to get her mother off her back.

"I just don't want you going hungry on your first day back at school," Joan said, "and less of the attitude, please."

"She doesn't look like she'll starve just yet," Frank said, and grinned over at Abbie.

Joan jerked her head up and shot Frank a dirty look across the table.

"It's gorgeous, Mam, but you'd feed an army with all this food.

There are *children starving* all over the world, you know," Cyril said as he suctioned down another sausage.

Abbie glanced over at her brother and believed that he must have some sort of tape worm.

"Well, that's not *my fault*," Joan said, defensively. "I just wanted you all to have a nice breakfast on your first day back," she said, frustrated with their lack of appreciation.

Joan stood up and furiously started stirring the porridge again.

"It's a mighty breakfast, Joan, isn't it, guys?" Frank said, and he gave Cyril a pleading look.

"It's the best, Mam. Just look at my plate," Cyril said, and held out the spotless plate and stood up to give her a hug.

Cyril regretted his earlier words. As he put his arms around Joan, they awkwardly collided. The saucepan did a sort of slow motion somersault out of Joan's hands and landed on Frank's lap. "*Jesus Christ!*" shouted Frank.

He leapt out of the chair as lumps of congealed porridge flew around the room, landing mainly on the crotch of his trousers.

"Oh, I'm so sorry Frank," Joan cried. "I ruin everything. I just wanted everything to be perfect today."

Frank's face burned red as a tomato as he jigged about the kitchen. Abbie resisted the urge to burst out laughing at the sight of him and clamped her hand over her mouth.

"No permanent damage there I hope," Frank said.

Frank looked down, grinning through gritted teeth as he disappeared like a scalded cat up the stairs. He collided with Johnny on the way down.

"What the hell's going on? I thought the house was burning down. Man, ye're unbelievable," Johnny said.

"Quit it Johnny, and out of my way. The house may not have burnt down but I'm at risk of being permanently maimed if I don't get *these trousers off*."

Frank shoved Johnny aside and made a beeline for his bedroom. Johnny paused on the stairs and suddenly heard his mother's cries from the kitchen.

"Feck's sake," Johnny said, and decided to retreat to his room until the drama had died down.

Downstairs, Joan was inconsolable as she looked at the mess on the floor.

"*Everything's ruined,*" she sobbed.

"Come on, Mam," Cyril said. "Just sit down for a few minutes. You've done enough already."

Cyril steered his mother towards the living room. Abbie, spotting her moment, abandoned her unfinished breakfast and escaped upstairs to change.

Joan sat on the couch with tears streaming down her face.

"Oh Cyril, I made such a mess of things. I can't seem to do anything right."

"Mam, it was just an accident. Relax, I'll clean it up," Cyril said, trying to pacify her.

"*Will you?* You're a star, Cyril, what would I do without you?"

Joan lay back on the couch. As she closed her eyes she was assaulted by memories of her past disasters. There was the time she forgot to pick up Cyril from school when he was six. Joan hardly had the energy to get out of bed most days back then. Then there was the time she set a chip pan on fire and was mortified when the fire brigade arrived after a passing neighbour heard her screams. A particular embarrassment was the fiasco of a ruined Christmas dinner because she forgot to put the oven on after one too many glasses of wine. The list went on and on.

"*Stop!*" Joan said, aloud, frustrated with the negative train of thoughts.

Joan glanced at the fireplace and her attention stopped at the framed black and white photo of herself and Frank on their honeymoon in London. The picture had been taken beside Big Ben and they were both grinning like Cheshire cats, a reflection of their state of newly wedded bliss.

"Those were the days," Joan said, saddened that they were never to return.

Everything had changed the day she met Frank. He had been besotted with her from day one and called her his porcelain doll. He had been a light when there was none in her life.

Joan stood up and walked over to take a closer look at the photo. She hardly recognised the happy-go-lucky girl. Joan looked as if she hadn't a care in the world. Her blonde hair curled beautifully around her face and her slim figure was emphasised by a wide belt that showed off her waist. They had their arms wound tightly around each other as they posed for the camera. A slimmer, tanned Frank looked back at her and it struck her that apart from his colouring, Cyril was the spitting image of his father, and not just in looks. He had definitely inherited his easy-going personality and that was something to be grateful for. It all seemed like a lifetime ago now, as she put the photo back in its place and sat down again. It was hard to believe that her adventurous spirit had often been too much for Frank. At times he had tried to rein her in. God help him, he had no idea what lay ahead back then. If he had, he might have done a runner.

"Here Mam, I just made a fresh cup," Cyril said, and left the mug down on the table beside her.

"Oh, you're a darling, Cyril. Thank you. I'll be out in a minute." Joan smiled, gratefully.

"There's no rush. It's all under control," Cyril said in a soft voice and then left the room.

Joan took a sip of her tea and inhaled deeply as she tried to remember one of her mantras.

"I am calm, centred and strong. I am calm, centred and strong," she said, closing her eyes and planting her feet firmly on the floor.

"Man, what the hell happened here?" Johnny asked.

Johnny rolled his eyes when he found Cyril bent over a pool of porridge, half-eaten rashers and sausages on the floor.

"Nothing," Cyril said.

"*Jesus.* Never a dull moment *in this place*," Johnny remarked.

He grabbed a couple of sausages, wrapped them in a slice of toast and wolfed them down.

"You could give me a hand rather than *stuffing your face!*" Cyril snapped, but was sorry when the words were out of his mouth.

He knew that food was a touchy subject with Johnny, but then again most subjects were these days.

"*Get lost.* I'm just having breakfast," Johnny retorted and poured himself a mug of tea. "You have to admit she's a bit of a head case. Where is she?" he asked.

"Keep it *down. She's in there,*" Cyril said, pointing to the living room. He quickly closed the kitchen door.

"Madhouse. You know, I think I must've been adopted. *Seriously man*, I'm nothing like either of them, I mean, *look* at me..." Johnny said, and pointed at himself as if it was fairly self-evident.

Cyril laughed. To be fair, Johnny didn't resemble anyone in the family and the postman jokes had done the rounds for years.

"Well maybe we could give you back then and get a refund," Cyril said, and gave him a playful punch on the shoulder.

"You're hilarious. You should be on the stage bro."

Johnny couldn't help smile at his brother. Cyril was one of the few people who could always get a smile out of him.

Upstairs, Abbie awkwardly pulled on her new uniform. She was relieved to have escaped eating the humongous breakfast Joan had prepared. She inspected herself closely in the mirror.

"Ugh, it's awful," Abbie said, turning sideways.

The pleated skirt was stiff and the material bunched strangely around her waist, giving her an almost apple like shape.

"Best to get it nice and roomy. It'll do you for the five years," Abbie said, mocking her Mam. "Yeah, but I'll look like a clown for the first four, Mam," Abbie argued.

Despite the skirt being taken up and in, it still managed to do three hundred and sixty degree rotations with the slightest movement.

"Get a move on, Abbie. I want to get a look at you all grown up," Frank shouted, and banged on her door as he made his way downstairs again. "Christ what a way to start the week," he muttered. Frank just hoped he hadn't done any permanent damage to the crown jewels.

"*I'm coming,*" Abbie called.

Abbie turned to take a final look in the mirror. With a final disapproving look at her reflection, she headed for the door. In an effort not to leave her father waiting, she confidently tried to take two steps at a time down the stairs. As her limbs were longer and harder to control after a growth spurt over the summer, Abbie stumbled, went over on her left ankle and landed awkwardly at the bottom of the stairs, hearing a crack. The pain was excruciating, and Abbie passed out.

"Jesus, Mary and Joseph. Jesus, Mary and Joseph!" Joan cried out.

Abbie came to and saw three worried faces looking down at her. "Oh, thank God you're alive," Joan said, relieved.

"Don't move a jot, Abbie. We don't know what the damage is," Frank said, and he scratched his head struggling to remember his first-aid training.

"Look at her ankle, *it's swelling up*!" Cyril remarked and pointed at the injured ankle.

"My poor Abbie," Joan sobbed.

"Take it easy, love," Frank said. "You're not helping things with the waterworks."

Frank gently pulled Joan to one side.

"Okay, Cyril, call an ambulance, will you?" Frank instructed. "I need to check her out."

"Dad it hurts," Abbie whimpered.

"It's okay, love. We'll have you right as rain in no time," Joan said.

"Joan, can you keep it down. I *can't think straight* with all the racket," Frank said.

"Well, she can talk and seems alert," Cyril said. He moved out to the porch to hear the 999 operator.

"*Give it* to me here, Cyril. I'll know what they're talking about," Frank said, warming to his role as paramedic. Frank believed that it was thanks to the man above that he had attended the first-aid course at work.

"Yes, sir. Looks like it might be broken alright," Frank said, turning to take a look at Abbie's ankle.

"Broken!" Joan remarked and was now inconsolable.

"Come on, Mam, sit down. Dad knows what he's doing," Cyril said, although he doubted that, but nonetheless, Cyril gently directed Joan back to the couch.

"Grand, yes, that's mighty. We'll see you then," Frank said. He put the phone down and gave Abbie a thumbs up. "All sorted, love. They're on their way. Now, where did Johnny go?"

Johnny was finishing the leftovers in the kitchen and jumped when he heard his name mentioned. Banging his cup on the table, he walked out to the hall.

"What's going on? Ow, that looks sore, sis," he said, hanging over the banister.

"*Out of the way* if that's all you've to say," Frank said, sharply.

"Fine by me. I was only saying. Bloody *Daddy's girl,*" Johnny muttered under his breath and marched off.

Seeing the ambulance reverse into the driveway, Frank grabbed hold of the banister and hoisted himself up.

"God dammit. Another shirt shrunk in the wash," he said, feeling the squeeze. Frank looked down at the moment a button popped on his shirt.

"Hi, I'm Ron. Where's the patient?" the burly, paramedic asked. He smiled as he hopped out of the ambulance and came into the house.

"Right in here, sir. Abbie's at the bottom of the stairs," Frank said, and then proceeded to give him a military style update on her condition.

"Aren't you the lucky girl that your Dad is a whizz at the first aid?" Ron asked. He smiled at Abbie and took her hand.

"Hello love, I'm Karen. How are you feeling?" the second paramedic asked.

Abbie heard a woman's voice and looked up to see a pretty blonde woman smiling kindly at her.

"We'll get you on the stretcher now and give you something for that pain," Ron added. "Please guys. I need you to move back a bit while we get her on the stretcher," Ron said, and waved Frank and Cyril out of the way while he and Karen manoeuvred awkwardly in the hall.

In a matter of minutes, Abbie was in the ambulance and they were ready to go.

"What's happening, Frank?" Joan asked, appearing at the front door, distraught.

"I'm going to the hospital with them. I'll buzz you later, love," Frank said. Frank gave Joan a quick peck on the cheek and rushed out to the ambulance. Frank then beckoned to Cyril.

"Stay here and keep an eye on things, will you?" he said in a low voice.

"Sure, Dad," Cyril said, and he re-joined Joan at the door.

"Oh what a morning it has been, Cyril…" Joan said.

Joan shook her head in disbelief as she watched the ambulance drive away. It wasn't even ten o'clock.

Johnny moved the dial on the radio but couldn't settle on anything worth listening to. First, chipper Ryan Tubridy full of the joys of life. It was enough to make him want to puke. He twiddled the knob, but the other stations weren't much better. Switching it off altogether, he lay back in the car seat and closed his eyes.

One thing Johnny was sure of was that life had rapidly gone downhill after Abbie was born. He was only three years old, but he was sure that he could remember the day they brought her home from hospital. From that day onward, the sting of rejection had grown. Johnny had to get out of the house. All that bloody drama over Abbie.

It had been a different story when he had broken his arm at her age. All he had heard was a lecture from his parents. He had jumped off the roof of the shed and it had hurt like hell, but it was his friend Jack who had dared him. He remembered Jack saying that it was worth ten quid to him, if he had the balls. Jack had even waved the note in front of his face.

"Bloody right I have the balls. A piece of cake," Johnny had said, folding his arms.

Feeling pretty cocky he had jumped without looking, missed the grass by inches and landed awkwardly on the concrete. He could still remember the loud crack as he hit the path, but it had been worth it just to see Jack's impressed face.

"*Fuck it,*" Johnny said.

Seeing the ambulance pull out of the driveway, he slipped out of the car, quietly let himself into the house and climbed the stairs to the safety of his bedroom.

TWO

They were met by a stifling wall of heat on entering the A&E department. As the automatic doors slid open, the acrid smell of disinfectant combined with stale sweat was overpowering, and Frank did his best not to gag.

"Christ almighty, this place is like a war zone," Frank said, shocked by his surroundings. "Hold your horses, Ron," Frank said, and pulled out a hanky, rubbing the beads of sweat from his face as he struggled to keep up with the trolley as it hurtled along. "You're busy in here today from the looks of it," he said to a nurse rushing past. "Jaysus, is this what our country has come to? Not even time for hello," Frank said.

They passed the waiting area that bulged to capacity. Every seat in the place was taken and the overflow had taken to sitting on the ground or supported themselves by leaning up against any available wall space. Frank was struck by the demeanour of the people, despair being the common expression on all their faces.

"Wherever the spoils of the Celtic Tiger had landed, it certainly wasn't in this hospital… it's more likely lining the pockets of corrupt bankers and builders," Frank muttered.

"*Dad,* where *are* you?" Abbie cried out.

Abbie's black curls bounced up and down on the trolley as she craned her neck to locate Frank.

"I'm right behind you," Frank said, but his words were lost in the sea of voices that surrounded them.

Frank did his best to catch up as the trolley continued through a set of double doors and into another waiting area, which was nearly worse. Not only were people penned in like cattle in a truck, but the noise was deafening, as patients writhed in pain and nurses called for assistance.

"We'll park you here for now," said Ron as he negotiated the trolley into a tight space beside the toilets. "There'll be someone down to see you shortly, Abbie."

"Thanks for your help," Frank said, hurrying.

"Oh, there you are, Frank. I thought we'd lost you. We'd better go. No rest for the wicked, as they say," Ron said.

"No, I'm right behind you," Frank gasped, leaning up against the wall.

Frank couldn't help but notice trollies lining every available wall space and patients of all description lying on them. Frank jumped when he felt someone grab his arm.

"You'll be lucky to make it out of here alive… I'm telling you. I've been here for a week," a patient said.

Frank turned around and made eye contact with a man who looked like he had come out the wrong end of a brawl and smelt like a brewery. Frank thought that he couldn't have been more than thirty years old. Despite the cuts and bruises, his body was definitely not that of an old man. Nevertheless, his face bore the tell-tale signs of someone who had experienced many horrors.

"How are you, sir? Are you alright there?" Frank asked.

"Well now, I'd hardly be here if I was alright now, would I? No offence, mister, but it's not exactly the Ritz, is it?" he said, and he let out a hollow laugh.

"I suppose you're right. I haven't been here in a long time myself, thanks be to God," Frank said.

"Mr Hughes?" a young female administrator called, standing over Abbie with a clipboard in hand. The name badge on her navy uniform said 'Joy', but Frank strongly suspected that she was definitely not, Joy by name, Joy by nature. She looked like she would rather stick pins in her eyes than deal with the unruly rabble that surrounded her.

"Yes?"

"Best of luck, sir," Frank said, and nodded goodbye to the young man.

"It's Paddy."

"Well, I hope you are out of here soon, Paddy," Frank said.

"I don't. At least I have a bed in here," Paddy cackled loudly.

"Mr Hughes," the administrator said, insistently. "I just want to confirm some details with you. This is your daughter, isn't it?"

"Yes, yes, is someone going to take a look at her?"

"We'll do that shortly. As I said, I just need to run through a few details with you first."

Frank proceeded to rhyme off the events of the morning. As he came to the end of all the questioning, he had a sinking feeling that they wouldn't be leaving anytime soon if Paddy was anything to go by.

"Now, Mr Hughes, as you can see, we're particularly busy in here today, but we'll look after… Abbie as soon as possible," Joy, the administrator said. She then turned and tightly smiled at Abbie, who in turn, nodded and attempted a smile though she felt more like crying. "We'll X-ray you as soon as possible," Joy said. She then tottered off in her high heels, leaving Frank and Abbie behind.

"She should be on the stage with that performance, love, shouldn't she? We didn't come down in the last shower," Frank said.

"Dad, I don't like it here. It smells, and there are so many people," Abbie cried.

Her dark hair was now matted with perspiration, and her eyes wide with fear as she took in the heart-breaking scenes of distress around her. Frank stroked her hair in an attempt to soothe Abbie, but the sight of his little girl in such pain only caused him to fall into his own grief, and soon his eyes began to well up with tears.

"Now, now, didn't the girl say you'll be having an X-ray soon, so that's a good sign, isn't it? We'll be out of here in no time."

Frank didn't like lying to her. He had given sermons around the kitchen table on this very topic, while Joan had quietly tut-tutted her disapproval.

Frank always insisted that there were to be no lies no matter what, and that the children could always tell him the truth and he in turn would do the same. Today, however, would have to be an exception to that rule. It was his baby girl after all, and Frank would do anything for her.

Frank leaned up against the wall, in anticipation of a long wait for an X-ray and his thoughts went to home.

****

The shrill sound of the doorbell echoed through the house.

"Oh, who could that be, Cyril?" Joan cried, pulling her dressing gown tightly around her as she sat at the kitchen table. Joan had planted herself there after the ambulance had left for the hospital, and she had been unable to move since then. Cyril sat opposite her, reluctant to leave her on her own.

"Can you answer it, please? I don't want anyone to see me like this," Joan said looking down in disapproval.

"Hello, Joan, Frank, is everything okay?" A high-pitched voice travelled down the hall and Joan sat bolt upright with fright.

"Who's that? Cyril, will you go out and check?" Joan jumped up and pushed Cyril into the hall, shutting the kitchen door behind him. Cyril almost collided with their nosy neighbour from two doors down, Bridie Lynch, who barrelled towards him down the hall.

"Oh Cyril, I saw an ambulance outside earlier on and I just wanted to check that everything is okay. The door was open, so I hope you don't mind that I let myself in. Did something happen?" she rattled, hardly pausing for breath.

Bridie Lynch was known to be a solid neighbour, once you could look past her brash exterior and judgemental attitude. Yet most locals gave her a wide berth, as her solidity didn't compensate for the amount of gossip she loved to spread.

"Hello, Mrs Lynch," Cyril said blocking her access down the hall.

"My God, it put the heart crossways in me. I'd have called earlier only I was up with May Flaherty," Bridie explained, referring to her new job as a carer. It was the perfect occupation for her inquisitive nature, giving her ample, juicy material to propagate.

"What happened?" Bridie said, itching to move past monosyllabic Cyril.

"There's nothing to worry about," Cyril said slowly and calmly.

"Is Frank sick?" Bridie asked, close to pushing him out of the way, so that she could gain entry to the kitchen, where she suspected she might have more luck with information.

"No, it's Abbie. She had a fall on the stairs this morning. She might have broken her ankle," Cyril explained.

"Oh, the poor love," Bridie sympathised.

"Dad went with her to the hospital. You know what it's like up there. It could be a long time before we hear anything."

"Oh, don't I know it. Is Joan here? Is she in the kitchen? Can I've a word, you know, woman to woman?" Bridie asked, determined to find out the real lay of the land.

"She is, but…" Cyril said, but he didn't have time to finish. Bridie finally pushed past him and walked straight into the kitchen, where Joan cowered in her seat, hoping not to be discovered. "Joan, oh my God. That's awful news. Cyril was just telling me," Bridie said, looking Joan up and down. The sight of Joan sitting in her dressing gown in the middle of the day wasn't lost on Bridie. She quickly closed the kitchen door behind her, leaving Cyril out in the cold.

"Hello Bridie," Joan said, feeling sick to the pit of her stomach at being caught half-undressed.

"It must have been an awful shock, you know, to have you still in your dressing gown at this hour?" Bridie said with blatant sarcasm.

"It was *actually*. You have no idea. She just tripped and fell down the stairs…" Joan said and shook herself. She was determined not to fall apart in front of nosy Bridie who had no problem spreading a story the length of the county in record time.

"That's terrible, Joan. And how did she manage that?" Bridie asked. "I don't know, Bridie. I was downstairs, you know, preparing breakfast for them all, when it happened," Joan said pointedly. However, Bridie wasn't having any of it. She pulled up a chair and settled in, determined to uncover any salacious detail that she could find. Joan sighed and rhymed off the events of the morning as clearly as she could remember, taking care to keep her raw emotions under check. When she had finished, she prayed that Cyril would march into the kitchen and save her from any further interrogation. It wasn't like him to leave her alone when she was upset. Joan didn't think she could take much more of Bridie Lynch.

"You can never be too careful. That's for sure, isn't it, Joan? Especially where children are concerned," Bridie interrupted Joan's thoughts with a bang.

"Yes, of course. Frank was fantastic though… you know…" Joan said. She knew she was on the verge of breaking down after such a callous encounter with Bridie and she looked at the door, willing Cyril to open it.

"Cyril, is that you?" Joan said to the closed door.

"Cyril, Cyril, are you there?" Joan cried out.

"Are you okay, Joan?" Bridie asked.

"Cyril," Joan shouted repeatedly.

"Oh, my dear, you don't seem well at all. Do you need a doctor? I'd no idea things were so bad, no idea at all," Bridie said, and Cyril opened the door just in time to hear her harsh words and to see his Mam's distressed expression.

"Mrs Lynch, I think it's best if you go now. We've a lot on today but thank you for calling."

"Oh, is it lunch time already?" Bridie said, looking at her watch. I'd better go myself. I've dinners to make and work to do. You'd think I should be finished for the day at this stage, after the busy morning I've had, but that's the way it goes for us working women. I mean, I know you wouldn't really know about that Joan…" Bridie said snidely. Cyril practically grabbed her by the elbow and escorted her out of the room.

"Give my best to Abbie, Joan. Let me know if I can do anything to help…" Bridie called out as Cyril dispatched her on the doorstep and slammed the door behind her. He went back into the kitchen to find Joan in tears again.

"Oh, I'm sorry, Mam. I tried to call the hospital but no luck, and Dad's not answering his mobile," Cyril explained.

"How could you leave me with her? She's awful, so she is," Joan sobbed.

"I really am sorry, Mam, don't mind her. She's a small-minded busybody and you shouldn't be giving her the time of day."

"I didn't really have any choice, did I? And to top it off, she saw me in my dressing gown. How mortifying!"

****

"Dad…" Abbie called, tugging on his shirt sleeves. "Dad…"

"Sorry, love, I was miles away," Frank said bringing his attention back to Abbie. His back ached from standing. What he wouldn't give for the little fold up chair from the garden shed. It was now almost two o'clock and there was no sign of an X-ray happening any time soon.

"I'm going to lose me marbles altogether if we're left here any longer," Frank muttered. He looked up and down the hallway, shaking his head.

"Dad, *that woman* keeps looking at me funny," Abbie whispered.

Frank followed Abbie's eyes to an older lady, who stood further down the corridor. She was laden down with bags and wearing what looked like forty coats.

"God help her. She probably has nowhere else to go," Frank said.

The woman waved over as Frank nodded at her. Taking his acknowledgement as an invitation, she started to shuffle towards them. Frank noticed how she stopped to check in with the patients as if she had some pastoral role in the place. As she approached them, Frank took in her brown beady eyes that told him she was no fool. Despite the warts and lines that marred her features and the pungent odour that was overpowering in such confined quarters, it was hard not to warm to her. Frank imagined that if life had gone differently for her, who knows, she could just as easily have ended up working in this hospital. He felt a shiver up his spine. It was a fine line for sure.

"Aren't you a beauty?" she cackled. Abbie recoiled as she stopped beside them, and her wizened hand stretched out to stroke her hair.

"You're a great woman all the same, looking out for everyone," Frank said in an attempt to deflect.

"What happened to you, love?" the woman asked.

Abbie was speechless and wrinkled up her nose. She was so close to her she could hardly breathe.

"She'd a bit of an accident this morning. Supposed to be starting secondary school and all today. Isn't that right Abbie? It must be four hours and Jaysus, not even an X-ray yet," Frank complained.

"You haven't seen the half of it," the woman said, leaning in close and whispering in Frank's ear. "I'm here all the time and it's only worse by the day. I do my bit, but I tell you, I'd shoot myself before I'd end up on one of those trollies. I'm Maura by the way."

A matronly looking woman interrupted their tête-à-tête.

"Excuse me, Mr Hughes, is it? I'm Fiona from Radiology. We're ready to X-ray Abbie. Sorry for the delay. I don't know what's going on *at all* today."

"Don't mind her. It's the same every day. *Mark my words, mark my words...*"

Maura then turned and moved on to the next patient, but not before she blew a kiss back at Abbie.

"Sorry about that interruption." Fiona said, looking dismissively after the elderly woman.

"It's okay," Frank said. He looked back at Maura, feeling a bit unsettled by the encounter.

"You'll have to wait outside during the X-ray Mr Hughes, but it won't take long. We'll take good care of you, Abbie."

"I'll be back in a few minutes, love. I've a few calls to make, but I won't be long. I'll just stretch me legs outside," Frank said.

Frank squeezed Abbie's hand knowing that they had another long wait ahead. Strolling out through the main doors, he took one look at the huddle of smokers in their dressing gowns, sucking on their cigarettes like they were the essence of life itself, and kept going. "Madhouse," he muttered.

Finding a quiet bench, he pulled out his phone and called the office.

"Liam. Sorry about not coming in today… Did you get my message? Well she's just having an X-ray… Sound, I'll do that. Righto. Appreciate it."

Hanging up, Frank counted his blessings that the boss was a decent man. It was only a few years ago that he thought he was washed up when the factory shut down. After sitting around the house for almost a year, he was saved by Liam Murray who owned the local builders providers. Over a few pints down the local, Liam was almost spitting nails as he bemoaned some of his young employees who wouldn't know a hard day's work if it bit them in the face.

"I'm telling you Frank, they hardly know how to chat to the customers, standing there looking as if they're bored out of their brains or staring at their phones. Business is hard enough these days without that carry on," Frank recalled Liam saying. "You and I are from the old stock, you know, customer is king, service is everything. I'm sick to the teeth of it. Give me a good solid man like yourself any day."

And so, Frank found himself employed by Liam Murray, in a supervisory role on the shop floor, much to the frustration of his younger colleagues. Yet, it wasn't long before customers and staff alike couldn't resist Frank's upbeat, jovial manner. A stroke of luck, he reminded himself and he wasn't going to mess it up. It didn't matter the request; he listened earnestly and did his best to have every customer leave the store satisfied. Luckily, Liam appreciated the regular repeat custom that Frank attracted, and gave Frank a pay rise fairly quickly.

"You and I are grafters, Frank, and like my old man before me, I appreciate a grafter," Frank recalled Liam saying.

Just as well, as going to college hadn't been on the cards for Frank. Whatever it took, he was staying in Liam Murray's good books. This was the first day he had missed since he started, but Liam was a family man like himself and family always came first.

"*Christ!*" Frank grimaced as he stood up, rubbed his back and walked back to find Abbie.

"Mr Hughes?" Fiona called, waiting for him with a disapproving look on her face as she stood next to Abbie.

In an instant, Frank was transported back to the bitch of a teacher who had made his life hell for years.

"Sorry, I had to make a work call," he said. Embarrassed, Frank turned away from her stern gaze.

Abbie smiled up at him from her trolley. What a trooper she was.

"We were wondering where you were. I'm afraid it's a break and the doctor has just taken a look at her. She'll be in a cast for a good few weeks. We're taking her to orthopaedics now. Are you coming with us?" Fiona asked.

"Of course I'm coming. *What else* would I be doing?" Frank asked.

"Dad, a cast, *can you believe it?*" Abbie remarked. Her eyes were shining. Frank could have sworn he heard the snooty Fiona mutter something about him, obviously having more important things to attend to. "The nerve," he whispered.

Frank felt a rush of blood to his face as Fiona turned her back on him and he obediently followed the trolley again as it weaved its way through the crowds. His phone buzzed in his pocket as they waited for the lift, and Frank fumbled in his pocket to answer it.

"God almighty," he muttered as the phone was tangled in his bundle of keys. Frank yanked on the phone and it shot out of his pocket, across the corridor and on to the floor before he had time to answer it. The lift doors opened just as Frank bent down to pick it up. As he turned to join Fiona and Abbie, who were waiting in the lift for him, he could have sworn that he saw Fiona roll her eyes.

"Is your phone okay, Dad?" Abbie asked.

"I'm sure it is love. Don't worry. I've it all under control," Frank said as he looked down at the cracked screen and then at Fiona, who seemed to smirk.

Frank clenched his fists as the doors closed. The familiar image of his old teacher sneering at him filled the lift.

****

Cyril hung up the phone and turned to Joan who still sat at the kitchen table in her dressing gown. Nervously fidgeting after her encounter with Bridie Lynch, she proceeded to make ribbons out of the beautifully laid napkins that had long been forgotten since breakfast.

"No answer again. It just went to message. I'll send him a text. You know what it's like up there, Mam. Ben Tracey was on a trolley for twenty-four hours after he broke his shoulder playing football..." Cyril said.

"*Stop it,* Cyril. I don't want to be hearing things like that," Joan insisted and put her hands over her ears.

"I just mean there's probably no news yet. It's still only two o'clock. That's like ten minutes in *that place*. Maybe I should go up there myself and check. What do you think?" Cyril asked.

Joan, however, didn't respond, but instead resumed her origami efforts until the table looked like it had been hit by a snowstorm.

"Leave it, Mam. Dad's with her. She'll be fine. Why don't you go and lie down?" Cyril pleaded.

"That's what I'm worried about. I should have gone with them in the first place. Poor Abbie. She must be terrified. Your father is great and all, but at times like this a girl needs her mother," Joan said.

Cyril thought that no girl needed a mother in this state but resisted saying that to his mother.

"I've a good mind to call the Joe Duffy show. What do you think? Things won't improve in this country unless we speak up," Joan said.

Joan turned on the radio as Cyril groaned.

"Joe Duffy is a moaner and so is everyone who calls in. What do you listen to that drivel for, Mam? It'll only bring you down."

"He's only trying to help. You're at school, Cyril. You don't hear half of what goes on these days. It's a disgrace, really it is. Oh, I don't know what to do. It's awful sitting here not knowing," Joan cried.

Cyril shoved a mug of tea in front of his Mam and distracted himself by making a stack of ham sandwiches. He knew there was no point arguing with her when she was like this.

"You know, I think I will lie down for a bit. Will you call me the minute you hear anything? I'll cook a nice dinner later as they're bound to be starving when they arrive home," Joan said.

Joan picked up her mug of tea and walked out of the kitchen. With the coast clear, Cyril reached across the table and turned off the radio.

At the top of the stairs Joan paused outside Johnny's room. She could feel the throbbing music reverberate through every cell of her body and was close to knocking on the door to tell him to turn it down but changed her mind. Walking to her own bedroom, she closed the door behind her in an attempt to block out the pounding sound. She put her mug on the locker beside her, lay back and closed her eyes.

Sleep had no intention of paying her a visit, however. Joan's racing thoughts were enough to scare off the hardiest of opponents. She ricocheted between plans of being the Florence Nightingale of nurses to Abbie to darker worries, and her body sagged with exhaustion as it chemically experienced every possibility without moving an inch.

Tossing and turning she knew it was no use. The sleeping tablets were in the en-suite, but she loathed to take one. Battling with Dr Kearney again, she had eventually given in and come home with enough tranquillisers to kill a horse. He had always insisted that they were to be taken only when things were too much for Joan, and Joan herself saw them as a standby. After all, he didn't recommend them every night, but exhaustion only made everything seem worse.

Joan remembered eventually caving in and fidgeting with her handbag as he had written out the prescription. She knew that old Dr Burke would never have prescribed them. He always took his time with Joan, even when babies were screaming to be seen in the waiting room. All she knew was that she always left feeling like she wasn't alone. Well, that time was gone.

Kicking off the bed covers, she slowly padded to the bathroom. With a cursory glance at her drawn face in the mirror, she dismissed her guilt and throwing caution to the wind, swallowed two. Now, please do your magic she begged.

Johnny heard her stop outside his door and flinched. Turning down the volume, he listened and heard the bedroom door click shut. He took a quick look at his phone.

"Lunchtime, finally," he said, as the loud rumblings from his stomach took over. Grabbing a sweatshirt from the musty pile on the floor, he sniffed it, retched and quickly pulled it on. He opened the door and glanced towards his parent's bedroom. Hearing soft rumbling snores, Johnny knew the coast was clear and went downstairs to the kitchen. His eyes lit up at the plate of sandwiches that would feed an army.

"Where were you?" Cyril asked, appearing at the door just as Johnny took a bite.

"*Give it a rest.* It looked like you and Dad had everything under control," Johnny said, and swallowed a mouthful.

"You *could've gone* to school, you know. Dad will *go mad* if he finds out."

"Why didn't you go in yourself then?" Johnny retorted.

"Dad asked me to stay home. Anyways, school is wasted on me. I'm no good at it. In any case, if I had brains to burn like you, I'd have my head in the books all the time. You can do anything you want Johnny, *seriously.*"

Johnny couldn't resist grinning at Cyril's words. He knew Cyril didn't have a jealous bone in his body.

"I heard her snoring upstairs you know. Some good she'll be when they come home," Johnny said.

"God almighty, Johnny. What did she ever do to you?" Cyril said perplexed.

"Just *forget it.* I'm going out for a while. Thanks for the sandwiches."

Johnny brushed past Cyril as he walked out to the hall and grabbed his coat. "You just don't understand. Nobody does," Johnny retorted.

Johnny banged the front door behind him. Pulling up his hood he turned right and took off in the direction of the local park to meet his friends. He dropped his head and followed the trail of hardened gum on the path that he knew by heart. Hearing a beep from his pocket he checked his phone. *Pick up some rollies,* Jack's text read.

"*Fuck's sake,*" Johnny said, and texted back.

Johnny weaved his way through the zigzag rows of colourful council houses that dotted his neighbourhood. He just turned the bend towards the coast road, when he heard his name being called.

"Hi there, Johnny," Joe Ward shouted, looking up from weeding his picture-perfect flower beds. Joe was a regular winner in the Tidy Towns Garden competition for his pristine garden, and neighbours had long given up hope of ever knocking him off his perch.

"Hi, Mr Ward," Johnny said, smiling. Johnny liked Joe Ward. He was a friend of his Dad's and had been the one to spot Johnny's potential for the boxing club. Joe had encouraged Johnny's Dad to let him join the local club. At the same time, it had been Joe who had recommended that Johnny take a break from the club when he had been caught using his fists outside of the ring once too often.

"And what are you up to these days, son?" Joe said.

"Not much, Mr Ward," Johnny answered.

"I hope you're making your parents proud, like a good fella," Joe said.

"Mmm," Johnny mumbled, looking at his feet.

"We might see you back in the club sometime? You were a real talent, you know. All you need is a bit of self-restraint. Isn't that right?" Joe hinted at Johnny. He could still see the fire that burnt brightly in Johnny's eyes.

"Yeah, I gotta go now, Mr Ward," Johnny laughed and walked away.

"Take it easy now, Johnny," Joe Ward called after him. Joe Ward had met a lot of young lads like Johnny in his lifetime. They were full of unbridled potential and just needed a bit of direction in life. Unfortunately, many of them were never given that direction. Instead they ended up on the dole and in the pub, or on the plane and out of the country, never to return.

Johnny walked the length of the coast road towards their local park, lost in thought about the great times he had had in the boxing club. They had only been cut short because he had knocked out one of the lads after a practise session, but in Johnny's eyes the guy had it coming to him.

Within fifteen minutes, Johnny had stopped off at the newsagents to pick up the Rizlas and he then joined his friends. They had constructed a makeshift living room behind a disused shed in the park and it was well away from the prying eyes of parents and the authorities. They had gradually furnished it with an eclectic mix of tyres, an old couch they found dumped in a skip, and pallets that fell off the back of a passing truck served as a table.

"Feckin' hell, about time. We're gasping here," Jack, his best friend said.

Jack had a shock of dark, thick hair that fell over his eyes, a strong nose that was too big for his face and jet blue eyes that were set closely together. He dressed flamboyantly, even adding a handkerchief to his school blazer or a scarf around his neck. Johnny thought that he had the look of a young debonair Oscar Wilde. Jack should have been an easy target for bullying, but everyone was intrigued by him and liked his easy charm.

"This is my last time. One of you *morons* better cough up the next time," Johnny replied.

Their gang of four had been formed a long time ago and their shared bond had become tighter, as they each in their own way rejected the system that was thrust upon them. It had become an almost daily habit to congregate after school and share a few joints. There wasn't much you couldn't solve under the influence of a bit of weed, they all agreed.

"You've more feckin' money than the lot of us put together, Jack!" Johnny argued, and threw the Rizla papers at Jack.

"You mean *my father* has more money than the lot of us put together. That wouldn't be hard," Jack remarked.

Jack laughed and then looked around to make sure the coast was clear. His long fingers went to work as they all hungrily watched his every move. Inhaling deeply, he lay back on the grass.

"Mother, that's good," Jack said and sighed.

"Give us a pull," Johnny said, and reached over and snatched the joint out of Jack's hand and sat down beside him.

"So, what happened to you today?" Liam O'Grady asked.

"You're one to talk. When was the last time you did a week straight?" Johnny shot back at him.

Liam was a puny looking teenager drowning in chains and leather. He turned to Johnny and grinned.

"Well, do you want to hear a good one?" Johnny asked.

He leaned forward on the couch, inviting them all to come closer and relished the thought of telling them every detail of his mostly concocted story. He got great mileage out of his mother's life.

"The mother had a bad start this morning again," Johnny began. They all laughed as they heard the familiar start to all of his stories. "It started with her dumping a bowl of porridge on top of Dad. Jesus, if you could've seen his face. I'd say his balls are like shrivelled walnuts by now," Johnny said, flicking the ashes off his spliff. "Then the frying pan went on fire and set her *totally doolally*. She was like *a mad one* running around screaming at the top of her lungs. I'm telling you, the neighbours must think we're total nutters."

Johnny felt himself reach a crescendo as he told them of the ambulance arriving, Abbie being whisked off to the hospital and his mother downing a load of tablets and taking to the bed.

"*Jesus* that's not funny. *How's Abbie?*" Jack asked. He looked at Johnny a bit strangely, causing him to squirm in his seat.

"Aw, she'll be grand. I'd say it's just a sprain. She's not home from hospital yet. You know what it's like up there."

They all went quiet as the joint was passed between them.

"Well, sounds like your mother could do with chilling out a bit," Fergus O'Reilly said, changing the subject.

Fergus was definitely the smartest of the lot of them. He was a year younger but had been moved ahead a class in second year. After years of being considered disruptive, it was eventually discovered he was bored. No one really knew what to do with him as he knew more than the teachers and pupils put together. He didn't know what to do with himself either.

"Does she smoke? You could tell her it's for medicinal purposes," Liam piped up.

"You know, it'll probably be legalised in the next few years. I guarantee you it would solve a lot of problems. Better than popping pills every day and buying into that lie. No one ever questions the motives of the big pharma or their fat profits. It's a total con job," Jack said.

Jack's voice was laced with cynicism. He came from a high achieving family and his father was a hospital consultant. Yet if there was one thing he was sure of in his short life so far, it was that he had no interest in following the pack.

"Don't start, Jack, for fuck's sake, I'm just in the zone…" Liam said, and slumped in one of the tyres.

Jack stood up. He walked up and down addressing his speech to the trees. Johnny laughed at the sight of his friend expounding, his shoulder length dark hair dancing with his every word. Jack flicked back his scarf and turned to them.

"You do know it's all a con job, don't you?" Jack's nostrils flared.

"*Chrissakes,* Jack, *what is?*" Fergus moaned.

"Everything. Did you hear that idiot Brown today? What a feckin' waste of space for a teacher. CAO points are all he talks about, and money. It'd wreck your head. And they wonder why the suicide rate is so high? Oh, that's right. Give them a few pills and they'll be grand. Does he think we're total eejits? The system is fucked and they're too blind to see it," Jack said.

None of them said a word, they just nodded. Jack knew what he was talking about. His older brother Paul had suffered a nervous breakdown only a year ago. According to Jack, Paul had played by the rules, worked his ass off in college and took up a high-powered banking job in London. Well now, ten years later he was back living at home and was just a shell of a person. He was only thirty-two years old.

****

Joan woke with a start. The phone rang downstairs. She strained to make out Cyril's voice, but it sounded miles away, like she was in a tunnel. Glancing at the clock, the bright red numerals stared back at her, as if to reprimand her for her slovenly behaviour, 18:00 hours.

"Oh God no, *it can't be.* I only lay down for half an hour," she moaned.

Drenched in sweat, she loosened her dressing gown, inhaling deeply. She looked over at Frank's side of the bed and saw his pyjamas neatly folded on top of the pillow. She felt her stomach lurch. As usual, Frank was the one to hold it all together, while she escaped to bed.

"Mam?" the voice sounded, as if it was in the room. "Mam, they'll be home in a couple of hours."

Joan could have sworn she called out, but there was no sound. Maybe I'm still dreaming she thought. Then she heard a knock on the door.

"Mam, *did you hear me?*" Cyril asked. Joan pinched herself hard and winced.

"Yes…" Joan said. She knew her voice sounded strange, as if she was drunk. "Come in. I must have fallen asleep," Joan said. Cyril stuck his head around the door.

"Sorry. I didn't mean to wake you. I just wanted to let you know…" Cyril said in a low voice.

"Good news and bad news?" Joan asked and tried to focus, but even with rubbing her eyes she saw two of him. Joan sat up in the bed.

"Take it easy. Abbie's fine, but her ankle is broken. Dad sounded totally fed up. He said it's like a zoo up there. Anyways, they'll be home in a couple of hours, that's the good news," Cyril said. "Oh thank god. I'll be down in a minute and I'll cook some dinner."

Joan went to stand, wobbled and sat back down on the edge of the bed. Cyril knew well the tell-tale signs and his heart went out to her. Opening his mouth to speak, he closed it again. He wanted to shout at her to stop going to that bloody doctor who just kept prescribing tablets. They hadn't helped her one iota from what he could see.

"I just need a minute, that's all," Joan said.

"Are you *okay?* There's no rush, they won't be home for ages," Cyril advised.

"I just need to have a shower, freshen up, I'll be fine. I'll make spaghetti, what do you think? Abbie likes spaghetti," Joan said.

"She'll love that, Mam."

Cyril kissed Joan on the cheek and quickly left the room. He hated seeing her like this.

Left alone with her thoughts, Joan moaned softly as the usual wave of guilt engulfed her after she took to her bed. It was a keen reminder of the weeks and months after Johnny's birth. It had been all she could do to make it out of bed or struggle downstairs in her dressing gown back then. The darkness of her depression had been so intense she couldn't verbalise it, not even to Frank. On top of that, Johnny didn't seem to sleep at all and was always crying.

Joan shivered. She would never forget that day as long as she lived. Frank had left her for half an hour to go to the supermarket and he arrived home to find Cyril crawling around on the landing, perilously close to the top of the stairs, and Johnny screaming to be fed in his cot. He had shaken her furiously as she lay almost comatose on the bed. Even when he had shouted at Joan, she had felt nothing, absolutely nothing. Who could ever understand that?

Joan remembered Deirdre, her counsellor saying to her, that it was likely that all the grief she had buried at the time of her mother's death surfaced and that it was too much for her at that point. She remembered her commenting that she was a child herself when her mother died. Deirdre told her that she had spent all her time trying to hold it together in an attempt to be the perfect wife and mother, but that it had all become too much. When she left the counsellor's office, her last words were 'you can't bury it forever' and those words seemed to have stayed with her despite numerous attempts to block them out along with all her grief. Joan knew that Deirdre was right. Still, she couldn't risk losing her family again. She just couldn't. No matter what it took, she had to keep it together.

Frank had been shaken by what he had witnessed, and he did his best to support her. If it hadn't been for his sister, Mona, who uprooted herself from her family in Dublin, they would never have managed with two children under the age of three. With their help Joan managed to keep going, but only just.

Joan dragged herself into the bathroom and ran the shower. Turning to look at her reflection, she frowned. Her face was puffy and red, the remnants of tears and sleep firmly etched on it. She leaned closer to inspect what looked to be a new collection of lines around her eyes. As she stepped into the shower, the hot jet of water pounded her body. A pleasant, but slightly torturous experience, Joan struggled to catch her breath as the water rained down on her. Turning it to cold was like an electric shock but it helped kick-start her. She hopped out of the shower and grabbed a towel, reassuring herself that she would be back to herself by the time they arrived home. Joan was very tempted to jump into her pyjamas again, but instead she put on a pair of navy slacks and a cream round-necked sweater, as she tried to look more together than she felt. She then pulled a comb through her hair. When Joan trudged downstairs and pushed open the kitchen door, she couldn't help smiling at the sight of the contents of the fridge on the countertop and Cyril staring at them with bemusement.

"I'll do that, love," Joan said, and nudged Cyril out of the way. Cyril sighed with relief.

"Are you sure?" Cyril asked.

"I'm fine. Will you go up to the shop and buy some garlic bread? Oh, and ice cream. Will you see if they have strawberry? It's Abbie's favourite."

Joan didn't recognise her own voice, but she was relieved that the gnawing anxiety in her chest had given way to a floaty feeling. This made it very hard to give the tablets up. Joan was, however, determined to tackle the subject again with Dr Kearney at her next appointment. Only last week she had mentioned taking mindfulness classes to him, but she could have sworn he threw his eyes up to heaven.

"I'm fine, Cyril, really I am," Joan said, staggering slightly.

Joan pulled on her apron and set to work.

THREE

By eight o'clock, dinner bubbled on the cooker, the fire was lit, and the TV played softly in the background. There was little sign of the drama that had unfolded earlier in the day. The front door opened, and Abbie limped in while holding onto Frank.

"Mam, *look at me.* I have a cast," Abbie called excitedly as she hobbled down the hall.

Joan opened the kitchen door and put her hand to her mouth. Abbie almost crashed to the floor in front of her as she tried to give a demonstration of her prowess on the crutches.

"Oh Abbie. Go easy or you'll hurt yourself," Joan said. She wiped her hands gingerly on her apron and opened her arms to embrace her daughter. "You've no idea how much I missed you. Cyril will tell you," Joan cried, and her voice quivered.

"*Jaysus*, it's good to be home. You've no idea, Joan, *I'm telling ya*, you've no idea," Frank said, and he followed them into the kitchen.

"Dad, it wasn't *that bad*… it was actually kind of fun," Abbie said, her eyes bright.

"*Not that bad?* You *have to be kiddin' me.* Don't get me started," Frank said, while ransacking the kitchen presses for a quick snack.

"Anyways, the main thing is our Abbie's going to be okay, but she's to keep that leg up for a few weeks…" he said, delighting in finding the peanut butter, "like a queen bee, isn't that right, Abbie?"

"Aw, you poor thing, let me see you, are you okay, love?" Joan asked and stroked Abbie's hair. "I've made spaghetti," Joan added, and kissed the top of Abbie's head.

Joan helped Abbie to negotiate the short distance to the kitchen table and helped her onto the chair. Joan reached down and lifted her leg onto a nearby chair and satisfied that she had done a mother's duty to perfection, Joan sat down herself.

"Cyril's gone to get ice cream," Joan said, rubbing Abbie's hand. "I was *so* worried about you all day, love."

Frank raised an eyebrow and awkwardly placed his slices of bread, peanut butter, plate and knife down on the table.

"Were you now?" Frank asked, and sank into a chair, rubbing his back. Joan glared at him, recognising the sarcasm in his voice.

"And *what* do you mean *by that? Of course*, I was worried..." Joan snapped.

"*Relax*, will you. It's been a long day. I think all we've had to eat is one of those bloody cardboard sandwiches. You wouldn't be long going from a visitor to a patient in that place, it's a madhouse," Frank complained.

"It can't be *that bad,* surely. I've heard the staff are great. Everyone says that... there was a woman on Joe Duffy the other day and she couldn't sing their praises enough..."

Joan neglected to say that the poor woman would have sung the praises of anyone who rescued her from a trolley after two days. "Aw, would you don't mind Joe Duffy. I'm sure he's never had to sit in A&E for a minute. *I'm tellin' you*, Joan, we saw it with our own eyes today," Frank said, and looked to Abbie for backup, but she had lost interest in the conversation.

Instead, Abbie busily manoeuvred her crutches, so she could escape to the living room. Joan felt tears sting the back of her eyes and filling a cold glass of water from the tap, she gulped it down quickly.

"Aw, don't get all upset now, Joan. You had to be there, *seriously*..." Frank implored.

"I'm not upset *for God's sake*, but you know you exaggerate sometimes," Joan said without turning around.

"*Exaggerate?* Well, the next time there's an emergency we'll let you see what it's like..."

"That's an awful thing to say. I just mean it's not easy when you're the one at home worrying either..." Joan said.

"Well, there is such a thing as a phone, *my dear*," Frank argued.

Cyril burst in the door before she had time to respond. "Well, *finally*, we thought you'd left the country, Dad. Where's the patient?" Cyril asked.

"Inside," Frank remarked.

Cyril sensed he had interrupted something and went to look for Abbie in the living room.

"Joan, *look*, we're all tired and I'm telling you, I have to have a shower and get rid of this smell," Frank said. He took a whiff of his shirt and stood up. "*Christ almighty. That's savage*, so it is… Come on give me a hug will you…" he said, and came up behind Joan, wrapped his arms around her waist and softly serenaded her.

"I've got you under my skin, I've got you deep in the heart of me…"

"You're something else Frank, you really are…" Joan tut-tutted, but she was glad to feel his arms around her.

A little later, they all sat down in the living room. Over dinner, Frank told them about the trollies, the drunks, and the waiting and waiting. He could always tell a story, and now that he was showered and eating, he was only raring to go.

"No, Joan, no more. I'm stuffed to the gills," Frank said, waving her away as she heaped more spaghetti onto his plate. He belched loudly, licked his lips and lay back on the living room couch. Abbie giggled beside him.

"Dad, you know, it's like… bad manners."

"No flies on you, eh?" Frank commented, and playfully nudged her. "Speakin' of manners, where's himself? I swear to God, there's always something," Frank said.

"What are you *looking at me for? I'm not* Johnny's keeper, but a wild guess, he's with Jack," Cyril said.

"They're some pair, those two," Frank said, and glanced at his watch. "For Chrissakes, *it's nine o'clock!* It's *not a hotel* we're running here…"

"Some hotel if you are…" Johnny said, and stuck his head in the door.

"*What time do you call this?*"

"Time for dinner, Dad, if you left any," Johnny said. "How did the trip to the maternity ward go?"

Johnny glanced at Frank, who now rubbed his tummy.

"What the… *watch it, Johnny*. This is the first decent bit of food I've eaten all day."

Frank felt the sting of Johnny's words. He wasn't going to succumb to the perils of the health care system like his father, Ted. He had gone into hospital for a fairly straightforward operation on his bowel five years before, contracted sepsis and left in a coffin. No, Frank was not going to meet his end like that. Luckily, vanity mostly kept his appetite in check and garnered him plenty of admiring glances from his female customers.

"Sit down, love. I've kept you a plate in the oven. I won't be a minute," Joan said.

Joan hopped up only too glad of the opportunity to stretch her legs and shake off the fog that began to descend again. Out in the kitchen, she splashed cold water on her face and gripped the edge of the sink. It started to dawn slowly on her. Abbie would be at home for the next few weeks and she only started a part-time job a couple of months ago on the urgings of old Dr Burke before he retired. He had told her that it was not good for anyone's mental health to be just sitting around all day and that it would do Joan the world of good to get out and meet new people. Joan remembered his words well. Frank had organised the part-time job with Peter, the head librarian who was an old friend from school. It was just a few hours a week in the local library, but it had been a stretch too far for her at times.

"Any chance of that dinner?" Johnny asked, standing next to her.

Joan turned and instinctively went to push the hair out of Johnny's eyes with her hand but held back when she saw him flinch. "I hope it's not all dried up," Johnny said and pretended to retch. "Well, you should have come home earlier. You know what your father is like when you're late," Joan said and then sniffed the air. "What's that awful stench, Johnny? It smells like a bonfire."

"Ya, Mam, it's a bonfire. There was a bonfire in the park," Johnny said, and turned and walked out of the kitchen throwing his eyes up to heaven.

Joan's shoulders sagged. Only the other night Frank had said it was a miracle that the Gardaí hadn't rolled up to the house with Johnny in tow. Although she argued with Frank then, she had now realised that he might be right. Joan had a sneaking feeling that Johnny dabbled in something illegal, but she couldn't bring herself to think about it.

"Now, this is more like it, a proper family meal together," Frank said, looking around the room.

From the expression on everyone else's face, it was clear they weren't sharing in his enthusiasm at being corralled into such close quarters. Frank and Joan were squashed on either side of Abbie on the red couch that had seen better days, and Cyril struggled to get comfortable in the armchair that was a hand-me-down from Frank's mother.

"Sit down there, Johnny, would you. You look like you're about to make a run for it," Frank said, and waved him into the chair. Johnny grunted and banged his plate down on the coffee table and grabbed a cushion to sit on.

"Now isn't this nice? All the experts are sayin' it you know…"

"Saying what Frank?" Joan asked, taking a gulp out of her tea.

She had decided against the camomile tonight in case Frank would be carrying her up the stairs as well as Abbie.

"You know, that it's all gone a bit mad with all the phones and stuff… nobody's talkin' anymore. That's the problem with the world these days. In my day, we always sat down and talked," Frank said.

Both Cyril and Johnny rolled their eyes.

"Here we go again," Cyril muttered under his breath and Johnny burst out laughing.

"What are you laughin' at? Traipsing in the door *at all hours* and not *a civil word in your head! Look at your mother slavin' away* over the dinner and not a word of thanks out of ya! *Jaysus*, where did I go wrong?"

"Aw, leave him be Frank," Joan said. She was not in the mood for another argument.

"Well, if we're in the sharing mode… Bill wants to take me on as an apprentice mechanic after I finish school," Cyril interrupted as he sprawled in front of the fireplace.

He had slightly twisted Bill's words, but he knew the offer was there. He had said that if things didn't work out in school that there was always a job for him at the garage, so it was the same thing. After all, Bill insisted that Cyril was a natural.

"*That's mighty*, Cyril. Isn't it, Joan?"

It was no secret that Cyril struggled with the books and a mechanic was a solid, respectable profession in Frank's eyes. There was always someone with a car that needed fixing.

"Of course, it is. Do you have to go to college for that? It's important to have a good education behind you in life. Isn't that what they're saying all the time on the radio?" Joan said.

"Mam. *Stop with the radio*, would you. You don't go to college to become a mechanic. Some good that would do you when some fella calls you and his car has broken down on the side of the road," Cyril said, frustrated.

"You could wave your piece of paper at him. I'd say that'd go down well," Johnny snorted and shovelled down another meatball.

"Look, it's better than that. I'll get work experience with Bill and I can make good money eventually. And the bonus is… it won't cost you anything."

Cyril did a silent drum roll.

"Exactly, that's what I like to hear, son. Are you hearing that, Johnny? We're not made of money you know."

"Fine by me, it's all a con job anyways. The whole bloody lot of it, you must see that!" Johnny said, and they all looked at Johnny confused.

"What's a con job?" Frank asked and sat forward.

"Oh no, don't get him started, Dad? Bloody everything's a con job according to him," Cyril said, and yawned.

"Exactement. The system is broken, and nobody gives a damn," Johnny said, paraphrasing Jack's speech in the park. His words were still ringing in Johnny's ears. The joint was wearing off now and there was a fire in Johnny's belly.

"Well, if you're talking about the healthcare system, you've a good point there, son. *Don't get me started*. It was *an almighty disgrace* up there today. The staff weren't the worst, well most of them, but they're just fightin' fire, that's all. Something's not right. That's for sure," Frank said and sat back on the couch.

"That's only the half of it," Johnny said and proceeded to tell them the sorry story of Jack's brother Matt, who was washed up before he'd lived at all, burnt out to a crisp. "He's like a vegetable, I'm telling you."

"*A vegetable?* That's an awful thing to say, Johnny. The poor boy," Joan said.

"Well, there's no point pretending. He just lies in bed all day and last week Jack found him wandering in the park in his bare feet."

"And what's wrong with *that?* He might just have wanted a bit of fresh air," Frank said.

"Aw, for feck's sake," Johnny groaned.

"Well, then maybe he should be in hospital if that's the case," Joan said, despondently.

"*What am I after just tellin' ye*? He'd be for the *birds altogether* if he ended up there!" Frank retorted and then ran his hands through his hair in frustration.

"I'm just saying, people can bury their heads in the sand all they like, but it's all breaking down. We're fucked basically," Johnny said. "God, did none of them see what was right in front of their eyes. They were all brainwashed."

"Language, Johnny," Frank said, but he couldn't help feeling pretty impressed by his young, rebellious son.

"You might be on to somethin' there alright, but sure what can we do. I try to do my bit at work and if my customers leave with a smile on their face, it's better than a kick up the arse. Isn't that right, Abbie?" Frank asked.

Frank looked down at Abbie, who struggled to keep her eyes open.

"Bring her up Frank, will you? The poor thing's exhausted. She's out for the count. We all are. It's been a day and a half, so it has," Joan said.

"In a minute, she's as grand there as in her bed. There's something I wanted to say, and I want to say it while we're all here." Frank cleared his throat.

"I was thinkin' about it today, you know, in the hospital," Frank said.

"What is it Frank?" Joan asked.

"I think we need a housekeeper," Frank said, firmly.

"A housekeeper?" Joan flinched.

"You know, what do they call them these days, au pairs is it?" Frank asked.

"What are you talking about?" Joan asked, shocked that her mothering and household skills were being brought into question.

"A young Spaniard is it, Dad? You're a dark horse all the same," Johnny said and grinned.

"I just mean, with Abbie laid up and you at the library Joan, we need some help. Only for a few weeks mind, until she's back on her feet," Frank insisted.

"*An au pair though?* I don't want someone living with us and taking over my kitchen."

What Joan really meant was that she no more wanted a young, pretty Spanish girl swanning around the house half-naked and batting her eyelids at Frank than a hole in the head. She had heard all about them. Marriages in tatters, husband shacked up in a flat with his floozy. No, she wasn't having that.

"No, no, there'd be no need for them to be livin' with us. I've just the right person in mind and if ye all agree, I'll ask her tomorrow," Frank said, feeling pleased with himself. "There isn't a drop of Spanish blood in her I'm fairly sure, not that there's anythin' wrong with the Spaniards. Sure, aren't we half Spanish ourselves?"

"God almighty, Dad, will you *spit it out. Who is it?* Is it that hot girl from down the road, you know, the one with the big…" Johnny said.

"Stop stirrin' it, Johnny. It's Mary O'Sullivan," Frank said.

Joan looked at him as if he had mentioned the devil incarnate.

"What? You can't be serious? You couldn't leave her alone with Abbie!" Joan shouted. Joan was on her feet.

"Take it easy. Of course, we could. Didn't she rear five children nearly on her own? What better woman, and she's right on our doorstep."

"Didn't you hear… you know… the stories…" she leaned over and whispered to him.

"*God almighty woman, what stories are you on about?* She's as sound as a pound," Frank remonstrated.

"Please, can we discuss this alone?" Joan pleaded but Frank continued.
"*Now look, Joan*, this concerns us all and time isn't on our side. We've only tomorrow and then I 'm back to work and so are you. *Do you want help or not?*"

"I suppose so."

"Well then…"

"I heard she's fond of the bottle and just rattles around the house all day," Joan said in a whisper.

"Well isn't that all the more reason… we'd be helpin' her too. Aren't we just after sayin' that the country's in an awful state? Wouldn't it be more in our line to look out for our neighbours?" Frank argued.

Joan slumped back on the couch, defeated.

"She was always a great worker and a great cook you know. I mean she's not a patch on you, Joan, but wouldn't it do for a few weeks?"
"Well, you have my vote." Johnny gave him a thumbs up.
"Aw, come on, Mam, Dad's right. What harm is it to get a bit of help? I'd say she's lonely. I only saw her the other day in her front garden, just her and the cat."

Cyril gave her his big puppy dog eyes that she could never resist. Just like Frank, Cyril had the softest, warmest, eyes. They were like two big pools of chocolate and Joan always caved in when combined with their easy charm. It was those eyes that had won Joan over from the very first day she met Frank.

"You know what they say about women and cats," Johnny said.

"*Give it a rest*, Johnny… So, what do you say?" Frank asked Joan.

Joan could feel Frank's eyes on her and there was silence while they all waited for her to respond.

"Well, maybe," Joan conceded.

"Yes, brilliant, I'll ask her tomorrow," Frank said.

"Okay," Joan said.

"She might say no, mind you… especially when she hears about you…" Frank said to Johnny in jest.

"*Feck off*, Dad. I take it that's family time done and dusted for today," Johnny said and picked up his plate and walked out the door.

"You're on the ball there, Dad, I'll give you that," Cyril said and walked over to kiss his mother goodnight. "It'll all work out fine, Mam, just you wait and see."

"I'd better get a move on myself and get this one to bed. Are you comin'?" Frank groaned as he bent over to pick up Abbie, trying not to wake her.

"Aw, look at her, Joan. She was a star today, you know."

Frank's eyes watered at the sight of his little daughter curled up in his arms, her cheeks flushed from sleep. He never thought they would see the day. After Johnny they had been lucky to keep the show on the road at all. It had been a rough few years, so when their little miracle came along, he knew there was a God for sure. Joan smiled at him.

"I'll follow you up. I'll just take a minute here and clear up the dishes."

"Now, don't be worryin'. Every cloud has a silver lining, love. Every cloud…" Frank repeated as he carried Abbie up the stairs.

Joan curled up on the couch enjoying the warmth left by their bodies and then pulled a blanket tightly around her. She didn't know about a silver lining. She had never felt so at sea. Nothing was working out the way Joan had hoped. Joan didn't really know what she had hoped, but this seemed a far cry from ideal. Mary O'Sullivan running the house. The neighbours would think she was useless. Joan couldn't forget what had been said about Peggy Maher, when Fr Brennan's housekeeper had offered to help her out around the house. God help the poor woman. Peggy Maher's husband had only gone on his usual bender for a few weeks and the last sighting of him was in a pub in Mayo. Peggy had four children under five, a full-time job and still they whispered awful things about her. Well, they would have a field day if they heard about Mary around the Hughes' house.

Joan wondered how it had all gone so wrong. Popping pills to cope with life, struggling to have a civil conversation with Johnny and hardly able to hold down a job. Joan was so tired that she didn't think she had the energy to walk upstairs. Her legs felt like lead and her head was thumping. Joan decided to close her eyes for just a few minutes.

It was hours later when she woke with a start. The room was cold and the fire dead. She shivered. Frank's parting words on his way to bed were still ringing in her ears - *every cloud, love.*

These words triggered a flashback of her last descent into darkness. Whenever the fog descended, often with no warning, it eradicated every bit of colour in Joan's life and left her paralysed. Joan was left with no words to explain how she felt, like she was dying inside.

The last episode had started with her idea to host a Christmas drinks party. Joan had desperately wanted to make Frank proud of her, to do what other wives seemed to do so easily. Despite his concerns, Joan had insisted, and by God she had sorely paid for that. It had looked to have great potential for about a half an hour. Neighbours, friends and Frank's work crew all mingling, high as kites with Christmas spirit. It was the 'high as kites' bit that ended up being the problem.

A couple of drunk lads from Frank's work had a bit of a skirmish at the sausage rolls and sent a table full of food flying. Peggy Maher had balled her eyes out and told anyone who listened about her husband's shenanigans. The upshot of it all was herself, who in a panic had taken one too many Xanax mixed with a few glasses of mulled wine and had ended up being escorted to bed at eight o'clock in front of all the guests. The indignity of it all. Joan shuddered at the memory. In public, they had always stuck to the faintly plausible story that Joan had been struck down with one of those twenty-four-hour bugs, but who were they fooling, especially when it lasted more like twenty-four days. It was the last ever Christmas party that they had attempted to host and now a forbidden topic of discussion.

Joan had fallen into such a slump afterwards that she had no problem getting Dr Kearney to increase her prescription. However, no amount of pills could eradicate the feeling of being a total failure. Joan felt that she was not only a failure as a wife and as a mother, but now was even a failure as a host. Joan thought that it was no wonder her father had sent her away after her mother died. She was just a failure, full stop. Every experience in life conspired to tell her

this.
Joan threw back the blanket and struggled to her feet.

Joan staggered out to the hall, feeling her way with every step. Stubbing her toe on the corner of the door, she smothered a scream. The house was deathly quiet, yet the hum of human life was palpable as they all slept upstairs. Life would get into gear again in the morning regardless, and she had to play her part. Still, there was something comforting about this quiet darkness and she wanted to hold on to it. Joan slowly tiptoed up the stairs, holding on to the banisters for support. Just as she rounded the corner at the top of the stairs, having successfully avoided the creaking floorboards, Joan heard a whimpering sound coming from Abbie's room and she pushed open the door.

"Abbie, it's Mam, what's wrong?" Joan asked and moved closer and now, acclimatised to the darkness, she made out the dark shape sitting up in bed with the blankets kicked off.

"I had a bad dream…"

"It's okay. I'm here. I just had one myself. Come on, move over, love…"

Joan lay down beside Abbie and pulled up the bedclothes.

"Do you want to tell me about it?" Joan asked, hugging Abbie tighter.

"It was awful. That scary woman from the hospital was chasing me and I couldn't get away… you know, because of my leg…"

"It's only a dream, Abbie. There was no scary woman in the hospital…"

"*Mam, there was*. She came over to us, she was like a witch."

"It just seems worse at night, that's all," Joan said.

Joan wasn't going to tell her that dark thoughts could haunt you at any time of the day or night. There didn't seem to be any rhyme or reason to it, from her experience.

"Will you stay with me for a while?" Abbie asked.

"Of course, I will. This is much better than listening to Dad snore," Joan said.

"I know, I can hear him in here sometimes. Do *all* men snore?"
"Well, I don't know about that, but I'd say a lot of them do. My father did, like a fog horn," Joan said, tucking the blanket around

Abbie, "my mother told me it was to torture women with no sleep, so that they wouldn't have the energy to be giving out to them."

"*No way*," Abbie said, and giggled.

"It's just a story. Your granny had plenty of those. She slept with me sometimes when I was your age… if I had a bad dream like you... now, time for sleep," Joan said, and closed her eyes.

Joan felt like she was back lying beside her own mother in bed. Little did she know then that it would be the happiest she would be in a long time. It had been brought to an all too abrupt end when her mother succumbed to cancer. Joan had only been thirteen, almost the same age that Abbie was now. She had been the one to find her when she crept out of her bed in the early hours, desperate for the company of her mother. However, Joan was too late. Joan's mother had passed away during the night and left Joan behind. No wonder her trust in life had all but disappeared after that cruel twist of fate.

FOUR

Joan hugged the steaming mug of tea against her chest. She smiled as she listened to Frank expound about his plans for the day. The awful fog of yesterday had lifted and she almost felt happy.

"After I drop the lads to school, I'll do a bit of a shop and then I'll pay Mary a visit," Frank said. Frank rubbed his hands together like he meant business.

"Please don't overdo it, Frank, you know what you're like when you're all gung-ho," Joan said.

"*Gung-ho?*" Frank asked, almost choking on his toast. "That's lovely coming from the *queen of high drama*."

"Please Frank, I'm only trying to help."

Joan threw the remains of her tea down the sink and busied herself washing the dishes that were piled high from the day before.

"Some help that is," Frank muttered into his cup.

"*What did you say?*" Joan snapped.

"Look at the time! Jaysus, we'll be late," Frank said, making a beeline for the door.

When Frank arrived at the supermarket the queue trailed down the aisles and there wasn't a sign of anyone behind the counter. That would never happen at Murray's, not if he had anything to do with it. He glanced around at the other shoppers in the queue, all quiet as mice, but with faces that would stop a clock. He thought of Johnny's outburst last night and couldn't deny there was a ring of truth in it. Everyone boiling with anger, but afraid to open their mouths.

"*Hello? Do you mind?*" Frank called over at the freckly boy, who pretended to stack shelves.

The boy seemed more interested in chatting up the young girl that was fiddling with her uniform and making eyes at him. Only for a manager appearing on the floor, Frank had no doubt he would still be standing there.

"Sorry for the delay, sir," the young lad said when he finally stood at the head of the queue. Frank knew that he no more meant it than the man in the moon. The boy was just going through the motions while the manager hovered over him.

"You could do with a few more staff from the looks of it," Frank said. "I've been *standing here* for at least ten minutes, you know, and *not a sign of anyone*."

Frank raised his voice for the benefit of the manager who intervened. He was not going to join the ranks of the disempowered.

"I'm very sorry, we've just had a few staff problems this morning," the manager said.

One of them is standing right beside you, Frank wanted to add, but kept his mouth shut. He had enough on his plate today without getting into an argument. The young lad had understood the message loud and clear from the looks of it, and Frank had bigger fish to fry to win over Mary. Frank picked up his shopping, marched out the door and made the short walk to Mary's house. Frank tried to remember the last time he had clapped eyes on her. As with all families from the area, they went back a long way. They had grown up just down the road from each other and had gotten on well though she had been a good ten years older than him. Their parents had been great friends and she a regular babysitter in the house.

Frank felt a wave of guilt as he thought about how long it had been since he had seen her. When her husband Tom was alive they visited often, but those days were long gone. He arrived at Mary's house, opened the gate and stopped to take it in. Mary had kept it in pristine condition and Frank couldn't help feeling a little embarrassed at how shabby they had let their own house become in comparison. But sometimes it had been all they could do to keep the show on the road.

Mary's little council house was within walking distance of the supermarket, which was a recent addition to the town and catered to the growing population that were now opting for life in the city. The locals couldn't believe the prices that many were willing to pay just to get a foothold in the area. Adapting to life in a box in the town centre was a compromise that now was preferable to life in suburbia for many exhausted commuters, and what had once been deemed the strange living habits of those in mainland Europe, was now sought after by many.

Frank ran his hands through his hair, rang the doorbell and waited. Mary was known for her sharp tongue, but Frank had known the soft-hearted woman that was underneath. Getting involved with them might be the last thing she was interested in, but there was no going back now.

"Good mornin', stranger," Frank said, grinning at her.

Mary was fixing her hair in a bun when she opened the door, hair that looked a lot greyer than he remembered. A network of fine lines now decorated her face, but there was no mistaking her. Mary was a big woman, and she had definitely added a few pounds over the years, giving her an almost cuddly appearance. Her soft, grey eyes took him in, but if she recognised him, she wasn't letting on. She just stood there staring at him.

"It's Frank, do you remember me, Ted Hughes son," Frank reminded her.

"*For God's sake*, I know who you are, Frank. *I haven't lost* my marbles just yet."

"How are you? You're lookin' mighty… really… you're lookin' mighty."

"I'm just wondering what has you at my doorstep at this hour of the morning, dressed up to the nines," Mary said. "Did something happen?"

"It's been a long time, way too long Mary and I feel bad about that, Jaysus I do."

"I assume these are for me," Mary said, and took the flowers out of Frank's hand.

"I take it there is some occasion I don't know about or you're after something? I didn't come down in the last shower you know…" "Aw Mary, don't be like that, would you," Frank pleaded, and shifted uneasily on his feet, thinking he might have made a big mistake. "I *did* want to talk to you actually, if you have a minute… I'd appreciate it."

Frank was sure he detected a slight flicker of amusement in her eyes. "Well, I suppose I better invite you in then," Mary said, and moved back to let him pass inside.

"Thanks."

Closing the front door behind them, Mary ushered Frank down the hall to the kitchen. He didn't need any directions, as the house was almost a replica of their own, one of many built in the 1950's.

"God, it's grand and cosy in here, Mary. You've done a great job with the place."

Frank surveyed the room, admiring the old Aga cooker in the corner that gave the room its own microclimate.

"You know, that was a present from Tom a long time ago. People would laugh at that nowadays, a cooker for a present, but it was one of the best things he ever bought me if you'd believe that."
"I'd say it was," Frank said. "There's great heat out of it all the same."

Frank hovered awkwardly at the door, not sure what to do with himself. He was no longer a regular caller, who could just plonk himself down in a seat, but he wasn't a total stranger either.

"Sit down there, Frank, and I'll make some tea. I can't wait to hear what has you at my door at this hour of the morning. Just clear a seat and throw those books over there," Mary said, and pointed to the piles of magazines lined up against the wall.

Frank sat down on the chair, feeling his shirt wet with perspiration from the walk and the welcome, or lack of it. He watched Mary as she made tea and sliced a cake, and his mouth watered. Mary wore a bright red dress that hung loosely on her large frame. Her silver hair gave her a sense of gravitas and Frank relaxed as he remembered the long history they shared. Frank had no idea if the stories of her sherry habit were true, but from what he could see, she hadn't changed too much at all.

"So, how are you Mary?" Frank asked, breaking the uncomfortable silence.

"How am I? All things considered I suppose I'm not too bad. You know Tom's dead twenty years. Can you believe that, Frank?"

Mary paused for a minute, stirring the pot of tea.

"*Jaysus*, I can't to be honest. How long were you married?"

"Well, if he was alive, we'd be fifty years, but it was thirty years when he had the heart attack," Mary said, speaking with the directness, for which she had always been known.

"He was a great man all the same..."

"He was... and he was a great man for the cards, until the very end, well, you knew that anyways. Would you believe, he sat up in his hospital bed playing cards with a friend the very day he died? That takes commitment doesn't it?" Mary said and smiled.

"And the children, how are they? You must've a load of grandchildren by now?"

Frank noticed her expression change and he knew he had hit a nerve.

"Well, I'm sure. I never see them or the children. What am I saying? They're no more children now, but that's how I'll always remember them. They get in touch when they need something, isn't that the way it goes?"

There was a faraway look in Mary's eyes as she sat down and poured the tea.

"You know, sometimes I wish we never had them," Mary said, and Frank almost choked on his piece of cake. "Aw, don't mind me. I don't really mean that. I know I was hard on them, but I did my best. It wasn't easy after Tom passed."

"I'm sure it wasn't. Jaysus you'd put most women to shame, rearin' five of them. They're not easy, I can tell ya that... and I've *only three*," Frank agreed.

"You know Frank, I thought they might understand when they grew older, had children of their own, that they might come back. Tom would have handled it better, that's for sure but it wasn't to be."

"Aw, *would you go away*. Tom wouldn't have known what to do with them. If you ask me, they're an ungrateful shower, the lot of them..."

Frank, like everyone else, had heard the stories going around about their marriage, that it was one borne out of convenience and proximity; a platonic relationship, but with five children arriving in quick succession that theory went out the window. Whatever their relationship, when Tom died, the children weren't long packing up and Mary was left alone, and alone she had been for the last twenty years from the looks of it.

"Now, don't mind me rabbiting on. I hardly see a soul, so when I do, I go on a bit. How are your lot?" Mary asked.

"Aw, they're grand, I suppose. We're not exactly the Waltons, but we manage."

Frank thought of the chaos in the house only yesterday. What should have been a happy day as they sent their children off to start a new year at school had turned into a fiasco, between Abbie's fall and Joan's melodrama.

"Who wants to be the Waltons Frank? I think it's far from the Waltons that any of us were reared," Mary said and smiled, and Frank noticed how attractive she still was, like the old Mary he remembered. "So now, do you want to tell me why you're really here?" Mary said, putting down her cup of tea.

"Well, I suppose I've a bit of a proposition to put to you," Frank said. Mary leaned forward, resting her elbows on the table.

"Go on, spit it out, Frank. I won't bite you know."

"Well, the thing is… Abbie had a bit of an accident…" Frank began. On seeing the look of shock on Mary's face, Frank quickly reacted. "No, *it's nothing awful*, thanks be to God, but she took a bit of a fall on the stairs yesterday and went and broke her ankle. The two of us were up in A&E for the day," Frank said, placing his cup down on the table. "Don't get me started on that place again or I'll have you here for a week."

"I'm sorry to hear that, the poor pet, and…" Mary said.

"Well yes, we could do with a bit of help to be honest. Abbie's going to be at home for a few weeks. Joan does a bit of work in the library and you know yourself, its' no easy job keepin' a house goin'…" Mary stirred in the chair.

"We'd pay you of course," Frank added.

"You want me *to look after Abbie*?" Mary asked in disbelief.

"Well her and the house, just a few hours here and there, what do you think?"

"You'll have more tea," Mary said, and hopped up to top up the pot with water while Frank waited for her answer. He didn't know if he would be going home with his tail between his legs or if she would jump at the offer.

"Well, Frank Hughes, you're a right turn up for the books, so you are," Mary said and sat back down looking as if she was mulling over his proposition.

"And? Will you give it a go? Just for a few weeks, that's all. You'd be doin' us a big favour, Mary, you really would," Frank said, leaning forward. Frank placed his hand on Mary's. "I know it might be askin' a lot and we haven't been great at keepin' in touch, but maybe it's a fresh start… for all of us."

"Take it easy, Frank. I will," Mary said.

"*You will!*"

"Yes, are you hard of hearing, Frank? Now, I get mass in the morning, so it'd be after that and I can do a bit of cooking, if you like, but one thing, I don't want to be overstepping, so only as long as Joan doesn't mind," Mary said, and placed her cup firmly down on the table. Mary looked directly at Frank. "You know we women like to be the captain of our own ships. We don't always like another woman butting in."

"You obviously haven't met Joan in a while," Frank said and laughed.

"What do you mean?"

"Well, she's had her ups and downs over the years. She wouldn't be great with the stress like, gets herself all worked up. You know, she was very depressed after Johnny was born and I don't think she's been the same since. Trust me, she's all for this."

"Oh right, I'm sorry to hear that. I'd no idea, *no idea at all.* God, it has been a long time, hasn't it, Frank?"

"It sure has, but we're here now, aren't we?" Frank added.

"So, what's your secret?" Mary asked as she scrutinised Frank's facial expression.

"What do you mean my secret? I'm an open book, Mary, always have been and always will be."

Mary roared laughing but caught herself when she saw the injured look on his face.

"I didn't mean it like that. I mean, you're always in good form, no matter what's going on. I remember you well as a child, you know, always into devilment and a big smile on your face."

Frank blushed. He had many memories of Mary saving his bacon when he had gotten into scraps as a young fella, and that had happened on more occasions than he liked to remember. Mary had always managed to smooth things over with his hot-tempered father.

"*Jaysus*, I don't know about that. You didn't see me in the hospital yesterday," Frank said and laughed. The memory of Fiona, the radiologist came to mind and he quickly changed the subject.

"You know my grandfather always said, try and accept the cards you've been dealt and play them out. Don't be lookin' at the other fella's hand… and I suppose that's what I do."

"Well, I'd say he was right, and you must be doing that. I think that's been half my problem."

The room went quiet as they both drifted away with their own thoughts. Frank glanced over at Mary who stared out the window and felt a surge of affection for this strong, independent woman who had been very good to him when he was a child. Mary felt an ache for those simple days when they had both been children. She thought about the path her life had taken afterwards and all the mistakes that she had made along the way.

"You should get out a bit more, Mary. You might even find a new man for yourself. There's plenty of them around who'd only be delighted to meet a fine woman like yourself," Frank said, trying to lighten the mood.

"Would you stop it?" Mary asked, and brushed the thought away with one stroke of her hand. "I'm way too old for that carry on, Frank… If I remember rightly, you'd a bit of an eye for the ladies when you were younger."

"I'd say it was more that they had an eye for me and some of them still do," Frank said, remembering many of the admiring looks he had received in his heyday.

"You wouldn't want to let Joan hear you talking like that," Mary chuckled.

"Now back to business. When do you want me to start?" Mary asked.

"What? Oh right, tomorrow by any chance?"

"Well, that's settled then. I'll be over after mass, is that okay?" Mary asked.

Mary stood up, shook the crumbs out of her dress and started to clear up the dishes.

"*Jaysus,* is that the time? You're some talker, Mary, so you are," Frank said, getting the message that it was time to be off.

"And you're some plámásar, Frank Hughes. Go on now, out of my sight and I'll see you tomorrow."

Frank stood up and looked around for the shopping bags he had left near the door. He picked them up and turned back to Mary.

"You've made my day, Mary, you really have. We really appreciate it, and you're stayin' for dinner tomorrow, no two ways about it," Frank said.

"I'll do better than that. I'll cook the dinner," Mary said.

"Jaysus, things are gettin' better by the minute," Frank said, skipping out the door.

Closing the door after Frank, Mary leaned up against it and smiled. Maybe this was just what she needed, a fresh start, something to get her teeth into again. She had a lot to do today, but she decided to celebrate first. She poured herself a sherry and sat down in her favourite chair, looking out on the back garden that still basked in all its summer glory.

"Aw, there you are, Boots" she said, and the big ginger cat, hopped up on her lap and settled in.

There had been no difficulty finding a name for the little kitten when she had found him. She had gone to put on her gardening boots and found him fast asleep in one of them.

"We're not used to visitors, are we?" Mary asked, affectionately scratching behind Boot's ears. Boots purred loudly in appreciation. "But things are looking up, Boots, I really think they are," Mary said.

Mary thought that maybe this was God's way of putting it all right. If her own family didn't want to have anything to do with her, then maybe the Hughes family had been sent to her to make up for it. The Lord did indeed work in mysterious ways. Mary thought that she must remember to light a candle for Tom tomorrow at mass. He was surely behind this sudden stroke of good fortune.

Frank, on the other hand, strolled home, feeling on top of the world. Mary's house was only around the corner from their own and he wasn't in any great hurry. His mission had been successful, and he wanted to replay it all in his head. His usual swagger took on even greater proportions as he delighted in how well things had gone. He unbuttoned his shirt and let the noonday sun warm his sallow skin. He wouldn't have looked out of place on the Riviera. It was still the height of summer by Irish standards and there was a buzz around town as people were out and about eager to catch the last rays of the year.

God, that visit had brought him back a few years. He couldn't shake the guilty feeling of leaving it so long, and now to ask her for a favour. Frank shook his head at the thoughts of it. Nevertheless, she had said yes.

"Feck it," Frank said, aloud.

All that bloody gossip about Mary and the sherry. She looked grand to him and he knew by the look of the place that she wasn't on the bottle all day. Jaysus, people were awful sometimes with the auld blather they spouted. Only last Easter the story circulated that she had arrived at the Good Friday ceremonies reeking of sherry and then proceeded to fall asleep and snore her head off. No amount of coughing or nudging could wake her up they said, and eventually it was left to Fr Brennan to try to rouse her when all the other parishioners had gone home. Frank didn't believe a word of it and even if she had overindulged and fell asleep, she wouldn't be the first. Fr Brennan's sermons were a challenge to the hardiest of souls. They would get on like a house on fire. They always had in the past and they would again.

****

"Oh God no, *shit, shit, shit,* this can't be happening. This *bloody phone,*" Joan said. She threw it across the bedroom and paced up and down, almost hyperventilating. "Calm down, breathe, breathe, in two, three, hold, out two, three. Remember what you learnt," Joan said.

Then she rushed to pick up the phone and checked to see if she really had sent the WhatsApp message. She groaned when she saw that she had.

Joan couldn't make head nor tail of all the groups and messages, which were mostly directed towards Abbie. Joan had sent a message to the "Basketball" group without any problem. It was only when she went to message Eileen that it had gone haywire. She had only bloody well gone and sent the message to the whole group.

"Abbie, do you know anything about deleting WhatsApp messages?" Joan shouted, running downstairs, her face burning at the thought of what she had just done. "*Abbie?*"

"What's wrong, Mam?" Abbie called, reluctantly looking up from her book as she lay sprawled on the living room couch.

"*Can you… can you delete WhatsApp messages?*" Joan asked, standing in front of her.

"No, I don't think so, as the ad says, when they're gone, they're gone," Abbie said.

"*What? That's a great help…* Will you tell your father to come upstairs as soon as he gets in. Where did he go? I thought he'd be back *ages* ago," Joan said and rushed upstairs.

When Frank opened the front door, ready to share his good news, he found an empty kitchen and a silent house. He walked through the kitchen and across the hall into the living room, where he found Abbie snuggled up with her book.

"Aw, there you are. You're the right little book worm, aren't you? Where's your mother?"

"She's looking for you, Dad," Abbie said, and gave her Dad the 'you're in trouble' look, which he knew only too well.

"What've I done *now*? Didn't I only go and get Mary O'Sullivan to agree to help out? That's a day's work done and it's only lunchtime," Frank argued.

Frank didn't need any trouble today when they were only getting back on their feet.

"I'm just telling you. She's looking for you, Dad, and she's in a bit of a… you know… a mood," Abbie whispered.

"Well I'm sorry to say, she can *feck off* with her mood today. I deserve a pat on the back, not a kick up the arse," Frank said.

Abbie giggled as he lifted his leg up in demonstration.

"*Frank, Frank is that you? Thank God.* I need to talk to you, now. It's urgent," Joan called.

Frank made his 'God help me' face to Abbie, who burst out laughing.

"*Jaysus,* you women will be the death of me. If I'm not back in half an hour, call an ambulance, will you? No, on second thoughts, that'd do more harm than good. Just say a prayer for me," Frank said as he climbed the stairs.

Joan dragged him into the bedroom as soon as he reached the landing.

"Why did you ever tell me that story? You better fix it, Frank. I'm warning you or I'll never be able to show my face again at basketball or anywhere."

"What the… Have you been on the sherry this morning?" Frank said and scratched his head.

"This is *no time for jokes*, Frank, I'm being serious," Joan said, pacing the room.

"Jaysus, will you calm down and make some sense woman."

"*Stop always telling me to calm down!* That won't help *anything*," Joan argued.

"Will you just sit down for a minute, Joan."

"No, *I can't* sit down. You don't understand. It's a total mess. I'm never using that bloody WhatsApp again."

Frank took a deep breath and determined that nothing was going to ruin his good mood after meeting Mary.

"What did you do *now*? Send a message to the pope tellin' him you fancy him?"

"*Stop it*, Frank! It's not funny. I told you, it's a *disaster*," Joan shouted.

Frank knew there was no point trying to calm her down. He just had to listen to the whole sorry story, and a sorry, stupid story it was, that didn't matter a jot. But you couldn't tell her that. A message meant for her friend, Eileen, had mysteriously ended up being sent to a group of mothers, whose children played basketball with Abbie. That didn't sound too bad until she went on to tell him the content of the message, and of course he would have to be the subject of it. "You should never have told me about Jane Corbett coming on to you," Joan shouted.

"Excuse-moi. I told you a funny story that's all, and it was a funny story, full stop. *Jaysus*, do you think I'd be tellin' you she shoved her boobs in me face if I was interested in her?"

"There's no need to be so crude, Frank," Joan said, her voice shaking as she entertained the thought of Frank falling for another woman.

"And now you go and tell half the town about it. Let me see the bloody message with my own eyes." Frank put his hand out for the phone. Joan handed it to him, feeling mortified at what she had written.

The message read:

Did you hear about Jane? She was all over Frank like a rash at the match. She doesn't waste her time. You better keep an eye on Dave.

"*Oh Christ,* Joan. *A right eejit* you make me look, that's for sure. Runnin' home to the wife as if I can't handle a bit of harmless flirtation," Frank complained.

"I didn't mean to send it *to everyone*," Joan said.

"You shouldn't be sendin' it to anyone," Frank argued.

"I know. *I know that now*. I don't know what got into me," Joan cried. She felt like such a fool.

"Did you *really think* there was anythin' more to it, *seriously?*" Frank asked.

Frank had been flattered by Jane Corbett's attention, but that was all it was. She definitely wasn't backwards about coming forwards. She batted her eyelashes at him and made up a story about a slow puncture. She was a good-looking woman and she didn't mind showing it off. It was only when she shoved her chest in his face as he bent down to take a look at the tyre that he had seen a lot more than her slow puncture.

Frank couldn't deny the little frisson of excitement that had run through him, but Frank knew well that you couldn't be too careful these days. He didn't want to be slapped with a lawsuit for just being polite. So, Frank had just smiled and re-joined the other parents at the side of the pitch. Everyone knew the story of Jane's husband setting up home with a young lad half his age, so you couldn't really blame her if she lost it for a bit. The poor woman had been left with two young children to rear on her own.

"You would think that *you of all people* would understand," Frank said.

"Me of all people? *What's that supposed to mean?*" Joan cried.

"Well, aren't you always on about women supporting each other and all that malarkey? Well, that seems to have gone *out the window* today." Joan put her face in her hands. She knew he was right. Jane wasn't the worst of all and had been very nice to her when some of the mothers hardly gave her a second glance. Joan was a lot older than many of them at fifty-five. At times, it felt like they were generations apart. Eileen too was lovely. She had gotten to know her at a yoga class, and she didn't seem to care that Joan was almost twenty years older than her.

"I know, you're right, but what are you going to do, Frank?"

"What *am I* going to do?" Frank shouted. "*For cryin' out loud*, I didn't send the *bloody message!* You're just goin' to have to grin and bear it. I won't be goin' to any basketball games for a while. *I can tell you that much.* Isn't it just as well that poor Abbie is laid up and won't be playin' any time soon?"

"Oh, you're right. That's a relief. I couldn't face them. I just couldn't face them."

"And do you not think that if I was goin' to have an affair, I'd have done it years ago?"

"That's *an awful thing* to say to your wife, Frank."

"Well, it's better sayin' it than doin' it, don't you think?" Frank remonstrated. Joan couldn't argue with that logic.

"And what about poor auld Jane. A bit of harmless banter and now she's a laughin' stock. You need to *think before you act*, Joan. It might be more in your line to take a few deep breaths before pickin' up the phone in the future! Now, just forget it! There's nothing we can do."

The phone rang and they both looked at each other. Joan grabbed it and held it out to Frank.

"Who is it?" Joan whispered. Frank peered at the phone as he held it close.

"It's Eileen, but leave it, Joan. Let sleeping dogs lie for a while. Let it go to message."

"Yes, you're right," Joan said.

"Could we send another message and maybe pretend it was a joke?" Joan looked at Frank who now sat at the side of the bed with his head in his hands.

"*Jaysus, in what world could it be seen as a joke?* He stood up and walked towards the door. "I need some air. And do you know *what?* I was only comin' home to tell you that things went great with Mary and she's only delighted to help out. She'll be here tomorrow after mass."

"Oh, right. That's great," Joan said.

Although she was disappointed, she resisted saying anything more, knowing whatever she said would only come out wrong. Mary was coming and there was nothing Joan could do about it. She didn't have a leg to stand on after all. When Frank closed the door after him, Joan reached for the phone. Joan needed to listen to Eileen's message.

FIVE

Eileen heard her phone ping and imagined it was a message about something else she had totally forgotten. She dropped her bags on the kitchen table and walked over to examine her colour-coded calendar on the fridge. She prided herself on keeping the show on the road, but recently she felt like things were slipping between the cracks. She kicked off her high heels and padded around the house.

Standing at five foot ten inches in her bare feet, Eileen towered over most women.

Although it had made her quite self-conscious when she was younger, her scrawny appearance had undergone a radical metamorphosis and by her early twenties, she was frequently compared to a young, taller Elizabeth Taylor.

Even now, in her late thirties, she was still a head-turner. She made herself a cup of herbal tea and sat down at the countertop and looked at her phone. It was a message from Joan. She would read it later. The house was silent, and she could feel herself relax as she gazed out the window at the back garden. Eileen thought that it was more like a well-furnished playground for her girls and Eileen felt her heart burst with love for them. She couldn't imagine a life without them now, though children had never been high up on her list of priorities when she was younger.

Eileen's eyes glazed over as she remembered what she had been like as a teenager, innocent and full of dreams. She had filled journals with her plans to travel the world, live in the countryside, and use the healing hands that she had been gifted with just like the women before her, with the exception of her mother. Her mother had just poo-pooed her fantastical ideas until Eileen had stopped talking about them altogether. Her mother always argued that Eileen should get her head out of the clouds and go and get herself a real job and a husband. That was the solution to all of life's problems in her mother's mind.

Eileen had hoped for marriage and children, but the professional career she had ended up in was not one she would have chosen for herself. Her father was a barrister and now here she was a solicitor. That was no accident of fate. Eileen imagined that she couldn't be the only person who had ended up living a life that followed convention, rather than pursuing their dreams.

Shaking herself, Eileen stood up and started preparing lunch. Nobody would be interested in hearing about her discontent. Eileen looked to have more than most could wish for in a lifetime. She had married a man that many women would have killed for, many of them almost had, doing their best to push her out of the picture. Nonetheless, Dave Danaher had pursued her relentlessly from first year in college and although she had given him the run around, dating lots of different guys, by the time they graduated she finally succumbed to his charms. Yet nowadays they seemed more like ships passing in the night. He had been the best-looking guy in their class at college and was now a successful barrister in town. Eileen was a solicitor in Clancy's, and they had two beautiful daughters.

To many it would be a fairy tale come true. They had married ten years ago, bought a beautiful detached house in an affluent part of town, and become the golden couple of their social circle. It was only when she was alone, that she couldn't escape the gnawing thoughts. It just wasn't enough anymore. Eileen finished preparing the chicken pasta salad and put it in the fridge for when the girls came home. She picked up her car keys and was ready to head out the door again after her short pit stop.

The school gates were her least favourite place in the world, full of fawning mothers whose eyes lit up at the sight of solicitor Eileen, married to barrister Dave. Her husband was well respected around town and she was astute enough to know that much of her popularity was down to the high status he held in professional circles. Going through the motions with the same old jaded, superficial conversations day after day was exhausting. Eileen had often contemplated telling these women how she truly felt, but she couldn't imagine any of them giving her the time of day if she did. For her girls' sakes she had kept the peace.

After all, Eileen's views didn't mix so well with the excited talk of holidays in the South of France, the latest collections in Brown Thomas or the most appropriate menu for the next dinner party.

The phone rang, just in time to break her from her cynical line of thought. Glancing at it, she saw it was Dave. Eileen picked up the phone.

"Dave… yes… I'm just on my way out the door… Okay, I'll leave dinner aside for you…" Eileen said, and the conversation ended as quickly as it began. Eileen looked at the phone and sighed on noticing Dave had hung up while she was still in mid-sentence.

Eileen remembered when he had used any excuse to hear her voice, sneaking out of meetings just to whisper down the phone that he loved her. Well, the cracks hadn't long been showing when the girls came along. Life just seemed to have become one giant to do list that was never completed and after collapsing into bed every night, it just started all over again the next day.

Eileen closed the front door behind her, stopping to take a quick look around their spacious front garden. A large water fountain and gazebo dominated the landscape, but there was still ample space to easily park at least a dozen cars. She breathed in the heady scent coming from the exotic floral display and sighed. As beautiful as it all was, it didn't do anything to quell the feeling of dis-ease that flooded her body. She hopped in the car, early for the school pick-up for a change, and arrived just in time to get a parking spot right outside the front gate. It wasn't easy to get out of a solicitor's practice in the middle of the day. There was always something urgently needed for court or a needy client who threatened to take their business elsewhere. If she saw another claim over whiplash or falling in the bathroom of the local chipper, she would lose her mind. She thought this was even more reason to get out of this profession as soon as possible. Eileen picked up her phone and read the message from Joan to the basketball group. She groaned as she realised the mistake Joan had made.

"Oh no," Eileen remarked. Eileen gave her a quick call, and when the phone rang out, she left Joan a message.

While theirs was an unlikely friendship that had started at a yoga class, they had gotten to know each other well and found out that their daughters were in the same class in school. Joan was nothing like the women in Eileen's social circle and although she was full of nervous energy that showed on her tiny frame and had her problems, Eileen thought her a refreshing change from the usual company she kept. Eileen had never laughed so much hearing about the disaster of a Christmas drinks party Joan and Frank had held. It sounded like great fun compared to all the boring ones she had attended. However, when Joan went on to tell her how depressed she often felt and how low she had sunk after the party, Eileen felt awful for making light of it and apologised profusely to Joan. And so their friendship grew, bonded by shared secrets and dreams that they would never dare tell another soul.

Eileen glanced out the window and spotted a huddle of women deep in conversation in the yard. It didn't take a mind reader to guess the subject of their gossip.

"Bitches," Eileen said, and hopped out of the car.

"Oh, hi Eileen," one of the mothers called out, signalling for her to join them.

"Oh, hi. How are you all? I'm in a bit of a rush," Eileen said casually, and brushed past, having no interest in adding any fuel to their fire.

"Did you get the message?" Lorna hissed. She was the usual ringleader of any bitchy get-together. "Is she on drugs? You know her, don't you Eileen? Is she all there? I mean, she must be *mortified.* Maybe it's age. She's well past fifty, isn't she?"

Eileen clenched her hands by her side and kept moving.

"Sorry, I haven't had time to check my messages. I don't mean to be rude, but you know me, I'm always chasing my tail. I'll catch up with you soon," Eileen said.

"Get a life," Eileen muttered under her breath, feeling frustrated with the constant, inane exchanges at the school gates. Eileen thought it typical that there was no mention of Jane at all.

They all knew Jane's husband had left her, but even when he was around, she flirted outrageously with all of the husbands. Eileen had caught her at a Christmas drinks party practically falling on top of Dave in the kitchen, but what was more unsettling was how comfortable he had looked in the situation. Jane came from a very high-profile family in the town, so Eileen knew that even if she had full on sex with one of the husbands on the basketball court, no one would have probably had a bad word to say about her.

"Hi, girls. Come on, into the car quick," Eileen said as they approached her.

"Mum, did you hear about Abbie?" Sophie asked, tugging at her sleeve.

"*What* about Abbie?" Eileen asked, gently shoving them into the back seat.

"She broke her ankle yesterday and she's going to miss the big match. She's one of our best players," Sophie moaned.

"*What?* I'd no idea. The poor girl," Eileen said, and hoped it might explain Joan's moment of madness.

"Can I visit her, please?" Sophie pleaded.

"*Of course*, when she's up to it. I didn't know you were that good friends," Eileen said.

It was only recently that Eileen and Joan had figured out their daughters were in the same class. It was hard to believe that after all those years at the school gates they had never even had a conversation.

"Well, we're new friends since we're on the same basketball team," Sophie explained.

"New friends are good," Eileen agreed. "Now, homework straight away when we get home, *okay*? I have a client coming in an hour."

"One of your crazy clients?" Amy asked, giggling.

"Stop it, Amy, they're not crazy."

Jesus, she could kill Dave. It had been funny initially, but now it was just insulting.

"Well, it was Dad who called them crazy," Amy said, feeling a bit hurt.

"I'm sure he did. Don't you know what your father is like, Amy? I'm sure he was just making a joke," Eileen said, through gritted teeth.

"I don't think he was joking, Mum. He called it new-agey stuff. *You should've seen his face*," Amy said, and turned up her nose imitating her father's expression.

"Amy, please..." Eileen raised her voice. "I'm sorry, it's just this traffic is crazy and I'm running late," Eileen apologised, annoyed at herself for raising her voice.

Eileen honked on the horn. So much for their agreement to raise their children to be open-minded and tolerant. Not much good if one of your parents was the furthest thing from it himself. Eileen decided that she was going to finally talk to Dave about it that evening when the girls were in bed.

****

At six o'clock, Eileen had finished with her client and lay on the massage table when she saw the phone flashing. An hour of no phones and no demands had been pure bliss. Eileen had hopped up on the table after her client left and loathed to move. Wearing a pair of leggings, an oversized T-shirt, and her hair pulled free of its ponytail, there was little sign of the professional woman from earlier in the day. Every muscle in her body relaxed and Eileen didn't want to leave her little cocoon. This was her room, and it was off-limits to the rest of the family. It had started out as an office and had morphed into a safe space for clients to let go of their worries. Despite their enormous house, it had still taken a bit of insistence before she had agreement from Dave that it was hers. Dave had argued that it was big enough for both of them and that they could share it, but Eileen didn't give in, despite being accused of being secretive. Eileen locked the door religiously and kept the key in a safe place.

Suddenly, the phone rang. Eileen looked over at the phone, hesitated, then thinking of Joan she reached out to answer it.

"Hello?"

"Oh Eileen, *thank God* you answered. I feel like such a fool. I *only* meant to send it to you..." Joan began.

Eileen sat up on the edge of the table having been yanked out of her lovely bubble.

"Joan, calm down. Yes, I saw it. It's not like you to be spreading gossip. I guessed it was mistake. Am I right?" Eileen asked.

"*Of course*, it was a mistake. I don't *know what I was thinking*. You know though, what with Abbie and all…"

"How is she? Sophie told me," Eileen said softly.

"She'd an awful fall, poor thing. She's in a cast and will be off school for a few weeks, but she'll be fine. It was an awful shock… but has anyone said anything to you about the message?"

Eileen heard Joan's voice shake and couldn't bring herself to mention the witch trial she had witnessed outside the school. "Not a word, Joan. I'd say they hardly noticed it. You know yourself, the messages never stop on that bloody WhatsApp," Eileen assured.

"I feel so bad about it and Frank isn't too impressed with me either," Joan confided.

"Aw, he'll get over it. In any event, it is Jane who should be embarrassed, coming on to someone else's husband in full view of everyone," Eileen laughed.

"I know, yet Frank doesn't seem to think so. He feels sorry for her and has wasted no time in telling me," Joan said.

"Aw, you know men. They lose all reason the minute a woman flashes a bit of cleavage at them," Eileen reassured her.

"You're right. I feel a bit better already. You know I'm mad about Frank, but with the way I've been over the years, I'm often surprised that he hasn't gone off with another woman. I don't know what I'd do if he left me," Joan said.

Eileen wanted to scream at her. She couldn't understand why women were so terrified of a man leaving them. So much for equality when a lot of women didn't even believe in it themselves.

"Joan, *for God's sake. Frank isn't going to leave you. Even a fool* can see he's crazy about you. Don't be making mountains out of molehills. At any rate, you would be fine if he did. We women are a lot stronger than we give ourselves credit for, and we need to start owning it," Eileen encouraged. "Are you there? Sorry, I didn't mean to lecture you… it's just been a long day."

"How do you do it, Eileen? You're *so brave*?" Joan said in a low voice.

Joan felt like pinching herself most of the time at the thought of Eileen being her friend. She would wake up one of these days and realise it had all been a dream. Women like Eileen just didn't have time for women like Joan.

"Don't be fooled, I have my moments, I can tell you. You know that well. Look at me, half afraid to admit to my husband that I want to leave my job. Some ad I am for female empowerment. Speaking of… are you free to be a guinea pig for my case studies any time soon?" Eileen asked.

"Of course. Did I tell you Frank has asked Mary, you know Mary O'Sullivan, to help out with Abbie? She's coming tomorrow," Joan said.

"*Mary O'Sullivan*, isn't she the woman who fell asleep at mass after drinking a bottle of sherry?"

"I know. I'm not sure how much help she'll be, but Frank's insisting. They go back a long way you know. She used to babysit him when he was a child," Joan explained.

"Enjoy it, Joan. I can't imagine Dave getting some woman in to help me. He thinks I have it easy as I'm working half days. Men have no idea. Look, I'll call you next week and arrange a date. I really have to get on top of these case studies, so we might try and make it a regular date. You'll love it, trust me. It's really relaxing if nothing else."

"Any afternoon really is good with me. I better go, Eileen. Frank's just back in the door and I've a bit of making up to do," Joan said.

"Okay, I'll get back to you with a date. Don't overdo it apologising to Frank, Joan. It was just a silly mistake. It is not a big deal at all. Bye," Eileen said.

"Thanks. See you soon, Eileen."

Eileen hung up the phone and lay back down with a smile on her face. It was hard not to find some of Joan's dramas funny. Eileen decided that she was on a mission now and was getting her case studies finished by the deadline in December. However, first things first, she was having a word with Dave. There would be no more making Eileen the butt of his jokes with the girls. It stopped now. By the time Eileen's downtime had ended and the dinner was cooked and eaten, Eileen heard the car in the driveway.

Dave felt like he had the weight of the world on his shoulders as he trudged up the driveway that day. He was only thirty-eight years old, but the years of long hours at work, were starting to take their toll. He was still handsome by any standard, with piercing blue eyes and a shock of thick, wavy hair that was strawberry blonde. Standing at six foot four inches tall, Dave was one of the few men who wasn't intimidated by Eileen's height.

Dave yawned as he put his key in the front door and imagined collapsing on the couch after dinner with a large glass of red wine in hand. Dave felt guilty for praying that the girls were in bed. He was crazy about them but just needed some quiet time this evening. He hoped that Eileen wouldn't have a million and one things to discuss with him. Sometimes it felt like he came home to another staff meeting. Dave felt that Eileen had no idea how stressful his job was and how everyone wanted a piece of him. They also had the pressure of a huge mortgage to pay off on the house. Renovating an old house was a project that neither of them had been prepared for and it was now a huge noose around their necks, along with the investments he had made that had gone pear-shaped.

Dave still couldn't believe that Eileen had decided to go part-time at work. That definitely wasn't going to pay the bills. Eileen was fast becoming unrecognisable from the high-achieving, social butterfly he had met in college. That was the girl he fell in love with.

"Dave, *is that you?*" Eileen called out, as he came in the door.

"Yes, I'll be down in a minute," Dave said.

He dropped his briefcase in the hall and went up the stairs. In their large bedroom, Dave pulled off his tie and sat down on the side of the bed.

"Jesus Christ," he groaned. He was only in the door and Eileen was looking for him.

"Dinner's ready," Eileen called from the bottom of the stairs, and after a couple of minutes, Dave slowly stood up and made his way down to the kitchen.

"What's all this? Is there a special occasion I forgot?" Dave said.

Despite his grumpy expression, Eileen couldn't help noticing how handsome he still was, even with the bags that were starting to form under his eyes and his expanding waistline. One look at the older barristers who worked with him was a good sign of where he was headed if he wasn't careful. Wining and dining were a necessary part of the job, he assured her, but Eileen began to wonder. The girls hardly saw him during the week, he was so late getting home.

"You could be a bit more enthusiastic," Eileen said with a hint of irritation in her voice.

"Sorry, it smells great, really it does. I'm just tired that's all," Dave said.

"It's roast chicken, but it's probably a bit dried up by now," Eileen said and pointedly looked at the clock.

"And a bottle of my favourite," Dave said. He casually picked up the red wine that she had left to breathe on the counter and poured them both a glass. "Come on. Am I missing something?" Dave asked. He took a sip of the wine and looked at her.

"Can't I just prepare a nice dinner for my husband without any ulterior motive?"

"I'm not complaining, Eileen, I just didn't expect it," Dave said as he sat down.

"How was work?" Eileen asked.

"Same old, you know yourself. You?" Dave responded.

"Much the same. Sophie really likes her new class. She's with all her friends," Eileen said.

"Oh, that's good."

"Sorry, they weren't up to see you. I sent them to bed early."

"No problem. This is really good, thanks," Dave said.

After a few minutes Dave pushed back his chair having finished his food. Dave was about to open his mouth to speak, yet thinking better of it, he clenched his jaw and said nothing. He glanced over at Eileen and quickly looked away, fearing that she might uncover all his secrets, if she looked in his eyes. He needed to talk to Con, their accountant before he said anything to Eileen, he decided. Eileen could feel Dave's eyes on her and focused instead on her glass of wine, inspecting it closely as if it was the most interesting thing in the world. She knew that she needed to talk to him tonight, but she didn't know if she had the energy. Sensing that Dave had looked away, she raised her eyes catching his side profile, as he stared straight ahead out the window. He looked tired too, she thought. Eileen wondered how constant tiredness and apathy had become their life and they weren't even forty. After a few minutes, Dave broke the silence.

"I just want to catch the news if you don't mind," Dave said, despondently. Dave stood up and half-heartedly went to clear the plates.

"It's alright. I'll look after the dishes and I'll follow you in," Eileen said.

When Dave had gone into the living room, Eileen gave herself a pep talk. She rehearsed what she wanted to say to him as she tidied up, feeling a flutter of nerves in her stomach. When she knew the news was over, Eileen picked up the bottle of wine and joined him in the living room. She generously refilled Dave's glass and she sat down beside him on the couch.

"Go easy. I've work tomorrow," Dave said.

"I wanted to talk to you about something," Eileen said, quietly.

"*Tonight?* Aw, *please Eileen*, I'm really tired. Can it *wait?*"

"It's nothing awful, Dave."

"It's just that I'm exhausted, Eileen."

Dave stretched out his long legs on the coffee table, raised his arms above his head and yawned. He prayed that Eileen would let it go for tonight. Dave was almost seeing double he was so tired, and he didn't trust what he might say when in this state.

"Well, if we *only talked* when we weren't exhausted, *we'd never talk*," Eileen snapped.

"Aw, *come on*, we talk plenty."

"We don't and please don't say the weekends as we just turn into a taxi service for the girls," Eileen continued before Dave had a chance to say anything.

"Okay, what is it? Seriously, I've a *really early* start tomorrow," Dave said and glanced at his phone to check the time.

"Well, you know the way I'm doing a Bio-energy course and I've qualified in Reiki…"

"Eileen you know that means *nothing* to me," Dave interrupted.

Eileen felt like he had punched her in the stomach, and she took a moment before continuing.

"What I wanted to say was, please stop saying to the girls that I'm into all this crazy stuff. *It's not on.*"

"*What?* I only ever made a few jokes, *come on. It's harmless,*" Dave said and laughed.

"Would it be harmless if I said that Daddy works with a load of chauvinistic men who think women are second class citizens?" Eileen retorted.

"*What's* gotten into you? That's a low blow," Dave said, surprised at her.

"Come on, you can't deny that some of them in there, seriously… I know, I've had to deal with them," Eileen said.

Eileen paused knowing she was only getting side-tracked.

"I'm sorry, Eileen, it's just that you are a beautiful woman. Some of them just can't handle it. It doesn't make them misogynists," Dave said. Eileen sighed in frustration.

"Look, it isn't about them. It's about you and me. I need you to support me, Dave," Eileen said, firmly.

"I do support you. I'm sorry if I don't get it. It's just that you've a great job in Clancy's. I don't understand why you stress yourself out by taking all this other stuff on."

"*It's not just other stuff.* That's the point. It's what I love, what I want to do with my life. I really don't think *you're getting it,*" Eileen persisted.

"No, I don't think I am," Dave said, and looked at her very sincerely.

"Look, I know it might come as a bit of surprise to you, but this is really important to me. Don't you remember all the workshops I did over the years?" Eileen argued.

"Sort of, but that's like me playing a round of golf. We do different things to relax," Dave said softly. He took his feet off the table and turned to face Eileen with the sincerest look he could muster on his face.

"Look, I won't joke about it with the girls in future okay? Can we drop it now?"

Dave turned towards the TV as if the conversation was over. "Oh God, how do I make this clear to you?" Eileen asked and cleared her throat. "I don't want to work as a solicitor anymore. I haven't for a long time. *I hate it* and it's *killing me* every day that I walk in the door of that office," Eileen said. Eileen paused and took a deep breath before continuing, willing herself to stay calm and measured. "Now, don't have a heart attack. I haven't quit or anything, but I'm working towards that when I qualify and can set up my own business. I've always wanted to work as a healer."

"Come again. You want to work as a healer? Seriously, *for fuck's sake, what does that mean? Jesus,* I agreed to you working part-time and now you're talking about giving up work altogether and turning into some *messiah*, who is going to save the world!"

"*You agreed to…*" Eileen cried. "*What do you mean* you agreed to? I don't have to ask permission *from you* to try something new. *You don't consult me on* everything you do. At least I actually *want to spend time* with our children…"

"That's beneath you, really it is. You know well *how bloody hard* I work to pay for all of this," Dave retorted.

"It was *you* who insisted we buy this *huge bloody mansion!*" Eileen snapped.

"You need to get a grip, really you do. I don't know what's been going on with you recently," Dave said.

"Well, maybe if you really loved me, you would try to understand."

"If I really *loved you? So now on top of everything else, I don't even love you?*"

"You know what I mean, Dave. Look, I'm sorry. That came out wrong, but it doesn't change the fact that you're not exactly supportive. I've always supported you in your career and I'd appreciate you doing the same."

"Jesus, I have supported you a hundred percent in becoming a solicitor and actually have encouraged you. To be honest, I always thought you were on track to become partner, *so forgive me* if I'm finding your recent behaviour a bit confusing."

Eileen felt a tingling sensation behind her eyes and knew she was in danger of bursting into tears. She stood up and paced the room.

"Yes, you've been very supportive of me being a solicitor, but I don't think you are hearing me. I don't want to do this anymore and I haven't for a number of years. I want to set up my own business. I would've preferred to do it with your backing but if not, I'll do it regardless."

Eileen felt weak at the knees and sat down again.

"*Oh, really*. And *who* is going to pay all the bills while you go find yourself? *Do you think we have money to burn?*" Dave angered.

"For God's sake, Dave, you earn plenty of money. I haven't given in my notice, but I will once I get my own business up and running. I really thought you might be happy for me. Obviously, that was a big mistake," Eileen said and slumped on the couch. Their conversation had veered out of control and Eileen didn't know how to get it back on track.

"I don't think you understand the situation. We can't afford it. Do you want us *to go bankrupt?*" Dave asked, and buried his head in his hands.

"*Bankrupt? What are you talking about?*"

"Well, I didn't want to bother you, but a few investments we made have gone belly up and let's just say we're not far off the bank turning up at the door to repossess the house. *Are you happy now?*" Dave said struggling to stay calm. He swallowed hard as he realised that the cat was out of the bag, and now there was no putting it back in.

"I didn't want to have to say it and definitely not like this, but there it is. *Now, are you glad we talked?*" Dave sat back on the couch and ran his fingers through his hair. Dave knew he was being nasty, but he couldn't help it. He had been under such stress, and there was only so much that a person could take. Dave knew that they shouldn't have had this conversation tonight, and he was right.

Eileen's head throbbed, and she felt like the walls were caving in. Having finally plucked up the courage to tell Dave about her plans it had all come crashing down. Eileen didn't understand what had just happened. She put her head in her hands and burst out crying.

SIX

Frank spotted the worried expression on Joan's face as he walked up the road. She stood at the front door waiting, and the nervous twitch in her shoulder was the tell-tale sign. As he approached the gate, Joan's face noticeably relaxed.

"Oh, *there* you are. I wondered where you went," Joan called.

"Didn't I tell you that I was going for a walk?" Frank said, and he walked slowly past her in the front door.

"I know. I'm so sorry, Frank, for the mess I've made, but I called Eileen and I feel a lot better now. She said that everyone will have forgotten about it in *no time*, that nobody reads half of those messages," Joan said, and followed Frank down the hall.

"*Jaysus, did she now? Well, isn't that great* all the same. If Eileen says it, then things are grand," Frank said, abruptly.

"Aw, Frank, *please* don't be like that. We've been through this already. I said I'm sorry. It was a mistake, but like you said, there's nothing we can do about it now."

"Well, *that's some turnaround.* You were sobbing on the bed when I left and now, you're all *c'est la vie.*"

"I just had time to think about things and get a bit of perspective while you were gone," Joan said proudly, remembering some of the advice from her burgeoning library of self-help books.

"*Oh, perspective is it?* And *where* was that perspective when you spilt the porridge on top of me the other day or when Johnny dyed his hair black! You didn't have a lot of perspective then if I remember rightly." Frank said as he walked into the kitchen with Joan following close behind him. Frank walked over to the fridge, opened it and took out the ingredients to start preparing his beef stroganoff speciality, the only dish he had mastered in his adult years. Anything, he thought, to distract from Joan's faux pas.

"Frank, what's gotten into you? I said I was sorry."

"Now Joan, I really want to get started on the dinner. Didn't I promise you that I'd cook my special tonight? It doesn't happen too often, so you might as well make the most of it."

Frank couldn't help smiling as he stood with his back to Joan, while he washed the vegetables under the tap.

"Just relax, love. It's been a long day. It's only a bloody message I suppose, not the end of the world," he added gently.

"Exactly," Joan said.

"And you can't really blame poor Jane, can you? I mean Tom Jones hasn't a patch on this..." Frank said, brushing his hands through his hair.

"*Stop it*, would you?" Joan giggled as Frank grabbed her around the waist and waltzed around the kitchen.

"You don't know how good you have it, Joan Hughes, you really don't," he whispered into her ear.

"Get a room will you, ugh. It's only six o'clock and you're at it already," Johnny sneered as he came in the back door.

"Wait 'til the women are trailing after you. You're a Hughes man after all. It'll be a different story then so it will," Frank jested, glad to forget any talk of phones and WhatsApp messages.

"*Get lost.* You're embarrassing," Johnny said and marched past them to pour himself a glass of water at the sink.

"*Jaysus*, what's wrong with your parents enjoying themselves? Wait until you meet the right girl, or boy even. It's all the same these days isn't it? Love is love. Isn't that right, Joan?"

Frank patted her on the backside.

"*Frank... Don't* be giving him ideas. He's only fifteen. Plenty of time for that, isn't that right?" Joan said, but Johnny brushed past her without a second glance.

"God, you're so lame, both of you. Remind me never to be seen in public with you," Johnny said. He threw his coat on a chair, kicked off his shoes and left.

"Dinner in half an hour okay, Johnny! No excuses," Frank called.

"I can't wait... and just for your information," Johnny said, sticking his head in the door, "I'm not gay, though sometimes it sounds quite appealing. If it means no more high maintenance women, I can see the attraction."

Joan turned to Frank with her mouth open and he put up his hand before she could get a word out.

"Don't Joan, just leave it," Frank said and turned back to preparing the dinner. Frank recognised the tell-tale smell and the bloodshot eyes, and he knew there was no point talking to Johnny if he was wasted.

"I just wish we could have a civil conversation, I really do," Joan said.

"I know, love. He's only trying to rise you and it works every single time."

"But…"

"But nothing. Let it go, love, and leave me get the dinner in peace." Joan walked out of the kitchen, knowing she wasn't going to get anywhere with Frank. She looked into the living room and seeing Abbie sprawled on the couch with a book in her hand she forgot about Johnny's words. Her daughter's face was scrunched up as she concentrated on what she read, but she looked up when she heard Joan come in.

"Hi, Mam," Abbie said.

"How's my baby doing?"

"Mam, I'm almost a teenager," Abbie complained.

"Well, you'll always be my baby. Can I sit down beside you for a minute?" Joan asked.

"Sure," Abbie said, and Joan sat down and put her arm around her.

"You're a star, you know that? You haven't complained once about your ankle and it must be very sore," Joan said, softly.

"I'm okay. Is there anything wrong, Mam?" Abbie asked.

"Nothing, love. I'm just happy that you're okay. You've no idea how worried I was yesterday," Joan said.

Joan leaned back on the couch and played with Abbie's curls. "Are you sure? Is it Johnny?" Abbie asked.

"Now, what makes you say that?" Joan asked, surprised.

"I know what he's like, Mam. He's the same to me. Saoirse told me her brother's just the same, *thick as*. I've decided that I don't care anymore," Abbie said, resolutely.

"It's just a phase you know, being a teenager," Joan said, but not very convincingly.

"Well, it's a pretty long phase, *like forever*. I think there might be something wrong with him, you know, in the head," Abby said.

"*Don't say that about your brother*, Abbie," Joan exclaimed.

"Well, I wish I'd a sister instead, like Sophie has," Abbie said with certainty. Her new friend Sophie seemed to have it all.

"I suppose we often want what we don't have. I'd love to have beautiful dark, shiny curls like you," Joan said, and kissed her on the top of her head.

"Dinner's ready," Frank called from the kitchen.

"Okay, I'll bring your dinner into you when we're finished. We can't have you walking on that leg, love."

"Thanks, Mam," Abbie said.

"*For the last time*, it's on the table." Frank said, and appeared at the living room door, his face matching the red tea towel thrown over his shoulder.

"Okay, I'm coming Frank," Joan said and stood up.

"Remember, not a word, Abbie," Joan whispered to her before following Frank into the kitchen.

"Where did Johnny go? Go on, Cyril, tell him to get a move on or that mangy dog next door will be getting his dinner," Frank angered and nudged him out of his seat.

Cyril reluctantly left his plate full of food and walked out to the bottom of the stairs.

"*Johnny, dinner, now!*" Cyril shouted and walked back into the kitchen.

"*God almighty*. Would you *go up and get him. I can roar at him myself*, but that doesn't seem to be gettin' much of a response!" Frank snapped.

"He's *not a child*, Dad. He'll come down when he's hungry," Cyril protested.

"I didn't go slavin' over my beef stroganoff *for nothing*. Now, will you *go up that stairs and* get him down here *before I give him what for*," Frank shouted, and pushed Cyril back out the door.

"Oh, go easy, Frank. It's not good for your blood pressure," Joan interrupted.

"*Jaysus*, Joan, what's not good for my blood pressure is cooking a dinner that isn't appreciated!"

Cyril bounded up the stairs and banged on Johnny's door. "*Dinner!*"

Cyril waited and while he waited, he couldn't help smiling at the handmade sign on the door, two fingers to anyone who might enter uninvited. That pretty much summed up Johnny.

"*Quit messing will you*, Johnny!"

On getting no response, Cyril pushed open the door to an empty room. It had been years since he was inside it, and he looked around. Nearly every inch of the wall was covered with posters full of angry looking faces. He stepped over piles of clothes and half-eaten food, standing on something that was unidentifiable. The bed was covered with second-hand records and Cyril bent down to take a look at them. He couldn't help laughing when he picked up an album that had Johnny Rotten from the Sex Pistols on the cover. Cyril knew he was Johnny's current idol. Placing the album back in its place, Cyril spied something fluffy sticking out from under the bed covers. If he didn't know better, he could have sworn it was a teddy bear. He was just about to take a look when he was distracted by a pungent pair of socks on Johnny's bedside locker.

"Jesus Christ, the smell!"

Cyril covered his nose with his sleeve and backed out of the room. He walked into the bathroom and craned his neck out the small window that looked on to the back garden. There was no sign of Johnny's bike, so Cyril knew there was no need to look any further for him.

"Well? *Where is he?*" Frank asked, looking up from his food when Cyril came back into the kitchen.

"No sign. He's not there," Cyril said, sitting down. By now, Cyril's appetite had taken a sharp dip.

"What do you mean not there? Sure, he only came in the door half an hour ago," Frank said dropping his fork. "Are you sure?"

"*Am I sure?* Yes, Dad. Unless he's hiding in the wardrobe, he's *definitely* not there."

Frank's face reddened and he looked at Joan.

"I'm sure he'll be home soon, Frank," Joan said, trying to keep the peace.

"He should be home now, not out gallivanting without a word to us. *I warned him*," Frank angered.

Frank stood up and looked out the window as if he expected to see Johnny walking up the path. Joan looked at Cyril hoping he might say something that helped.

"He might have texted me, if he had to go out," Cyril said, and put his plate in the sink.

Cyril's appetite had now definitely gone, and he went to get his phone out of his jacket pocket.

"For *Chrissakes*, where would a fifteen-year-old have to go in such a panic at this hour and wouldn't it be more in his line just to tell us rather than sending *bloody messages to you*…" Frank spluttered. "It's not on. Well?" Frank asked and looked at Cyril expectantly.

"Nothing, really. Just something about a book and Jack. He won't be long," Cyril said, casually.

"*A feckin' book!* Does he think *I came down in the last shower?* When has *that fella* ever picked up a book?"

"Don't shoot the messenger. It has nothing to do with me," Cyril said and made a face.

He knew exactly where Johnny was right now. The stories about the two of them were doing the rounds at school, but Cyril wasn't going to be the one to break the news at home, though he couldn't understand how his parents couldn't see what was right under their noses.

"Sorry, son. You're right." Frank said, and patted Cyril on the back.

"I'm telling you, love, I'm having a word with him when he gets home. I'm not spending my time making dinners and he couldn't be bothered turning up," Frank said, and started clearing away the plates.

"He probably just thought he'd be out and back before you noticed," Cyril said.

"Well, that didn't work out so well for him, did it now? *Jaysus*, every time I'm in good form, something bloody happens in this house. I thought we'd be celebrating, what with Mary comin' tomorrow. She'll think we're a crowd of lunatics, with this carry on."

Frank banged the dishes into the sink.

"Frank, we're not a crowd of lunatics. And she's no holy Mary herself, just because she goes to mass every day. We've all heard the stories about her."

Frank stopped what he was doing and turned to face them both. "Well, I can tell you one thing. I saw her with me own eyes today, and there's nothing wrong with her and she wasn't half-flutered for your information. In fact, she was in great form and the house was spotless," Frank said, lifting the bottle of Fairy liquid, "and *what* are you two laughing at?" Frank asked.

"Nothing. Pink suits you, Dad. Doesn't it, Mam?" Cyril smothered a laugh as he took in the sight of his Dad expounding in his pink rubber gloves.

Joan stood up. She was sick to the teeth listening to Frank rave on about Mary.

"I'm going in to see Abbie. Seeing as it is a rare occasion that you're in the kitchen Frank, I'll leave you to it. You can have the junk room tonight," Joan said, and marched out leaving Frank staring after her.

They had christened the small room at the back of the house the junk room when they first moved in. And it had stayed the junk room. Frank had done a lot of wheeling and dealing to furnish the room for under half-nothing, and it showed. Nevertheless, it served as an overflow room when they were grating on each other's nerves.

It wouldn't matter if they hung chandeliers from the ceiling, it would forever be known as the junk room.

"What's gotten into her?" Frank asked and looked at Cyril flabbergasted.

"Maybe you should go a bit easy with praising Mary, Dad."

"*What?* Isn't *she the one* doing us a favour? God, I can't figure women out sometimes."

"Sometimes?" Cyril slagged him.

"You're right, son. I can't figure them out at all."

Frank washed the dishes as Cyril dried, and in that hour that they spent together in the kitchen they talked about everything from school to girlfriends and women in general, to the state of affairs of the nation.

Once they were finished, Frank pulled off his rubber gloves and left the kitchen.

"Is there any sign of him yet? It's quarter past nine," Frank said, walking into the living room where Joan and Abbie were watching a movie. Frank struggled to keep his frustration at bay, not wanting to upset his two favourite girls. He just prayed that Johnny wasn't in any trouble.

"He's not answering his phone all evening. *Where in God's name could he be?*" Frank said, trying to keep a lid on his worst fears.

"Dad, I can't see," Abbie complained as she strained to see the television.

"*I mean it,* Joan. The one night I wanted to put me feet up and relax and he has to go AWOL," Frank continued, moving behind the armchair, totally unaware that Joan was fast asleep.

"I don't know why you're always worrying about him, Dad. He always comes home in the end," Abbie said, throwing her eyes to heaven.

"Why didn't you call me, Frank? I didn't know it was that late. I'll call Jack's mother," Joan said and stirred in her seat. She opened her eyes and leaned forward on the chair.

"No, *you won't. I'm calling* him myself again. And he better bloody pick up this time!" Frank declared, and he walked out to the hall to get his phone.

"You know, he often stays at Jack's and does his homework…" Joan called after him.

"Aw, come on, love. Do you really believe that?" Frank walked back in with the phone to his ear.

"It's ringing out again. *That bloody eejit.* Listen!" Frank snapped and held the phone out so they could hear it.

"Dad?" Johnny's voice sounded faint on the other end of the line. Frank put the phone to his ear and Joan listened in.

"Johnny? What the… stop it, Joan," Frank said, and pushed her away.

"Where are you? It's half bloody nine, you know."

"On my way. I can't talk now."

"Where are you son?" Frank asked again.

"Ten minutes tops. On the way," Johnny said and hung up. "Did you hear that? And you think he was doing his homework. It sounded more like he was out on the town. And what were you pinching me for?"

"There's no point getting angry with him, Frank. You don't know what might have happened," Joan answered.

Frank shook his head. One minute she was up to high doh over nothing, and now here she was as cool as a cucumber and her son out half the night. He went out to the kitchen and finished his beer with one mouthful. He had a sneaking suspicion that something was going on with Johnny, and the dread that rumbled in his belly told him it wasn't something good. Frank ran his hands through his hair and paced the kitchen. The foreboding feeling was still familiar as he remembered his own father waiting for him at home. He rubbed his face recalling where the punch had landed after he had come home late one night. No words were ever spoken as his father's fists always did the talking. Frank had vowed he would never be a carbon copy of him, no matter what. Frank told Joan some of the stories and she had cried, but there were some too harrowing to verbalise. The recurrent nightmare that still visited him from time to time was the night when he had been locked in the shed, when he was only twelve years old. Frank shivered and walked out to the hall. He was not going to repeat the sins of the past.

When Cyril and Johnny were only young boys, he had imagined coming of age conversations with them, sharing his wisdom over their first pint and listening to their worries with a supportive pat on the back. Frank didn't know how well he had done at that so far, but he definitely was not his father's son, and Frank never would be if he could help it.

Frank jumped when the doorbell rang, almost dropping his bottle of beer. It was a rare occasion that anyone rang on the front door, with friends and neighbours always entering by the back. Joan hovered at the living room door and Frank waved her back. Frank put the bottle down on the hall table and taking a look in the mirror, he opened the door. Standing before him was a huge, middle-aged Garda in uniform, and Johnny sloped up the driveway behind him with his hands jammed in his pockets. Johnny came to a standstill behind the Garda, trying to steer clear of the glare from the light in the porch.

"Mr Hughes, good evening. I'm Garda Reilly."

The Garda put out his hand to Frank, who stared open-mouthed at him. Frank thought he had the look of a hardy farmer, with a head of sandy hair, hands the size of shovels and a ruddy complexion, which hadn't been helped by his encounter with Johnny. Frank glared at Johnny who, from what he could see, looked meek and pale-faced in comparison as he tried to hide in the shadows. "Hello, Garda. And what brings you here at this hour?" Frank asked.

He wasn't going to admit that he had imagined this very moment many times in his head.

"Well, Mr Hughes. I'm afraid that I found your son in the middle of a fight down in the park, and he was laying into some poor lad big time. If I hadn't come along, I don't know what damage he might have done. It could have been a lot worse if I hadn't arrived on the scene." Garda Reilly cleared his throat and straightened his uniform jacket, preparing himself for another parent who wouldn't accept that their darling son or daughter had been up to no good.

Frank tried to catch Johnny's eye, but he looked at his feet. "I'm telling you now, if the lad had ended up in A&E and his parents pressed charges, it would be a very different story, a very different story altogether," Garda Reilly said, shaking his head. Frank was distracted for a minute as he saw the curtains twitch in Bridie Lynch's front room across the road. That was all they needed. Every dog on the street would be talking about them in jig time if she had anything to do with it.

"He started it, Dad. McCabe is a pig, and I only tried to help Jack." Johnny insisted. Frank turned his attention back to the scene unfolding in front of him.

"Easy does it, Johnny. Go inside and let me have a word with Garda Reilly."

Johnny shuffled in the door. As the hall light shone on his face, Frank took in the cut over his eye and his grazed knuckles. Joan and Abbie had heard the voices and huddled in the hall to watch. As

Johnny walked past, a knowing look of déjà vu passed between them.

"Now, Garda, what's all this about? Young Johnny has never given us a day's trouble in his life," Frank said, putting on his best look of disbelief as he scratched his head in confusion.

"Well, he gave some fella, I think Brian McCabe he said his name was, a right leathering in the park. He wasn't the only one involved, but he was fired up. Has he any problems with anger at home or at school?" He looked over Frank's shoulder as if he expected to find an explanation in the house. Frank was tempted to say that anger was Johnny's middle name since the day he was born, but he held his tongue.

"*Jaysus,* he's never given his mother or me an ounce of trouble. Are you sure it was him? It just isn't like our Johnny to be getting into fights."

"It was him, alright. I saw him with my own eyes. He's not easy to miss with that head of red hair. I can tell you that what I witnessed this evening was far from good behaviour," Garda Reilly assured him.

"He has never hurt a fly in his life. We've no time for violence in this house, don't we not, Joan?" Frank asked and turned to Joan for moral support, but she had disappeared down the hall with Johnny. Frank could feel his momentum quickly fading as he struggled to defend his unpredictable son on his own.

"He's always been one to stand up for the underdog. Maybe that explains it," Frank said, his words lacking any real conviction. Garda Reilly looked at him with disbelief.

"In my experience, Mr Hughes, when young fellas start down this road of violence, it can be a slippery slope. I would urge you to have a chat with him. If there's a next time, which I hope there isn't, he may not be so lucky. You wouldn't want him ending up with a record, would you?" Garda Reilly cautioned.

"Aw, now, hold your horses. I can assure you that nothing of the sort goes on in this house. We're peaceful people and we have reared our children to be the same," Frank said, struggling to stay calm.

"I'm glad to hear it, but he'd an awful temper on him this evening and I'm just giving you the heads up. I just hope that I never have to arrive at your door again like this."

"Well, that makes two of us. It might be worth paying the parents of Brian McCabe a visit. He's no holy Joe from what I've heard, but I appreciate you bringing Johnny home all the same," Frank said.

Frank turned and closed the door, afraid that he might say too much. He stood in the hall and caught his breath.

"Jesus Christ," Frank muttered.

The day that they had secretly dreaded for years had finally arrived. The anger that had been boiling away inside Johnny had found an outlet and Frank shuddered to think of the damage he might have done. Years of pent up anger exploding was not a pretty sight. He would never forget his own father when the anger erupted. His eyes bulged and a large vein throbbed on the side of his head. He had been a walking time bomb every day.

Garda Reilly slowly walked back to the squad car with a heaviness in his step. He shook his head as he wondered how parents could be so blind when it came to their own children.

On the other side of that door, Frank walked into the kitchen and found Joan cleaning Johnny's cuts and bruises, while he sat staring into space.

"Look at him, Frank. I hope that Guard is going to catch whoever is responsible for this," Joan said, rubbing Johnny's cuts with antiseptic.

"Johnny… I want to have a word with you in private," Frank said.

Johnny pushed Joan's hand away impatiently. He stood up and followed Frank out to the junk room.

"Okay, spit it out. Tell me what happened," Frank said and sat back in the armchair, doing his best to appear open and receptive.

Frank pointed Johnny towards the small couch across from him and cleared his throat. Frank felt a wave of protectiveness as he looked at his son, who was so angry with the world. The adrenaline came at him in waves across the room. Frank's own father had been addicted to it and the feeling of power it gave him. Frank pointed at the gash above Johnny's eye.

"That looks sore," he said, affectionately.

"It's grand. I'm telling you, it was McCabe's fault, Dad. He's an animal and I was only trying to help Jack," Johnny said without a shred of remorse.

"*Aw Jaysus*, do you hear yourself? You could've ended up in jail. Do you realise that? And that's aside from the fact that you just disappeared without a word," Frank said as calmly as he could.

A silence opened up as they both were afraid of saying something they might regret. Eventually Johnny spoke.

"*I'm sorry*, okay. Jack texted me and he needed my help. It's a long story..."

"*Go on*. I'm all ears," Frank said, curious to hear what elaborate tale Johnny might have concocted this time.

"He owed McCabe money, that's all. He didn't have it and McCabe wasn't happy. Jesus, Dad, the guy's a head the ball. When I got there, he had him pinned up against the wall. I wasn't just going to leave Jack and walk away," Johnny said.

Frank knew only too well that his son could well pack a punch. He had been in the local boxing club when he was younger and the coach had assured them that he showed great promise, but that he needed to mature a bit. Reading between the lines, what he really meant was that Johnny was well up for kicking the shit out of anyone, no problem. Frank didn't know whether to be proud or disappointed at the remark, but Johnny hadn't lasted long there in any event. When he had taken to having boxing matches outside the ring, Frank had been politely asked by the club organisers to give Johnny a break for a while.

"Well, you could have called me. You'd have saved us all a lot of trouble."

"*Seriously*, Dad, what good could you do at home, while Jack had the shit kicked out of him?"

"I'm just telling you from experience. Violence never solves anything, trust me. And why was he borrowing money off him in the first place? You can tell me you know. I won't judge."

Frank waited for Johnny to spit it out but when Johnny wasn't answering, he didn't push him. Frank had decided a long time ago that unlike his own father, he would never use brute force with his children. He would do his best to let them know they could always confide in him, he would earn their trust, not demand it.

"There are other ways to make a difference in life you know, without using your fists. How are you any better than Brian McCabe if you behave just like him?" Frank continued.

"It's not fair, Dad. The cops won't touch him, just because his father's a judge and he knows it," Johnny said.

Frank forced back a smile. He couldn't help feeling proud of Johnny. Whatever problems he had cowardice wasn't one of them.

"All I'm saying is, you don't know your own strength. Garda Reilly said you were really layin' into him. Do you want to end up in *jail* before you *even finish school*?"

"I'm just sick of the likes of McCabe getting off scot free all the time. No one does anything about guys like him, but the minute I step out of line, they want to stick cuffs on me. The whole system of justice is a joke in this country," Johnny argued.

"Well, you might be right there, son, but you can't sort it out by getting into fights. The cops will be keepin' an eye on you from now on and so will I. So, you better stay out of trouble," Frank said.

Frank looked at Johnny's downcast face and resisted the urge to get up and walk across the room and hug him. He still knew that he needed to be firm.

"Do you hear me?" Frank warned. "You know, Johnny, I've seen plenty of violence in my own life and it never ended well. Believe me when I tell you that."

"I get it, Dad," Johnny said.

There are other ways and you're a smart lad. Why not stick your head in the books and figure out another way of making your mark on the world? I know you have it in you, son, I really do. I believe in you. Do you hear me Johnny? I believe in you." Frank just managed to finish the sentence as his voice cracked. He would have given anything to hear those words even once from his own father.

"Okay," Johnny said, feeling a bit embarrassed by his Dad's outburst. Johnny stood up to go and hesitated at the door.

"You should have seen McCabe though? He won't mess with me again…" he grinned full of pride.

"*Christ*, will you get off to bed? The lot of you have me mithered. What will Mary make of us at all?" Frank said, and stood up, wondering if anything he said had registered at all with his wayward son.

Frank pushed Johnny out the door and went to join Joan in the kitchen. Joan at the kitchen table, sipping on a herbal tea that did little to calm her anxiety.

"Oh, there you are, Frank. What took you so long? What happened?" Joan spoke so fast that her words were garbled.

"Take it easy. It's all sorted, love. I had a good man to man with him and he won't be steppin' out of line any time soon. I can tell you that for sure."

Frank rubbed his hands together, glad that he had finished their chat without losing his cool. He had smelt the pot wafting off Johnny, but he hadn't been able to face that conversation.

"Oh, that's great, but I really hope they catch the culprit. It's a disgrace, really it is," Joan said.

Frank didn't mention that the culprit was upstairs in their house feeling delighted with himself.

"It is indeed. Now, I'm off to bed. I'm getting too old for all this madness."

Frank pecked Joan on the cheek and then slowly climbed the stairs.

Johnny heard his father's footsteps on the stairs and sank back on the bed, knowing he had a lucky escape. He hadn't told him the whole story. It was true he had come to Jack's defence, but they both owed McCabe a lot of money and they had to come up with it fast.

SEVEN

Mary woke, alarmed at the darkness setting in. She looked at her watch and saw that it was nearly three o'clock in the afternoon. The weather had taken a turn for the worse with lashing rain and wind bringing a premature end to the day. She jumped out of the chair, sending Boots flying with a yowl. Visibly unimpressed, he slinked over to the heat of the Aga stove to resume his sleep.

"*God almighty*, look at the *time*, Boots. We're way behind," Mary yelped.

Mary knew it might sound daft to some, but she really wanted to make a good impression with the Hughes family. Having spent the last twenty years on her own, busying herself with the garden and odd jobs in the church, her life had often felt more like a cruel existence rather than a fulfilling experience. It pained Mary to dredge up her many regrets, and despite everything, Mary knew she had done her best in the circumstances.

"Well just maybe, this is a chance for a fresh start," Mary said, and stroked the appreciative cat. She then filled his bowl with water. Mary sat back down on the tatty but comfortable armchair and pulled on her lace up boots. She thought about Frank's words and remembered how she had reared five children and assured herself, that experience would automatically kick in as soon as she walked through the Hughes' door. Mary stood up and searched the room for a pen and some paper, so she could make out a shopping list.

Bending down, Mary sifted through the pile of magazines that Frank had moved, hoping to find one of the notebooks that she used for her recipes and herbal remedies.

Mary groaned as she felt her joints creak with the effort, but nonetheless continued to rummage around in the pile and gasped as an old housekeeping notebook of her mother's fell out on the floor. She had searched high and low for it in the house and had just been coming to terms with the fact that she might have thrown it out by mistake. She leaned on the table and pulled herself up onto a chair. Mary placed the notebook on the table, taking a minute to look at her mother's writing on the cover. Emotion stirred in her and Mary pulled a tissue from her sleeve and dabbed her eyes. Slowly, she opened it and read the message that her mother had inscribed for her daughter on the inside cover.

To Mary,
My very brave and beautiful daughter. I wish you every happiness in life.
With all my love,
Mam.

Mary caught her breath as she felt the loving presence of her mother in the room. It was a long time since she had read the message, a message that her mother would have taken thought and time to write, as evidenced by her warm words and perfect handwriting. She put her hand to her chest as a sharp stab of pain reminded her of her loss. It felt as real in that moment as it had all those years ago. Tears flowed as the pain that she had pushed down for years erupted suddenly, a tsunami of emotion that would not be quelled.

Mary let the emotion freely express itself and after about ten minutes, the storm eventually subsided. Mary felt exhausted but knew that a heavy burden had been lifted from her. Gradually, a wide smile crept across her face. Mary looked out the window to see the sun emerge from behind the clouds and a rainbow parade its glory across the sky.

"Thank you, Mam," Mary whispered.

Mary was left in no doubt that her mother was doing everything she could to help her only daughter right now. It was more than her mother had been capable of doing while she was alive, she had struggled to carry her own burdens.

Feeling a surge of energy, she set about writing a list of what she needed to buy. As she did so, flashbacks of a different life came into focus - the children crawling around under her feet as she wrote out her daily shopping list, bickering as they did their homework beside her at the table and a baby roaring to be fed while she tried to keep on top of everything. There had been little need of lists when they had all grown up and moved away. Any important matters were easily recorded on her calendar on the wall.

After some further thought, Mary settled on an Irish stew and an apple tart for dinner at the Hughes. Although she loved baking, Mary had found it hard to stay enthusiastic when the final result, however nice, always ended up in the bin with only one or two slices eaten.

"There, there, Boots," Mary said, leaning down to stroke her cat, "we'll get through this together."

Mary could easily empathise with those who lived alone, whether by choice or a twist of fate. A solitary lifestyle that might be a dream to busy, overburdened parents, lost its attraction when it became the norm every day and the only opportunity to exercise your vocal cords was to shout at Judge Judy or exchange pleasantries with the checkout girl in the supermarket.

Standing up, Mary closed the notebook and placed it in a prominent position on her bookshelf. Then she went out to the hall to inspect her face in the mirror. Despite her puffy appearance, Mary recognised a light in her eyes that hadn't been there for a long time and she felt a new spring in her step. Mary tidied her hair in a bun and went back into the kitchen to gather up her shopping bags. Inspecting her selection of coats in the wardrobe under the stairs, she opted for her bright red raincoat.

Despite life's hardships, Mary had always been attracted to colour. When she felt particularly low, it had helped to mask her sadness. Even more than that, she knew it was a cry for attention from a world that had little time for older people. After a year of mourning for Tom, she had cleared out not only his, but her entire wardrobe and vowed to never wear anything black again. The end result was often a mishmash of clashing garish colours, but at least she was no longer invisible. If the attention she received was looks normally reserved for someone who was deemed mad or eccentric, she could live with that, but today Mary felt different.

"Yes, you'll do just fine," Mary said, looking at her reflection.

Mary smiled as she pulled on the bright red coat that accurately reflected how she felt, full of life and energy.

"Look after the place, Boots, I won't be long. I'll bring back your favourite dinner, a special treat today," Mary said.

Boots stirred, looked up at her and nodded his approval and Mary smiled back at him.

"What would I do without you all the same, you little rascal?" Mary said, closing the kitchen door.

Boots had been a life saver when Mary had been at a particularly low ebb. Mary pulled the front door behind her and set off to do her shopping.

Hoping the supermarket wouldn't be packed to the gills with office workers she hurried along, head bent against the beating rain. At the door of the supermarket, Mary grabbed a basket and referring to her list, she quickly collected everything she needed and queued for the cashier.

"God be with the days when it took me an hour to get home," Mary said, not recognising a single person in the supermarket. "Be careful what you wish for Mary," she reminded herself and smiled. Just then, she fixed her attention on a striking-looking woman and two young girls just in front of her and smiled as she watched a battle ensue at the sweet stand with the hassled mother eventually giving in. Mary remembered those days well. She could have sworn she recognised the woman. Mary knew she was staring but couldn't help herself. She recognised the woman from a photograph in the local newspaper. This woman had been with one of the Danaher son's, Mary was sure of it.

Tom had worked for the well-known business family when they had were just married. The Danaher's had owned a large hardware store in town which they eventually sold to an international chain, and the elder Danaher wasn't long joining the social elite. It was a status conferred by his sudden wealth and not an accident of birth. Tom had great respect for him and had talked about him often. He had worked his way up from the shop floor, but it was said that his children were spoilt, jumped-up brats. The beautiful woman standing in front of her looked to be married to one of these jumped-up brats if memory served her correctly. Standing here in the supermarket, Mary thought she looked like any other stressed out mother trying to get through the day in one piece.

Mary was lost in thought as she walked the short journey home. Only for her shopping bags anchoring her to dry land, she would have been blown into the river. Her house had a spectacular view of the water, and she knew it was a wonderful luxury that many couldn't afford these days. No doubt once she passed away, her family would be quick to sell up and make a tidy sum of money for themselves. There would be no sentimentality, it would just be a very sensible, profitable business transaction.

"Well, they can do what they like then," she mumbled, "but there's no chance of them *committing me* to a nursing home. I'll take my last breath in this house, if it's the last thing I do," Mary said.

If Mary's children weren't careful, she might change her will and leave nothing to them. Tom had left the house to her to do with as she pleased, but no doubt he thought that their children would be the beneficiaries. Well, he hadn't seen how they deserted her one by one, like rats on a sinking ship. If the Hughes' played their cards right, who knows, they might get a nice little windfall someday.

Propelled by the strong westerly wind, Mary almost fell in the front door of her house. Boots looked up as she opened the door, none too impressed with the cold draught of air. He gave her a look that could kill. He might as well have been saying what the feck are you doing bringing half the river into the kitchen and drenching me at the same time?

"Aw, Boots, its well for you half-asleep all day," Mary said.

She dropped her shopping, wiped herself down with a towel and picked up the phone to Frank. Mary quickly cleared her throat while she waited for him to answer.

"Hi Frank? It's Mary. Can you hear me?"

"Hello, hello? Who is this?" Frank shouted.

"It's Mary, Frank. Have you forgotten me *already?*"

"Of course, I haven't forgotten. For Chrissakes, Mary, I can hardly hear you. I'm out for a walk."

"God, you picked some day for a walk, Frank," Mary said and looked out the window at the rain that beat down again.

"It's grand. A bit of rain never harmed anyone," Frank said.

"I just wanted to check, it's half past ten tomorrow morning that you want me, Frank?" Mary said. Mary drummed her fingers on the table as she waited for him to reply.

"It is indeed. You're a lifesaver, Mary. Is everything okay?" Frank asked.

"Everything's fine. I was just double-checking. I'll see you tomorrow, Frank," Mary said, and hung up the phone.

Mary began making pastry and couldn't help chuckling at the memories of a young Frank who had been a real livewire, always full of devilment and cut knees. He had been a handful anytime she babysat, but totally irresistible. Frank could always wrap any woman around his little finger and still could from the looks of it. She would never forget the day he brought a bunch of school pals home, and they broke a window in the neighbour's glass house, on purpose, she was fairly sure as she saw them taking aim in the back garden. Frank wasn't long conjuring up some convoluted story that had the neighbour almost sorry for him and ready to take the blame herself. It was those brown eyes that always stole the show and melted the heart of any woman, neighbour or otherwise, and forgiveness was then only a few steps away.

Mary laughed thinking of all the falls she had taken for him over the years. She was no stranger to the stories about Frank's father, but thankfully he had stopped short of ever laying a hand on her. Mary had done well to avoid her own father as it was.

"You know what Boots, it's a fresh start for both of us. You'll have the place to yourself and I might bring you with me one of the days if you behave yourself," Mary said and smiled.

The cat purred and gobbled down the leftover pastry she threw on the floor. If it meant more food for him, he wasn't complaining. The windows steamed up as the kitchen reached sauna-like temperatures, and when Mary headed to bed, she felt that it had been a very good day indeed.

****

At exactly 10.30 am on Wednesday morning, Mary rang the doorbell of the Hughes house. She had rushed from mass with Fr Brennan, who kept it to a tight twenty minutes during the week and had still ended up with time to spare. Standing on the doorstep, Mary surveyed her surroundings and took in the jaded appearance. The front garden was just a square patch of grass that looked to get the bare minimum of care and there wasn't a flower or shrub in sight. Mary turned back to the front door taking in the green paint that was now starting to peel. She couldn't help feeling a bit disappointed. However bad things had been in her own life, keeping her house and garden in order had been her saving grace. Even if it was only a façade at times, it had helped her retain some semblance of control. Whatever was going on with the Hughes family, their house needed a bit of TLC.

Mary was just about to ring again when the door flew open and Joan Hughes greeted her. If being given the once-over suspiciously was a greeting, this was a mighty one. Mary was surprised to see that Joan was a dainty-like thing up close and even smaller than she had remembered. Mary watched Joan's blue eyes dart nervously as she spoke, and there were two spots of red on her cheeks, the only colour on an otherwise very pale complexion. Beautiful blonde curls softened her appearance and Mary, noticing the strained expression on Joan's face, imagined that she would be very pretty if she just relaxed a bit.

"Hello, Mrs O'Sullivan. Do come in. We're expecting you" Joan said.

"Hi, Joan. Lovely to see you. It's been quite a while, quite a while indeed."

Mary picked up her shopping bags and followed Joan through to the kitchen.

"Oh my God, Mary, there was no need to bring so much with you. *We do have* food here you know," Joan said and laughed, but Mary didn't miss the dig in her comment.

"Oh, of course you do. I just thought with you both working and Frank did ask me to help. I was going to make dinner, but if you'd prefer not, that's fine by me," Mary said, hearing the condescension in Joan's voice.

"No, no. Seeing as you've brought everything with you, I suppose you might as well cook," Joan said.

Mary held her tongue. She was sorely tempted to give Joan Hughes a piece of her mind and march home with her groceries, but she remembered what had happened yesterday afternoon and the beautiful feeling of her mother's presence, so she smiled warmly at Joan instead. Tom's words also rang in her ears. He had always been telling her to cool it and to think before she opened her mouth.

"I'll give you a quick tour before I go to work. Abbie is in the living room and the boys are at school. I should be back around four thirty or five, and we usually have dinner about six when Frank is home," Joan said, her shoulder twitching.

"That's fine. Any jobs you need doing around the house?" Mary asked, glancing around at the cluttered kitchen.

"Well, if you wouldn't mind doing a bit of hoovering and if you could put a wash on," Joan said and pointed at the overflowing laundry basket. Only if you feel able for it."

"Of course, I'm happy to. That's why I'm here as I said, Joan. Frank *did ask me*, you know, and I wouldn't have said yes if I wasn't up to it."

Mary looked closely at Joan and noticed her trembling like a frightened rabbit.

"Okay, well, thank you. He just gets carried away with himself sometimes. You know the way… I just hope he didn't put you under any pressure… you know… to say yes… it's only that I'm working… other than that obviously… I'd take care of things…" Joan stuttered, having been taken aback by Mary's directness.

"*Of course,* you would," Mary said as she took off her coat and rolled up her sleeves.

Mary softened having realised that Joan was a lot more fragile than she might dare to admit.

"We've just had a lot going on recently," Joan explained as she recalled the guards arriving at the door the night before.

"You have indeed by the sounds of it. How's Abbie doing?" Mary asked.

"She's *so brave*. I'm so proud of her, but it was an awful shock," Joan said and trembled.

Mary could see that despite her funny notions, Joan deeply loved her young daughter. Mary followed Joan as she led the way to the small living room across the hall.

"Abbie, Mrs O'Sullivan is here, you remember her, love, don't you? She's going to stay with you while Dad and I are at work," Joan said softly.

"Oh hello, Mrs O'Sullivan," Abbie said, brightly.

Mary looked at her and thought she was the cutest thing with her beautiful dark curls and hypnotic green eyes. She was reminded of her own Bernice when she was a little girl, and she felt a lump in her throat as she thought of her youngest daughter. Hardened by life and an ignoramus of a husband, her beauty had quickly dimmed. Years of excessive smoking and worrying hadn't helped and the signs of a life full of heartache were etched deeply on her face. She hoped little Abbie's life would be a happier one than her daughter's had turned out to be.

"How's the patient doing? That cast must be a tonne weight," Mary remarked.

Abbie lifted her leg theatrically, warming instantly to Mary and the attention.

"No, it's quite light actually, just a bit like, itchy," Abbie said, proudly.

"Well, I'm here at your beck and call while your parents are at work, so make the most of it," Mary said and smiled.

"I best be off. Is that okay, Mrs O'Sullivan? Abbie will tell you where everything is," Joan said and gave Abbie a kiss, despite feeling uncomfortable with the intimacy that seemed to be already developing between the pair.

"Call me, Mary, please. I haven't been called Mrs O'Sullivan in a long time Joan," Mary said.

"The boys might be back before me, but they'll do their own thing, so you don't need to worry about them," Joan said.

Joan picked up her coat and bag, itching to get out of the house. She didn't like this arrangement one bit, and with Mary of all people. Well, she would soon see what it was like doing all the housework and looking after Abbie. From what Joan had heard, it had just been herself and her cat for years. She would get some shock that was for sure.

When the door closed behind Joan, Mary sat down across from Abbie.

"We'll have a great time together won't we? I'll get a bit of work done and then I'm all yours," Mary said.

"Okay," Abbie said, surprised.

Abbie hadn't expected Mrs O'Sullivan to be interested in her at all. Her mother had said she was a bit strange and wasn't used to company. Well, this woman seemed the total opposite.

"Do you like to read?" Mary said, pointing at the pile of the books on the table beside Abbie.

"I love to, but I've nearly all of them finished," Abbie said and picked up one of the books and flicked through it.

"Well, *good for you.* It's one of the best things you can do for yourself, that's for sure," Mary said.

Mary was delighted to see that Abbie wasn't like all the children she had heard about, who when left to their own devices literally sat looking at a screen all day. She stood up and checked her watch.

"Now, I best tidy up in the kitchen and start getting dinner ready. I'll fix us some lunch then and we can have a chat," Mary said, plumping the cushions and picking up the newspapers that were strewn on the floor. "Do you need anything?" she asked.

"No. I'm good, thanks. That's Dad by the way. He's always leaving his newspapers everywhere. He drives Mam mad," Abbie said, and rolled her eyes, imitating her mother's fed up expression.

"I'm sure he does," Mary said, leaving the room. Mary had a fair idea that a lot of things might drive Joan mad.

By one o'clock Mary had the kitchen sparkling, her stew simmering on the cooker and a wash on the line. She fixed them both a ham sandwich, a glass of orange juice for Abbie, a strong mug of sugary tea for herself and they sat together in the living room.

"So, tell me about yourself, Abbie," Mary said, genuinely wanting to know.

Mary took a gulp of her drink and sat back in the chair opposite Abbie. Seeing that she had a captive and interested audience, Abbie dropped her sandwich on the plate and started to talk excitedly. Even though her parents asked her questions, she often had the feeling that they quickly drifted off to their own worries. Over the course of the afternoon she told Mary about school, her friends, hobbies and worries. She was propelled along by the momentum of Mary's enthusiasm. Mary asked questions, looked Abbie in the eye and she didn't shake her head in disagreement or interrupt. Mary just listened. Mary told Abbie that she had been a primary school teacher years ago and that she missed it now.

"What do you do now, Mrs O'Sullivan?" Abbie asked.

"Mary, please call me, Mary, Abbie. You're only making me older than I already feel. If we're going to get to know each other, you must call me Mary."

"Okay, Mary. What do you do every day?" Abbie asked.

Abbie felt like she had gained entry to the world of adulthood and her expression was genuinely curious.

"Well, that's a good question, Abbie. I'm not sure to be honest. All my family are gone, but I do love spending time in my garden and reading. I go to mass and I watch a bit of TV. I sound an awful bore, don't I?"

Mary cringed as she saw Abbie's almost pitying expression. "Aren't you ever lonely?" Abbie asked.

Abbie was unable to imagine a life without her family, even if Johnny was unbearable most of the time. She knew the rhythm of her home and she couldn't picture it any other way.

"Well Abbie, nobody has asked me that in a long time. Yes, I suppose I am, but I get on with life as best I can. It's not all that bad. I do have my cat Boots," Mary said and smiled.

Mary felt very content and was still basking in the memory of coming across her mother's notebook yesterday. Another day, in a different mood, she might have told Abbie that our so-called modern, disposable Irish society had you cast aside when you passed your sell-by-date. Elderly burdens that had once been cherished treasures were now kept out of sight and out of mind, as nursing homes were filled to capacity. Mary knew that was an exaggeration, but up until Frank had arrived on her doorstep, she had lived a lonely, purposeless life.

"I can be your friend if you like. I know I'm a lot younger than you, but I don't mind if you don't. I'd like to be your friend," Abbie said, warmly.

Mary was touched by this little girl who seemed mature beyond her years and nothing like her delicate mother Joan. Sadly, as Mary had often seen in her many years teaching, there were a lot of children who took on the role of a parent in the relationship, a role often thrust upon them well before their time, when their own parents weren't able to fulfil it.

"Well, Abbie, that's one of the nicest things anyone has said to me in a long time. I don't want you to be feeling sorry for me now. I do like being on my own most of the time, but I would be delighted to be your friend," Mary said and then paused to compose herself.

The last thing Mary wanted was Frank and Joan thinking that she had spent the day moaning to their young daughter.

"I mean it, so don't be worrying about me. I have Boots and we get on just fine. You'd love him, so you would."

"Will you bring him here some day? He's probably lonely without you," Abbie said, and her eyes flickered with affection.
"I might just do that," Mary said warmly.

It was half five that evening when Joan opened the front door and was transported on a nostalgic trip down memory lane. For a moment she imagined that she had arrived home from school to find her mother humming away as she made the dinner. Mary had her back to her as she bustled around the kitchen and dinner bubbled on the cooker. She looked around and noticed that the place was spotless, and there was a pile of washing neatly folded on a chair. She suppressed a smile of delight and cleared her throat.

"Oh hello, Joan. I didn't hear you come in. How was your day?" Mary asked, wiping her hands on her apron.

"It was a busy day," Joan sighed.

Joan had been frustrated by the never-ending queue of customers that didn't give her any time to catch up on her own reading. Any cover with a beautiful romantic heroine always caught her eye and the library was full of romantic heroines. Today she hadn't been near any of them.

"I'm sure it's tough, Joan. Modern life isn't easy on women. Even I can see that," Mary empathised.

"I'm not complaining you know, but I have to say that it can be very stressful at times, not like the old days," Mary said and then saw Joan's dismissive look, but decided to let it go.

God knows, Mary was done with judging people. It had cost her a lot of relationships along the way.

"I'll just lie down for half an hour if you don't mind, get a bit of rest," Joan said, catching a yawn with her hand.

"Not at all. You do that, Joan. Well deserved it is, I'm sure," Mary encouraged.

Mary resisted the urge to run the old tape in her head. That tape would have said that Joan didn't know the first thing about stress and probably spent more time in bed than most people. However, Mary didn't say that, because she had said goodbye to the old Mary and thrown that tape out.

By half past six, they were all seated around the kitchen table and there was a hum of contentment as they all tucked in.

"It's been the best day like ever, and look," Abbie said and stuck out her arm to show off her colourful plastic bracelet. "Look what Mary bought me," Abbie said, and shoved the bracelet in Joan's face.

Frank looked around the table, delighted that dinner was going off without a hitch. They all almost looked happy. He had been the instigator of this great idea to ask Mary to help out, and no one could argue that it had been anything other than genius. He took in Cyril and Johnny with their heads down, licking their lips. Abbie was full of the joys, bouncing up and down on her seat and although Joan was a bit subdued, she would be hard pushed to find anything to complain about.

Frank looked over at Mary and tried to figure out what she thought of it all. She had a neutral almost disinterested expression on her face, but little did he know that inside she was beaming. Mary was beside herself at the sight of all the empty plates. Mary had forgotten the buzz she felt when feeding a family, a family that appreciated her efforts. Her own lot had been totally ungrateful, getting up from the table with hardly a word of thanks. Mary looked up and caught Frank gazing at her and decided to change the subject on to more neutral grounds.

"Guess who I saw in the supermarket today right in front of me in the queue? Frank you'd remember Pat Danaher, Tom used to work for him," Mary interjected.

"*Sure, of course, I do.* I could have sworn he was dead though," Frank said, seriously.

"Not him, but his daughter-in-law, a beautiful woman. I think she's married to the son, Dave. Isn't he a barrister or judge? I'm sure I saw the two of them in the paper last week at some event. Well, she stood right in front of me with two lovely little girls, her daughters, I assume. I didn't think they lived around here. I've heard he's nothing like his father. He was a great man, so he was," Mary said.

"Oh, that must be my good friend, Eileen," Joan said.

"That's gas. Weren't you just on the phone to Eileen the other day?" Frank said, winking at Joan.

"She's in my yoga class, Mary. I don't know her husband, but she's *so lovely*. We've become very good friends," Joan said and put her head in the air trying to ignore any reference to the WhatsApp message.

"Oh, is that right? Isn't it a small world all the same? Well, she looked a bit hassled, but I'm not surprised as the two girls were doing their best to clean out the sweet counter," Mary said and laughed.

"Isn't Sophie in your class, Abbie?" Joan asked, tapping her on the arm to get her attention.

"Yes, Mam. You know she is. She's on my basketball team," Abbie said impatiently.

"They live out in Barna, Mary," Joan said pointedly.

"Barna is it? Well, *isn't it well for some*," Mary said.

EIGHT

Eileen had finally fallen asleep in the early hours and Dave was long gone from the house when she was woken by the alarm clock. A momentary feeling of serenity was quickly replaced by the memory of their argument the night before. She stretched out on the bed and tried to remember when the conversation had gone so wrong. Eileen had started by telling him about her plans and had ended up hearing about their likely bankruptcy. Throwing back the covers, she sat on the side of the bed and shook her head at the madness that had unfolded. She reached over and grabbed her silky dressing gown off the chair. Eileen stood up, pulled it tight around her and found her Ugg slippers near the wardrobe.

Pulling them on, Eileen plodded downstairs to make coffee while the house was still quiet. Very soon she sipped on the strong coffee, staring out the large double doors to the garden, trying to process all that had happened. This time of day was her favourite usually; a time that was ripe with possibility. However, today she was just full of an anger that had quickly replaced the shock she had felt earlier.

"*For feck's sake,*" Eileen quipped.

Eileen looked around their palatial home. She knew they both earned a lot more than most people, particularly her friend Joan and her husband. Yet, here they were with the threat of their house being taken and it didn't sound like Dave had planned on telling her anytime soon. Eileen thought of all the years in college and the long hours working and wondered what it had all been for. They had been the golden couple of their class and still were in most peoples' eyes. Yet, God knows what he had been up to. She pictured the school gates and the stories that would do the rounds when it got out.

"Wait until the school mums get wind of it," Eileen muttered. "I know what they'll say before they even open their mouths."

Eileen took another sip from her coffee, but not even the strong brew could give her a boost this morning.

"I must've been living in la-la land not to see what was right in front of my eyes," Eileen said, and stared vacantly out the double doors again.

Well, maybe she had been living in denial, but she hardly saw Dave these days. Any time they spent together was usually at some function or other for his work, and they were always in the company of others. If they ever had a moment alone, it was reserved for updates on schedules and synchronising their movements, so that nothing was missed. They were a well-oiled machine, but somewhere along the line the cracks had started to appear.

Eileen walked over to the sideboard and let her eyes stray to the collection of framed photographs that told the story of their life together. From their college graduation to Amy's christening, it was all recorded in print. To an outsider they might look like the picture-perfect family, but it was all a lie. Eileen lifted her hand, coming very close to sweeping all the photos on to the floor, but thinking of Sophie and Amy, she dropped it again.

Eileen and Dave had once been each other's greatest cheerleaders. She knew she wasn't imagining it. Everybody said they were perfect for each other and it had felt like that. Eileen thought about all the plans they had made when they were first dating. Dave had always talked about becoming a barrister, having a family and then selling up at some point and moving to the countryside when the children were reared.

Well, that possibility looked more remote by the minute. From what little he had said last night, they could be paying the mortgage on their bloody awful house for many years to come.

"Mum, why didn't you wake us? We'll be late for school," Sophie said, appearing at the kitchen door.

Eileen turned to her daughter and was struck by her resemblance to Dave. Sophie was very tall for her age and had the same thick, strawberry blonde hair as her Dad.

"Come here, love," Eileen said and held out her arms to her tall, lanky daughter. It wouldn't be long before she was towering over her in her bare feet.

"Are you okay, Mum?" Sophie asked.

"I'm fine. What time is it?" Eileen said, hugging Sophie tightly.

"Half eight. We're *dead* late, you know," Sophie said, expecting Eileen to panic.

"Sorry love, I just lost track of time. Look, it's not the end of the world if we're late for one day in our lives."

Eileen just didn't have it in her today to keep everything on track.

"I'm just going to have a quick shower. Make sure you have some cereal and get some for Amy while you're at it. Is she awake?" Eileen asked, letting go of Sophie.

"Yes, but she's not out of bed yet."

"Give her a call, will you? We'll be on the road in half an hour, so make sure you're dressed and ready. We'll pick something up for your lunch on the way; whatever you want," Eileen said and walked upstairs and into the en-suite.

Eileen turned on the high-tech shower and relaxed under the jet of warm water. The strong injection of caffeine into her system combined with the pounding water wasn't long jolting her back to life. Eileen decided to get through the day and resume her conversation with Dave later on. This time, she would be more prepared and calm. They could talk through whatever problems they had. If they stuck together, they could handle anything. Last night had just been a case of bad timing.

In fifteen minutes, they were all in the car and ready to go. After stopping at the local deli to pick up lunch for both of the girls, Eileen dropped them at school and drove to the office. It was on these days that Eileen was glad of her designated parking space underground. Eileen checked the time as she took the lift to the fourth floor, where Clancy Solicitors was based. Seeing it was half nine, she felt pleased with herself that she was only half an hour late. Still, there was no slipping in unnoticed as Eileen had hoped. Meg, their bossy receptionist had an agitated look on her face when she walked through the door.

"Pat was looking for you, Eileen," Meg said, and nodded towards his office with a look that meant, now.

It was Pat Clancy's law firm and Eileen knew she had been lucky to get a job with them. He had even agreed to her request to go part-time, but they both knew well that he was getting his money's worth.

Eileen did more work in those hours than many did in a day. Eileen had even brought work home on occasion and constantly had to remind herself that her part-time hours were reflected in her greatly reduced payslip.

"What's up, Meg?" Eileen asked.

"*Look*, I don't know, *I'm just telling you* that I've seen him in better humour."

"God almighty, that's all I need on the one day I'm late. Thanks for the heads up though," Eileen said.

Eileen found it hard not to like Meg. She acted like she ruled the roost, but Meg had saved her bacon on many the occasion. Their relationship didn't really go beyond the office as they were worlds apart in many ways, yet at work they had formed a firm bond. Meg was only in her twenties and still living life like it was party central. How she turned up in the office every morning looking as fresh as a daisy was beyond Eileen. Eileen dropped her briefcase and coat in her office and knocked on Pat's door.

"*Yes*," Pat's booming voice answered. Eileen opened the door and stepped into his office.

"Pat, sorry I'm late. There were a few hiccups at home. I'll make sure to make up the time."

"Don't worry about it, Eileen. We have a bigger problem to deal with," Pat said. "I've just had a call from Fran Daly and he's not happy at all. In fact, he is threatening to pull his business," Pat said.

"*What?*" Eileen asked, surprised. Eileen had dealt with Fran Daly for years and although he was a cantankerous bastard, she had always managed to pacify him and rein in his outbursts. "I've been nothing, but grovelling to him, Pat. *You know that.* No one else in the office would go near him with a ten-foot barge pole and *I've* put up with his abuse for years without a word of complaint."

Fran Daly ran a very successful chain of toy stores and was known for being a difficult employer.

"I know that Eileen, but this is business and he says his business is suffering because of us, or more to the point, you."

"What? He can't be serious," Eileen said.

"He was deadly serious when I spoke to him. You know the case you are dealing with, the guy who is suing him for wrongful dismissal?"

"Yes, I know it only too well. He has me hounded every minute of every day, so that I hardly have time to deal with anything else. What's the problem?" Eileen asked, sitting down in the seat opposite Pat.

"Well, he's saying that you didn't get papers down to the courthouse on time yesterday and now he's facing a fine. The final straw, he said in a number of slip-ups on this case and he's only mentioning it now, because it's starting to cost him money."

Pat stared at her waiting for an explanation.

"What the… *That is a total lie.* I sent those papers out just before I left yesterday. I remember it distinctly and he has never mentioned any other concerns to me. I'm telling you the truth, Pat," Eileen said emphatically.

"I'm not doubting you, however, he is one of our biggest clients, and we can't afford to lose him. I'm sorry but you're going to have to grovel a bit more. I suggest you get on the phone ASAP and do whatever it takes. Now, I've another meeting, so I'm trusting that I can leave this in your hands," Pat said.

Pat picked up the phone to make it clear that their discussion was over. Eileen knew not to push Pat. She took his cue and left the room.

"Bloody Fran Daly," Eileen cursed, as she walked back to her office. Eileen needed him on her case like a hole in the head today. Ironically, if all had gone well with Dave last night, she might just have told Frank Daly to get lost, whatever the consequences, but that wasn't looking like an option just now. Eileen closed the door of her office, sat down at the desk and went over the details of his file, trying to figure out what had gone wrong. They were within walking distance of the courthouse and she remembered that she had been on her way to drop off the papers when Maggie, one of the secretaries said she was going shortly and had offered to drop them in for her.

"Jesus Christ!" Eileen shouted.

One of the paralegals looked up at her from across the corridor. It didn't help that they had glass doors and soundproofing was non-existent in the office. Eileen waved at her and smiled apologetically. Maggie must have forgotten. She could ring the courthouse and double-check, but if Fran Daly said he had been fined, well likely the papers had been late. It was Maggie's fault, not that she could really blame her. It wasn't her responsibility after all. Maggie was a tough nut and wouldn't back down easy, still at the same time Eileen could always tell if she lied.

Maggie had that tell-tale sign of pushing her hair behind her ears and clearing her throat. It was a dead giveaway. Well, she had to find out as Fran Daly wasn't going to go away that easy. Eileen left her desk and walked down the corridor to the cubicle where Maggie sat with the other secretaries.

"Maggie, can I have a quick word?" Eileen asked, and leaned over the partition, not wanting to make a big deal in front of the other girls. Maggie downed her Dictaphone and looked up at Eileen with an 'I'm in the middle of something very important, so this better be more important' look.

"I just wanted to double-check. You know those papers for Fran Daly that had to be at the courthouse by 2 pm sharp yesterday and you offered to take them…" Eileen said, pointedly.

"What papers? Oh yeah, I brought them down alright along with a lot of other papers, as I always do," Maggie said and resumed her typing.

"Okay. I'm not doubting you. It's just that they're saying they didn't get them on time. I need to clear this up with him this morning. Seemingly he's been on to Pat and he's not happy. I just need to have all the facts before I call him. Did you get delayed for any reason? It's okay if you did. I just need to know," Eileen said, firmly.

"Eileen, I'm telling you I dropped them in. I left here at quarter to two. I stopped briefly to talk to Ger…"

Eileen almost groaned. Ger had to be the most talkative postman that had ever walked the planet.

"Then I went straight to the courthouse," Maggie said and flicked her hair back and pushed it behind her ears. Eileen had all the information she needed.

"That's fine, Maggie. Thanks," Eileen said, and she marched back to her office fuming.

Meg, having witnessed the exchange, gave Eileen a shake of her head as she walked past, only confirming her suspicions. Well, feck Maggie anyways. There was nothing for it but to grovel again to Fran Daly. She couldn't land Maggie in it, so she would just have to ride out the abuse and hope that he would overlook it this one time. She had no idea what Pat meant by the final straw. This was the first she knew of any problems. Back in her office, Eileen took a moment and then picked up the phone.

"Hello, can I speak to Mr Daly please? Yes, I'll hold."

Eileen fiddled with a pen while she waited for Fran to come on the line.

"Mr Daly here."

"Hello, Mr Daly. It's Eileen from Clancy's. I just heard the news and I wanted to talk to you straight away about it. Pat has filled me in and all I can say is that I went down to the courthouse myself with the papers, so I'm at a loss to figure out what might have gone wrong. I really am very sorry for any trouble."

"Well, hello Eileen. How are you?" Fran asked.

Fran's voice was very upbeat, and Eileen was a bit thrown as she expected to get a right bollocking.

"Yes, it was very embarrassing, but I managed to get the fine quashed. It took a bit of persuading, but you know with my standing in the town, they were quick to see reason. I'm sorry that I had to throw Clancy's under the bus, but I had to do what was necessary to sort things out. All is fair in love and war, isn't that right?"

Eileen felt like being sick listening to the sarcasm drip off his words.

"I have to say that I'm surprised at you though. You're usually on top of things, so it was the last thing I expected."

"Well as I said, Fran, I'm really sorry. As far as I was concerned, they were dropped in on time, but I take full responsibility for what happened. What can I do to make things up to you?"

As soon as the words were out of her mouth, Eileen regretted them. She knew Fran didn't waste any opportunity when it came to women. He had never outright come on to her, but like a lot of men, he seemed to think it was okay to ogle without a shred of embarrassment. Well, Eileen had years of practise dealing with men like that and when called for, Eileen could have a thick skin and a quick tongue.

"Well, seeing as you mention it, Eileen, I really want to sit down and go through everything with you. We have a lot on at the moment, and I want to make sure everything is in order."

"Absolutely, Mr Daly. I totally agree. When suits?"

"Now that I think of it, I have a late meeting in town today. How about we get an early dinner in that new place, Mancini's? We could kill two birds and go through everything then," Fran quickly replied, spotting his opportunity.

"Or how about I call by your office first thing tomorrow?" Eileen suggested.

"It's better for me this evening. I'm sure you'll make it, Eileen, a resourceful girl like you. It is very important that we go through everything as soon as possible," Fran insisted.

"I'll have to check with Dave and see if I can get a babysitter at such short notice, Mr Daly," Eileen said.

"I trust you'll make arrangements. Let's say half past six in Mancini's. I'll get Grace in the office to book it. See you then," Fran said, and hung up.

"*What a bastard*," Eileen remarked.

The nerve of him assuming that she would just drop everything outside her working hours for him. Eileen held the phone in her hand, about to call back and postpone, but she knew she was on thin ice with Pat. He would be none too impressed if she turned down one of their biggest clients. Eileen wouldn't put it past Fran to concoct the whole story about a fine and threatening to move his business as a way to wangle dinner with her. She decided she would go this one time, but Eileen was out of there by nine o'clock at the latest.

Eileen picked up the phone, this time to fill Dave in.

"Hi Sandra, is Dave there?"

"Oh, hi Eileen. How are you? I'm afraid he's in a meeting and won't be back until after lunch. Can I get him to call you?"

"Thanks. That would be great. I have to go here I'm afraid, it's all go in the office, but lovely to talk to you," Eileen said.

"You too, Eileen. It's been ages. We would all love to see you and those two gorgeous girls of yours if you get time to call in one of the days," Sandra said.

"Yes, that would be lovely, once I can find a free slot in their busy schedules," Eileen jested.

"Great. Look forward to it. Bye then, Eileen," Sandra said.

"Bye, Sandra," Eileen said and put the phone down. She was glad to have avoided a long conversation with gushing Sandra. She had no intention of calling to Dave's office. All the girls who worked there fawned over him. It was embarrassing to watch, but Dave lapped it all up. Eileen felt more frustrated with women by the day, hanging on the attentions of any man that would look their way. Picking up the phone again to call their babysitter, Dawn, Eileen cursed Fran Daly for messing up her day.

"Oh, hi Dawn, how are you? Would you be free this evening at six... just for a few hours, it's a work thing?... I know, last minute as always… you're a star, see you then.

Thank God," Eileen said as she hung up. Dawn had saved her bacon yet again.

Eileen stood up and closed the door of her office. Her whole morning was now hijacked by Fran Daly. Despite his transparent efforts at charm he was no walkover. Eileen knew she had to be on her toes for this meeting. Fran would likely want to get business out of the way first and then Eileen would have to endure his fawning and slobbering. God, when did she become so cynical and angry? Any other day she would have dealt with Fran Daly without a second thought, and now here she was like a schoolgirl, all nervous and jittery.

Eileen decided to fill Pat in on the latest developments with Fran Daly. She knew she couldn't afford to get in Pat's bad books, especially after the bombshell that Dave had dropped only last night. Eileen left her desk and walked down the corridor to Pat's office.

Eileen could see through the glass wall that Pat was free and knocked on the door, feeling proud of herself for nipping the problem in the bud.

Pat was almost beside himself when Eileen told him the news.

"I knew you'd sort it out. That's great news, Eileen. Now make sure to put it on our account. I don't want him thinking we're cheapskates," Pat said.

Eileen was close to saying that it was Fran Daly, who was the greatest cheapskate of all time, but instead bit her tongue. Fran was known to put his hand in his pocket on only the rarest of occasions. No wonder he was loaded. Eileen had to suck it up this time because of Maggie. She would never rely on her for anything important again, that was for sure.

At six o'clock that evening Eileen was ready to leave the house. A two-minute telephone conversation with Dave had told her that his mood hadn't much improved. He hadn't the remotest bit of interest in her problems with Fran Daly, and after a few impatient grunts he just hung up the phone. There was little chance of picking up on their conversation this evening, and it was probably just as well from the sounds of it.

"Bye, girls. Be good for Dawn and bed early," Eileen said.

"Bye, Mum," Sophie said.

"Bye, Mum," Amy said.

Eileen turned back to blow them a kiss, but they were giggling over something Dawn had said, and Eileen silently left. Eileen's heart lurched. It never failed to when she left them. It wasn't easy pretending to have it all. The greatest con job ever in her book. She drove into town and parked near the restaurant. Eileen decided she would have the one glass of wine, but only to be sociable. She needed to keep her wits about her. Eileen had gone for a business look, taking great pains in choosing her clothes. She had opted for a navy dress with a buttoned-up collar. Eileen had added a pair of earrings and a cream coat and kept her hair tied up in the loose knot she wore at work.

Fran Daly was bouncing up and down on his heels in reception when she arrived. He wore a sports jacket and chinos. In his early sixties, his excessive lifestyle had clearly left its mark. He bordered on obese, not helped by his short stature, and a network of blue veins ran through his swarthy complexion. Eileen thought that at the rate he was going, he wouldn't have long left to enjoy his great wealth. He still had a heavy smoking habit and the scent of tobacco overpowered any aftershave he might have doused himself in. He looked a lot more casual than he normally did at work meetings, where he regularly rotated his extensive collection of double-breasted pinstripe suits. So much for a business meeting beforehand in town, Eileen thought. Fran had the distinct look of a man who had showered and changed for a night on the tiles.

"Now, I thought we'd have a drink here and go through everything before we have dinner," Fran said, directing Eileen to a quiet little booth away from prying eyes.

"Certainly, Mr Daly. I brought your file with me. I went through it this morning and I have a few things I want to clarify, if that's okay with you?"

Eileen reached into her bag and opened the file on the table.

"Well, aren't you the organised little lady. What will you have to drink? Will you join me in a gin and tonic?" Fran asked, not looking remotely concerned about business or any blunders Eileen supposedly had made.

"Thanks, just a sparkling water," Eileen said directly to the waiter who now stood over them. "I'm driving, so I'll just have a glass of wine with dinner, thank you," Eileen said, softly.

"I'll be taking a taxi home, so I'm happy to drop you off on the way. You live out in Barna, don't you? I'm not far from there myself," Fran said.

Eileen could feel a shiver going up her spine at his attempt at familiarity and had no intention of taking a taxi home with him. After half an hour of going through the file, Eileen cleared her throat as Fran launched into his second gin and tonic.

"Mr Daly…"

"Fran, Eileen. I keep telling you to call me Fran," he said, taking a greedy gulp out of his drink.

"Fran, I just wanted to make sure all is okay with us. I mean in terms of how I'm handling your account. I just had the impression from Pat this morning that there were a number of things bothering you, and needless to say, I was very surprised. It was the first I had heard of it and it caught me a bit off guard, if you know what I mean. I trust that if there is anything you're unhappy with, you would come to me directly," Eileen said, and gave him her brightest smile, when what she really wanted to do was stick a fork in his bloodshot, leering eyes.

"*Bothering me?* No, I don't think so. I don't recall that *at all.* Are you sure Pat didn't pick it up wrong? I mean, I was a bit concerned with the fine and all, but I have no recollection of raising any other concerns. Now you don't worry your pretty head Eileen, as far as I'm concerned, we're good, indeed we're great. Now let's move into the restaurant to eat. I'm starving," Fran said.

With that Fran stood up and pushed back his seat before she could say anything further. He was giddy, and the alcohol had only served to loosen him up. They were shown to one of the best tables in the restaurant and once they were seated, Eileen tried to bring the conversation back to business.

"Well, I'm glad to hear it, Fran. At Clancy's, we take great pride in meeting our clients' professional needs and with over ten years' experience in the practice, I can honestly tell you that I am proud to say that I have never had a word of complaint from my clients. I'm glad to hear you're satisfied with the level of service you're getting," Eileen said. Fran waved his hand as if to dismiss her words.

"Speaking of service, *where the hell* is the waiter gone when you want to order? All is fine, Eileen, please accept my reassurances. Now let's enjoy our dinner."

Fran insisted on topping up her glass if she took the slightest sip of her wine. Eileen turned to her glass of water instead, so that she wouldn't be over the limit before the main course.

Fran made a big palaver over the menu and the choice of wine and insisted they had three courses. He greedily devoured a large steak with all the trimmings, while Eileen stuck to fish. If he had been a good friend, Eileen might have given him a friendly bit of advice about his diet, but they would never be friends. Despite her protestations, Fran insisted on ordering a second bottle of wine even though he had drunk most of the first one. Eileen was mortified as she watched him drone on about the wine to the very tolerant waiter. However, Fran's efforts at appearing the seasoned sommelier failed dismally. Finally, when they had finished dessert and Eileen had endured enough of his crude jokes and innuendo, Eileen looked at her watch.

"Oh, is that the time? I really do need to get going, Fran. I told the babysitter I wouldn't be late and it's already half past nine," Eileen said, and put her napkin on the plate to indicate that she was finished and ready to go home.

"Now, now, Eileen. Hold your horses. How often do you dine out with a client? I'm just going to have a brandy for the road and then we'll make tracks. Will you join me?" Fran said, starting to slur his words.

Eileen wondered how some men could think slobbering drunkenness was an attractive quality. Maybe it was just the Dutch courage that skewed their judgement, she reasoned. Fran wasn't paying any attention to the obvious look of disdain on her face. The prospect of sitting with Dave in their living room was becoming more appealing by the minute, whatever his mood. He wasn't a big drinker and although he might be disinterested, he definitely wasn't crude.

"Just a peppermint tea for me then and really after that I must get going," Eileen said, firmly.

"*A what? What in God's name is a peppermint tea?* That doesn't sound like a proper drink *at all*," Fran said and looked at the waiter.

"Well, that's what the lady ordered, so that's what she shall have," the waiter remarked.

While the waiter prepared their drinks, Fran went outside for his third cigarette of the evening. Eileen quickly paid the bill using the company credit card.

"I've always been meaning to say it to you, Eileen, Dave is a very lucky man, a very lucky man indeed. How did he manage to catch such a beautiful woman as yourself?" Fran gushed freely, as he sat back down at the table.

"You're too kind, Fran. It is I who feel lucky to have met Dave. He's a fantastic husband and great with the girls," Eileen said and took out her phone to show him a photo of the family, but Fran just brushed it away and reached across the table grabbing her hand. "You know, I'm very lucky to have such a gorgeous woman working on my account. I think we're a match made in heaven."

Fran threw back his head and laughed loudly at what he thought was a very funny remark. Eileen pulled her hand back and pretended to check something in her bag. It took all the restraint she could muster not to punch him in the face. From the corner of her eye, she saw the waiter keeping tabs on their table and she was grateful. No doubt he had seen plenty of men like Fran.

"Fran, I *really do* have to go. I think that was Dave texting me to check where I am. He'll be worried if I don't get home soon," Eileen said and tried to keep the irritation out of her voice.

After another ten minutes of tedious chit-chat and dodging his attempts to grab her hand again, they finally stood up to leave. She was mortified as the waiter stopped her at the door.

"Is everything okay, Miss?" he whispered in her ear, with a knowing look on his face.

"Oh yes, thank you. I'm fine," Eileen said, softly.

Eileen was tempted to say more, but Fran turned to see where she was and almost lost his footing on the steps. Feeling embarrassed, Eileen practically shoved him out the door in front of her. "Jesus, you can't see a thing out here. I could sue them for everything they have, I'm telling you. That'd make them sit up."

"Come on, Fran. Time to go home," Eileen insisted.

She whispered sorry to the waiter and pushed Fran from behind. Eileen wouldn't make the mistake of agreeing to have dinner with him again.

"Look, I'm going past your house on the way. I'll give you a lift. I'm just parked up the road," Eileen said, going against the hum from her gut that told her to get away from him as quickly as possible. Looking at him staggering it was hard not to be concerned for his welfare. Eileen led the way and Fran followed her obediently.

"Ten minutes and I'll be rid of him," Eileen reassured herself. "You're a fine woman, a fine woman all the same," Fran muttered as they reached her car and he fell against it.

Eileen opened the passenger door, gave him a push, and he fell on to the seat. She made her way round to the driver's seat.

"Can you move over Fran, so I can actually drive the car?" Eileen snapped.

Fran straightened himself slightly and lay back against the headrest. He tried to speak but what came out was totally incoherent. Eileen turned the heat up high and started the car. Glancing over, she was relieved when she saw his head drop to his chest and heard a snoring sound. Pat Clancy would want to be paying her a lot more to put up with the likes of this. She wouldn't be long telling him so. Eileen drove along the coast road and feeling it was safe to relax, she opened the driver's window and breathed in the fresh night air. Between the heat and the stench of alcohol, cigarette smoke and perspiration from her passenger, she felt a bit nauseous. However, she wasn't long regretting that decision. The blast of sea air only had the effect of rousing Fran from his stupor.

"Ah, you're the best Eileen, you really are." Fran reached across and put his hand on her knee.

"Fran, please. I'll have you home now shortly."

She cursed him under her breath and removed his hand. He wasn't deterred that easily though. As they rounded a bend, he slumped on top of her and his hand wandered over again, this time landing higher up on her thigh.

"Get your *hands off me*, Fran. This is not on," Eileen said.

Eileen just about managed to control the car and dodge his hands at the same time.

"Aw, you're all the same. Batting your eyelashes and flashing your boobs and then like butter wouldn't melt… Now, stop playing shy. I know you want it."

Fran reached over and grabbed her breast and slobbered on her neck. Instinctively Eileen's elbow went up and she caught him on the side of the face.

"Jesus Christ. What did you do that for? I was only being friendly. You like it rough then do you?" Fran asked, excited. He made a lunge at her.

With the car swerving dangerously, Eileen's heart felt like it was going to explode out of her chest. Eileen took a quick look in the rearview mirror and seeing the coast was clear, she pulled to a halt at the side of the road. It all happened so fast after that. Knowing there was no way she could lean across and open the passenger door to push him out without being assaulted further, she put on her hazard lights and jumped out of the driver's seat. Coming around to the passenger side, she pulled open the door. Fran who had been lying against the door, fell out on top of her and roared laughing.

"Jesus, *you're a feisty one.*"

With all the strength she could muster, Eileen dragged him onto the grass verge at the edge of the road and he rolled over onto his back.

"What the fuck, what the fuck are you doing?" Fran roared, now woken from his drunken coma.

"You're no gentleman, Mr Daly. You're an animal. How dare you? I should bring charges against you for your behaviour. I never want to set eyes on you again, you sorry excuse for a man," Eileen shouted and sat back in the car, slammed the door and drove off.

Eileen took a quick look over her shoulder and saw that he had staggered to his feet. He could crawl home for all she cared. She had been chatted up and leered at, but Eileen had never been felt up like a piece of meat. Eileen shook badly and just a mile from home she pulled the car over to the side of the road and burst into tears. Eileen stayed there for a long time crying and finally, when there were no more tears left, she started up the car and drove home.

Eileen suddenly realised that she had left Fran Daly on the side of the road and that in his state of inebriation he could easily stagger out onto oncoming traffic. A driver wouldn't have a chance of seeing him in the dark. There was no way in hell she was going back to check. Eileen called the Guards and told them what had happened. "No, I don't want to press charges. I just wanted to let you know he is so drunk that he could easily be knocked down," Eileen said and struggled to get the words out without breaking down again.

Despite the concern of the lovely Guard on the other end of the phone, Eileen insisted that she was okay. Eileen just wanted to get home, close the door and pretend that the evening had never happened.

NINE

When Eileen closed the front door behind her on this Wednesday night she glanced at the clock in the hall and saw that it was half past eleven. Like an amnesiac, she struggled to account for the previous hours. Eileen remembered looking at her phone in the restaurant just before they left, and she could have sworn it was only half past nine at night. Eileen couldn't believe that it had taken her two hours to be free of Fran Daly and arrive home.

While the house slept, totally unaware of what had happened, Eileen went straight for the drinks cabinet in the living room and poured a large brandy. She looked down at her shaking hands and clasped the glass tight to steady herself. The residual warmth of the living room led her to the couch, and she curled up, pulling her cream coat tight around her. Eileen would have given anything for a hug from Dave and to spit out every detail of her sordid story. Eileen needed to vomit out all the ugliness but felt paralysed to say or do anything.

Eileen knew that it had been a long time since they had been each other's confidantes, but it didn't matter tonight. She just needed the comfort of another human being. Sitting in the dark, Eileen felt very alone. She finished her brandy and when she could no longer keep her eyes open, she lay back against the couch. Eileen slept fitfully and when she woke hours later, stirred by the early morning chill, it was dawn and the house was still quiet.

Shivering, Eileen saw that it was half past six on the clock on the mantelpiece, and she decided to shower and change before anyone was up. She didn't fancy explaining why she was still in a dress and high heels at this hour of the morning. Eileen stood up feeling stiff and walked slowly out into the hall. Taking a quick look in the mirror on her way upstairs she almost jumped at the sight. Two panda eyes stared back at her and streaks of mascara ran down her cheeks. It couldn't have been a more different picture to the confident businesswoman, who had walked out the door the evening before.

As Eileen walked up the stairs, the voice in her head took charge and told her that she had to be strong and resolute today. She was telling Pat the bare essentials, but she was making it clear that she could no longer have Fran Daly as a client. This was business and whatever the outcome she would stand up for herself. She paused at the top of the stairs and decided to use the main bathroom, as she didn't want to wake Dave and have to explain herself. Eileen quietly closed the door and stripped off her clothes. She stepped under the hot jet of water and let it rain over every inch of her body. Reaching for the loofah brush that was on the ledge, she scrubbed every inch of her body. Eileen was not raped, but she felt as if she had been defiled in a way that made her sick to her stomach. She remembered the feel of Fran Daly's hands on her body and retched.

Eileen jumped from the shower and vomited repeatedly into the toilet until there was nothing left, but the sting of bile. Shivering, she grabbed a towel and wrapped it tightly around her and collapsed onto the toilet. How could this have happened to her of all people? After taking a few deep breaths, she stood up and opened the door. She listened for any sound and then tiptoed up the corridor to their bedroom. Eileen slipped into the room, praying she wouldn't wake Dave. All she wanted to do was to crawl into bed and bury her head for at least an hour.

"You're up early. I didn't hear you come in last night," Dave said and stirred in the bed and rubbed his eyes.

"Yeah. It went on a bit late… I've a lot on today too," Eileen blurted out as she grabbed her dressing gown off the back of the chair. "I could do you with your help…"

"I'll drop the girls if you like," Dave offered, swinging his legs out of the bed and stretching.

"That'd be great, thanks."

Eileen turned her back to him as she pulled on her dressing gown and swallowed hard to stem the tears. Every molecule in her body wanted to break down and run into his arms, but she resisted. Eileen knew she needed nerves of steel today. She had to hold it together when she spoke to Pat. She didn't want Pat thinking she was some over-emotional woman who couldn't handle herself. So she kept her back to Dave, knowing that one look at him, and she would likely break down all over again. From the day they met his piercing blue eyes had always stopped her in her tracks. If a hybrid of Robert Redford and Paul Newman ever existed, Dave came pretty close to being it.

"I'll call the girls and I'll see you downstairs," Eileen said and quickly left the room without looking at him.

Dave sighed, feeling a sting of guilt for the bombshell he had landed on her on Tuesday night. He showered quickly, changed into his suit and joined the others in the kitchen for breakfast. One look at Eileen and he knew she wasn't herself. She sat silently nursing a cup of coffee with a distant look in her eyes, while the girls chattered over her head.

"Come on, girls. Grab your coats or we'll be late," Dave said, as he gulped down a coffee and pulled on his coat. Eileen didn't react. "I've Jeff's birthday tonight, remember? I'll be home first to change but dinner is at eight."

Dave picked up his keys and turned to her.

"Did you hear me Eileen?" he asked, feeling worried about her. Eileen looked up at him blankly. "Jeff's birthday tonight?" Dave repeated.

"Oh yeah, that's fine. I'm looking forward to an evening on the couch with the girls," Eileen said and stood up. She kissed Sophie and Amy before Dave shoved them out the door.

When she heard the front door close, Eileen stood up, threw her untouched breakfast in the bin and went upstairs to change. She pulled her reliable red suit out of the wardrobe, covered her tired complexion with plenty of makeup and pulled her hair back in a high knot. She felt like a walking cliché, but she didn't care. The term power dressing hadn't been coined without good reason, and she had used it to her advantage many times, especially with men. She had never apologised for that. Eileen knew that Pat didn't appreciate displays of emotion, especially tears, so under no circumstances could she cry today.

"You can bawl your eyes out all you want once you are out of the office, but you will not let Fran Daly away with this," Eileen said and tried to muster all her strength as she said the words out loud, but she wasn't feeling it.

Her efforts at being assertive and strong in life hadn't always been well-received, often attracting bitchy comments from women and snide comments from spurned men.

An hour later, Eileen parked her car and took the lift up to Clancy Solicitors. She dropped her coat and bag in her office and then went straight to reception. There was no way she could do any work until she spoke to Pat.

"Maggie, is Pat in his office?" Eileen asked. She put her hands in her pockets, so that Maggie wouldn't see them shaking. Eileen looked around nervously, almost expecting Fran Daly to wander into the office, all smiles.

"You look fantastic as usual, you bitch," Maggie joked. "Are you okay, Eileen? You don't seem yourself."

"I'm okay, thanks. I just need to talk to Pat. It's urgent," Eileen said. Maggie took a quick look at her diary and turned back to Eileen. "It's not a great day today. He's a lot on, Eileen. Would it hold?" "No, I need to speak to him, Maggie, this morning," Eileen said in a strong tone, which left Maggie in no doubt that she wasn't taking no for an answer.

"Let me see what I can do, and I'll give you a buzz shortly." "Thanks so much. I owe you big time, Maggie," Eileen said and smiled, relief written all over her face.

"You sure do, and you can start by buying me a glass of wine one of the days. I haven't seen you in an age."

"You're on. It's just been a bit crazy, but I promise, soon," Eileen said and gave her a weak smile and walked back to her office.

A few minutes later her phone rang.

"Pat will see you at eleven o'clock. First and second round is on you," Maggie laughed.

"You're a star. Thanks Maggie," Eileen said and fiddled around with paperwork until near eleven o'clock and then walked up the corridor and knocked on Pat's door.

"Hi Pat. Thanks for seeing me," Eileen said and walked into his office. Eileen took a seat across from his desk and settled her hands on her lap. She didn't feel it, but she knew she looked the part.

"Maggie said you needed to speak to me urgently. Is everything okay?" Pat asked.

"No, Pat, it's not okay and I need to talk to you about it," Eileen said.

Her throat felt dry and she thought her voice might break. "Okay that sounds ominous, what is it?" Pat asked and Eileen relaxed a little seeing the concerned look on his face.

"I've something important to tell you, Pat, and I'd appreciate it if you would just hear me out before saying anything."

"Jesus Eileen, you're worrying me now," Pat said, sitting forward. "I can't have Fran Daly as a client any longer. I don't want to go into the details but suffice it to say, that he is no gentleman. Meeting him yesterday evening was a big mistake, Pat. He was totally unprofessional. There is no way I can work with somebody like that," Eileen said. Eileen felt her heart thumping in her chest as she recalled the encounter.

"Slow down, Eileen. What are you saying? I just had a phone call from him earlier and he sang your praises. He said you were a total professional. I can tell you, he has forgotten all mention of the fine or indeed any other complaint he might have had," Pat said and sat back in his chair, thinking it had all been a fuss over nothing.

"What? What did you just say?" Eileen asked. She could feel her world turning upside down.

"Eileen, are you okay? I'm just after saying that Fran is delighted with us and specifically with you. Am I missing something here?"

"Yes, *you are missing something. That man*, if you could call him a man, is an asshole. I don't want to go into all the details but trust me when I tell you, that yesterday evening was not a success. If you call being blind drunk and practically assaulting your solicitor a success, well then maybe in his eyes it was. I can certainly say that from my point of view *it was not.* I have *never been more humiliated in my life*," Eileen said, upset.

She had hoped it was out of character, a one-off, but obviously that was not the case. This was par for the course for him. "Eileen, please, just slow down a bit. Are you sure you're not reading too much into it? I know he likes a few drinks and can be crude, but you've always been well able to handle yourself. He's harmless. You know that as well as I do. That's why you have always been one of our best solicitors. You can separate the professional from the personal and still do the job," Pat said.

Pat looked at his computer as if he was checking something and then looked back at her. Eileen knew he was losing interest in the conversation. Pat was treating her like she was a little girl having a tantrum. Eileen sat forward, resting her arms on his desk as she tried to hammer her point home. She kept her voice low and even.

"I'm not reading too much into anything, Pat. In fact, if anything, I'm downplaying his behaviour. Fran Daly has no idea how to separate the professional from the personal. He behaved despicably, and that's being kind. I'm not having him as my client anymore and that is my final word," Eileen said and raised her voice.

"I'm really sorry if he didn't behave himself last night, really I am, and I won't ever ask you to have dinner with him again, *but surely* you can see this was a one-off. I'm sure he's feeling embarrassed about it. That's why he rang me this morning. He felt guilty and was impressed with how well you handled yourself. From now on it will just be business, and if he crosses a line with you in future, I'll back you up one hundred percent," Pat affirmed.

"He's not feeling *a shred of embarrassment*. He doesn't think he did anything wrong, Pat, and that, to be honest, is even more shocking. I really thought you would take my side on this, *after all the years that I have worked with you*. This is my final word and I hope you respect it. I will not *under any circumstances* be working with Mr Fran Daly ever again."

It had taken all Eileen's strength to say what she just had, and now it looked like she was on her own.

"Eileen, calm down. I really think you need to take a few days. Take tomorrow off and think about what you're saying. As I said before, Fran Daly is our largest client and we cannot afford to lose him, but lose him we will if you refuse to work with him. This is very serious, so I'm going to end our conversation now and advise you to think about your words and the repercussions. We will pick this up again on Monday. I assume by then you will have had a bit of time and distance to reflect and see some sense."

Eileen sat back in the chair and shook her head in disbelief. Then she stood up and straightened her jacket in an effort to regain control.

"Thanks for your time, Pat. I'll talk to you on Monday. Have a good weekend," Eileen said. With that she turned and walked out.

It was a mistake putting Pat Clancy on a pedestal. It looked like when push came to shove, he chose money over morals. Eileen picked up her mobile and saw that she had a missed call from Joan. It would have to wait. Eileen decided to book a restaurant for Saturday night. She had to talk to Dave, and it was now urgent. Watching the clock for the rest of the morning, it took every ounce of her energy to stay in the office until lunchtime. When the clock finally struck one, Eileen grabbed her things and practically ran out the door.

Eileen stopped on her way home to buy groceries. Still fuming from her meeting with Pat, she came very close to decking an unsuspecting man in the queue, who had smiled shyly at her. He practically turned on his heels when she glowered back at him. Eileen had no problem spotting the difference between an admiring glance and a sleazy eyeing up, the intention was always clear from their eyes. She knew the poor man had only been paying her a compliment, but today was too little too late. Any other time, Eileen would have just politely smiled, but he had met her on the wrong day.

When she walked in the door at home, Eileen dropped the shopping in the kitchen and went straight upstairs. She lost no time scrubbing off all her makeup and changing her clothes. She had never been one for the fashion parade that was the school run and today especially, she didn't care one iota what she looked like. She pulled on her loose yoga pants, a long white T-shirt and tied her hair in a ponytail. It was still warm enough for her flip-flops, so she slipped them on and straight away felt more herself as she walked back downstairs and made a cup of tea. She now looked like the laid-back hippy twin of the power dressing woman who had gone out to work that morning. If I never have to wear a suit one more day in my life, she thought, it won't be a day too soon.

Eileen's old clothes, like her old friendships now felt like they didn't fit anymore. She wouldn't forget in a hurry the coffee morning she had endured at Dave's insistence last month. It was a regular date for all the wives of his colleagues, and she had avoided most of them. Never again, she said to herself afterwards. Dave had no interest when she told him that they were a bunch of airheads and had nothing to talk about but clothes, holidays, and the latest gossip about who cheated on whom.

She would take an afternoon with any of her new-found friends, who had more substance and depth than the shallow women she met every day. Eileen had never felt more at home than the day she walked into her Bio-energy training course. She was no longer Eileen the beautiful solicitor with the perfect husband and children. She was just Eileen and she didn't have to pretend. These people understood her. It had nothing to do with how she looked or what she did. Maybe it wasn't Dave's fault that he didn't understand. He had married an earlier version of Eileen, but she couldn't help it if she had changed.

Eileen picked up her car keys and was on her way out the door to pick up the girls when her mother, Caroline Murphy rang to fill her in on the latest gossip.

"Eileen, I was wondering if something was wrong. I haven't heard from you in ages…" Caroline said.

"Mum, *look*, I can't stay on long. I have to pick up the girls," Eileen said.

"I don't know *why* you answer the phone and then say you don't have time to talk…" Caroline replied.

"I'm sorry, Mum. It's just been a busy week. How are you?"

"I'm not talking to you, Eileen, if you're racing out the door. Oh, by the way, your father saw Dave the other night in Keoghs. He was at a retirement do," Caroline said. Eileen knew her mother was waiting for encouragement.

"Oh, right," Eileen said.

"He was chatting to this young…"

"*Look*, Mum. I don't have time to talk about Dave's conversations in the pub. You know Keoghs is his haunt. But speaking of socialising, is there any chance you could babysit on Saturday night? It's really important, I wouldn't ask otherwise," Eileen said.

"Oh, I don't know…"

"You don't have to come here. They could stay the night with you and Dad. They'd love to see you and you know they're no bother now…"

There was a prolonged silence at the other end of the phone, and Eileen silently waited, hoping she would say yes.

"Your father and I aren't as young as we used to be, Eileen, but I do love seeing the girls. Okay, but don't make a habit out of it," Caroline answered.

"Thanks, Mum. I'll give you a call before I drop them over."

A habit out of it? If her mother babysat twice a year, she thought she overdid it.

"Is everything okay, Eileen?"

"What do you mean?"

"With you and Dave. He's treating you well, I hope?"

"Yes, what do you mean?" Eileen asked and almost choked on her words. She couldn't imagine that her mother knew anything.

"Never mind, Eileen. I'll see you on Saturday then."

Her mother hung up abruptly, which she usually did when there was no chance of hearing any juicy gossip. Eileen wasn't totally surprised as her mother had never been Dave's number one fan. In her world, he was still only one generation from the shop floor, and she had higher aspirations for her only daughter. It should have been a comforting thought to Eileen, but she dismissed it. Having the same world view as her mother was something she had always railed against, specifically when it came to her choice of husband. She picked up her keys and ran out the door to pick up the girls, late as usual.

Later that evening, the sounds of the girls chatter greeted Dave as he opened the front door at half past six. Life was definitely not going to plan, and Dave had no idea what to do. He collapsed on the couch and the girls hopped on top of him, telling him all about their day. Despite his mood, today Dave found their voices soothing and he welcomed the distraction of their world as he let all his worries go.

Granted, he might not receive a prize for being the most available father, but when he was with them, he was with them.

The experts called it being present and he prided himself on being totally present on the rare occasions when he was in their company. He always threw his phone in the dish in the hall when he came in the door and he didn't look at it again while he was with them. If he was honest, it was likely more therapeutic for him than them. He looked up and saw Eileen watching them fondly from the doorway.

"Hi," Eileen said, enjoying seeing him with the girls.

One thing she didn't doubt was that he was a great father. Eileen remembered when Dave used to light up like that at the mere sight of her. Well, maybe this weekend they could try and go back to that. She vowed to be attentive and charming, but most importantly, honest. There was no chance of any real intimacy again unless she was truthful about what went on in her life.

"Hi," Dave said and extricated himself from the girls and stood up. "I have to shower, girls, but I'll be back down to hear the next instalment of this exciting story, Amy."

Dave kissed her affectionately and Eileen could have sworn she saw tears in his eyes.

"Can I talk to you before you go out?" Eileen said as he brushed past on his way upstairs.

"Sure. Just give me half an hour," Dave said.

"It's a surprise, a nice one I hope," Eileen said silently to his retreating figure.

When he reappeared in the kitchen half an hour later, Eileen was ready to make her announcement.

"I've booked us a table in Bon Appetit," she said.

Eileen looked at him as he leaned up against the sink with a glass of water and thought how handsome he looked. His light blue shirt magnified the bewitching effect of his eyes, and if she was any other woman, she would have been green at the thought of him going out on the town without her. However, that was not her, it never had been. Maybe that was half the problem. He had always said that he had loved her independent streak, but maybe it now just seemed like indifference.

"*Bon Appetit?* What's the occasion?" Dave asked.

Eileen wanted to say that she would have booked Mancini's, but that was off limits after Wednesday night.

"Well, I think we need to talk, don't you?" Eileen asked, but seeing his anxious expression she added, "look, I don't want to fight. Can we just talk and listen to each other, Dave? Mum has agreed to babysit, so it's all sorted."

"Okay, okay. We could just stay in. I'm pretty exhausted, but if you insist…"

Eileen had that determined look and Dave knew better than to argue when she was like that.

"I do. We need to leave the house for a change. Look, the girls have a party on Saturday. Why don't you have a lie-in Saturday morning and chill out for the day. I've to go into town and then I'll drop them off with Mum after the party. I think that's a fair deal, don't you?"

"Okay, thanks. I'd appreciate catching up on some sleep alright," he said. "Now I need to make a move."

As he walked towards the door, Dave stopped to kiss her on the forehead and put his arms around her. Eileen froze in his embrace, unable to explain her reaction. Dave pulled away and went to say goodnight to the girls on his way out the door.

****

"Isn't it great all the same, Joan?" Frank shouted from the en-suite as he doused himself in aftershave. It was Friday morning and he felt very pleased with how things were working out with Mary. "Did you hear me, love?" Frank asked, walking into the bedroom. "Yes, I heard you, Frank," Joan said and sighed, her confidence now at an all-time low as she listened to him extol Mary's virtues for the umpteenth time. "I don't know. I mean, only for I'm working, I don't see the point, really I don't," she said. Joan shook her head as she pulled on her dressing gown and tied it tightly.

"*Jaysus*, you're a hard one to please. I thought I did you a bit of a favour organising help."

"I know, but she's not as young as she used to be Frank. It's only been two days. I don't know…" Joan argued.

"Would you stop? You can't say I'm not looking sharp," Frank said proudly and pointed to the shirt that Mary had perfectly pressed.

"Well, thanks very much. You'd think I did nothing around the house."

"*No one* is saying that, for *Chrissakes*. Look love, I was only trying to make life easier for you," Frank said, exasperated.

"I know, I know," Joan retorted, and sat down on the side of the bed and took a deep breath. "Oh, I don't know what's wrong with me. I'm not feeling the best today."

"Now, don't go saying it's her cooking. I saw you lapping it up last night," Frank said and took a final admiring look in the bedroom mirror before he picked up his wallet from the bedside locker.

"Would you please keep out of my hair and go to work, Frank? I just need a few minutes alone," Joan said and waved him away as he bent down to kiss her goodbye.

"Okay, have it your way. Now, those two better be ready for school," Frank said and went out on to the landing and knocked on Cyril and Johnny's bedroom doors.

"Lads, downstairs *now*. I'm goin' with or without you."

Hearing no answer from either of them, Frank went downstairs and found Cyril standing in the kitchen hungrily devouring a slice of toast covered in butter and jam.

"About time, ready to go when you are, Dad," Cyril joked.

"Very funny. Where's Johnny?" Frank asked, looking around

"He's in the car."

"In the car?" Frank said in disbelief. Johnny waiting to be driven to school was definitely a first in their house. Frank wondered if his pep talk on Wednesday night might actually have had an impact on his hard-to-reach son.

"Come on then. Don't you be the one holdin' us up so," Frank said. He gave Cyril an affectionate clip around the ear and a light shove down the hall in front of him.

Johnny sat in the car waiting for his Dad and Cyril. He needed a bit of headspace to put his thoughts in order. Johnny knew he was walking a fine line between trying to sort out their mess with McCabe, and at the same time not wanting to end up in any more trouble with the law. They were almost there, Johnny reasoned to himself. They just had to find the money somehow and pay him off. Then they were home free.

Seeing his Dad and Cyril coming out the front door, he sat up straight and quickly plastered a smile on his face.

Joan, hearing the car pull out of the driveway was left alone with her thoughts and rising anxiety. She felt her shoulder starting to twitch and the germ of a hard knot developing in her stomach. Joan buried her head in her hands, willing herself to keep it together.

'You're useless! Even an old woman like Mary O'Sullivan can do more than you. Look at her, running your house, everything spick and span. You can hardly dress yourself. Frank is regretting the day he married you,' the voice inside Joan's head said.

"Stop!" Joan shouted, but the voice in her head only increased in volume.

'You're a failure, always have been, always will be,' the voice continued.

Joan jumped up and opened the wardrobe to inspect herself in the full-length mirror. A pale, worried face looked back and she could have sworn she saw her heart pounding through her dressing gown. Joan knew she should do her breathing exercises, but her mind was racing. The litany of cruel commentary just went on and on, and she felt worn out before the day had started. Joan would just have to wait for it to wear itself out and she was left strung out, as always. Surely any psychotherapist worth their salt would trace her problems back to her mother's death, but no one had been able to help her out of that hole.

Joan went into the en-suite and turned on the tap. She threw cold water on her face and quickly grabbed a towel to dry her face and still the tremor in her hands. There was nothing for it but to make the phone call. She went back into the bedroom and knowing that the house was empty, she picked up the phone from the bedside locker.

"Hi Peter. It's Joan. Sorry, but… I won't be able to make it in today. I'm not feeling well. I'm sure I'll be back tomorrow. Sorry again." Joan left a message on the library's answering machine. She had worked out that calling before they opened meant that she could avoid any awkward conversations or admissions of her precarious state of mind. Feeling embarrassed, Joan hopped in the shower to blot it out. Peter was just another person to add to the list of people who were frustrated with her.

Joan scrubbed her body furiously with a loofah brush until her skin was bright red and tingling. When she had done her best to obliterate every awful thought, Joan turned off the water and stepped out of the shower. She grabbed the towel she had left on the radiator and briskly rubbed herself dry. Finding her dressing gown at the back of the door, she pulled it on and tied it at the waist. She brushed out her damp hair, leaving it to dry naturally and went out to the adjoining bedroom to check on Abbie.

"Abbie, are you awake?" Joan asked, knocking gently on the door. There was no response, so she opened the door.

"Abbie?" Joan called.

Joan walked over to the bed to find Abbie curled in a ball with the duvet tucked tightly around her. The only thing visible was a few stray dark curls and Joan smiled.

"What time is it?" Abbie asked, pulling the covers down. Abbie stretched her arms over her head.

"Half past eight, did I wake you, love?" Joan asked and reached across the bed and hugged Abbie, pressing her face into her hair. The sweet smell always comforted Joan.

"Are you okay, Mam?" Abbie asked and sat up in bed propping herself up with her pillow.

"I'm not feeling a hundred percent, so I'm going to take the day off work. How about I make your favourite for breakfast? Just the two of us, before Mary arrives," Joan asked.

Joan hoped Abbie would jump at the opportunity to spend time alone with her mother.

"Okay. You know, Mary is a lot nicer than I thought she would be," Abbie said thoughtfully as she gazed out the window. Joan flinched at the mention of Mary and changed the subject.

"Do you need a hand?" Joan asked.

"No, it's super easy with the crutches. I don't want to lose my independence, you know."

Joan looked at Abbie, guessing that Mary was behind her spirited words.

"*Really?*" Joan asked.

"Yes, Mary said that it's important for women to be strong and independent."

"*Did she* now? It's also important to be a lady, Abbie. Men like women who have manners and they like to look after them, like your Dad looks after me."

"Does he? *Dad?*" Abbie remarked and burst out laughing.

"Yes, of course he does. He does need a push every now and then, but he does his best," Joan said.

"Well, I think Mary's right. I'm able to fend for myself," Abbie said and grabbed her crutches and swung her legs off the side of the bed.

Joan sighed. Mary was making a fairly serious imprint on her daughter even after two days. She didn't want her to end up a man-hating feminist before she was even a teenager.

"Breakfast in ten minutes, *okay*," Joan said more sharply than she intended.

"*I wasn't trying* to annoy you, Mam," Abbie said and sat back on the bed feeling impatient with her mother.

"I know, love. Don't mind me. It's just one of those days. Now don't be long," Joan said.

Joan stood up and walked to the door, closing it behind her. She didn't want to hear any more about the wonder that was Mary. For the life of her Joan couldn't understand what a seventy-year-old woman and a twelve-year-old girl could have in common. From the sounds of it, plotting the next wave of feminism might be their common ground. Joan decided that she was going to find out today, even if it meant eavesdropping on their little tête-à-têtes.

TEN

When Joan came downstairs, she found the kitchen looking like it had been abandoned in an emergency, so she piled all the dirty plates up in the sink for Mary. Joan took time to set the table, wanting it to be just perfect for her alone time with her only daughter. Joan retrieved Abbie's favourite childhood cup from the back of the press and placed it centre stage on the table. Then she started to prepare the eggs with added milk, just as Abbie liked them.

By the time Abbie hopped in the door the table was set, and Joan served out the scrambled eggs.

"I was thinking, Abbie. You should have a friend to visit, maybe Sophie? Would you like that?" Joan asked and sat down across from Abbie.

"Yeah, I suppose so," Abbie replied.

"I thought you'd be dying to see some friends. Are you not bored *at all?*" Joan asked.

"No, not really. It's only been a few days and Mary…" Abbie started.

"I know, Abbie. Mary is so much fun," Joan said sarcastically. Abbie's head jerked up.

"Yes, she is actually. *What's wrong with that? Why don't you like her?*"

Joan sensed the irritation in Abbie's voice and paused as she thought about the question. She did like Mary, but it wasn't easy watching another woman cosy up to Abbie and run the house like a five-star hotel.

"It's just that I thought, you know… that you might like to see girls your own age. That's all."

"Maybe next week. Mary's bringing some old photographs over today to show me," Abbie said. "I'll meet Sophie next week, Mam."

"Photographs? My God, you're right busy bees the pair of you."

Joan put down her knife and fork and pushed her almost untouched plate to one side. She was rapidly losing her appetite.

"Dad says you have to go back for a check-up next week? You might be out of that cast in a few weeks. Wouldn't that be great?" Joan asked.

"I suppose. As long I don't end up on a trolley again for hours though. There was an awful lot of old people lying on trollies. Mary said that hospital is the worst place to go if you're old. That you only end up sicker or you die."

"I don't know if Mary is right, love, though I've heard some awful stories on the radio. You won't be going back to A&E. You'll have a proper appointment with a doctor," Joan said as she poured Abbie a glass of orange juice.

"Did you know that Mary's Granny lived with them when she was old?"

"No, I didn't," Joan said.

Joan thought she would scream if she heard Mary's name mentioned again. It looked like there was no escaping her anywhere in the house. Joan stood up and started to clear away the dishes.

"She didn't have to go to hospital, because she had a family to look after her," Abbie explained.

"Well, life is different now, Abbie, and people are busy and working long hours, so they don't have time to be looking after Grannies and Grandads. Mary comes from a different time," Joan insisted.

"Well, it isn't right, Mam. Isn't Mary looking after me? If she is ever sick, we should look after her. It's only fair," Abbie retorted.

"You're very thoughtful, Abbie, but wait until you grow up and you have a job and a family of your own. It's a different story then. Life isn't as simple as you think when you are a child."

The doorbell rang and interrupted their conversation.

"It can't be her already. It's *not even* ten o'clock," Joan yelped and quickly walked out to the hall and opened the front door. She found Mary standing on the doorstep, an apparition of blazing colour. She was laden down with bags of groceries and bustled in past Joan and down the hall. Leaving them down on the kitchen table, she turned around to face them both.

"Oh, thank God. That's a relief. They weigh a ton. I'm not as young as I used to be, that's for sure. I'd have carried double that, not a problem when I was younger."

Mary smiled at Joan who had followed her down the hall with her mouth open.

"Sorry, where are my manners? Good Morning to you both," Mary said and tossed Abbie's hair affectionately. "How's my partner in crime today?" she asked.

Joan rolled her eyes and looked at the two of them as thick as thieves.

"I came downstairs on my own on the crutches. What do you think of that?" Abbie asked, and raised her arms triumphantly.

"You're a trooper, really you are. Isn't she, Joan?"

Mary registered Joan standing in her dressing gown in the middle of the kitchen. Joan looked like she was going nowhere fast.

"Are you okay, Joan? You look a bit pale," Mary said, concerned.

"I don't know what it is, but I'm not feeling the best today to be honest," Joan answered.

"Have you been sick? Is it one of those vomiting bugs?" Mary asked.

"No, it's definitely not that," Joan said and stuck her nose up at the suggestion, "but I might lie down for a while. It's okay if you want to go home though, you know…"

"I'm happy to stay and help out, but whatever you want Joan," Mary said lightly, as if she didn't care either way. The room went quiet as they both figured out their next move.

"Please stay, Mary. Can she, Mam?" Abbie asked, and looked from one to the other with a stubborn glint in her eyes.

Abbie wouldn't give in easily, Joan knew. With each passing day, she witnessed Abbie change before her eyes as she approached her teenage years.

"It's probably best you stay then, Mary. I'm not up to much today. I mean if it was any other day…" Joan said.

"That's fine. Haven't I the food bought so it'd be a waste otherwise. That's settled then," Mary said and pulled on her apron and set to work on the dishes. Mary knew she had been a bit extravagant with the shopping, but she had been so excited at the prospect of cooking for a family that she had found it hard to rein it in. However, she tempered her worries by reminding herself that Frank was paying her.

"Great, now you can lie down, Mam. Mary will stay with me," Abbie said and smiled, delighted that Mary was staying.

Joan nodded feeling defeated. The morning wasn't turning out the way she had planned.

"You go on to bed, Joan. I'll bring you up some lunch later. I won't bother you. I'll just knock and leave it outside," Mary insisted and before she knew what happened, Joan found herself being waved out of the room and up the stairs to her bedroom.

When she was upstairs, Joan sat on the bed, wondering how she had ended up confined to her bedroom while Mary and Abbie bonded in the kitchen. Nothing ever seemed to turn out the way she intended. There was the time she had planned to surprise Johnny on his birthday and had actually baked a cake, but it fell flat and it was Frank who had saved the day. In a mad panic after work he had found a bakery open and convinced them to add a personalised message for Johnny. Frank had insisted it was no bother, but when he arrived home dripping in perspiration and gulped back a beer in one go, it was obvious it had been.

The words of her favourite counsellor, Deirdre, rang in her ears. Joan had listened in awe as Deirdre told her that she needed to do things, like find her voice and speak her truth.

"It'll eat you up if you don't, Joan," Joan whispered, remembering her words.

Listening to the noises coming from downstairs, Joan knew that Mary had no such problems. She could hear her voice booming away in the kitchen as she chatted and laughed with Abbie. Mary seemed so capable, so full of energy and she must be at least fifteen years older than her. All the older women Joan remembered had died young or ended up decrepit and demented. Frank's mother had spent her final days living with them, propped up in a wheelchair by the fire, babbling away to no one in particular, and her own mother hadn't made it past forty. This was a new perspective on female ageing that she had never contemplated.

As the sound of Abbie's tinkling laughter floated into the room, Joan lay back on the bed and was reminded of a time when she had laughed like that. It was long before children had arrived, when it was just herself and Frank. Joan had been carried along with his love of Irish music. They had visited almost every venue in the country, and he would drag her out to dance, twirling her so fast that her hair whipped round her face and she couldn't stop laughing. Joan had felt free as a bird.

Joan decided that she had to find a way back to that woman. From the looks of it, she wouldn't be long losing Abbie if she didn't pull herself together. It felt like she had already lost Johnny. Well, it was now or never with Mary looking like she was only too ready to fill her shoes. Joan turned on her side savouring the memory of her happy days. She drifted off to sleep and a few hours later she woke from the sound of creaking on the landing. She climbed out of bed and listened at the door. When she heard the footsteps retreat down the stairs, Joan opened the door and saw a tray with sandwiches and a pot of tea. It was Mary's doing, obviously, and she choked up as she picked up the tray and went back into the bedroom.

Downstairs, Abbie pored over Mary's photographs, fascinated with every detail. She quizzed her on every person in them and their story.

"They all look so happy," Abbie said, sounding surprised.

"I suppose they do look happy… people pretend sometimes, you know, when they are having their photograph taken. It doesn't always tell you the whole story," Mary explained.

Mary had no intention of upsetting Abbie with the story of her childhood. She picked up one of the photographs of her parents and looked closely at her father. He looked nothing like the man she remembered growing up, the man who had beaten her mother senseless on many occasions while Mary had cowered behind the couch, too traumatised to move.

"I know what you mean. Mam always looks much happier in photographs," Abbie said, and Mary noticed the sadness in her voice. "I sometimes see her crying, like the other day. I came into the living room, but she just turned away and said she was fine. I know she wasn't," Abbie said.

"She probably was just worried about you, I mean, you did break your ankle," Mary said and tried to find the right words to console her.

"Maybe, but I've seen her crying plenty of times. She doesn't always know I see her though," Abbie responded. "I often think it might be something I've done."

"*What* are you talking about?"

"I know I can be a bit grumpy sometimes… I am impatient with her."

"Oh, Abbie. Please don't say that. That couldn't be further from the truth," Mary said and reached over and clasped Abbie's hand in hers.

"But how do you know? You haven't seen her Mary," Abbie whispered.

"I just do. You've done nothing wrong, trust me. Grown-ups can be sad, just like children."

"I know, but I just wish I could make her happy."

"Aw, Abbie, you being alive makes her happy. Do you not see that? The minute I walked in the door I could see that your mother would throw herself in front of a bus for you."

"Do you think so?" Abbie said and looked up at Mary, her eyes searching hers for reassurance.

"Of course. She absolutely adores you. I'm a mother and I know that for sure. You're everything to her. There is absolutely nothing you could do that would make her stop loving you. Do you hear me?" Mary said in a raised voice, knowing she spoke the truth. Abbie laughed.

"That's the spirit. Now, let's have that cup of hot chocolate."

Mary stood up to put on the kettle, relieved to change the subject. Joan almost tripped in her hurry to go back upstairs and away from the conversation she had just overheard. She struggled to keep the tray steady and dropped it on the bed as soon as she was back in the safety of her bedroom. Closing the door behind her, she exhaled and sank to the floor. She couldn't ignore the strange feeling of solidarity that swept over her as she listened to Mary sing her praises.

Aside from her own mother, her opportunities for bonding with other women had been few and far between in life. Yet her face burned as pangs of jealousy and irritation surfaced, railing against her softness.

"What was Mary doing talking to Abbie in such an intimate way in the first place? She hardly knows her. It's none of her business. She's *my* daughter. How could Abbie confide in Mary so easily anyway? How could she tell her such private things and betray her own mother?" Joan asked herself at an almost frantic pace.

Joan put her hands over her ears and tried to block out the judgemental, confusing voice in her head. Her overwhelming feeling was one of sadness. Abbie was upset and worried about her. So much so, that she had gone as far as confiding in a woman she hardly knew. Struggling to her feet, Joan rushed into the bathroom and leaned over the toilet. She dry retched until her stomach muscles hurt and then, dropping the lid, Joan sat on the toilet seat with her head in her hands. Whatever happened, she had to make it up to Abbie.

Mary's kind words stayed with Joan for the rest of the day. As she dressed to join them downstairs that evening, she decided that despite her conflicting emotions Joan would keep an open mind about Mary.

Frank was the first to arrive home at five o'clock. Armed with a bottle of sherry to thank Mary, a few beers for himself and a bottle of wine that might accompany dinner, he was in a mood to celebrate. Frank opened the back door and was assaulted by the most appetising smells.

"Somethin's cookin' in the kitchen, somethin's steamin' up the air…" Frank belted out as he entered the kitchen.

"Go easy, Frank. You'll wake the dead," Mary said, stirring her sauce.

"You're not long layin' down the law. That's the Mary O'Sullivan I remember. So, what's on the menu today?" Frank asked and leaned over her shoulder.

"What do you think? It's Friday and you know I'm a good Irish catholic, so take a wild guess."

"Well, I'm guessin' it's not steak," Frank remarked.

"Hilarious. It's salmon actually," Mary said and smiled.

"Nothin' wrong with a nice bit a salmon in my book. Where's Joan?" Frank asked looking around.

"She's upstairs I think," Mary said.

Mary knew that whatever went on between Frank and Joan, she knew they had one of those marriages that would last for ever. "Speak of the devil. How are you feeling, love?" Frank asked and smiled. He walked over to give Joan a kiss as she walked into the kitchen.

"I was just telling Frank that you went upstairs," Mary said while she peeled the potatoes. The room went quiet except for the sound of dinner bubbling on the cooker. Frank looked at Joan.

"Yes, I was upstairs. I feel a lot better now. Dinner smells great, Mary," Joan said, setting the table.

"And where are those two lugs? Are they not home yet? Mary I'm tellin' you, you couldn't be up to the pair of them," Frank said and stuck his finger in the sauce. Mary quickly slapped his hand away.

"Thanks, Dad." Cyril sauntered into the kitchen, still in his garage overalls. His face was streaked with oil and he was grinning from ear to ear. "I'm not Johnny, you know. We're chalk and cheese as you say so yourself," Cyril said, washing the grime off his hands.

"Where is he anyways?" Frank asked.

"How should *I* know? I don't see him from one end of the day to the other."

"Is he not home yet? You won't believe it, Mary. Johnny was…" Frank started.

"Frank, please, will you just go inside and sit down," Joan said and shoved a beer in his hand and pushed him towards the door. "Will you leave me, *woman.* I'm tryin' to talk to Mary," Frank retorted.

Joan gave in and sat down at the table. It looked like Mary was going to know every sordid detail about their family before the week was out.

"We had the bloody guards at the door the other night, would you believe that? And guess who they had in tow? Yes, our Johnny," Frank said, taking a slug of his beer.

"*The guards? What happened?*" Mary asked and almost dropped the pot of potatoes on the floor.

"Don't ask. I'll just say that our Johnny can pack a punch so he can…" Frank said. He couldn't resist a smile at the thought of his son standing up for his friend.

"Frank! We don't condone violence, Mary, *not at all,*" Joan interjected.

"To be fair, he was only helpin' out a friend but…"

Frank decided not to share all the gory details of the episode. "Anyways, I'm a man of principle, always have been, always will be, so he's under orders to behave himself and be home early. I'm givin' him a call, Joan, and he better bloody answer."

Frank stood up and went out to the back garden. Joan poured herself a glass of wine from the bottle Frank had left on the table, sat down and closed her eyes.

****

"Feckin' hell. Don't say anything, Johnny, I'm warning you."

Johnny and Jack were sitting on the wall outside school after study. Brian McCabe stopped in front of them, feeling brave with the support of his entourage.

"You two better come up with the money or I'll finish you off next time," Brian said.

"You were the lucky one, McCabe. I'd have finished you off only for the cops arriving," Johnny sneered at him.

"Go easy," Jack nudged him.

"Don't worry, asshole. You'll have your money and we won't be doing business with you again. That stuff you gave us last time was crap," Johnny said and hopped off the wall. McCabe grabbed him by the collar.

"Go on… *I dare you.* I'd have you on your back in seconds," Johnny said, egging him on as he saw their teacher Mr Green approaching.

McCabe was just about to punch him when he caught sight of the teacher.

"You're fucking dead if ye don't come up with the money. You have a week," Brian threatened.

"Everything okay here, lads? I want no messing on school grounds. Do you hear me? Now, go on home the lot of you."

"Nothing going on here, Sir. Just stopping for a friendly chat," McCabe said, and signalling to his minions he took off down the road.

"You two, as well," Mr Green said. He was one of the few teachers who didn't fear the wrath of parents, no matter who they were.

"We're on our way, sir," Jack reassured him as they started to walk in the direction of the park.

"Jesus, Johnny. Will you watch it with McCabe. You know he's a head-the-ball. We just need to pay him off and be finished with him."

"I know, but I hate the guy. Just because his father's a judge, he thinks he's above the law."

As they arrived at their den, Johnny picked up a rock, took aim at the shed and proceeded to shatter one of the windows.

"What the fuck, Johnny?"

"Just imagining it's McCabe's head. Take it easy. It's just an old shed. Nobody uses it," Johnny reassured. Johnny felt his phone vibrate in his pocket and looked at it.

"Feck it. I have to go. That's the old man," Johnny said and answered the phone.

"…Yeah, I'm on the way," Johnny said. He nodded at Jack and walked away in the direction of home. Jack looked after him trying to figure out his friend. Sometimes he was like a man possessed.

At home, Frank hung up the phone and stepped inside the house.

"He's on his way," Frank said and then proceeded to pour a glass of wine for Mary.

"Oh, I shouldn't Frank, it's only, what time is it?" Mary said and picked up the glass, taking a large gulp of the wine.

"Ah, would you go on, Mary. It's Friday night and it's seven o'clock, wine o'clock, that's what the women call it these days, isn't that right, Joan?"

Joan kicked him under the table but cracked a small smile as she did it.

"It looks like beer o'clock to me," Mary said and winked at Joan, feeling a slight thawing in the atmosphere between them.

"There you are, son. Good man…" Frank said as Johnny appeared at the door.

There was a giddy atmosphere around the table. Mary's addition to the house had ensured they all made an effort to put their best side out. Frank was in his usual Friday evening good humour, Mary was just delighted to be part of their little community and Joan was determined not to let the side, or Abbie, down again. Frank locked eyes with Joan, but they both quickly looked away, neither ready to acknowledge the truth about their youngest son.

Dinner went off without a hitch.

"Now lads, once we're finished here, we'll have a bit of music. What do you think, Mary?" Frank said and nudged her.

"What are you looking at me for?" Mary laughed as she went to fill the dishwasher.

"Well, I'm off to find my accordion and warm up. I'll leave you ladies to do what you do best," Frank said, standing up from the table.

Mary gave him a swipe with the tea towel on his way out the door. A feed of alcohol had given him an itch that needed scratching. Inebriation was all the encouragement Frank needed tonight and an enthusiastic audience. Mary and Joan were left alone in the kitchen as the children scattered to their own corners of the house. They cleaned up in an easy silence and after a few minutes Joan opened her mouth.

"I just wanted to say, Mary…" Joan said and felt like she might choke on her words.

"What is it, Joan? I know there's something on your mind. Please say it out. I've actually been wanting to talk to you on your own too, but haven't had the chance until now," Mary said.

"Oh, really."

"Look, I know it must be a bit strange, another woman coming into your house, and an older one at that. But it was Frank who asked me to help out, what with you both being busy and Abbie off school. I'm not trying to take over or anything. You're doing me a favour actually."

"Oh, right," Joan said and felt the wind taken out of her sails.

"If you have a problem with it, I totally understand, and we don't have to say it to Frank. I can make up some excuse and that'll be that," Mary said. Mary stopped what she was doing and looked Joan in the eye.

"Yes, I mean no, I don't want you to leave. I wasn't too sure, you know, about it at the start, but I was wrong, and Abbie really likes you."

"Joan, I'm a novelty. I'm mad about her, but I can tell you one thing that's for sure, she adores you," Mary reassured.

They stood facing each other and their eyes met. In those few seconds, a new understanding was reached, and the tide started to turn in their relationship.

"And thanks for, you know, with Frank. I feel a bit… you know, I feel a bit down sometimes. I don't like to worry him," Joan said and bit her lip.

"You don't have to explain anything to me, Joan. I've been there myself. You're not on your own, you know," Mary said. On hearing Frank coming down the stairs, she put a hand on Joan's arm and looked her straight in the eye. "Just know that if you ever want to talk, I'm here. I'm not the worst listener in the world," Mary said and smiled.

Joan wanted to hug her but was stopped by Frank arriving back with his accordion in tow.

"Now ladies, it's time to leave the dishes and to put your feet up. Frank Hughes is here to entertain you."

They moved to the living room and to an outsider Mary and Joan looked like bosom buddies as they sat beside each other on the couch, sipping wine and singing along to the music. Frank finished his set with a rousing rendition of 'The Rose of Tralee'. He dedicated it to Mary, knowing her people were from Kerry. The week had come to a better conclusion than any of them could have imagined.

Mary was floating on air when she came home from the Hughes' house on Friday night, so much so, that she regaled Boots with a blow by blow of the night. Mary roused him from his sleep by the Aga, bundled him up and settled him on her lap in the armchair. "That was so much fun, Boots. You wouldn't believe it," Mary remarked.

Mary didn't believe it herself. She couldn't remember the last time she had enjoyed herself so much. Mary had forgotten the pleasures of a noisy family dinner as everyone fought to have their voice heard. However, the highlight had been when Frank took out his accordion afterwards and treated herself and Joan to a little concert. She stroked Boots who purred with contentment and told him every detail of the night.

"God, it brought me back. It really brought me back, Boots," Mary said, delighted.

And it had. It stirred up memories of her mother singing in the kitchen or even at bedtime when she sang to her until she fell asleep. Music had helped them both survive a life that had otherwise been marred by atrocities; atrocities that Mary had done her best to block out. Mary brushed away the memory and decided to have a nightcap.

"Sorry, Boots. I'll just be a minute," Mary said. Boots let out a screech, objecting to being unsettled from his owner's lap. "My bloody arthritis," Mary cried out and she rubbed her back.

Mary took a tumbler glass from the press, poured a finger full of sherry, hesitated and then filled it halfway to the top.

"We'll save the posh glasses for when we have visitors. Isn't that right, Boots?"

Boots hopped up on Mary's lap the minute she had settled herself back in the chair. Mary smiled and marvelled at the turn her life had taken, and when she had least expected it.

"Just a little nightcap to celebrate a good day," Mary said.

Mary knew she had drunk enough earlier, but arriving home to a quiet house after the lively home she had been in was almost too much to bear. Mary rubbed Boot's coat as she drifted away with her thoughts. She had lived in fear of this moment; the moment that she might let herself become too close to anyone else. Mary must remember that the arrangement with the Hughes was only temporary and soon enough she would be back on her own again. "Thank God you came along, Boots. At least we have each other." Mary leaned over and kissed the cat who loved all the unexpected attention he was receiving so late in the night. Finishing the last of her sherry, she lay back in the chair and closed her eyes.

Time passed quickly and soon it was morning and in all that time, Mary slept soundly in the chair. One could say that it was probably the best Mary had slept in years.

"*Good God, is it morning?*" Mary asked, waking with a start.

She looked at the clock on the wall and couldn't believe it was eleven o'clock the next day. She hadn't slept so late in a long time. Mary opened the back door for Boots, who looked at her with such disdain that she apologised profusely. He didn't even acknowledge her as he strutted past with his head held high in the air.

"I'm so sorry, Boots. I don't know what happened to me," Mary said. Mary immediately boiled the kettle and made herself a cup of tea and sat down. With each sip of the hot liquid, Mary felt more human and was ready to make a plan for the day. She needed to do something to mark this new direction her life had taken.

Once Mary had eaten a light breakfast of toast and marmalade, she went upstairs and pulled down the steps to the small attic. Mary would spend the weekend clearing out the clutter of her old life. She would hold on to some photographs and a few other sentimental items, but it was time to say goodbye to everything else. Mary was determined that by the time she went back to the Hughes family, she would be finally free of all the baggage that had been holding her back for so long.

Mary spent the weekend traipsing up and down the stairs, poring over every item she uncovered. She shed a few more tears as she found old birthday cards from her parents, a reminder of the charade of happy families Mary had played along with at the forceful request of her father, but mainly to keep her mother happy.

When she had a pile so high that it hardly fitted in the bin, Mary decided that a little bonfire would be the most fitting way to say goodbye to her old life. Mary wasn't a stranger to a bit of ritual. She pulled on her coat and wellies and with Boots looking on beside her, Mary held her own little cremation ceremony in the garden. Mary watched the past disintegrate to ash and then finished by cleansing the house with sage and opening all the windows.

Now, feeling a lot lighter in herself, Mary set out to the supermarket in the evening, eager to prepare for the week ahead.

ELEVEN

Eileen's weekend was different to any weekend she had experienced in all her years with Dave. On Saturday morning, Eileen prepared herself for the day with a hot shower while the children ate their breakfast downstairs. She was soon dressed and passed Dave asleep in bed before tiptoeing out of the room and downstairs to the kitchen.

"Mum, I don't want to go. *Please* can we stay home? *I'm not going.* I *refuse* to go," Amy announced as Eileen entered the kitchen.

Eileen knew Amy was sky high, no doubt as a result of the sugar feast Amy had indulged in for breakfast, while Eileen herself had been in the shower. She threw a blind eye at weekends, but the tantrums were exhausting. Eileen tried not to laugh as she watched her stamp her feet on the kitchen tiles, her dark wispy hair flying in all directions.

"Amy, you know Gran is really looking forward to having you stay. She'll have lots of treats if you're good. You always love it when you go."

Amy always took time to warm to an idea. Sophie, on the other hand, would hop on a plane with the first stranger who asked.

"Please, please. I want to stay here with you and Dad," Amy insisted, her face growing red.

"Dad and I won't be here. We're going out. So, I'm afraid Amy, you have to go. Please do this one thing for me. I promise you, you'll have a great time. She's ordering pizza and you're going to watch a movie. Do you really want to miss that?"

Amy scrunched up her face as she weighed up her options.

"And you have a party this afternoon. Haven't you all the luck this weekend?" Eileen added, hoping that would push her over the line.

Normally parties would set Amy through the roof, but their neighbour's child, Claire, was diabetic. A bouncy castle and a clown were planned to compensate for the lack of sugar.

"I'll think about it, Mum," Amy said seriously, as she flounced out the door to the living room.

"Of course, darling. I wouldn't want you missing out on all the fun, that's all," Eileen called.

Eileen knew she had taken a turn and would come around. It was the same pattern every time. A manic high, followed by a cranky low and then back on an even keel. She just had to drop them off in the afternoon and Grandad was going to pick them up from the party.

****

At eight o'clock Eileen and Dave sat facing each other in the salubrious surroundings of Bon Appetit. It was an exclusive restaurant with a laid-back feel. It was helped by soft lighting and gentle music playing in the background. The ambience may have been intended to relax customers, but it also facilitated private conversations like the one they were about to have. Intimacies could be shared in comfort without the risk of being overheard. As they were shown to their table, Eileen and Dave drew plenty of admiring glances from customers; looks they hardly noticed anymore.

They were seated at a prized window seat that Eileen hadn't even asked for when she made the booking. Just the mere mention of the Danaher surname bestowed many untold benefits. It was one of the best tables with spectacular views of the fast-flowing river that ran through town. Colourful fishing boats bobbed up and down on the water, tied up in their resting place for the night.

"This is nice, isn't it?" Eileen commented when they were settled.

"Yes, it is. Thanks for suggesting it," Dave said and smiled.

The waiter brought them menus and they ordered a bottle of wine before choosing their food. It was an old habit of theirs. When they needed to talk about something important the unwritten rule was that they didn't tackle it until they had finished their starters and a glass of wine. Thawing out time, they called it. Eileen looked over at Dave as he flicked through the menu and thought that he looked rested. His blonde wavy hair was a bit darker with the years, but there were no signs of it receding. He had looked like a surfer in college and there was no doubt that his killer megawatt smile had helped his career. After a few minutes of chit-chat the waiter was back at their table to take their orders. When they were left alone, Eileen picked her moment.

"I've something to tell you, Dave, about, you know, about dinner with Fran Daly," Eileen began.

"What about him?" Dave reached for the basket of bread and thickly covered a slice with butter.

"He's been difficult recently and Pat wanted me to make peace with him. That's why I had to go, but it didn't go well at all," Eileen said.

"What do you mean?" Dave asked and looked up while munching on a slice of bread.

"He ended up atrociously drunk over dinner. I could handle him in the restaurant, but he practically assaulted me in the car on the way home."

"What do you mean in the car? *You gave him a lift home? Jesus,* Eileen," Dave said, sharply. "Sorry, I just mean that it's never a good idea to give a male client a lift home. You just can't be too careful these days, you know that," Dave added.

"Aw, come on. I didn't think things were that bad. I had no intention of giving him a lift, but by the time we left the restaurant he was so drunk, he staggered all over the place. I was parked nearby, so I just thought it would be easier than trying to put him in a taxi," Eileen explained.

"That was *his bloody problem*," Dave retorted.

"He assaulted me in the car, Dave," Eileen said.

Eileen proceeded to tell him what had happened, stumbling on the words as she relayed everything. Dave stiffened with every word.

"*Jesus Christ,* Eileen. *The bastard. Why didn't you tell me before now?* He should have been arrested, *you know that."*

Dave then lowered his voice to a whisper, aware that a few people had looked over at them. "I hope you told Pat what happened. He'd tell the fucker where to go."

"That is what I'm trying to tell you. I did tell him, but he acted like I was just exaggerating. Would you believe that Fran rang Pat before I arrived at work singing my praises and pretending like nothing had ever happened?" Eileen said and shook her head. "If I refuse to work with him, he will pull his account. Pat has given me the weekend to think about it, but I think I'm going to lose my job, unless I toe the line."

"*What?* No way. I'll talk to him, Eileen. *That's not fucking on*. Oh God, this is all a mess," Dave said and buried his head in his hands, realising the implications of what had happened.

"Are you okay?" Dave reached across the table, just like Fran had and she almost pulled away, but stopped herself.

"I don't know to be honest. I did ring the guards, because even though he's a pervert, I didn't want it on my conscience if he was knocked down. I told them I didn't want to press charges, but now, oh, I don't know," Eileen said, and her voice trembled.

"I'm so sorry, Eileen," Dave said, softly.

"What I need to tell you is that I'm handing in my notice on Monday. I mean, unless Pat does a total turnaround, which I know he won't. I cannot and will not betray myself by working with that bastard again. I know he has done this before. I'll find some other work until I have my own paying clients," Eileen said, pulling herself together.

"Giving in your notice?"

"What other choice do I have, Dave?" Eileen asked. "Pat has made it plain that he won't accept no for an answer."

"*Why didn't* you report him to the guards? *For Chrissakes, Eileen.* If he was arrested, Pat would have no choice but to drop him. Now, he still has the upper hand and you just look like a hysterical woman."

"*A hysterical woman?* Is that how you see me? I'm just after telling you what happened and *that's all you have to say. Really Dave.*"

Eileen threw her napkin on the table.

"Look, I didn't mean it like that. I meant that you didn't report him and now he's off scot-free. Don't you see that? And you end up losing your job. How is that fair? Like you said, it's not his first time and I'm sure you're not the first woman. I've heard stories too."

"I don't know if I can. I know that might seem crazy, but…"

Eileen's eyes filled with tears, but she tried her best not to cry in a restaurant full of people.

"You know, I've taken the sleazy looks and comments all my life, but I draw the line at anything physical. It could have been a lot worse, Dave, if I hadn't dragged him out of the car. I know I'm not making sense, but at the moment this is all I can do."

"It's okay. I'm sorry. I've no idea what it must be like. Men are assholes, you know that Eileen," Dave said, and he looked at her with such sympathy that she surprised herself by bursting out laughing.

"Yeah, they are," Eileen said in agreement. "God, it's such a relief to tell you. Well, I'm glad you're not one of the assholes," Eileen said.

In that moment, Eileen saw something flicker across Dave's face, but she couldn't place what it was.

"Now, while we're at it, will you talk to me about our finances?"

"Oh, Eileen, I've made such a mess of things. *Really,* I have. I'm so sorry. I'm such an idiot," Dave confessed.

"Talk to me Dave. However bad, I need to know what's going on. I came clean with you."

"Well, I made a few investments that I didn't tell you about. I thought you would just worry, and Jeff told me they were a sure thing. I really thought it would all be fine, but it's a disaster. I didn't want to say anything until I knew how bad it was, but I spoke to him on Friday and it doesn't look good at all," Dave continued.

"How bad?"

"Let's just say that you leaving your job couldn't come at a worse time. We have a lot of debt now and I don't know how to climb out of this hole… We could lose the house," Dave said in a low voice.
"How could you not tell me about this? *Jesus*, Dave. *I'm your wife.* How long has this been going on for?"

"A year or more. I really am sorry."

"Is that why you're always home so late and have been so distracted?" Eileen asked.

"Well, yes. I suppose so. Well, partially…"

"Look, I don't care about the house, Dave. Can't we buy a smaller one? Or rent out rooms, do Airbnb? There are lots of ways these days to supplement our income. If I'm not working in Clancy's I can do something else. Even if you don't want to hear this, I'll be qualified soon as a therapist and will be able to see clients. I can use one of the rooms downstairs."

Eileen reached out her hand to Dave.

"I don't deserve you, Eileen. Really, I don't. I'm such a fool. I never deserved you. I couldn't believe it when you finally agreed to go out with me all those years ago," Dave said on the verge of tears.

Eileen had a sneaking suspicion that there was more going on, but their food arrived at the table just as she was about to say something. She let it go. They had covered enough ground for one night.

*****

The following Monday morning, Frank was busy serving a customer at work when he heard a voice that he hadn't heard in a long time. It bore the tell-tale sound of a local but was laced with an unmistakable American twang. He looked up to see Séamus Feeney standing in front of him.

"Well, Frank Hughes. I haven't seen you in an age. You're looking swell. Are you working here now?" Séamus asked.

"What the…" Frank said. Frank gave the customer her change and came out from behind the counter and gave Séamus a hug. "Well, if it isn't yourself? You're a sight for sore eyes. It must be five years or more since you've been back on a visit?" Frank remarked.

"Oh, it's at least five years I'd say, Frank. I haven't been home in a long time, too long actually," Seamus said with a wistful look in his eyes.

Séamus had left Ireland many years before, hoping to make a living abroad. Music was his life and he wasn't long becoming an international success, only returning home for holidays and to catch up with family and friends. He and Frank had played in many a dark shebeen over the years when they were both a lot younger.

"Are you back in town for a gig? I thought you'd have bigger fish to fry than slumming it here with us," Frank said.

"I'm back home for a vacation, Frank, a long one. I think I've been in every corner of the world at this stage. I can't complain, but I'm beat. Do you know when I first left Galway? Forty years ago, would you believe that?"

"I wouldn't. *Jaysus*, you're making me feel old."

"You and me both," Séamus said. "America's been very good to me and it was my base for a long time, but there's nowhere like home, to be honest."

Séamus had cleaned windows for a living before a career on the world stage beckoned. Although he took his craft very seriously, the same couldn't be said for the media frenzy that went with it. Frank looked at him and couldn't help feeling a bit jealous. Séamus' long corkscrew curls were still a burnished copper and his face, although a bit more weather-beaten, had a healthy glow. His eyes held the spark of a contented man.

"Well, the bit of travel hasn't done you any harm. You haven't aged a day," Frank said.

Séamus was tall, but the weight he carried in the past, courtesy of barrels of Guinness, was now replaced by a lean, wiry physique.

"I gave up the booze a few years back, Frank. Best thing I ever did. Jesus, I couldn't go anywhere but people were buying me pints, even the Japanese, who by the way, love the Irish music. I was on a downward spiral with it. The music suffered and one of them had to go, so it was an easy decision."

"Well, fair play to you all the same," Frank said and clapped him on the back.

"How are you? Are you playing at all? You were great on the accordion, Frank," Séamus added.

"Would you believe that the first time I played in years was the other night for the wife and Mary, you know, Mary O'Sullivan?"

"I do indeed," Séamus said and smiled at the memory of a young Mary and her mother who had been beautiful singers.

"We had some craic, Séamus. I was just thinking she must be at least seventy if she's a day and she can still hold a note."

"Her mother was a great singer, the father was a whole other story though… but never mind that," Séamus said, and he shook his head.

"Come over here and sit down for a minute, will you. I'm just about to take a break," Frank said and led the way to a coffee area in the corner of the shop. They ordered a pot of tea and sat up at the counter.

"You can't beat a Barry's," Séamus said and sighed as he lifted up his cup and savoured the taste.

"So, tell me, how are the family, Frank?"

"Devil a bit wrong with them, Séamus. Poor Abbie broke her ankle last week, but she's doing grand. Cyril is car mad and wants to be a mechanic, Johnny is… well, what can I say… he's us driven cracked and it's hard to know what to do. He had a run in with the guards the other night," Frank said, feeling the urge to confide in Séamus who he thought might understand.

"Sorry to hear that Frank. That can't be easy," Séamus nodded, having plenty of experience in that department.

"To be honest, it's been comin' for a long time. I wouldn't be sayin' it to Joan now, but…" Frank said with a nudge and wink, "the apple doesn't fall far from the tree. I was no angel myself, so I can't be too hard on him. Mary is helpin' out for a while and it's been the best thing ever. Even Joan is warmin' to her."

"Ah, your awesome wife, Joan. How is *she* doing?" Seamus asked.

"Depends on the day you're asking. I'm mad about her, but you know yourself, some women suffer a bit from the nerves… the doctor has her on tablets," Frank admitted, knowing he could trust Séamus.

As Frank talked easily to Séamus, it brought back memories of how close they had once been when they were younger. Frank realised that he had missed the company of his old friend, much more than he had realised.

"That's a bummer, Frank, you know, everyone in the States is on something. No surprise that Trump was elected. Most of the population were on some drug or other when they voted," Séamus said and laughed so loudly people turned in their seats. "Sorry, in bad taste I know, but you have to laugh, don't you?"

"That's for sure. What else can you do?" Frank said, draining his cup.

"On a brighter note," Séamus said, "I'm playing in Tigh Neachtain now, every Wednesday night with some of the old guys. We could do with an accordion player. Will you join us?"

"Me? Aw, I don't know. I'd be fairly rusty you know."

"It's like riding a bike, Frank. And bring that son, Johnny, along. It might do him some good. Before I found music, I was lost. I was so angry I came close to breaking the windows I was cleaning. It might keep the cops off his back."

Séamus was surprised at how easily he talked about his past, a past that he had been desperate to forget. It looked like the years of therapy in America had healed some of those old wounds.

"Thanks, though I wouldn't hold my breath," Frank said. "You know, since I've the accordion down from the attic, I might just give it a go," he said and then glanced at his watch and stood up. "Sorry, Séamus, but I better head back to work. You take your time here."

Frank put out his hand to his old friend.

"I better be going myself," Séamus said, "I actually did come in here to buy something. I'm fixing up the home place, but that's awesome Frank. That's just awesome. See you Wednesday then."

Séamus gave Frank a firm handshake and disappeared down one of the aisles. Frank watched him walk away thinking that he sure had the cut of a yank about him, laid back and oozing positivity. Well, between Mary and now Séamus appearing, things were surely looking up.

At home, Joan was going through a good patch. The weekend had passed without any problems and by Monday evening, the house was quiet. Mary had left a huge pot of casserole for them and all the washing and cleaning was done. The sun was shining, so Joan grabbed a blanket and brought her cup of tea out to the back garden to relax on the sun lounger. It had been her routine during the summer when the weather permitted. Frank had cobbled together a little patio area with some of his buddies and it was perfect for the sun trap the garden became during summer evenings.

Joan tried to imagine she was on holidays as she closed her eyes and felt the heat warm her body. A smile crossed her face as she remembered Friday night and the spectacle of Frank standing on the table singing at the top of his voice. It was a long time since she had enjoyed an evening as much. Mary had been far from the sherry swilling, sharp-tongued shrew that she had imagined. Joan blushed as she remembered some of the awful stories she had spread about Mary, many of them without any foundation. The woman she had laughed and chatted with was warm and caring. Mary reminded Joan of her own mother if she was honest and Joan had sorely missed her mother's presence all these years. It would be good to have another friend in her life, even if Mary was fifteen years older than her, Joan didn't care. Many of the women her own age had no interest in her. Apart from Eileen, she sorely lacked in that department. Frank had always been her everything from the day she met him.

Joan was from a small village outside Cork, the daughter of a placid farmer and a gregarious mother. Her childhood had been happy until everything changed when her mother died when she was just thirteen years old. Joan was left alone with her father, a man of few words and even less emotion. Joan had to grow up quickly. It fell to her to assume her mother's role, but it hadn't been a great success as Joan was only young and had none of her mother's strength and vigour.

It wasn't long before her father installed a new Mrs O' Connor in the household. She was a local spinster woman, who had no great interest in rearing someone else's child. Joan put her hands to her face as she recalled the horror of it all. Joan wasn't long becoming an outsider in her own home, living with the constant fear of being sent away. Anxiety and headaches became the norm as she tiptoed around her new step-mother and grief-stricken father.

There was no room for Joan's sadness in those years, and so she buried it away as best as she could, only to have it manifest in panic attacks and periods of depression when she grew older. Finally, at sixteen years of age, they decided it would be best if Joan took a job in Galway and arranged lodgings for Joan there.

As Joan sat on the bus as it wound its way to the city that would be her new home, she had toyed with the idea of ending it all. No one would notice if a strange girl from the country disappeared. Luckily, before Joan had a chance to entertain the idea any further, she met Frank, colliding with him at a bus stop. He had been besotted with her from day one, and it wasn't long before marriage and children became her life. There was one thing Joan was sure of - Frank had saved her life that day.

Joan was stirred from her memory by her son standing at the back door.

"Mam, did you see my blue shirt? Is it washed?" Cyril asked. He stood, rubbing a towel through his hair.

"What?" Joan asked.

"My shirt, is it washed?" Cyril asked.

"Oh, you look very handsome, Cyril," Joan said and sat up shielding her eyes from the sun with her hand.

All Joan could see was the glare, but it was safe enough to assume, as Cyril always looked handsome no matter what.

"Aw, Mam, come on. *I'm in a hurry*," Cyril said.

Cyril was going on his first date, but he had no intention of telling any of them. He couldn't believe that the most stunning girl he had ever seen in his life had only gone and arrived in the garage with her father. Her name was Linda, she had told him. She looked like a porcelain doll, with a mass of red hair that tumbled down past her shoulders. Her eyes hypnotised him. Cyril couldn't be sure what colour they were as they seemed to change with her mood. The day they met they were so bright he could have sworn they were the golden yellow of a meadow on a summer's day. When she opened her mouth it was another story. Loud and brash, he was instantly drawn to this feisty girl who was nothing like the women in his family. She was tall and lanky like him and had the body of an athlete. Without a bother she had asked him out, not even considering that he might decline. Once Linda had his number, she had snapchatted him like crazy all week with endless pictures of her every movement.

"*Where* are you going *on a Monday*, Cyril?" Joan fussed.

"Just the cinema… with a friend," Cyril said casually, turning his face towards the sun.

"The cinema? I didn't think you liked the cinema very much."

"Everyone likes the cinema, *Mam*."

"Well, don't be late home. It's a school night and you know what your father is like."

"I won't," Cyril answered, knowing well it was his mother who would be walking the floorboards if he was late. "Now, can you *please* tell me where my shirt is?"

"Did you check your wardrobe? Mary did all the washing and ironing before the weekend. It must be there," Joan said and lay back on the lounger.

"Finally! Thank you. Couldn't you *have told me that* at the beginning?" Cyril threw the towel over his shoulder and walked back towards the house.

"Are you sure you're not going with a girl and that's what has you all excited?" Joan called after him. Joan would have loved to see Cyril with a girlfriend.

"*I'm not all excited!*" Cyril retorted and closed the door behind him. He didn't fall into that trap. Going back to his room he was delighted to find the pressed shirt hanging in his wardrobe. Clean clothes hanging in the wardrobe was a first in their house. Cyril felt his heart thumping as he dressed. Linda had just seen him in a pair of dirty overalls in the garage. If she had taken a shine to him then, he might stand a good chance of impressing her tonight.

A half an hour later, Joan just nodded off when her mobile phone rang. She was jolted out of her sun-induced drowsiness by the sound of Eileen's business-like voice. Joan had just been thinking about her and her advice about meditation. Eileen had even given her a CD as a present for her birthday and given her instructions on what to do.

"Hello, are you there, Joan?"

"Yes, sorry Eileen, I was miles away."

"Apologies, I'm only coming back to you now. It's been a bit crazy. Would tomorrow suit to be my guinea pig?" Eileen asked.

"You haven't heard anything, you know, about the message?" Joan ignored Eileen's question. Eileen sighed.

"Heard anything? No, of course not. That's all forgotten, Joan. I just wanted to ask if tomorrow is okay for you," Eileen said, impatiently.

Events over the last few days had given her the impetus to push on with her case studies.

"Oh, right. Yes, I think so. I'm not working tomorrow," Joan said.

"Great, I'll be there by three if that's okay?" Eileen said.

"Yes, that's fine. Did I tell you about Mary, Eileen? It's actually working out really well. She's really quite nice, not cracked at all."

"That's great. I'm sure it's a relief that she's not cracked. *Look*, I can't talk now. We'll catch up tomorrow," Eileen said.

"Oh, okay then. See you tomorrow," Joan said, feeling the familiar sting of rejection at the call being cut short.

It was all in Joan's head, but old habits weren't easily changed. Knowing that Frank would be in the door shortly, Joan was glad of the distraction and went to heat up the casserole. She was just opening the back door, berating the critical housemate in her head, when Frank burst into the kitchen from the hall.

"You'll never guess who I met today, Joan. A blast from the past it was. I'm tellin' you, a blast from the past," Frank said, struggling to catch his breath.

"Go easy, Frank. Are you okay? You know what the doctor said. Your heart… "

"Would you don't mind my heart? I'm just after a walk, that's all. Didn't the good auld Doc tell me to exercise more and isn't that what I'm after doing," Frank said and wiped his forehead with a handkerchief.

"Well go on then, tell me would you. Who did you meet?" Joan asked.

"Séamus Feeney. Imagine, Séamus Feeney. Sure, it's been years, five if it's a day. He just saunters into the shop this mornin', not a bother on him."

"*Séamus Feeney? The* Séamus Feeney?" Joan asked, almost dropping the pot on the floor. She banged it down on top of the cooker.

"*Isn't that what I'm after saying woman?* Are you listenin' to me at *all?*" Frank asked and paced the room with excitement.

"The fiddle player?" Joan asked.

"Yes, the fiddle player. Don't say you don't remember him. Sure, didn't we travel half the country to see him," Frank said.

"Of course, I remember him, Frank. He was on The Late Late Show last year. *Oh, that's marvellous.* What's he doing home from America?"

"He's home for a break," he said. "I'm tellin' you, it's better he's lookin'. He's even given up the drink. Would you credit that? *Séamus Feeney off the drink?*" Frank exclaimed.

Joan couldn't imagine it at all. The last time Joan had seen Séamus, she was pregnant with Johnny and they had gone to see him in concert in Dublin. He had played as brilliantly as ever, but when they met him after in a pub, he was knocking back the pints as fast as they were being bought for him. By the time they pushed through the crowd to talk to him he was three sheets to the wind. He just kept hugging them and saying that the old friends were the best.

"Did he ever marry at all?"

"Well, I think he'd have mentioned it. Don't you? Anyways, he must be pushin' seventy. Who'd have him now?" Frank retorted.

"He was *so* handsome, Frank. Any woman would be lucky to have him," Joan said with a dreamy expression on her face.

"Well, I don't think he's married, so don't be gettin' any ideas. How could you keep a marriage goin' if you're in a different country every week? But I'm tellin' you, he looks younger than he did when he was fifty."

"Well, if that's the case, Frank Hughes, maybe you should consider giving up the drink yourself. If he's such a good ad for it and all."

Joan smiled to herself as she stirred the casserole. Frank had walked himself into that one.

"What *would I be givin' up* when all I have is the odd pint on a Saturday night? Weren't you the one downin' the wine the other night?" Frank remarked.

Joan was grateful that Frank wasn't a big drinker. His natural charisma didn't need any bolstering from alcohol.

"I was not *downing the wine.* I had two glasses at the most, and we had company, so that's different. You're talking through your hat, Frank Hughes."

Joan turned from the cooker and brushing her hair back from her face, she stood squarely facing Frank with a defiant look on her face. Frank loved when Joan was gutsy and full of spirit. Grabbing her by the waist, he waltzed her around the kitchen bellowing: "I've got you under my skin, I've got you deep in the heart of me…"

"Frank, will you *get a hold of yourself,*" Joan said and giggled, her eyes shining brightly. As their eyes locked, they both silently shared the same thought. If only she could be like this all the time; full of life and free of fear.

"Not again. Jesus, do you two wait until I come home to start at it?" Johnny said and stormed through the kitchen.

"Christ almighty, wouldn't it be worse if we were roarin' and shoutin' when you came home?" Frank bellowed.

"You must be joking. Nobody wants to see their parents at it. It's *disgusting.* You should be locked up," Johnny said and curled his lip in disgust.

"At it? *Jaysus,* I thought I was just havin' a dance with your mother. I didn't know that was a crime these days."

"You're hilarious," Johnny said, grumpily.

Johnny and Jack had only a week to find the money for McCabe and they hadn't a penny between them. He still couldn't figure out why Jack couldn't siphon some off from his parents' stash without them even noticing.

"Watch it. Do you *hear me?* You're on thin ice after last week," Frank said.

Frank's attempt at seriousness was half-hearted. He was feeling in too good a mood after bumping into Séamus.

"Go on, out of my sight, will you," Frank said, and he gave Johnny a playful shove towards the door.

"Aw, leave him be Frank," Joan said and reached out to hug Johnny, but he bypassed her and slipped out of the room.

"*Jaysus,* Joan, how many times have I to ask you not to disagree with me in front of the children? *We need to be on the same page,*" Frank reprimanded.

Good old Ken from work had shared that wisdom. "On the same page, is it?" Joan asked and giggled as she served up the casserole.

"It's *no laughing matter,* Joan. Givin' mixed messages only confuses children."

"Okay, Frank, I understand. Now, will you tell me more about Séamus Feeney? Is he staying for long?" Joan asked and put the plate down in front of him and sat down at the table. Frank swallowed a large spoonful before answering.

"Well, you're not going to believe this, but he's only gone and asked me to play with him in Tigh Neachtain," Frank said.

"He wants *you* to play with him!"

"Yes. Don't sound so surprised," Frank said and wiped his mouth with his hand.

"Frank, *please*," Joan said and hopped up to grab a serviette from the press and shoved it on his lap.

"I'm tellin' you, the man above is up to something, Joan. Only Friday night I have the itch to play after years and years, and now *Séamus Feeney* turns up out of the blue."

"Oh my God, Frank, that's amazing. If people hear that he's back playing in town, you won't make it in the door. You know he's a celebrity nowadays," Joan said and was already having visions of Frank on stage with Séamus, the crowd in raptures.

Joan would casually turn and say to the person beside her, *that's my husband up there with Séamus Feeney, you know*, and they would be so jealous of her.

"So, I'm thinkin' of going along this Wednesday. What do you think?" Frank asked. "You could come too. We could ask Mary as well. She's not a bad auld singer and might even give us a bar or two. Séamus said she's as good as her mother was."

"*Mary?* Oh, I don't know if it would be her scene *at all.* A noisy pub and loud music?" Joan said and twitched nervously.

"Are you talkin' about yourself now or Mary? Sure, didn't she sing in pubs for years, not a bother on her," Frank remarked.

"Still, that's a long time ago, she's a lot older now…"

"We're all a lot older, my dear, if we take that attitude we might as well roll over and die."

Frank sat back in the chair and rubbed his belly. He could almost reach out and touch the memories of being on stage, they were still so vivid. Frank had loved everything about it, from the energy generated by the enthusiastic crowd to the meeting of minds with his fellow musicians. He had never tired of it. It was just that the demands of family life had taken over and some of the musicians had moved abroad, like Séamus, as they tried to forge a successful career for themselves.

"You know well that Mary would love it. *Come on.* You can be my groupies," Frank said and grinned.

"Okay, whatever you say, Frank," Joan said.

"All she can do is say no. Oh, and Séamus said it might be good for Johnny, a bit of distraction you know. He was no angel himself when he was younger, our Séamus."

"*You told him* about Johnny and *the guards?* Oh, how could you, Frank? He'll think we're an awful shower, in trouble with the law."

"What? Are you jokin'? Séamus had more run-ins with the law than hot dinners when he was on the booze. I'm tellin' you, he's the last one to judge. Anyways, I'd say the chances of Johnny comin' with us are pretty slim, *don't you?*"

Joan knew he was right. Whatever about Mary coming, Johnny was a whole other kettle of fish.

"See ya!" Cyril shouted from the hallway, "I'm off!"

"Don't be home late. It's a school night!" Joan called.

"Where's he going?" Frank asked.

"Oh, he's going to the cinema with a friend," Joan said.

"A friend? Would she happen to be a girlfriend by any chance?"

"Oh, Frank!"

It wasn't long before Cyril was at the cinema. They had agreed to meet outside on the steps and Linda was so late, Cyril doubted she would turn up at all. He felt like a spare part, waiting on his own, watching all the laughing, loved-up couples make their way to the ticket office. Cyril was close to giving up and heading home when Linda rocked up. He couldn't miss her long limbs and blazing red hair as Linda came hurtling across the road. Linda was all apologies, but it didn't matter. When she batted her long dark lashes at Cyril, he was a goner. It was then that Cyril knew Linda had the power to break his heart, and that he would do almost anything for her.

Cyril couldn't believe his luck that Linda sat beside him at the cinema, making her way through a large box of popcorn.

Linda laughed and munched her way through the movie, elbowing him every now and then at something funny.

"This is hilarious, isn't it? I'm so glad we came," Linda said before she was back in the throes of it as Cyril lost her to the giant screen.

Walking home afterwards, Linda didn't stop talking. With anyone else it would have been madly irritating, but her exuberance made Cyril giddy. It was like she radiated light, and all he wanted to do was be near Linda and bask in its glow. Cyril felt excited and shy at the same time. He found it much easier to lose himself in the workings of a car than try to think of something smart or funny to say to girls.

Cyril was a sensitive soul and many years of witnessing his mother's fragile demeanour had only given him an even gentler manner. Although polite and very witty when you knew him, Cyril was cautious, believing all girls were prone to volatile moods. He had never in his life met or imagined a girl like Linda.

"Did you know that my parents want me to do some awful boring degree in university, like business or law? I mean could you imagine anything worse, Cyril, could you?" Linda rattled on.

"Oh, are you going to college then?" Cyril asked. He didn't know if a college girl would ever have an interest in a lowly mechanic.

"*No way*. Well, not to university anyway. They don't know yet, but I have bigger plans. I'm going to be a designer, and design clothes better than that Posh Spice one. I make a lot of my own clothes, didn't you know?" Linda said, took off her coat, swung it over her shoulder and sashayed down the road. "What do you think?" she asked and flashed her eyes at him.

She wore a short sleeved, red shift dress with a pattern of dogs on it and Cyril hadn't noticed it until now.

"Did you really make that? *That's amazing*," Cyril said, confidently. "So, what do you have to do to be a designer? Do you have to go to classes?"

"Well, I've been doing my research and there is a course in the Technical College in town. That's definitely my number one choice on the CAO form, though my parents don't know it yet. It drives me crazy that they think they know what's best for me, and yet they don't even ask me what I want," Linda said.

Cyril nodded furiously as he listened to Linda. She articulated everything he had felt for a long time but hadn't been able to say out loud. Finally, another person who wasn't obsessed with CAO points and hell-bent on going to university. This girl spoke his language.

"I think they just want what's best for them or at least they want to be able to boast to their friends. They're awful snobs, you know. I don't know how I ended up with them as parents. We couldn't be more different," Linda said, and Cyril laughed.

Most parents were snobs he thought, except for his father. They packaged it up as a desire to see their children do well in life, but often it was just about their own unfulfilled dreams.

"I know what you mean. Well, my Dad is fine, but I think Mam wants me to go to university as well. Just because she didn't go, she has this idea that everyone has to go to university nowadays. I'm not. Bill is taking me on as an apprentice mechanic and I'll be earning money before half our class even have their degree. As it is, he pays me for helping out when I can at weekends and holidays."

"Good for you, Cyril. I can see we're on the same wavelength. We'll conquer the world together!" Linda said and laughed out loud as she linked his arm.

They continued walking and as they arrived at the gate of her house, Linda turned to Cyril, and before he knew what happened, Linda reached up and planted a big, sloppy kiss on his lips.

"Thank you, Cyril Hughes. I had a great time. I think we're going to have a lot of fun together, don't you?"

Without waiting for an answer, Linda disappeared up the driveway and into her house. Cyril stayed rooted to the spot, putting his fingers to his lips. If this is what it feels like to be in love, he thought, well then, I'm in – hook, line and sinker.

TWELVE

Dave fumed when he put down the phone to Eileen on Monday afternoon. Her words were still ringing in his ears. This was all he needed. She was officially on the job market as of two weeks from today. He knew that she would pick something up in one of the practices around town, and Eileen was determined to start calling around that day, but Dave couldn't help feeling betrayed. It wasn't that he felt completely betrayed by Eileen, he knew what happened, he felt betrayed by Pat and by Fran Daly. Dave couldn't do anything about these other men, and that's what gnawed at him. He was angry, and this anger was multiplied when he thought of how his supposed trusty advisors had betrayed him with grand ideas of how Eileen and Dave's investments were going to turn over a major profit and fast. Dave was so angry with himself now. Eileen's words were ringing in his ears. She had said that between the two of them, they knew a fair few people and it wouldn't be that hard for her to find another solicitor position. Dave simply didn't know who to trust anymore.

Dave didn't have to meet Con, his accountant, to know that their situation was dire. He had been so close to putting the house in Eileen's name years ago, but she wouldn't have it. Eileen assured him that it wasn't the way to start a marriage. Dave hadn't been completely honest about the reason he wanted to put the house in Eileen's name, and now he had put everything in jeopardy. He hadn't told her that he had been investing their money in different schemes for a lot longer than a year, and although things had gone quite well for a while, particularly during the Celtic tiger, it had been a different story since then.

"Jesus Christ!" Dave shouted in his empty office. On top of everything else, he now had Julie to deal with as well. "Fuck!" he shouted. Dave grabbed his coat and ran out the door. It was only ten minutes from his office, and he could text her on the way. He didn't need her going off on one today of all days.

Dave walked through town lost in thought as he planned what he would say. He had tried to extricate himself from Julie's charms many times, only to end up booking nights away for the two of them down the country. Eileen never asked any questions when he told her it was work. She had never been the jealous type, only laughing when women openly flirted with him in company.

Dave was so preoccupied that he didn't see the elderly woman walking towards him on the footpath, laden down with shopping.

"I'm so sorry," Dave said as he bumped into her.

"Not at all. I wasn't looking where I was going," Mary said and smiled at him as she passed by.

As the bright autumn evening reflected Mary's own optimistic state of mind, she decided to stop just across from her house to take in the beautiful view of the river. A pair of loved-up swans glided elegantly along the water, a sight that would invite serenity to even the most tortured of souls. The swans bobbed along, carried by the current of the water and as she stood there it struck Mary, that like the swans, her life too could be easier if she let herself be carried by the currents that ran through it. Mary was determined to make the most of every opportunity that came her way from now on, and she gave thanks for living in such a beautiful place. Mary contentedly closed her eyes, enjoying the feeling of the warm evening sun on her face.

"Feck it," Dave shouted into the river as he continued on his way, and his thoughts drifted back to Julie. It wasn't his fault that Julie came along at just the right time, or more like wrong time. It was a moment of weakness, but Julie was persistent and adoring. She didn't make it easy to say no.

Julie was a secretary in the courthouse. They had bumped into each other occasionally and shared pleasantries, but that had been it. She was much shorter than Eileen, but she had a curvaceous figure that could match Marilyn Monroe in her heyday. It was obvious she considered herself a ringer for the star, dying and cutting her hair to complete the likeness. Julie's sexy, flirtatious nature was impossible to resist. It had started with her casually brushing against him in the lift or lightly touching his arm and laughing at something he said, though for the life of him Dave couldn't see what was so funny. There was no denying the chemistry between them. It hadn't taken a lot to light that match, and once it was lit there had been no going back.

Dave arrived at the small deserted car park that was the usual venue for their rendezvous when they needed to talk. It was a shrewd choice, tucked away from prying eyes and the hustle and bustle of town. Perched on the edge of the river, it had a spectacular view for a car park. There was no sign of Julie when he arrived. He checked his phone and saw that she had texted him. She would be late. It was a beautiful balmy evening, so throwing his jacket over his shoulder, Dave decided to pass the time by taking a walk along by the riverbank. He needed to calm his nerves and clear his head.

Vivid images of the fateful night when he had first betrayed his wife flashed before his eyes, and he felt a rush of guilt like he never had before now. It had all been so predictable. It was the annual office Christmas party over a year ago and Julie was well game. He had had a fight with Eileen before he went out and in a bad mood, he drank way too much. Fertile ground for an affair. The minute he sat down in the restaurant Dave knew without a doubt where the night was headed.

Julie squeezed in beside him and hung on his every word all night. Dave couldn't remember when Eileen had last looked at him like that. Julie looked amazing in a snugly fitted red velvet dress that bordered just on the right side of trashy. When they went to a local pub after the meal, he had a few pints with his colleagues but found himself missing Julie's bubbly company. She had joined some of the girls from the office on the makeshift dance floor, and every now and then Julie glanced in his direction. As the night progressed and they all were drunk, their group of twelve splintered, and nobody spotted him leaving with Julie who was fairly unsteady on her teetering high heels. Julie latched on to him for balance as Dave walked her to her city centre apartment. Julie made it known that her flatmate was away for the weekend. Without waiting to be persuaded, he joined her for a night cap and a lot more. Julie was adventurous in the bed department, or maybe it was that she was different, either way she made Dave feel like an Italian stallion and he couldn't pass that up. Eileen never even heard him sneak into bed at all hours of the night. However, she took great pleasure slagging him the following morning as he nursed a whopper of a hangover and a lot more.

Dave's face burned red at the memory. Turning, he saw Julie frantically waving at him from the car park. He walked towards her, mentally preparing the words to tell her that it was definitely over this time. He had vowed that he would never turn out like his father yet here he was, almost a cardboard cut-out. As he moved closer their eyes met, and they both knew what was coming.

"No, Dave. Please, don't do this."

Dave stopped in front of her and gently took her hands in his.

"Julie, I'm sorry, but we can't do this anymore. We *just can't.* I've too much going on."

Julie wriggled out of his grasp and took a step back.

"I thought we were happy. You said so yourself only last week," Julie cried.

"*Calm down*, Julie. People will hear us. Look this isn't just about us. I've a wife and family."

"A wife that you told me you had nothing in common with. You said you weren't happy. I wouldn't have wasted my time if I thought there was no hope," Julie spat at him.

"Aw, come on, Julie. You knew the score from day one. I told you I wouldn't leave her. You knew I was married and I'm sorry to say it, but that was your decision."

Dave looked around to make sure that they hadn't attracted an audience.

"That's *a horrible thing* to say. How could you be *so nasty*?"

"You'll thank me for this in the long run, trust me you will. To be honest, I never understood what a twenty-eight-year-old girl saw in a man who was unavailable and ten years older. You must have loads of guys after you."

"But I love you, Dave. Don't you see that? I loved you from the first day I saw you. You've always known that," Julie said tearfully.

"What about all those things you said to me? Didn't they mean anything?"

Julie hadn't held out much hope of it lasting, but that was before he had whisked her away for romantic nights in hotels and bought her expensive gifts. It wasn't just that. He had shared his hopes and dreams with her and she with him.

"Of course, they did," Dave said gently, "but everything's changed now. I have to go. I've things to discuss with Eileen and she'll be wondering where I am," Dave said and turned to walk away, and Julie grabbed his arm. Dave looked around, hoping that no one would see the two of them together. He saw a solitary figure a distance away, someone he didn't recognise.

Mary didn't know how long she had been standing there, when she was jolted back to the present by the sound of raised voices in the small car park adjacent to the river. Mary opened her eyes and squinted. It was still bright, and in the distance Mary made out a couple having what looked to be a lovers tiff. Finding it hard to resist the spectacle in front of her, she stayed glued to the spot as they shouted at each other and then passionately kissed. Mary felt like she had just wandered on to a movie set.

"*Please*, don't leave. We can work this out. *I promise*, I won't be too demanding. Just please say it's not over, *please*," Julie cried. She looked so sad and almost childlike as she stood in front of Dave. He reached out and hugged her. Before he knew it they were kissing, and she clung to him like a drowning woman. Dave broke free from her embrace.

"*Look*. We just need to cool things down for a while," Dave said, caving in. "*Like I said*, it is not just about Eileen. There are the girls to think about and financially we're having a few problems. I can't go into it but trust me when I tell you that I have it up to here."

Dave raised his hand to his forehead, uncertain of his next move. He quickly looked around and then he saw his exit route.

"I'll be in touch, but I really have to go now," Dave said and left.

Julie stood staring after him as he walked out of the car park. She wiped her face and went back to her car. Julie though that if she just was to give it a bit of time, Dave would come around. He always did in her eyes.

As Mary stayed watching the scene unfold, she noticed the man suddenly tear himself away and walk out of the car park. Before Mary could make a move, he marched right by her with a face like thunder. He was so distracted that Mary knew he hadn't even noticed her. Yet, Mary felt a flicker of recognition and she furiously wracked her brain as she tried to remember why he looked so familiar.

"Yes, it's that Danaher fella from the paper," Mary said aloud, when he was gone.

They had only been talking about him last week at the Hughes house. Joan was a friend of his wife Eileen if memory served her correctly. She was sure she was the beautiful woman she kept seeing at the supermarket. Well, the woman she looked at now who stood with her mouth open didn't look anything like his dark-haired wife. Life was full of surprises that was for sure. Mary wondered if Eileen knew what her husband was up to on a Monday evening. Well, she wasn't going to be the one to enlighten her, considering Mary didn't know the woman from Adam. Mary picked up her shopping bags and crossed the road to home.

"Fuck's sake!" Dave cursed as he walked back to his car that was parked near the office.

That hadn't gone to plan at all. It was well past eight o' clock when Dave eventually put his key in the front door of his home. He expected Eileen to be waiting for him, ready to launch an attack so he jumped in first.

"I'm sorry, I'm sorry. I was delayed just as I was on my way out the door."

Dave dropped his briefcase in the hall and walked into the kitchen just as Eileen looked up from cleaning the floor.

"That's funny. I rang the office and they said you were gone since half past five," Eileen remarked.

Eileen's voice was strangely calm, and Dave didn't detect any hint of accusation.

"Yes, that was the plan, but then, you know yourself, I'm just on my way out the door when Tony nabs me," Dave responded.

Tony Canavan was a solicitor that he dealt with a lot, so Dave hoped it sounded legitimate.

"Oh, right. Two hours ago," Eileen said, snidely. "That must have been pretty important."

"It was just about a client," Dave explained. The lies dripping off his tongue more easily now.

"I ate with the girls earlier," Eileen said. "There's a plate in the oven for you. I'll put them to bed, and we can talk then," she said. The tone of her voice made it clear that it wasn't up for discussion.

"I want to play with Daddy. Why are you always home so late?" Amy hurtled into the kitchen and threw herself at Dave.

"Come here, angel," Dave said and picked her up, smothering her with kisses.

Eileen softened as she watched them together.

"I'm going to help Sophie with her homework. I'll leave you two to catch up," Eileen said and looked at Dave.

Dave looked exhausted, but Eileen didn't care. They were meant to be a partnership, and Eileen felt tired of carrying the bulk of the child-rearing responsibility. Eileen slumped on the couch beside Sophie who had flown through her homework as usual. Laid-back Sophie, who was nothing like her sister in looks or temperament, Eileen had visions of her packing up and leaving home once she turned eighteen. Not because of any falling out with them, but more because she could. She had a self-sufficiency that seemed unnatural for a child her age, but it was also a relief at times.

"Are you okay, Mum?"

"I am love, just tired that's all," Eileen said and pulled Sophie to her and hugged her. She needed a breather for half an hour before she talked to Dave.

When everything had settled down and the children were in their beds, Eileen opened a bottle of wine in the kitchen.

"So, I'll be leaving Clancy's in a couple of weeks," Eileen said, pouring herself a glass of wine. Dave took a glass from the press, sat down at the kitchen table and poured himself a glass of wine too.

Dave lifted his fork and proceeded to eat his, by now, overcooked dinner.

"Did you hear me, Dave?" Eileen asked.

Dave had his head down taking a mouthful of spaghetti.

"Yes, give me a second, *will you*. I'm eating," Dave retorted, taking another mouthful. After a minute or two, he pushed back his plate and looked up, indicating that he was ready to talk.

"Did you hear what I said?" Eileen asked impatiently.

"Yes, you told me on the phone. I don't think I could forget that in a hurry."

Dave pushed back his chair, stretched his legs and took a large mouthful of wine.

"Jesus, Dave, do you have any interest in what actually happened to me? That asshole Fran Daly assaulted me, and Pat is willing to let me go as an employee rather than lose him as a client. These are the times we live in it seems," Eileen angered.

"I'm sorry, Eileen, really I am," Dave said and struggled to look her in the eye.

"Anyways, it looks like I might have another job, part-time in Davitts," Eileen said. She let the words hang in mid-air and then continued. "They specialise in family law, which I'm not crazy about, but it will do until I have my own business up and running. They're a small practice, but I've always liked Clare. It'll be a breath of fresh air to work for a woman for a change. She might actually *listen to me*," Eileen said.

"What?"

Dave played back his meeting with Julie. Fuck it, he was on thin ice. If Eileen picked up a whiff of it, he was finished. Dave had been very close to spitting it out on Saturday night, but had just stopped himself on time. He looked up at Eileen who decided to fill the dishwasher. Eileen stood with her back to Dave.

"What are you doing*? I thought we were talking*," Dave remarked.

"So did I, but I'm not interested in talking to myself, Dave."

Eileen banged the dishes as she jammed them into the dishwasher.

"It's just work. I've a lot on my mind right now," Dave said.

"You've a lot on you mind. *Really?* And would it surprise you to know that I have a lot on *my mind?* I mean considering everything that has just happened," Eileen yelled, feeling completely unappreciated. Dave stood up from the table, carried his empty plate over to the dishwasher and then sat back down.

"Sorry," Dave said, cursing his slip up.

"Please sit down. I promise I'll listen to you. That's great news about Davitts, really it is."

Softening slightly, Eileen put down the tea towel and re-joined him at the table.

"I really am happy for you, you know about the new job," Dave added.

"Okay. Now, can you tell me what exactly is going on with our finances, Dave?" Eileen rested her hands on the table as she tried to regain her composure.

"I'm meeting Con, but not until later in the week. We'll have the full picture then," Dave said, and cleared his throat before continuing.

"I think we have to face the prospect that we might have to sell the house. It's the last thing I want to do but…"

"How bad is it Dave?" Eileen voice was calm and measured. "It's bad."

"Are we talking bankruptcy?"

"To be honest, I don't know, but all of our savings are gone and more. If we sell the house it will go some way towards paying off our debts and might buy us some time," Dave said and looked crestfallen.

"*Our debts?* I knew absolutely *nothing* about what you were up to. *Jesus Christ*, Dave, what sort of marriage is this? I'm really beginning to wonder."

"If I could take it all back, I would," Dave said, remorsefully.

"*Really*, the marriage and all?" Eileen snapped.

"No, you know what I mean."

"Well, that's very convenient. Do you understand? I don't think you do. I think you're just pretty pissed off that you had to come clean. And as you might have guessed, I'm pretty pissed off with men this week, in fact I'm majorly pissed off."

Eileen stopped and took a mouthful of wine.

"We need some new ground rules, Dave, whatever happens. Total honesty and transparency from now on. Do you hear me?"

"Yes, of course."

"To be honest, it's a bit of a joke having to even suggest it, but it looks like that's where we're at. I still can't understand what possessed you. You must have talked to someone, seeing as you weren't talking to me. Was nobody a voice of sense in your ear?"

Dave squirmed in his seat as he listened to Eileen. Although he knew she was right, it wasn't easy receiving a dressing down for being so stupid.

"It all just seemed too good at the time and the returns had been great for other investors I spoke to. I just invested at the wrong time, I imagine," Dave said.

Dave wasn't going to admit that there had been plenty of dissenting voices, but he had been carried away with the idea of making a tidy profit that would pay off their mortgage and more. He had even considered buying a little place in Dublin, an apartment for his trysts with Julie.

"Too good is right, that's for sure. Well, I'm going to suggest that we sell the house regardless. Property prices are good, and we bought at a good time. You know, I never really liked this house and we don't need all this space. I mean *it's ridiculous.* We could have another family living with us and it would *still be too big,*" Eileen said, gesturing with her arms.

"I agree. Let me talk to Con on Thursday and I'll have all the facts. I'll tell him we're planning on selling regardless. But we also have to figure out where we're going to live. It's still going to cost us to buy somewhere new. Any profit is going to have to go towards… my debts."

Eileen was tempted to say that her parents would be well placed to help with a deposit on another house, but she decided not to unless she had to. His family wasn't short of a bob or two either, but his father was dead, and Dave and his mother had never been close. Well, he may just have to bury his pride and beg if it came to it.

"Okay, well that's sorted then. We're selling the house and we'll see how the land lies after you talk to Con. All going well, I'm starting a new job in a couple of weeks, so we have made some progress. Now, I'm going to bed. It's been a hell of a day, or should I say days, and I'm exhausted," Eileen said, and stood up and left the kitchen.

Left alone, Dave felt like crying. Eileen had been his best friend and confidante from the day they met. He had always told her everything. Now, here he was carrying a huge secret and she was the last person he could tell. Something had irrevocably changed in their marriage. It may have been a long time brewing but tonight was proof that they were no longer as solid as they used to be. He stood up and poured the dregs of his wine down the sink and slowly climbed the stairs to bed.

THIRTEEN

On Tuesday afternoon, Eileen parked her car by the sea. She reached over to the passenger seat for her jacket and grabbing her sunglasses, she hopped out of the car and locked the door behind her. She had a luxurious hour to herself before she was due at Joan's house. She breathed deeply as she felt the warm breeze on her face, and she set out to walk the length of the promenade. Eileen had left the girls at home with Dawn, the babysitter and resolved to do this more often, so that she could have a bracing sea walk where she could be alone with her thoughts. Eileen picked up the pace as her mind tried to make sense of the whirlwind that had been the last week.

It didn't matter the time of year, once the sun shone people appeared in their droves, taking advantage of their local Costa del Sol. Having grown up in Galway, Eileen wondered how many times she must have trodden this path. It must be in the thousands, she calculated. After her excruciating hangover on Sunday morning she could definitely have done with it. Eileen groaned as she remembered Dave opening another bottle of wine when they got home from their meal at Bon Appetit. She had protested, but only mildly. The prospect of forgetting all her troubles for a while was too much of a temptation. She paid for it the next day, however, waking with a bellyful of anxiety and a very hazy memory of their conversation.

Eileen kicked the wall at the end of the promenade with great force as she recalled their conversation after her meeting with Pat the day before. Eileen just couldn't escape the nagging feeling that she didn't know everything that Dave was at. Something didn't feel right. Eileen was almost back to her car when she felt her phone vibrate in her pocket. She sat down on the nearest bench to read the text message. It was Joan checking that she would call, and she texted her back to say she would be there in half an hour. Eileen sat looking at the choppy sea and realised that she had stopped in exactly the spot where Dave had first asked her out, almost fifteen years earlier. Sitting looking at the very rock that they had been sitting on, everything hit Eileen like a ton of bricks, Fran Daly's assault on her, their financial problems and the enormous chasm that had developed between Eileen and Dave. Eileen cried again and felt her tears whipped away by the strong wind that had developed. She hurried back to the car, glad of the protection of her sunglasses. As Eileen sat in the driver's seat, she wondered if she could be having a breakdown. Eileen had cried nearly every day since last Thursday and she couldn't stop.

When Eileen arrived at Joan's house five minutes later, Joan stood on the doorstep waiting for her. Eileen took a quick look in the car mirror and noticing her smudged mascara, she rubbed a tissue under her eyes. She put on her best smile and hopped out of the car.

"Hi Eileen," Joan said and waved from the door.

"Hi Joan."

Eileen walked towards the house and then firmly hugged Joan.

"Are you okay?" Joan asked when they separated. Eileen's face had a healthy flush and she could have passed for a teenager in her jeans and T-shirt, but Joan quickly recognised the pained expression that she so often wore herself. "Really, is everything okay, Eileen?" Joan asked again.

Eileen's lip quivered as she tried to keep it together.

"I've had better days, Joan."

Eileen brushed her hair off her face and looked away in the distance. She could feel tears rising again and furiously brushed them away.

"What is it?" Joan said, softly. "Come on in and we can have a chat."

Joan led Eileen by the elbow down the hall and before Eileen knew what had happened, she was sat at the kitchen table spilling her guts out. After what felt like an eternity, Eileen stopped and took a breath. She had given Joan a blow by blow account of the last week and now she almost felt like laughing. Unloading all her problems had left her with just a giddy feeling of relief.

"I'm so sorry, Eileen. Really, I am," Joan said, compassionately.

Eileen thought she might start crying again. Joan had just sat and listened and hadn't interrupted once or tried to tell her what to do.

Quietly Joan stood up, poured Eileen a glass of water and then she sat back down, her eyes totally focused on her friend.

"I don't know what to do, Joan. One part of me wants to bury anything to do with Fran Daly so deep and never talk about it again, but that hasn't worked so far as you can see. And I'm waking up in a sweat every night," Eileen said. "Another part of me just wants to make the *asshole* pay and report him to the guards. I spend my time talking about female empowerment and now when push comes to shove, I'm dithering."

"It's only been a few days Eileen, don't be so hard on yourself," Joan said who couldn't believe the strength of the woman sitting across from her. Joan had no doubt that she herself would have been locked up and in a strait jacket by now if it was her.

"I know, but I've no interest in being a victim. I don't want anyone else knowing my business, but at the same time, things won't change unless women speak out. He's done this before Joan, I'm sure of it."

Eileen's voice grew stronger.

"What makes you say that?" Joan asked.

"I just know it. Call it a sixth sense. He's a predator. The way he planned it all and then totally playing innocent the next day, calling Pat to sing my praises. It was too polished," Eileen said.

"God, that's awful. He deserves to be locked up. And you know, everyone in town thinks he's a saint. Frank is always on about him," Joan said.

"Please don't say anything, Joan. I don't want anyone else knowing, not until I decide what I'm going to do."

"Of course, sorry. I didn't think," Joan said.

Just then they heard the back door open and Eileen jumped out of her seat.

"Bathroom?" Eileen asked Joan and looked towards the hall.

"Just at the top of the stairs. That's probably, Cyril. He won't be in the way for long," Joan said. She stood up and pointed the way to Eileen who disappeared up the stairs. The kitchen door opened, and Cyril bounded in.

"Hi, Mam. I'm starving," Cyril said and started rifling through the presses.

"Cyril, I need a bit of privacy," Joan said in a hushed tone as she followed him around the kitchen.

"What are you whispering for?" Cyril asked and looked at her, trying to work out what might be going on with her this time.

"My friend, Eileen, is here. She's in the bathroom but she'll be back in a minute. I need you to make yourself scarce for a while," Joan said and pushed him towards the door.

"Okay, hold your horses. I just want to grab something to eat," Cyril said and escaped her grasp and grabbed a slice of Mary's Apple tart from the counter.

"Cyril, *I mean it*. It's important, *please*," Joan pleaded, while keeping one eye on the door.

"What's with all the secrecy? Have you a drug deal going down? I won't breathe a word, I promise," Cyril whispered and grinned. Cyril disappeared into the living room.

Eileen, who had been waiting until the coast was clear, crept down the stairs into the kitchen and picked up her coat from the chair.

"Joan, I'll go. I didn't realise the time and I don't want to hold you up. I'm so sorry, you didn't even get a treatment what with all my drama," Eileen said.

"Please stay, Eileen. It's fine. Cyril has gone in to see Abbie. We'll go into the back room where we won't be disturbed. Frank won't be home for another hour anyways," Joan said, but Eileen hesitated. "Come on. You can do a treatment on me any day," Joan said and smiled. Joan led the way down the hall.

Eileen, happy to let Joan take control for a change, quietly followed her into the cosy room.

"Eileen, I won't breathe a word. I promise," Joan said, eager to be seen as a trustworthy confidante.

"I know you won't. I had to give in my notice. You understand, don't you?" Eileen said.

"Of course, to be honest I don't know how you're still standing what with everything that has happened. I *really* am so sorry you had to go through all that," Joan said, close to tears.

"You're a great listener, you know. Thank you. I don't have too many of them in my life right now," Eileen said and reached over and took Joan's hand. They smiled warmly at each other. "Well, I think you're very brave for doing the right thing," Joan said in awe of her.

"I wish Pat did, but of course, when the person who assaults you happens to be a major, wealthy client, it changes everything. My boss doesn't have the moral balls to tell him to fuck off," Eileen said angrily, and Joan flinched at the sudden change in her mood. "Sorry. One minute I'm crying, the next fit to kill someone."

"Can I do anything?" Joan asked.

"You've done so much already just by listening to me, Joan." Eileen stood up and checked her watch. "You know, it might sound crazy, what with all that has happened, but I have a niggling feeling that there's more. Whatever happens, I just hope that we don't lose everything."

As Joan walked her to the front door, the strains of Cyril and Abbie's laughter followed them from the living room.

"You're doing something right, Joan, judging by that laughter," Eileen said.

"Oh, I don't know. They've always gotten on great. It's Johnny I worry about."

The two friends embraced at the door and as Eileen walked down the path, Joan called after her.

"I'm here, Eileen, any time. Just give me a call," Joan said and then closed the front door.

Joan leaned up against the door and took a deep breath. God, if such awful things could happen to a person like Eileen, no one was safe.

****

"So, how are we going to come up with the money in four days? Can you get it?" Johnny asked, secretly hoping that Jack would pay off their debt, or at least his family would.

It was already Tuesday and they only had until Friday to pay off the debt.

"I'll pay you back, *I promise,* but I haven't a bean these days and I can't ask Mam and Dad," Johnny said, pacing the room.

Jack lay on his bed, staring at the ceiling and thinking about his brother Liam.

"I'm not asking my parents for money to pay for a supply of pot if that's what you think. Not exactly the dream for their golden son, is it?" Jack said, reading Johnny's mind.

"Very funny, man. What about one of your brothers? They're all loaded, aren't they?" Johnny asked. He couldn't understand why Jack made such a big deal of it.

"*Jesus,* Johnny. *It doesn't matter* if they're loaded. It's not the money, it's *what the money is for,*" Jack said.

Jack was sick to the teeth of all the pep talks he had gotten from his eldest brother Liam. He had been a bit of a wild child himself, but he had copped himself on and now ran his own chain of successful restaurants. Jack wouldn't forget their most recent conversation in a hurry. Liam's words were etched in his memory. Liam had told him that if he hadn't given up the stuff, he would still be going nowhere fast. Liam didn't mind Jack experimenting, but he assured him that it would eat every ounce of ambition and energy that Jack had. Jack had argued that he wasn't about to fall prey to drugs, but Liam hadn't bought it. Liam had assured Jack that he had seen plenty of guys who had ideologies and twenty years later were still talking about all their big plans. Liam had told Jack that they only stumbled from one dead-end job to another or stayed on the dole.

"Liam will kill me if I told him I needed money to pay this debt," Jack said.

Liam had told Jack about a friend who had just been found dead from a heroin overdose, and he had always had all the same excuses as Jack. Liam told him how easy it was to end up taking hard drugs, with one thing leading onto another and before Jack would know it, he would be heading down the wrong path at a rapid pace.

"So, *what* are we going to do? *Are you listening to me?*" Johnny shouted, interrupting Jack's thoughts. Jack sat up on the bed and adopted a serious tone of voice.

"*Look*, Liam will give me the money, but it will be the last time. He won't give us a job next summer or ever if we don't quit. Maybe now with McCabe on our backs, it's a good time to get out of the game," Jack said.

"*Fuck* McCabe! Who *gives a damn* about him? We'll have nothing to do with him after Friday," Johnny snapped.

"Johnny, I'm serious. I'm not spending my life on the dole, thanks very much," Jack said.

"Relax, will you. Who said anything about the dole? I want to run my own business, like Liam someday. I'm definitely not working for some gobshite boss in an office that's for sure," Johnny said.

"He doesn't take any shit, so you better clean yourself up if you want to work for Liam. He only fired a waiter last week because he was half an hour late for his shift," Jack said.

"Piss off!" Johnny retorted.

"I'm *serious.* That'll be you within a week the rate you're going," Jack said and stretched out his legs and kicked Johnny as he paced the room. "Why don't you stick to booze? Oh, on second thoughts, don't do that," Jack said and laughed.

"Get lost," Johnny said, wanting to forget that incident.

None of them would forget last Halloween. It was enough to put Johnny off alcohol for life. A combination of Tequila and pot had caused him to temporarily lose his mind. Jack and the lads had told him that it was a miracle he wasn't arrested. Johnny had a vague memory of Fergal O'Brien roaring at him, but after that it was a blank. Johnny was a man on a mission. They told him that he had set fire to a garden in the park. It had been named after a local businessman who had allocated money for it in his will, for the benefit of his local community, but Johnny thought it was just a ploy to get his name on a plaque, so that he would be remembered forever.

Nobody could stop Johnny and it was only when they heard sirens in the distance and the flames had taken hold, that the lads managed to pull him away and make their escape. Jack had shown him the article in the local newspaper afterwards and the coverage on social media. There was public outrage at the act of vandalism, but luckily for Johnny, the perpetrator was never identified. He had steered clear of tequila after that. He didn't argue with Jack, but he knew that he would never have done that after smoking a joint.

"Jesus, you're making me dizzy. I'll get the money this last time, but it's the end of the line, *okay*," Jack insisted.

"Okay, I appreciate it, man," Johnny said and looked at his watch. "*Shit*, I'm late. The old man said he'd pick me up on the way home," Johnny said and grabbed his schoolbag and coat.

"Keeping tabs on you now, are they?" Jack called and laughed as Johnny ran downstairs and out the front door.

By the time Johnny reached the car, he was red in the face and out of breath.

"There you are. I thought I'd be sendin' a search party out after you," Frank said, doing his best to sound light-hearted when all he wanted to do was give his fiery son a kick up the arse as he sat in to the car beside him. "Well?" Frank asked.

"Aw, come on. I'm not *that* late," Johnny retorted.

"Well, you're *not early*, that's for sure. You're skatin' on thin ice these days. *Do you hear me?*"

"Okay," Johnny said sulkily and stuck in his earphones.

Frank did his best to keep his cool as he started the car. The smell of pot was overpowering in such a confined space, and he rolled down the window as he started to choke. Frank tried to remember some of Ken's wisdom. He had plenty of experience with his own rebellious son from the sounds of it. Frank replayed his wise words as he drove in silence.

Ken had advised him to keep the lines of communication open one day, when Frank confided in him on their coffee break at work. Ken had trained as a counsellor by night after his own experience with a son, who had come very close to ending his life in the river, only to be spotted by a passer-by who raised the alarm. Ken had been determined to equip himself with the skills that might prevent another incident. Ken constantly advised Frank to talk to Johnny and never to interrogate.

"Just talk," Frank muttered. "Get to know him and what's going on in his head," Frank continued, repeating Ken's words.

Frank glanced over at his son and his heart went out to him. He recognised the anger and confusion that were etched on Johnny's face. It could have been him thirty years ago. He pulled up at the house, and Johnny whipped off his headphones and went to open the car door.

"Hang on there for a minute," Frank said firmly.

"*Aw, Dad. What is it?* I'm *starving*," Johnny said and kept his hand on the door handle.

"Just a minute. I wanted to ask you if you remember Séamus Feeney at all," Frank said.

"*Who?*" Johnny asked, totally disinterested.

"Séamus Feeney, he's from down the road but has lived in America for years. He's a famous fiddle player now. Actually, I played in a band with him years ago," Frank said, proudly.

"You, in a band?"

"Yes, your auld man was in a band. What do you think of that?"

"I think you might be losing it, Dad," Johnny said and opened the door.

"Losin' it, am I? Hold on there for a minute," Frank said and grabbed Johnny's arm.

Frank reached into the glove compartment and took out the photograph that he had searched high and low for the night before.

"So, who does that look like?" Frank asked and he shoved the photo into Johnny's hand.

"*Jesus.* Are you *serious?* Sorry, Dad, but you're not exactly rock' n' roll material," Johnny said and laughed.

"It was *a Trad band.* We were the coolest thing back then," he said in a hushed tone, "and the women were mad for us."

"Ugh, why are you telling me all this?" Johnny asked.

"He's back in town and I'm playing with him tomorrow in O' Brien's. If you don't believe me, come along and see for yourself. He's a genius. I'm telling you, son," Frank said.

Frank couldn't take his eyes off the photo that transported him back to the good old days.

"Can I go now?" Johnny asked. Frank sighed and looked at him.

"So will you come?" Frank asked casually. Sounding like he didn't care usually had the most impact on Johnny.

"I'll think about it, okay, but I'm not promising anything, Dad."

Johnny left the car and slammed the door behind him.

"Well, it's a start," Frank said, hoping that Séamus' idea might take root. He put the photograph back in the glove compartment for safe keeping and followed Johnny into the house.

****

Cyril was one of the first out of the school gates as always. Cyril couldn't wait for the day that he would finally bid goodbye to teachers and schoolbooks forever.

"Hey handsome, did you miss me?" Linda asked, standing right outside the school gate waiting for him. Noticing the look on Cyril's face, she linked his arm and laughed.

"Hi, this is a nice surprise," Cyril said and pulled her along quickly.

Though delighted to see her, Cyril wanted to keep Linda to himself for now and well away from the prying eyes of his school mates.

"Let's go as far away from these school gates as possible," Cyril said.

"Come on then. Let's head to the beach," Linda suggested.

"*The beach?* It's the *middle of September*. It *is* Galway you know," Cyril said, laughing at her enthusiasm.

"It's a gorgeous day for a swim. It's glorious, trust me. You'll feel amazing after with all those endorphins and all."

"I haven't been in the sea for years, but why not?" Cyril said, eager to join in her excitement.

They took off in the direction of the beach which was just a short stroll from Cyril's school. Cyril couldn't take his eyes off her. She looked taller and thinner in the school uniform that she had definitely outgrown and as she bounded along beside him, he smelt the fresh scent of apples off her hair.

When they arrived at the beach, Linda led the way to a quiet spot away from all the daily swimmers. She dropped her bag, stripped down to her underwear and dived straight into the water.

"It's gorgeous, Cyril, trust me," Linda shouted, but Cyril could only stand watching her with his mouth open. "I'm telling you, dive in. It's much easier that way," Linda instructed. Not wanting to look soft, he stripped down to his underwear and belly flopped into the water.

"Bloody hell, it's freezing," Cyril shouted, trying to catch his breath from the cold shock.

"Keep moving. You'll warm up in a minute. Those poor feckers from the midlands would kill for this. Do you ever see them in the summer? They have that look in their eye as they charge like mad ones into the water," Linda said and shrieked with laughter.

"Very funny, well, I don't think any of them would be stripping off today, only the local lunatics," Cyril said.

"Be careful who you're calling a lunatic. It's not polite to call your girlfriend a lunatic," Linda remarked and grinned at him as she swam towards the shore.

Cyril could have sworn he heard her say the word girlfriend and smiled. He followed her out of the water, wrapping his arms around himself in an effort to warm up.

They both lay down on the rocks to dry off under the September sun, and Cyril turned on his side to look at her properly.

Linda's red hair glinted in the sun and her pale skin looked almost translucent. Her body was lean and strong, no doubt a result of her adventurous nature. Cyril lay on his back and luxuriated in the sunshine on his body. She was right about how lucky they were to have this on their doorstep. He had forgotten how good it was, and it was even more special when all the tourists had gone home.

"When did you start swimming in the sea?" Cyril asked and sat up. Linda put her hand up to shield her eyes from the sun and stared right at him.

"Oh, a few years ago. I swim all year round now. Not every day, but at least once a week," Julie said.

"Wow, that's impressive," Cyril said.

Linda sat up, pulled on her shirt and turned to him with an intense expression on her face.

"Being serious, I suffered really badly from anxiety before. Every day I had a constant knot in my stomach, and my chest was pounding. It started in first year at school," Linda confided.

"*You?*" Cyril asked in disbelief.

"I know. Everyone says the same thing. Personally, I put it down to feeling smothered by the system," Linda said animatedly as she sat cross legged facing him.

"You sound just like Johnny," Cyril said.

"Who's Johnny?"

"My brother, the rebel without a cause."

"That's funny. Did I ever tell you that? You're funny, Cyril."

"Yes, I'm a comedian, alright. In our house you need a sense of humour, trust me," Cyril said. Cyril couldn't help thinking of all the drama in their house over the last few days and wondered what Linda would make of it all if she knew.

"Well, the bottom line is once I started swimming, things started to change for me. That and making my own decisions."

"You're the last person I'd imagine suffering from anxiety. Are you better now?" Cyril asked, uncertain of what to say.

"Well, I suppose I am. I know what I want to do and I'm happy about that. Not everyone's exactly over the moon about it though."

"What do you mean? Your parents must be happy that you're feeling better?" Cyril asked.

"Sort of, but I have a secret to share with you. People are happy for you, but only as long as you're playing by their rules. Most people are sheep, they're afraid to think for themselves, to live the life they really want to live. So when you do it, it freaks them out," Linda said, fired up.

"You're a lot wiser than you look, if you don't mind me saying so," Cyril remarked. Cyril looked at her in amazement.

"Not at all. Most people think I'm bats, so that's definitely a compliment. Now, come on or I'll be in trouble if I'm late home," Linda said.

They pulled on their clothes over their damp underwear and climbed back up onto the footpath. Linda slipped her hand in his as they walked along, each of them lost in their own thoughts.

"Call me," Linda said when they arrived at her gate.

This time, Linda pecked him on the cheek and sprinted up the driveway, turning to blow him a kiss before she disappeared in her front door. Cyril waved and turned to retrace his steps towards the beach and home. Linda's house was in the opposite direction, and he was now a good half-hour walk from his own. He couldn't stop thinking about her words as he strolled along. Maybe Linda was right. Just look at his own mother. She meant well, but she was dead set on him going to university. It didn't matter that all he had ever wanted was to be a mechanic. Everyone said they wanted you to be happy, the problem was it was their version of happy they were talking about.

****

"Hi Joan, how was your day?" Mary asked and made a pot of tea, delighted with the rare chance to have a chat with her on her own.

"Okay, I suppose. It's very busy these days at work," Joan said.

Joan sat down at the kitchen table, slipped off her shoes and rubbed her feet. She had spent half the day filling the shelves with books and her feet were aching. This wasn't what Joan had envisaged when she had taken a job in the library. She felt like a glorified porter.

"Are you looking forward to tonight in Tigh Neachtain?" Mary asked and poured her a cup of tea and placed a slice of apple tart on the table in front of her.

"Thanks," Joan said and took a sip and sighed with contentment. "I don't know to be honest. I used to love going to gigs with Frank, but that was years ago. I haven't been out socially in I don't know how long…"

Joan put her hand on her stomach and grimaced. Just the mere thought of a noisy pub and it was in flitters.

"Well, I know how you feel. I don't stir out much at all since Tom died. Believe it or not, that's twenty years ago now. I know that sounds crazy, but you know yourself once you get into a rut, it can be hard to shake it. I've been a bit of a hermit until I started coming to your house," Mary said.

Joan sat up in her chair. Mary sounded a bit like a kindred spirit.

"I'd no idea. You should join us tonight. Frank would really like it, and I would too. I really would," Joan assured.

The thought of standing on her own in a crowded pub was enough to cause her to break out in a rash. Frank wouldn't get it if Joan told him, try as he might to understand. He was a natural extrovert and always the life and soul of the party.

"Well, only if I wouldn't be intruding. Are you sure?" Mary asked and stirred with excitement.

"Yes, please come. It starts at eight. Frank will probably go earlier to set up. Why don't you head home a bit early this evening and call back at seven thirty. We could walk up together," Joan said brightly.

"Perfect. We'll have a great night, Joan. Two young ones out on the town," Mary jested and they both laughed at the idea.

"I meant to ask you. You're friends with Eileen Danaher aren't you?" Mary asked.

Seeing as they were getting on so well, Mary felt brave enough to throw caution to the wind and raise the subject.

"Yes, she was just here yesterday," Joan said, still reeling from the shock of Eileen's news. "She's very gifted you know, a healer. She's training at the moment, some sort of energy work and I'm her guinea pig. You'd never think it of her, would you?"

"That's for sure. She looks so professional and business-like. It just goes to show that looks can be deceiving, can't they? Did I tell you that my Tom worked for the older Mr Danaher years ago? He had great time for him, a hard worker and very fair he always said."

"I don't know her husband at all Mary. She is a solicitor, you know, but she wants to change career. She hates it now. We just met at a yoga class and then we found out that Abbie and her daughter Sophie play basketball together. She's so nice. I mean I'm years older than her and I didn't think she'd have any interest in me to be honest."

Joan played with the slice of tart that she had hardly touched. Joan still found it hard to believe that she and Eileen were friends. When she said it out loud to Mary, she almost felt like she must be talking about someone else.

"Well Joan, look at the two of us sitting here chatting and I'm at least fifteen years older *than you.* I don't think it's about age at all. You either click with someone or you don't. It sounds like you click just fine."

Mary was tempted to probe further but knew not to push her luck. She finally had bonded with Joan and didn't want to risk seeming like a busy body.

"I suppose we do," Joan said and smiled at the thought of having two new friends. Joan put down her fork and leaned across the table.

"She's going through a tough time, Mary. I can't say anything, but my heart goes out to her. It really does..." Joan said and then paused.

"Oh, I'm sorry to hear that. Is it her husband by any chance?" Mary asked, knowing that she may have overstepped the mark, but she felt she had to say something after what she had witnessed on Monday.

"Her husband? Um, well he's got a lot of financial problems if that's what you mean. But that's not..." Joan stopped, feeling guilty. She couldn't tell Mary everything. She knew she shouldn't be saying anything at all.

"Please don't tell anyone, Mary. I promised Eileen I wouldn't breathe a word and now here I am. God, I'm not doing a very good job as her friend."

Joan looked down feeling embarrassed.

"Financial problems?" Mary said. "Of course, I won't say anything. That's awful."

Mary grabbed her coat from the back of the chair and quickly pulled it on.

"Is everything okay?" Joan asked.

"Of course, it is. Now, I better get home if I'm to be back here at half seven. I'll see you then, Joan," Mary said. She desperately needed fresh air.

On the walk home, Mary played back the scene she had witnessed on Monday evening. Mary didn't know Eileen Danaher at all, but now she felt like a traitor. The poor woman had no idea that her problems were far bigger than financial ones, but Mary couldn't say anything. It wasn't her business. If there was one thing Mary O'Sullivan prided herself on, it was on not being a gossip.

FOURTEEN

As Mary and Joan opened the doors of the pub that evening, they were met with an almighty din. Tigh Neachtain was hopping as it hadn't taken long for word to circulate that Séamus Feeney was back in town. Joan spotted Frank fiddling with wires on the stage and waved at him.

"Do you see him, Mary?" Joan asked, feeling proud.

"I do indeed. You better keep an eye on him, Joan, or he'll be getting ideas about himself."

"Do you mean more ideas?" Joan asked and giggled.

"God, its bedlam in here. Follow me, Joan."

Joan stuck close to Mary as she pushed and shoved her way towards the bar, using her handbag as a weapon. This woman surprised her more by the day.

Joan had done a double take when she opened the door to Mary after she had gone home to change. The apparition on her doorstep looked years younger and definitely more colourful. Mary had let her hair down revealing a thick mass of silver waves. Her blue floaty dress was complemented by a colourful beaded necklace and a golden shawl. A dab of red lipstick and some eye shadow nicely highlighted her soft, round features. Joan hardly recognised this woman who had lived a solitary existence down the road. Joan looked down at her own clothes and wanted to cry.

"Boring," she cried out, safe in the knowledge that no one could hear her.

Joan felt more suited to a secretarial job than a night in the pub. Her blonde curls softly framed her face and made her look years younger than she was, but she had erred on the side of caution and chosen a sensible pair of black slacks, flat shoes and a blue shirt buttoned up to the neck.

"Well, what a sight for sore eyes you two are. I'll be the envy of all the men in the place," Frank said, having spotted them coming in the door.

"Go away with your plámás, Frank. We're here to listen to a bit of music that's all," Mary said and gave him a playful slap on the arm.

Joan strained to hear their conversation. She could feel every cell in her body vibrating from the noise and wondered how she would stick it when the music started. She had once loved this environment and the music, but that was a long time ago. She looked around at the crowds and felt a knot in her stomach.

"What'll ye have to drink? A sherry, Mary, and a white wine for you, Joan?" Frank asked.

"A brandy for me, Frank. How often am I out?" Mary announced.

"*Jaysus*, you're in some form tonight, Mary… Are you alright there, love?"

"It's so busy, Frank. I can't hear a thing," Joan cried.

She threw a dirty look as people elbowed her on the way to the bar, but it went ignored. You didn't turn up at a gig like this if you were looking for personal space.

"A glass of wine will sort you out. Just hold on there a minute," Frank said and let a roar at the barman.

Within minutes, Frank handed them their drinks. The two women looked at each other and smiled.

"To a great night," Mary saluted and clinked her glass against Joan's and almost drained her brandy in one go.

Joan followed suit, but just took a sip. She had taken a Xanax before coming out and didn't want to risk another episode like the disastrous Christmas party.

"Okay, ladies. Follow me. I'll make sure you have a bird's eye view of the stage."

They followed Frank through the heaving crowds to a top corner of the bar. It was a spot that was normally reserved for older locals and musicians. Tonight, they were both.

"I'll bring Séamus over afterwards. He's dyin' to meet the pair of you," Frank said, directing his words at Mary, who blushed. Mary felt like a million dollars. The nights of sitting at home in her quiet little house with Boots seemed like a distant memory now.

"Did Johnny come?" Frank asked and turned to Joan. Joan detected a glimmer of hope in Frank's eyes and couldn't tell him that Johnny had responded with just a grunt when she asked him.

"He said he'd probably follow us down later. I'm sure he will," Joan said, sincerely hoping that Johnny could do this one thing for his father even if he couldn't be bothered to do it for her.

"I hope so. I'd love him to meet Séamus," Frank said and kissed her on the cheek. He then left to join the band on stage.

"I'm sure he'll come," Mary said, seeing Joan's expression change when Frank was gone.

"I don't know, I really don't know, but I hope for Frank's sake that he does."

"Let's just enjoy the concert. You've done all you can," Mary said, and Joan nodded.

Once the music started even the older locals came to life. Joan allowed herself to be carried away with the crowd and the music.

"Aw, go on. You'll give us a dance," an older man said to Mary.

Mary turned to the outstretched hand and looked at the man who wished to escort her onto the floor.

"Thanks very much, but I'm grand. I'm only listening to the music tonight," Mary said and laughed.

"Jesus, you're a tough woman. All I'm looking for is a bit of a twirl around the floor," the man said.

"There isn't room to swing a cat here," Mary said, tapping her foot with the rhythm.

"Knock that back and you won't be long joining me on the floor," the man said.

He handed her a brandy and as the night wore on the drinks kept appearing, which Mary amply accepted. Mary couldn't remember the last time she had so much fun. She smiled at Joan who had her arms folded tightly and looked like a tightly wound spring.

"This is great, isn't it, Joan?" Mary remarked.

Joan remained beside her nursing her glass of wine.

"It is. I think I'll just have a quick look to see if Johnny's here," Joan said.

Joan disappeared into the crowd with an anxious look on her face and Mary sighed, turning back to the stage. She had secretly hoped that a few glasses of wine might loosen Joan's tongue and she would learn a bit more about Eileen and the state of her marriage, but it didn't look like that was going to happen. When Joan reappeared a few minutes later she smiled and her face relaxed.

"He's down the back. Frank will be delighted," Joan said proudly.

Mary didn't hear her as she sang loudly along at the top of her voice while fending off the advances of her new friend. Mary was now on first name terms with beer-bellied, generously perspiring Paddy, who leaned up against her, hoping he wouldn't be going home alone. Mary laughed when he suggested that he would make a great addition to her life and her bed.

"Paddy, I'm very content in my life and in the comfort of my own bed but thank you for the offer. Now, will you leave an old woman to enjoy the music!"

Mary looked at Joan and rolled her eyes. If this was the type of man that waited for her out in the world, she gladly took her lonely existence as it was. No doubt, like a lot of widowed men, he just wanted someone to mother him and replace the wife he had lost a few years back. Mary had no interest in waiting hand and foot on some helpless pensioner. Give her an independent, charming man who didn't need his slippers handed to him and she might reconsider.

"Aw, Mary, don't be so hard will you? Just think about it. We could have a grand old time together," Paddy said, and Mary gently shoved him away.

"Go on home now, Paddy. You won't even remember me tomorrow, I can guarantee you that," Mary said.

Joan felt a sting of jealousy as she watched Mary easily flirting and batting off the attention of her admirer, as if it was par for the course. Joan quickly turned her attention to the stage, her face red with embarrassment. Paddy only had eyes for her silver-haired companion. She couldn't resist glancing back at the scene unfolding beside her, and a reluctant smile crept across her face as she watched Mary hold Paddy in her thrall. It was hard not to be impressed.

Doing her best to follow suit, Joan swept her blond curls back off her face, put her hand on her hip and shot a bright smile at the other men propping up the bar beside Paddy. However, she might as well have been invisible for all the attention they gave her. She looked away feeling the familiar stab of rejection and was relieved to see Frank approaching through the crowds with Seamus in tow. Joan had no idea that despite her best efforts, she would never be attractive to the aimless older man who was adrift without a woman to keep the show on the road. They were only drawn to the strong bossy types like Mary, women who would mother them.

"Jesus, we can't leave you alone for a minute but you're chattin' up all the men," Frank said.

"Aw, stop it, Frank. Have you seen the state of them?" Mary remarked and stepped back from the bar just in time to escape Paddy's wandering hands. Frank and Séamus burst out laughing at the sight.

"Ladies, you remember Séamus?" Frank asked.

Seamus towered over Frank as he stood behind him.

"This couldn't be the Mary O'Halloran I remember. If you are, you haven't aged a day," Séamus said, stretching out his large suntanned hand.

"Hello, Séamus. You're too kind," Mary said and blushed. Mary shook his hand. He was much more handsome than she remembered. His pale blue eyes held her gaze for just a little longer than was necessary. Séamus' corkscrew curls bounced up and down as he talked, and she softened at the lilting sound of his American twang. If it had been Séamus dragging her out to dance tonight instead of Paddy, Mary might just have said yes. Mary had a fleeting sensation of cheating on Tom, but it didn't last. Tom was long gone she reminded herself.

"I think the last time I saw you was at Tom's funeral and that's not today or yesterday, Séamus. It's twenty years ago, so I'm afraid I have indeed aged. The concert was just fantastic. Wasn't it, Joan?"

Joan, delighted to have Frank back beside her, stuck her hand out to Séamus.

"And Joan, aren't you just the picture. You're like a movie star," Séamus said, and Joan blushed at the compliment.

"Would you go easy there now, Séamus? You're surely layin' on it thick with the ladies."

"You're only jealous, Frank," Mary said with a glint in her eye.

"Isn't that right, Séamus?" Mary asked.

Mary felt the fire of the brandy in her belly as she spoke. Séamus roared laughing, enjoying Mary's feistiness. She was nothing like the woman he remembered who had been straitlaced, serious and at the beck and call of her sensible husband.

"Easy there now, Mary. No more brandy for you tonight," Frank said, trying to take her glass. Mary shooed him away.

"I'm perfectly fine, Frank. Don't mind him, Séamus. Are you enjoying being home?"

"It's awesome, Mary and there's nothing like playing in front of a home crowd. It doesn't matter the corners of the earth I've played in; nothing beats it. This man might join us from now on, won't you?"

Séamus threw his arm around Frank's shoulder.

"What do you mean?" Joan asked, looking at Frank for an explanation.

"I'm not goin' anywhere, love. Séamus just means here in Tigh Neachtain. Isn't that right?"

"Don't worry at all, Joan. I'm not planning on kidnapping your husband. I've seen enough of the world for now. I'm on a bit of a vacation and just want to play the odd gig in town."

"See, there's no need to be worryin'. I'm not leavin' you all alone," Frank said and put his arm around her.

"Stop it, Frank. I'd manage fine, don't you worry," Joan stated confidently. She was tired of being seen as fragile.

"Who are you and what did you do with my wife?" Frank boomed and they all laughed.

"Please, don't talk to me like I'm a child, especially in public," Joan pleaded with Frank when they were out of earshot of Mary and Séamus as they were reacquainting.

"Would you stop. I was only messin'," Frank said. He took a mouthful from the creamy pint of Guinness the barman handed to him. "Did one of those auld lads come on to you? Is that what's goin' on? Are you planning on leaving me?" Frank jested.

"*God almighty*, Frank," Joan cried. "If only."

Looking over at the drunken men slurring their words Joan thought she must be losing her marbles. Was she really jealous that they had paid more attention to Mary than her? Joan needed her head examined. She looked back at Frank who stared at her. Her eyes softened. He was streets ahead of any of them. He wasn't exactly in his prime, but he would give an ageing Tom Jones a run for his money. His shirt was soaked through with perspiration and his tummy hung over his trousers, but he only had eyes for Joan. She leaned in and gave Frank a quick kiss on the lips.

"You were great tonight," Joan said. Frank was at a loss for words and did the only thing he knew to do at that moment and knocked back his pint.

Séamus beckoned the barman for a drink. He took a long sip from his pint of water and then turned to look at Mary.

"So, tell me, do you still sing?" he asked, and Mary laughed.

"Aw, go on. Will you sing one song with me for the road?" Séamus asked.

Frank tells me you sing like a bird, even better than your mother, and she sure could sing."

"Oh, I don't know. It's been years since I sang in public. I don't know what Frank has been saying to you."

Mary couldn't help feeling a little excited at the prospect. Séamus could be very persuasive. Mary though that this was probably par for the course with him. Americans were known to be very charming and well able to dish out the compliments when they wanted. Well, Séamus had spent most of his life over there, so he was bound to have picked up some of their tricks.

"I wouldn't know what to sing."

"The West's Awake, Mary," Frank shouted, overhearing their conversation. "Didn't we sing it the other night?"

"Did we?" Mary asked, having forgotten.

"Okay, let's give it a blast and you'll join us as well, Frank," Séamus said and walked up to the stage to find his fiddle.

"Well, look who the cat dragged in," Frank said and grinned. He nudged Joan as Johnny walked towards them.

"He could look so handsome, Frank. If he just dressed a bit better and smiled," Joan said as she looked at Johnny marching towards them.

Johnny was dressed head to toe in black and sported a pair of Doc Martens and his signature scowl.

"Don't say anything to him, Joan. I'm warnin' you. At least he's here," Frank said.

"I know. I just mean…" Joan said and sighed.

"Ah, there you are son. Did you see us?" Frank asked and put his arm around Johnny.

"I did and I've to hand it to you, Dad, you're not bad for an auld lad," Johnny said. "That guy Séamus though is genius."

"He is indeed. Wait a minute and I'll introduce you," Frank said.

"You look very handsome tonight, Johnny," Joan said and went to brush his long fringe out of his eyes.

"*Mam, leave it will you,*" Johnny retorted and recoiled at her touch.

"Now, Johnny. We're in company," Frank said and turned to introduce Séamus.

Johnny took one look at the famous musician standing in front of him and felt his face redden as he tried to think of something smart to say.

"Well, *who* do we've here? I take it you are the famous, Johnny, I've been hearing all about," Séamus said. Johnny straightened up, eager to impress the musician he had heard all about.

"I've to say Mr…" Johnny said.

"Call me, Séamus, son."

"I've to say, Séamus, that was *mega. I mean it.* That was off the charts."

"Oh, right. I'm taking that as a thumbs-up," Séamus said and laughed.

"Now, will you join us, Johnny? Mary here is going to give us a song and your father and I are going to help her along. Isn't that right Frank?"

"I can't play *anything*," Johnny said.

"We'll have to do something about that. We all have a gift. Music saved my life I'm telling you, and it allowed me to travel the world.

There are a lot worse ways to make a living in my book, so you should think about it, I mean only if it floats your boat… Whatever it is, we all have a gift and the trick is to find it before time runs out," Séamus said softly. "That's if you don't mind me saying so," Séamus said. He turned to Frank.

"Not at all, Séamus. As you said so yourself, there are a lot worse ways to earn a livin'," Frank said and beamed over at Joan, who wasn't so impressed with the advice.

Johnny watched enthralled as Seamus started them off on the fiddle and then Frank and Mary joined in. Mary surprised herself by remembering every word of The West's Awake and the few stragglers that were still left in the pub gathered round. Johnny looked at their adoring faces and he knew right there and then that he would give anything to have that sort of effect on people.

As the night drew to a close, they congregated on the path outside Tigh Neachtain saying their goodbyes.

"Some night, Séamus. It brought me back, I'm telling you," Frank said and slapped Séamus on the back. "Wasn't it, Joan?" Frank asked.

"Yes. Thanks, Seamus. Very enjoyable," Joan said. Joan's gaze was already on the road for home.

"This is only the beginning. I want to see you down here every week. *Right?* No excuses," Séamus said.

Mary looked over at Joan's surprised face and burst out laughing. "We're not used to the direct ways of you yanks, Séamus, but I like it. We beat around the bush way too much here in Ireland."

"*Who* are you calling a *yank,* Mary O'Sullivan? I'm more a local than the lot of you put together. The Feeney's go back generations in this town," Séamus said and threw his arm around Mary light-heartedly.

The gesture wasn't lost on Joan who elbowed Frank.

"We'll be off then," Frank said. "Come on, son."

"I'll walk down with you, Mary. We can't have you wandering the streets on your own at night," Séamus said casually.

Séamus and Mary bid goodbye to the Hughes and strolled down the road in the direction of her house.

"There might be somethin' in it after all, Joan," Frank said, as the Hughes walked down the road in the opposite direction to Séamus and Mary.

"Can we stop here for a minute, Mary? Let's take in the view," Séamus asked.

They stood in silence at the railings and gazed out at the river. The full moon cast a shimmering light on the water and bathed the town in a silvery glow. In the distance, the buildings they knew so well were silhouetted against the night sky like in a painting. It was a mesmerising scene and they both went quiet as they took it in.

"I had forgotten how beautiful it is here," Séamus said, breaking the silence between them.

Séamus sounded almost regretful, as if he had just remembered the charm of his hometown, a place that he had left with a belly full of anger. Séamus remembered it as a different place back then, steeped in intolerance, oppression and full of begrudgery. True appreciation of his talent had only come after he was a success on the international circuit.

"It is, isn't it? I don't appreciate it enough and I'm living just across the road," Mary said.

Mary felt embarrassed thinking about how she holed herself up and drew the curtains once darkness set in. Tonight had definitely shown her that there was a whole other world out there.

"I'm with you on that. I'm seventy-five and I'm only stopping to smell the roses now. I've worked non-stop for most of my life. I love the music, but I've missed out on a lot of other things, you know, family and…"

"I understand," Mary said.

"I felt I had to prove something. That's why I left Ireland. But I think I'm finally copping on. Life is meant to be enjoyed. It's about the journey as they say, don't you think?"

"I suppose you're right. I hadn't thought of it like that. Well, if that's the case, I can't say I've done a great job of it myself," Mary replied. "I spent most of my life trying to prove that I didn't need anyone. How sad is that?" she said and laughed softly.

Séamus looked at Mary and wondered what her life had been like all these years. It hadn't been all plain sailing for her either from the sounds of it.

"I'm not far behind you on that score. I think we all do it when we've been hurt. That's why I fitted right into America. Everyone's out for themselves, the next deal, the big buck, that's what matters. Don't get me wrong. It was very good to me… but it's a sad way to live, Mary. It's the pits," Séamus admitted.

"I wouldn't know, I mean, about the money, Séamus," Mary said and smiled. "I'm the queen of rowing your own canoe. Ask anyone around here. They'd say that I'm as odd as two left shoes, that I'd bite your head off if you came near me."

"Get outta here. I think you're awesome, Mary."

"You know, only for Frank asking me to help out, I definitely wouldn't be here tonight. It might sound a bit silly to you, but it has given me a new lease of life."

"Of course, it has. We all need to feel useful, or what's the point?" They walked onwards and before they knew it, they found themselves outside Mary's gate.

"It looks like I'm finally learning to slow down and maybe you're starting to gear up. We might just meet in the middle," Séamus said. Mary blushed as Seamus pecked her on the cheek and turned to walk away. He stopped as if he had just remembered something.

"I want to see you down in Tigh Neachtain on Saturday night, okay? We're doing a fundraiser and it should be good fun. I'm not taking no for answer, and be prepared to give us a song."

Mary was left speechless as she watched this tall, wise man with his kind face stroll down the road. Mary felt like pinching herself to see if it all was real.

Frank could feel his heart beating at the rate of ninety as they came in the door from Tigh Neachtain. The adrenaline rush from being on stage still coursed through his veins.

"*What a night! Jaysus,* what a night, Joan," Frank said,

Frank poured a large glass of water from the kitchen tap. He gulped it down in one go and smacked his lips. Frank's shirt was drenched with perspiration and he shivered involuntarily as it felt cold against his skin. Joan walked past Frank without uttering so much as a word. Struggling out of her coat, she draped it on the back of a chair and then she went out to the hall where she exchanged her sensible shoes for a pair of comfy slippers.

"Has Johnny gone to bed?" Frank called out.

"Will you *keep it down*, Frank? *Yes,* Johnny's gone to bed. The whole house is asleep," Joan snapped and sighed heavily as she walked into the kitchen to sit down at the table.

Joan still felt bruised by her experience in the pub.

"Wasn't that a great night all the same? I'd forgotten what it was like. *Mighty craic.* You might have a celebrity on your hands if you're not careful, love," Frank jested and leaned against the sink, grinning like a Cheshire cat.

"Can you put the kettle on, Frank?" Joan said crankily.

"*What's wrong with you?*"

"*Nothing's wrong.* It was a great night, Frank. Really it was," she said without an ounce of enthusiasm.

"Well, it doesn't sound like it. You'd think we just came from a funeral with the look on your face," Frank barked.

"I'm just tired that's all. Don't give out to me. I'm not in the mood."

"Not in the mood? We're just after a great night in Tigh Neachtain. *God almighty, woman, what's eatin' you?* Will you just come out *and say it?*"

"Will you just put on the kettle, Frank?" Joan pleaded.

Frank filled the kettle, shoving it back down on its base with a loud bang.

"Frank, for God's sake, the children are in bed. Will you go easy?"

"Would you mind tellin' me what has you in such a mood?" Frank asked.

"Nothing. I'm just tired that's all. I enjoyed the night, but it's been a long time since I've been out in a busy pub. I'm worn out."

Frank held his breath and certain words he was tempted to shout at her. He occupied himself making the tea and when he felt his anger defuse, he sat down at the table.

"Frank, not the mugs! You know the tea tastes better in a china cup."

"God almighty, woman. *At this hour of the night,* what does it matter?" Frank struggled to his feet and resurrected the china cups and saucers from the press.

"There we go," Frank said through gritted teeth as he put them on the table. He brought the pot of tea over to the table and set it down to draw. "Wasn't Mary in great form all the same? I haven't seen her as happy in years," he said.

"Well, to be fair, we haven't exactly seen her in years," Joan said dismissively.

"Exactly. It's about time she had a bit of fun too. Mass and the shops aren't exactly great craic."

Frank thought of the look on Mary's face as she laughed and sang along to the music. It had been a great sight to behold after all these years.

"God, she hasn't that hard a life, Frank," Joan said and knew she sounded like a petulant child.

Joan couldn't help thinking that only a week ago they were the ones doing Mary a favour. Now here she was, the life and soul of the party and Joan the sad wallflower. Joan felt a failure again and the condemning voice of negativity rang in her ears like a broken record. Joan was on the verge of tears. Her stomach churned and her palms felt damp to the touch as she unsuccessfully fought the nasty roommate in her head.

All she could think of was Mary and Frank in their element in the pub. Frank had his job and the accordion, Mary had the singing, Cyril had his cars and Eileen seemed to be finding her true vocation, despite all her problems.

"Why are you being so hard on her, Joan? Isn't it good to see her havin' a bit of fun?"

"It is. I'm sorry."

Joan opened her mouth again to explain, but she couldn't find the words. Frank had been with her through thick and thin and she couldn't risk dumping more of her worries on him.

"What do you make of herself and Séamus?" Frank asked with a glint in his eye.

"They seemed to be talking alright, but they were probably just being polite," Joan said, regaining her composure while she sipped on her tea.

"Talking? Séamus was mad about her. Are you blind, Joan? Sure, he hardly left her side at the bar. I think I might just have done a bit of matchmaking," Frank declared proudly.

"They're a bit old, Frank. I don't think Mary is looking to meet anyone, and Séamus could be gone away again in no time."

"He's not going anywhere soon. He told me so himself. Wouldn't it be nice for both of them to have a bit a company? They don't have to marry, sure nobody ties the knot anymore," Frank said as he drained the last of his tea from the cup.

"Would you slow down? They only just met."

"Look, just 'cos you're lucky enough to have me, will you spare a thought for the poor auld creatures that have nobody."

"You're full of yourself," Joan remarked, trying not to smile.

Frank's upbeat demeanour nearly always managed to cheer Joan up, except for on her very low days, when no one could reach her. Joan reminded herself that she should be thanking her lucky stars for Frank. Not all women were so lucky.

"I'm only tryin' to help. How about asking them to dinner on Friday? Mary will be here anyways and Séamus is on his own, so it'd be a nice thank you, you know, for tonight? Just casual," Frank said and stood up.

"Oh, I don't know. They mightn't like being set up."

"*What's wrong* with you, woman? They had a ball together tonight. We're just helpin' things along a bit."

"You don't know anything about Séamus, Frank. Maybe he has a girlfriend or a wife?"

"*You what?* I doubt he'd have been all over Mary if there was another woman in the picture. It's only dinner. If nothin' happens, nothin' happens," Frank insisted.

"Are you going to cook? Seeing as you're the one inviting them," Joan asked, and Frank couldn't miss the sarcasm in her voice.

"You know well that Mary cooks the dinner, Joan. All you have to do is put a smile on your face, look pretty, as you always do, and let nature take its course."

Frank rubbed his hands together, totally unaware of the impact of his throwaway words. Joan bit her lip and stood up to wash her tea down the sink. With her back turned to Frank she repressed a scream, a scream that she had held in for a very long time, a scream to be seen, to be heard, to be understood.

"Well?" Frank asked.

"Alright, have it your way, but don't come crying to me if it all goes pear-shaped," Joan said, knowing there was no point arguing with him. Frank was like a dog with a bone when he made his mind up about something.

"Pear-shaped? God almighty, woman. We'll have a great night, so we will. I'll ask Séamus tomorrow. Now, will you come on to bed?"

FIFTEEN

Eileen's plans were starting to fall into place. On Thursday morning, she sat in her office after coming off the phone to Clare from Davitt's Solicitors.

"Meet me for coffee on Friday, Eileen. We'll work out the details then."

Eileen let out a deep sigh of relief. She had just been offered a job. For the first time in ages, Eileen felt somewhat hopeful about the future, despite their financial problems. The main cloud on the horizon was Fran Daly getting away scot free, because she hadn't the guts to report him.

"Hold it together, Eileen," she lectured herself.

If he assaulted or did worse to some other woman, she would never forgive herself. A younger, less experienced woman might feel intimidated by his wealth and power and just give in, but she had no excuse for letting him off the hook. At least, she acknowledged to herself, she had taken the first step and talked about it. Arriving on Joan's doorstep only the other day, she had been determined that she wouldn't breathe a word about what happened, but she had just gone and spilled out every gory detail.

Eileen looked at the files on her desk. She was supposed to have everything in order before she finished, but she couldn't concentrate. Eileen stopped what she was doing and stared into space.

"Bloody men!" she cried out and slammed the files on the floor.

Between Dave and Fran Daly, she had it up to here with them. She must have been on another planet to miss all the clues that seemed so obvious now. Eileen replayed the scenes in her mind when there was a knock on her office door. She jumped, startled by the intrusion. Eileen had been keeping well below the radar at work trying to finish out her days as quickly as possible. She checked her diary to see if she had forgotten an appointment, but Eileen already knew that she had no meetings scheduled today.

"Yes, who is it?" Eileen said hesitantly.

The door slowly opened, and Fran Daly silently entered her office and closed the door behind him. He was dressed in one of his business suits that strained under his weight, and his thinning grey hair was oiled back in place. Eileen almost gagged at the sight of him. Fran looked a sight more together than when Eileen last saw him stumbling to his feet on the side of the road just a week ago. Eileen saw his faux sophistication and charm as a cleverly constructed cover for the predator inside. It was as clear as day to her now, and Eileen shivered at this realisation.

"Well, hello, Eileen. It is good to see you. It really is," Fran said. Eileen stared at him, lost for words. "I hope you don't mind my intrusion. I'm sure you're busy. I just wanted to have a quick word with you in private. I won't take up much of your time."

Fran walked over to the bookshelf, casually picked up a framed family photograph of Eileen with Dave and the girls on holiday and let out a sniffle of laughter.

"Such happy campers," Fran remarked.

"Excuse me!" Eileen said, struggling to find her voice.

"Oh, I'm just admiring the lovely family photo, Eileen. Who'd have thought?"

"What?" Eileen asked in shock.

"Oh, nothing. I actually called by to wish you well. I must say I was very disappointed to hear the news from Pat. I mean you and I always worked well together. To be honest, I was a bit annoyed initially," Fran said. He smirked as he took a seat at her desk. "You know being left in the lurch and all, but I understand you've family commitments to take care of," Fran said.

Eileen stared at him and sank further back in her chair. It was a minute before she could actually speak.

"Mr Daly. What… what are you doing in my office?"

"As I said, I just wanted to wish you the best of luck for the future. We worked well together professionally and I'm sorry to see it end," Fran said.

Eileen took in his jovial demeanour and measured words and thought she might be losing her mind.

"Am I missing something here? Have you no memory of what happened last Wednesday night?"

"Are you okay, Eileen?" Fran asked, and casually picked some dust off his suit jacket and then stared at her without blinking.

"No, I'm not. Were you so blind drunk that you *can't remember*?"

"I'm at a loss here, Eileen," Fran said calmly. "It was a very enjoyable night as far as I'm concerned. I actually wanted to thank you properly for it. Yet, I'm not sure I understand what's going on here. Pat did say you were under a bit of pressure. I only dropped by to let you know that you'll be missed and to wish you well," Fran said loudly, and Eileen immediately knew it was for the benefit of anyone in the office who might be within earshot.

"You understand very well. Do *not* attempt to play games with me. You assaulted me last Wednesday night. You would not take no for an answer, no matter how many times I said it. *I don't care how much alcohol you consumed, nothing, I mean nothing excuses your behaviour.* To be honest, I'm in total shock that you have the nerve to turn up here *in my office!*"

Eileen folded her arms as she tried to steady herself. For as long as she lived, she would never forget the look that flickered across his face. For a fleeting moment the mask slipped. His eyes bulged and his nostrils flared. He was consumed with hatred. It was only for a second and then he composed himself, looking at Eileen like she was some deluded little girl.

"I came here to see you with the best of intentions. Be very careful what you're saying Eileen. I mean it. Be very, very careful. You're a solicitor and I'm sure I don't have to remind you of the consequences of slandering someone's good name," Fran threatened.

"*Slandering?* Are you being serious?"

A strange coldness entered his eyes and lowering his voice he practically spat at her across the desk.

"You don't know who you are dealing with. I can tell you that I'm far better as a friend than an enemy. I've been nothing but generous towards you and this practice, and I don't take kindly to untrue accusations being made about my character. I'm telling you, you better stop with this madness now."

Fran spoke with the practise of a man who had made this speech before. He rattled off the words with such fluidity that it appeared he had convinced himself of their truth.

"Madness?" Eileen retorted in a raised voice. Eileen was frustrated that she was just able to parrot back his words.

"Yes. I've dinner with business associates all the time and none of them have ever been so insulting. In fact, I'm having dinner with my accountant Marjory Hynes this evening. I've never had a word of complaint from her," Fran said smugly.

He licked his lips and a smile crept across his face. Eileen felt her blood turn cold and she shot out of her chair, almost upending it in the process.

"I'm asking you to leave my office *now*, Mr Daly, and I hope *I never set eyes on you again!* I'm not some *silly little girl* that you can threaten. I know well what happened last Wednesday night and count yourself lucky that I didn't call the guards on you. It would be a very different story if I had."

Her heart thumped so loudly that she was sure he could hear it. Instead he just burst out laughing in her face.

"I'm afraid, Eileen, I'm not sure what has gotten into you. You obviously have a lot going on at home, I mean every dog on the street has heard the stories about Dave."

Eileen's face paled and she thought she might faint. Surely, Fran Daly didn't know about their financial problems on top of everything else.

"My husband has nothing to do with this!"

"Really? I'd say he has a lot to do with it," Fran remarked and chuckled, enjoying watching Eileen squirm. "I'll put your outburst down to all the stress that you must be under. Problems in a marriage are never easy."

"*What?*" Eileen asked. She felt like she had been punched. "How *dare you* involve my husband? It has *nothing to do with what you did* and I might add that our financial situation is none of your business."

"Your financial situation? I don't know anything about the state of your finances, Eileen."

"What are you talking about?"

"You really want me to spell it out?"

"Yes, and then please leave my office."

"Sorry to be the bearer of bad news but it's hardly a state secret that your husband can't keep it in his pants."

With a triumphant look, knowing Eileen had no idea what Fran was talking about, Fran turned and walked out of the office.

Eileen felt like she had been punched. She was rooted to the spot as she processed Fran Daly's words. Eventually, Eileen sat down at her desk and tried to piece together the fragments of their conversation. Firstly, he had the gall to act as if she had made up some story. Then, Fran was talking about her marriage and what Eileen thought were Dave's financial problems. What did he mean by 'can't keep it in his pants'? Surely even Fran wouldn't stoop so low to make up such a far-fetched story just to distract from his own behaviour. Eileen needed some air. She had another hour to go at work, but she didn't care. Eileen grabbed her jacket from the back of the chair and in a daze, she took the lift to the ground floor. Eileen didn't know where she was going, she just knew that she had to keep moving.

Walking aimlessly down the street, Eileen's legs tried to keep pace with her racing thoughts. In the end, Eileen wore herself out, and collapsed on a bench at the edge of the river and stared out at the water. It had felt like things couldn't be any worse. Now, here she was with potentially more bad news. Yet, Eileen didn't want to let herself go there. It was more likely that Fran Daly had been vindictive enough to make those things up.

It just couldn't be true.

"Dave, of all people. There's no way," Eileen said.

Dave had been crazy about her. There wasn't a chance in hell of him straying. Even when women had thrown themselves at him in social situations, he couldn't have cared less. It just wasn't him. Eileen picked up the phone and was about to call her mother but put it back in her bag. She didn't need her 'I told you so' right now. Joan would likely be at work, but Eileen thought that she had dumped enough on her already. Hadn't they only been talking about the man-eater Jane Corbett coming on to Frank and once upon a time to Dave?

"Please God, he hadn't got mixed up with her," Eileen said.

Eileen looked across the river to the town where life continued as normal. She saw people going about their daily business none the wiser to her heartache. Eileen had never felt so alone and cried. Eileen jumped at the sound of footsteps and quickly wiped her face.

"Hello, I don't mean to intrude…"

Eileen looked up to see a tall, elderly man with kind eyes looking back at her with genuine concern.

"I just wanted to check if you're okay?" He added with a smile.

"Thank you. There's no point saying I'm fine while I'm sitting here with tears running down my face. I must look like an awful mess," Eileen said. She took a tissue from her bag and blew her nose.

"Far from it. Can I do anything? I'm in no rush if you want to talk. I'm Séamus by the way," the man said.

Eileen edged over on the bench making it clear that he could sit down. Séamus accepted Eileen's request and sat next to her.

"What's so bad that you're camped out here like it's the end of the world?" Séamus asked.

Eileen turned to look at him properly, feeling relieved that his accent wasn't local.

"Do you have all day?" Eileen asked through her tears.

"Well, I do as it happens, but I'm sure it can't be all that bad."

"Oh, I don't know. Maybe you're right. It's probably not as bad as it seems right now, but my mind is racing so much I can't see the wood from the trees," Eileen said.

"Why don't you tell me, that is if you want to? Speaking from experience, talking helps. Better out than in they say."

"I hope that's true," Eileen said and for the third time this week Eileen went on to tell someone everything that had happened, but on this occasion, Eileen finished off with the new bombshell that Fran Daly had landed on her.

Eileen smiled timidly when she finished, feeling a bit better. Séamus sat quietly for a short while before responding.

"It sounds like you have a lot going on alright. If you want my advice, for what it's worth, the first thing I would advise is talking to your husband. Don't go down a rabbit hole until you have all the facts. That man, Fran Daly is it?" Séamus asked. Eileen nodded.

"Well, if you can call him a man, he should be shot. We're not all like that, you know. At least you won't have to deal with him again, if that's any consolation," Séamus offered.

"Oh, it is. I know it doesn't look like it, but I'm normally a very strong woman. I'm usually the one consoling other women," Eileen said.

"I'm sure you are, but none of us escape hard times. I've had my own struggles and it would take a lot longer than a day to tell you all of them. It does improve, but you *do* need support. It's always much easier with a bit of help," Séamus said and stretched to make eye contact with Eileen. "It doesn't matter who it is or even if you have to pay someone. You *can't* do it *on your own*."

As they sat in silence on the bench, Eileen was struck by Séamus' words. Eileen realised that she didn't have a lot of solid people she could turn to, when push came to shove. Eileen was grateful for Joan and realised she was probably the best friend in her life right now.

"Well, you've been a great help. I can't thank you enough. I'm Eileen by the way," Eileen said, and put out her hand.

Séamus shook her hand.

"Thank you, Séamus. You're an angel."

****

Across the city, Mary found a quiet house when she arrived at the Hughes. She slipped in the back door that Frank now left open for her on his way out to work. Finding an empty kitchen which bore the tell-tale signs of the inhabitants' last movements, she felt like an intruder. Mary sat down at the kitchen table and guessed that Frank and Joan hadn't gone straight to bed when they arrived in from the pub the night before. A stale pot of tea still lay on the table.

Mary felt a slight wrench as she remembered the late-night chats she had enjoyed with Tom. It was one of the many things she missed without the presence of a partner in her life.

"Enough of that," Mary said, not wishing to feel sorry for herself any longer.

Mary heard the chair creak as she stood up to find her apron and rubber gloves. Indulging in sweet treats to quell her loneliness hadn't done her physical shape any favours. She tied the apron tightly and patted her middle. She sighed as she felt some extra padding that had been added in the last few weeks as she cooked and baked like a woman possessed. For the next hour, Mary scrubbed, brushed, washed and polished every available surface until her hair and skin were damp from the effort. She gave a last rub of the cloth to the table and stood back to admire her handiwork.

"Oh, there you are, Joan. You'll have a cup of tea," Mary said, wiping her hand across her forehead.

"Morning. It looks like you've been busy," Joan said and looked around at the sparkling kitchen.

"Have you the day off today?" Mary asked.

"Yes, thank God. A leak," Joan said.

Joan was relieved when she woke up to a text message from Peter saying that the library was closed, and she had turned over for a second blissful sleep. Joan sat down and watched as Mary prepared a light breakfast in minutes.

"Thanks so much for last night. Really, I haven't had such fun and such a sore head in years," Mary said as she bustled around the kitchen, preparing scrambled eggs and toast.

Mary had carefully washed and dried the best china and was quick to notice Joan's look of approval as she set the table and stuck the tea cosy on the teapot.

"That's good you enjoyed it," Joan said, wondering what the gossipmongers would make of it if they saw Mary O'Sullivan now.

"Did you enjoy the night?" Mary asked, adding more toast to Joan's plate.

"I won't, Mary, thanks. I've enough here," Joan said, waving the toast away. Joan could feel her waistband tightening with Mary's generous portion sizes. "I did enjoy it… I think. To be honest, I found the crowds a bit much. It's been a long time since I've been out socially," Joan confessed, nibbling on her toast.

"You and me both," Mary said, placing her elbows on the table.

"Well, I'm glad you were. Otherwise, I would have been standing there all night on my own," Joan said and blushed, feeling embarrassed at the admission.

"It looks like it worked out for both of us then," Mary said emphatically. "These last couple of weeks have been fantastic for me, Joan. I actually feel a bit useful again. Before I was just clocking in time until the man above decided to turn the lights off," Mary admitted.

Mary had no problem speaking honestly to Joan. The barriers between them had gradually dissolved and she actually found it a great relief to reveal how she truly felt.

"I'm sure you've heard the stories about me, Joan. I'm no fool. I mightn't be out much, but *even I know* what people say. That I'm half cracked, fond of the jar and that I have full-scale conversations with myself," Mary said, and Joan giggled at Mary's candour.

"Maybe I was all of those things, but I did what I needed to survive. I'd be lost without Boots, now, and don't say it, Joan, I know the jokes…"

"Weren't you a teacher?" Joan asked, curious to know more about her.

"I was, but that was when women had to give up their jobs when they married. How ridiculous was that when you think of it? Though to be honest, I think some women would be delighted if that was the case now. Don't you?" Mary said and they both laughed. "I'd be shot for saying that in public, wouldn't I?" Mary remarked.

The two women were beginning to see that they had a lot more in common than they had originally assumed.

"I just don't know that I could have reared five children and spent all day in school with a whole class of them. I'd surely have been locked up," Mary said and shook her head at the thought.

"Well, I definitely wouldn't have been able for it. I…" Joan hesitated, and her shoulder twitched furiously.

"It's okay, Joan," Mary assured her.

"I was depressed, you know… after Johnny was born. It was awful. I couldn't drag myself out of bed for days on end. I wouldn't have survived without Frank," Joan said, shocked by her own honesty.

Mary's sincerity had unlocked something, and Joan said things she never would have imagined in a million years sharing with anyone other than Frank.

"I'm sorry, Joan," Mary said and reached over and took Joan's hand. "That must have been so hard. Everyone has their cross, don't they? Just look at me. I have five children and not one of them contacts me or comes to visit. I know I didn't do a great job rearing them, but all the same it's not easy," Mary said.

"That's awful. Why don't they keep in touch?" Joan asked. "I don't know. I suppose over time we just stopped talking. I was very hard on them at times," Mary said and looked at the floor, embarrassed by her admission.

"It's not an excuse, but I didn't have the best childhood growing up. Tom was as soft as anything with them, so I suppose I made up for it, and boy did I? I said some awful things, Joan."

Mary cringed at the memory of the shouting matches in the house. She didn't recognise the woman she was back then anymore. Mary would have given anything to rewrite history, and her words, but she knew it could only ever be wishful thinking.

"It's too late now. Too much water under the bridge as they say. Now, I'm rambling on. I better head to the shops," Mary said. She stood up from the table and cleared the dishes.

"Well, I think they sound very selfish," Joan said, bringing her cup and plate to the sink. "Oh, before you go, I wanted to tell you something."

"What is it?" Mary asked.

"Frank wanted it to be a surprise, but I think you should know," Joan confided.

"What? God, you've me interested now. What's the surprise?" Mary asked, standing with her hands firmly planted on her hips.

"Well, I don't know if it's that great. We want you to stay for dinner tomorrow night. Frank's inviting Séamus to join us too. I hope you don't mind," Joan said.

"*Séamus?*" Mary exclaimed, holding on to the door. "*What* is that husband of yours up to? I hope he's not trying to play matchmaker," Mary scolded, though secretly pleased.

"I told him you had no interest and that he was a busybody, but he wasn't having any of it. I don't know if he's asked him yet. I can tell him not to, if you'd prefer," Joan offered, but judging by Mary's now pink cheeks, she guessed there would be no need.

"Not at all. He's good company and I like him but that's all. As long as he doesn't mind, I don't," Mary said.

That afternoon Séamus found his way to his favourite coffee shop in town. It was a traditional tea and sandwiches place mainly frequented by older adults. He loved to sit in his favourite seat by the window, enjoying an uninterrupted view of Shop Street and the hustle and bustle of daily life. However, on this particular afternoon, Séamus was shaken by his meeting with the woman by the river. He stared into his mug of coffee and was rapidly transported back to one of the most painful moments of his own life.

On that very same spot forty years ago, he had cried his eyes out and despaired of ever finding his place in the world. It was after a feed of drink and many years of pain that the fast-flowing river had almost lured him in. Only for a few friends catching up with him on their way home, it could have been a story with a very different ending. Séamus eyes filled up at the memory and he let the tears run down his face unchecked. He smiled through his tears. It was just a memory, he reminded himself. Séamus scratched his head and took another sip of coffee.

Since arriving home, he had been shocked at number of stories of bodies turning up in the river. Before he left, there had been the odd story of a drunken person falling in the water or a fisherman meeting his end in a storm, but that was the height of it. Now, it looked like it was a city full of prosperity and a sea full of pain and despair. Something didn't add up. He stood up from the table to pay his bill.

As Séamus walked back towards home his thoughts turned to Mary. Meeting her again last night had wakened something in him that Séamus thought died a long time ago. His last girlfriend, an actress from the Bronx, had been as fond of the jar as Séamus had been, and they had never stood a chance. That had been more than ten years ago, and he had been scarred by the experience. By the time Séamus had broken up with her, she had stolen a lot of money from him. Séamus hadn't been in a hurry to meet anyone else and had enough work to do putting his own life back on track.

Séamus stopped at the bench where he had chatted to the woman called Eileen and looked around. Feeling the heat of the sun on his face, he smiled with contentment. Séamus marvelled at the transformation in the city when the sun was shining. The dank, depressed town that he remembered growing up in now had an energy that was usually reserved for mainland Europe or cities like New York. Séamus thought of the tourists, students, buskers and locals that mingled together easily, and he felt a surge of pride that he had never felt before. There was a confidence about the people and an optimism in the mood. Séamus couldn't help feeling hopeful as he watched the swans glide gracefully on the river and heard the friendly chatter that was a hallmark of the city. Despite its now cosmopolitan status, it was still a small town and in Séamus' eyes, it was the colourful, eclectic community that made it special. If Séamus was really honest, it was colourful, eclectic Mary that now made it extra special for him.

On that same Thursday afternoon, Brian McCabe approached Johnny and Jack. He hovered over them both as they walked out the school gates and then he made his move.

"I'm looking forward to payday tomorrow," Brian McCabe said with an accompanied irritating smirk. "A deal is a deal, so you better show up. Seven o'clock, the usual spot."

"*Piss off*, would you," Johnny hissed at him, walking faster to escape him.

"Don't be late, loser, or else," McCabe shouted, making a punching sound with his fist as his friends egged him on.

"Wait up, Johnny," Jack called, running to catch up as Johnny marched down the hill at great speed.

"What's gotten into you?" Jack panted as he caught up with him.

"I'm just *fucking sick of him*. Every day *the same bullshit.* Why did you choose him of all people?" Johnny growled.

"*Me?* I didn't go near the guy. I can't stand him. Are you serious?" Jack retorted and roughly tugged on Johnny's jacket bringing him to a standstill.

"Hold up there. Now, have your facts straight before you start pointing the finger," Jack shouted.

They stood looking at each other, both red-faced with frustration. "Trouble in paradise," McCabe said and passed by with his gang, enjoying the sight of the two friends at loggerheads.

"*I told you to piss of, McCabe, and I won't say it again*," Johnny snapped and squared up to Brian McCabe, almost touching noses with him.

Brian McCabe wasn't much taller than Johnny and definitely not as skilled with his fists. Everyone knew who would come out the victor in a straight-up competition between the two.

"Johnny, for the last time will you leave it?" Jack asked and nudged him. "Can't we just hold tight until tomorrow, pay them off and be done with it? Stick to the boxing club if you need to punch someone so badly."

Jack felt his patience rapidly wearing thin with Johnny. His brother Liam had given him the money to pay off their debt, but he had been very clear about the conditions. Jack could still hear his thundering voice ringing in his ears.

Liam's bark was worse than his bite. All Jack wanted was to be like him, self-made and with a social conscience. Liam was doing something worthwhile with his success, unlike his materialistic parents.

"Okay, okay. *Give it a rest*," Johnny moaned.

"I had to beg for the money and it's the last time. Liam made me feel this big," Jack said, gesturing with his fingers.

"Okay, I said. Just hold tight until tomorrow," Johnny said and grinned at Jack as he parroted his words back to him.

"You're hilarious," Jack said. He couldn't help laughing at his impression of him.

"Did I tell you I was at a gig in Tigh Neachtain last night?" Johnny asked, beaming as he waited to see Jack's reaction.

"*A gig? You?*" Jack asked, and then roared with laughter.

"Yes. *Piss off.* Séamus Feeney. He's a trad musician. Plays the fiddle. He's class. He goes back a long way with the old man. Dad was on stage with him."

"Feck off. That's pretty cool."

"Yeah. The place was buzzing," Johnny said, feeling pleased with himself.

"Why didn't you ask me along, moron?"

"I thought it'd be crap to be honest, but it was pretty mega. He's offered to help if I want to make it in the music business," Johnny said, unable to help himself from embellishing what actually had transpired.

"So, you've found your calling then?" Jack asked and punched him on the arm playfully. "Pity you can't sing or play an instrument though."

"I used to play the drums and I was pretty good, for your information," Johnny said.

Johnny's parents hadn't agreed, with his mother calling it an awful racket, but what did she know about music? It had ended up being more therapy than pleasure as he regularly disappeared to the shed to drum out his frustrations with the world.

"Well, he's playing every Wednesday night, so you can join me if you like," Johnny said.

"I might just do that. Who'd have thought it? Johnny Hughes, a musician. Well, you'll need to go easy on the drugs if you don't want to go the same way as the likes of Kurt Cobain."

"*Piss off*, would you. You're one to talk. I was only saying."

Thursday afternoon heralded a different kind of experience for Eileen's husband Dave, who sat at the desk in his office. He couldn't escape Julie at work and if anything, she went out of her way to cross paths with him. Hearing a noise from outside his office, he swivelled back around in his seat and saw her bending over talking to his secretary Rita right outside his office.

"*Feck's sake* stop walking past in that tight skirt," Dave muttered.

Dave swivelled in his chair and did his best to put any sight or thoughts of Julie out of his mind.

"Rita, can you fetch me a coffee, please?" Dave asked as he picked up the phone.

"Sure, Dave. Won't be a minute," Rita said.

There was a coffee shop downstairs from the office. He usually went down himself after Eileen had given him an earful for treating his secretary as his maid, but today was an exception. He had to avoid Julie. As Rita left, Julie turned and smiled at him and did her best sexy walk back to her office.

"Jesus Christ!" Dave groaned. "Did she not get that it was over?"

Julie's clothes seemed to be even tighter and shorter as she lost no opportunity to show him what he was missing. Dave felt her lure even stronger now that things were not so well at home.

Dave dialled Eileen's number and waited, but there was no response. He put the phone down again. Dave had wanted to tell Eileen that he had met Con that day, and although things were pretty dire, it didn't look like he and Eileen would have to declare bankruptcy. The only thing was that they would definitely have to sell the house, but Eileen was comfortable enough with that. As one load lifted off his shoulder, Dave saw another walking down the hallway, and he knew this would not be as easy to offload.

Suddenly, Dave's phone lit up on the desk and one glance told him it was Eileen. For some reason, Dave panicked. He took a look at the notes on his desk after meeting Con and let it ring out. Dave wanted to go through them one more time before he talked to Eileen. Dave's phone beeped again, and he picked it up to see a message from Eileen. He sat back and groaned. She was being insistent whatever it was about. 'Can you meet me in Grey's at five thirty? It's important,' the message read.

"Fuck," Dave blurted out. He had actually been considering asking Julie for a drink after work in Grey's Hotel. They met there occasionally, because of the convenient private booths that hid them from prying eyes. It was the perfect place for illicit liaisons, and an ironic choice for Eileen. Dave replied to the text from Eileen and told Eileen he would be there.

A few hours later, Eileen walked through the reception of Grey's hotel. She was deep in thought about her meeting with Séamus. It might just have been the therapy she needed before talking to Dave. Arriving early, Eileen slipped into a quiet booth in the bar, took a breath and let her shoulders relax. Feeling warm from the walk, she took off her camel coat and folded it on the seat beside her. Eileen took out her compact and checked her makeup in the mirror.

Eileen felt nervous as she rehearsed what she wanted to say, remembering Fran Daly's cruel words. Eileen decided that she would ask Dave straight out if he had told her everything. Eileen wouldn't jump to any conclusions, but she wouldn't let him off the hook either. Eileen was not leaving this hotel tonight until she was sure she had the truth. There would be no hysterics or drama, it wouldn't help anything. She just needed to know the truth.

Eileen's life as she knew it seemed to be on a track to self-destruct and some part of her had already taken the hand brake off and was ready to just let go.

"Hi. Sorry. Am I late?" Dave asked and slipped into the seat opposite her. "It took me a few minutes to find you. It's like a maze in here with all the nooks and crannies," he said.

Dave furtively looked around and then picked up the wine menu and flicked through it.

"You're fine. I just arrived here a bit early. It's been a crazy day and I wanted a few minutes of quiet," Eileen said.

As if on cue, a waiter appeared to take their order.

"Well, hello, Mr Danaher. How are you? What can I bring you and the lady this evening?" the waiter asked.

Eileen watched Dave flinch at the waiter's words.

"I'll have a red wine, please," Eileen said, taking the lead.

"I'll have the same, a Rioja if you have it," Dave asked, closing the menu.

Dave knew only too well they did, having drank copious glasses of it with Julie. Eileen nodded at the waiter to make it two.

"So, this is where you go to when you're *working late*," Eileen said, doing her utmost to keep her tone light.

"Ah, you know, just it's a handy spot sometimes for meetings or a work drink. You know the way these hotels are. Cosying up to their customers is all part of the business," Dave said casually and straightened his tie.

Eileen smiled to herself and folded the napkin. Eileen made small talk about the girls until their drinks came, and they could talk without interruption. When the wine finally arrived and the waiter left, they both took a large gulp.

"So, you wanted to talk, it sounded urgent. Is everything okay?" Dave asked, rubbing his hand along the five o'clock shadow on his face.

"You know that everything is far from okay, Dave," Eileen said and flashed him a humourless smile and sat back. "First things first. How did it go with Con?"

Dave took another gulp from his wine.

"Well, it's not great but one bit of good news is that we won't have to declare bankruptcy," Dave said. He waited for some encouraging words, but Eileen just stared at him blankly.

"We'll have to sell up and look for somewhere smaller. It's going to be a different life to the one we've been living, Eileen. We'll have to cut back. I'll have a lot of debts for years to come. But we can make it through this and I promise you, I'll never be so stupid again. I've learnt my lesson. I'm so sorry that you have to suffer because of my mistakes."

Dave had practised his speech on the way from work and he was relieved to finish it. Judging by the strained looked on his face, Eileen knew that Dave was genuinely sorry.

"I'm glad that we're not going to be bankrupt, at least I think I am. At the same time, I can't help wondering if it would be for the best. We could wipe the slate clean and start again. No assets, but no debts either. Just a fresh start. I know that might sound mad, but what sort of a life will it be paying off all that money for the rest of our lives?" Eileen reasoned.

"I'm earning good money and you can too. Bankruptcy isn't a walk in the park either, Eileen. I thought that we would sell the cottage in Clare and that will help clear a lot of the debts. With both houses sold, our creditors would be kept happy and we would have the capacity to pay the remaining outstanding debts over time. I've gone through it all with Con. He agrees. What do you think?"

"I suppose so," Eileen said and played with her napkin as she thought about it, and then she looked him squarely in the eye. "I need you to be totally honest, Dave. Are you telling me everything?" Eileen asked with as much confidence as she could muster.

Dave almost choked as he drained the last of his wine. There was no way that she could know anything about Julie, he assured himself.

"*What do you mean? I've just told you* that I met with Con. If you don't believe I'm telling you the full story, then talk to him yourself."

"I'm assuming everything is above board with Con. Yet to be fair, you haven't exactly been honest with me for quite a while. Don't you think I've every right to be sceptical? Are there any other surprises that you have up your sleeve? If there are, I'm telling you now is the time to put them out on the table. It's the only chance we have. I'm willing to go along with your plan, but I need to know everything," Eileen said. She wouldn't be side-tracked with stories of Con the accountant. Eileen was well aware of Dave's prowess in a court room and his ability to spin a very credible story, even out of the sparsest of facts.

"I cannot and will not stick with you in this marriage if you are lying to me about anything else. That's the bottom line," Eileen said.

Eileen searched his face for a reaction, but apart from looking quite pale, she couldn't figure out what Dave thought.

"Yes, I'm telling you everything. Look, I know I've been an asshole about the new business you want to set up. I'm truly sorry about that. It may take a bit of time, but I will support you one hundred percent with it from now on, I promise. Can you just bear with me for a while until we have some of this mess sorted?" Dave loosened his tie, hoping she couldn't see the perspiration that now seeped through his shirt.

"I truly am so sorry, Eileen. I'll make it up to you, I promise."

"I'm glad to hear that you're finally willing to support me," Eileen snapped, "but it's going to take a lot of time before I can trust you again. Do you understand?" Eileen took a deep breath before continuing. She could tell by the beads of perspiration on his forehead that he felt under pressure.

"I don't want the girls to sense that anything is wrong, so we will act as normal at home. You're going to have to bear with me while I try and come to terms with it. It's a big blow, you know, after all our time together..."

Dave's phone rang.

"I'm sorry. Do you mind if I take this? It's a client, we've a meeting tomorrow. I won't be long." He stood up without waiting for a reaction and walked towards reception.

"Would it have mattered if I said no?" Eileen said to the empty seat. Feeling exhausted, she beckoned for the bill so that they could leave when he returned.

"Here's your bill and the manager thought you might want this back?" The waiter handed Eileen an expensive red silk scarf. "Excuse me?"

"It was handed in by a customer a few weeks ago, after you left. I wasn't here myself, but the manager on duty held on to it. He said it was Mr Danaher's table. It looks expensive, so he thought you might want it back," the waiter said and smiled.

Eileen returned the smile and then paid the bill. She sat staring at the scarf for a few seconds, trying to compute what it meant. It certainly wasn't her scarf and it smelt of a perfume that she had never worn.

"Is that manager on duty this evening?" Eileen reacted quickly, hoping Dave would take his time on the phone.

"Yes, he is. He's... actually, that's him." The young waiter pointed at a man in uniform who walked towards them from the direction of reception.

"Can I have a word?" Eileen asked and the young waiter beckoned to the manager who approached the table.

"Hello... Mr O'Dowd," Eileen said, looking at his polished name badge.

"I just wanted to check something with you. I think this scarf that you found might belong to a colleague of my husband's. Can you recall what she looked like by any chance? I just wanted to let her know."

"Oh... right," the manager said, stumbling on his words. Eileen gave him an appreciative smile.

"Well, I think so. I'm nearly sure it was a blonde girl, yes definitely she was blonde," the manager said and stopped short, as if suddenly realising he may have divulged too much information.

"Oh right, yes. That's definitely her. Thank you for your time," Eileen said trying to keep her voice steady. As the manager walked away from the table, Eileen knew that the scarf wasn't indisputable evidence of an affair. However, when combined with Fran Daly's revelations, it looked decidedly probable. Eileen knew her instincts had been right. She was definitely on to something.

SIXTEEN

Dave hung up the phone and immediately ran into the toilets of Grey's Hotel and splashed cold water on his face.

"Jesus Christ, that was a close call," Dave said, looking in the mirror.

An ashen coloured face stared back at him. It didn't look like Eileen had suspected anything when he answered the phone. He thought then that he had jumped up so quickly from the table, she probably didn't have time to notice. The bloody chances that Julie would call him when Dave was sitting having a drink with his wife in Grey's Hotel, of all places. Dave had told her not to call him ever, but it seemed she didn't want to play ball anymore.

"What a bloody mess," Dave said and sighed as he wiped his face with the paper towel. He looked around, relieved that he had the place to himself.

"She hadn't been long hanging up the phone when I told her who I was with… *but bloody hell*, only after I agreed to meet her," he said to his reflection in the mirror.

Dave fobbed her off with promises of a quick drink tomorrow after work, but he was determined to duck out of that. Whatever happened, he had to avoid her going totally loco and ringing Eileen. Dave heard about women who did that, just lost the plot and created a shitstorm. What a fool he had been to think that Julie would be any different? Just as well he had told her that it was over. It wasn't fun anymore and she definitely wasn't worth losing his family for.

Dave checked himself in the mirror one last time and walked back to the bar. He would suggest they have another drink, chill out and soon they would be back to normal. Eileen always relaxed after a few glasses of wine.

As he walked towards their booth, he saw her holding something in her hands, and it was only as he moved closer to the table that it became clear. The colour drained from his face. She was holding the scarf he had bought for Julie.

"Who owns the scarf, Dave?" Eileen asked. Her cheeks were pink, but her voice steady as she asked the question.

Dave sat back down and cleared his throat.

"What do you mean?" Dave asked, trying to maintain his composure.

"I mean exactly that. *Who* owns the scarf?" Eileen asked again. "How would *I know* who owns the scarf? Just leave it here. The barman will find it. I'm sure people forget things all the time," Dave said.

Practised in the art of thinking on his feet, Dave didn't want her giving it to any of the barmen just in case it jogged their memory. It's only a scarf. It proves nothing, he reassured himself.

"I think the barman found it already. That's why he handed it to *me*. Any idea why he might think it's mine?"

Dave looked at the scarf bobbing up and down in her trembling hand and swallowed hard.

"I don't understand, Eileen. Is it yours?" Dave asked innocently.

"No. It's not mine and you *know damn well it's not*."

"Calm down *for God's sake*. People are looking at us. Look let's go home and we can talk there. I know it's been a tough few days," Dave said.

"*Don't you dare!* Do you *hear me*?"

Eileen put her hands flat on the table in front of her, calmly inspected them and lowered her voice.

"Don't dare talk to me like I'm one of those fawning, airhead secretaries that work for you. Please give me a bit more credit than that. I already asked you if you had told me everything and I'm giving you one last opportunity. So, whose is the red scarf?"

"*What is up with you? What's the big deal about a scarf?* People leave scarves behind all the time!"

"Do I have to go and look for the manager again, who told me it belonged to the *blonde* lady you were with? I'm sure he'll put us straight. And before you say anything, Dave," Eileen said and put her hand up to stop him interrupting, "I advise you to think twice. Not only did I have to deal with the embarrassment of your girlfriend's scarf being handed to me, but I also had to face the indignity only this morning, of Fran Daly, *Fran Daly of all people*, telling me that it is common knowledge that my husband can't keep it in his pants," Eileen angered.

Dave's mouth dropped open as he listened to her deliver the words with icy coldness. Dave went to speak, but nothing came out. In the silence that opened up, their eyes locked. No words were needed as the look they exchanged said everything. They were teetering on the edge of a place they might not come back from. Then surprising both himself and Eileen, Dave burst out crying.

"I'm sorry, I'm so sorry. It was a stupid mistake and I regret it so much. If I could do anything to take it back, Eileen, I would. Please, forgive me. It's over and I've told her it's over..."

Dave's voice trailed off and he buried his head in his hands. He was annoyed at himself for being so pathetic, but he couldn't stop crying - crying for being caught, crying for what he might lose, crying for the mess that he had made of everything.

"Who is she?" Eileen said stonily.

"Nobody, just a girl in the office," David said, his voice was just above a whisper.

"*Nobody?* I'm sure she'd love to hear you say that. *Who* in the office? I want *a name*, Dave," Eileen insisted.

"Julie, Julie Mahon," Dave said.

Eileen knew straight away who it was. Hadn't they only joked a few years back that she would be the dream woman for any man going through a mid-life crisis?

"How long?"

"A year."

"A year? For an affair that supposedly meant, or should I say means nothing, it sounds like *a pretty long time*. Can you just tell me one thing? Did you stop at any point to think of me or your two young daughters?" Eileen asked.

"Of course, I did. If I could take it all back I would. I'm so sorry, but we can come through this. It's over. I'm telling you, it is over," Dave cried.

Dave looked up at Eileen with tear-filled eyes.

"So, let me make sure I have this right. *You've not only almost bankrupt us*, but you go and top it off by *having an affair*. Is there anything else I should know?"

"Nothing," Dave said, barely audible.

"Listen to me, Dave. I'm only going to say this once. I'm going home to the girls now and you can do whatever you like. I'm sure Julie would put you up, just *don't you dare set foot in the house tonight*," Eileen said in disgust. "I can't look at you and I don't want the girls upset."

"*Please* say we can work it out. *Please*, Eileen. I don't know what I'd do without you," Dave cried.

Eileen picked up her bag, tossed the scarf in his direction and walked out of the hotel. Disoriented after the conversation, Eileen couldn't remember where she had parked the car. Out on the street, she walked aimlessly until it finally came to her. She had left it in the multi-storey carpark near the hotel. Retracing her steps, she hardly could believe what had just happened. Soon Eileen was safely sitting in the driver's seat of her car. Eileen lay back, leaning her head against the headrest and let reality wash over her.

"Fuck him, fuck him!" Eileen yelled and pummelled the steering wheel furiously.

Fran Daly, as awful as he was, had been right. God if he knew, likely every dog in the street knew. Step by step Eileen walked through the extent of Dave's deception in her head. Dave had started squandering their money God knows when, and now they were on the verge of bankruptcy. In the middle of all that he had found time to start an affair. There was also the added humiliation that Dave had picked Julie, of all people, from his office. Julie must have thought she hit the jackpot, snagging herself a hotshot barrister, so much for female solidarity.

Eileen started up the engine and almost crashed the car into the barriers on the way out of the car park. Steadying herself, she replayed any clues she might have missed on the journey home. All those conferences and meetings that had him staying away at night. It was likely that all of it had been lies. Lies, lies, a life built on lies. Eileen pulled in at the side of the road, just like she had a week earlier after the incident with Fran Daly. This time Eileen didn't cry but rather felt numb and robotic.

Thursday evening traffic whizzed by as Eileen sat in the car. It felt like hours had passed as Eileen lost herself in the rhythmic *whoosh* of the cars. When Eileen looked at her watch it was eight o'clock. It was only an hour since she left the hotel. Eileen couldn't wipe the image of Dave staring speechless at her out of her head. Dave had often been remote and preoccupied, but Eileen had never taken him to be a liar. Eileen felt an overwhelming urge to see the girls. They were the only thing that made sense right now. She started the car and five minutes later pulled up in their driveway.

"Hi Dawn, hi girls," Eileen called out as she charged into the house at full speed. Eileen had never been so happy to see her children cuddled up on the couch watching TV.

"Did you eat dinner?" Eileen asked and looked at Dawn.

"Dad's not home yet. We're just watching a movie. Can we stay up until the end, please? It's only half an hour more," Amy begged, hopping up and down on the couch.

"Okay, just a half hour," Eileen said and walked over to the couch, stretching out her arms for a badly needed hug.

"Mum, you're in the way," Amy said, wriggling out of her grasp as she strained to see the TV.

"That's a lovely reception to come home to," Eileen said lightly, turning to smile at Dawn. "Thanks so much for coming at such short notice. You can go home now, unless you want to watch the end of the movie."

"Please stay, please," the girls said in unison, and Eileen nodded at Dawn.

None of them had seemed to notice that anything was amiss. Eileen obviously was a better actor than she thought.

"Your Dad won't be home tonight. He's had to go away with work, but he said to tell you that he loves you very much and that you're to go to bed early," Eileen said.

She could feel tears burn the back of her eyes as she said the words. Would there ever be a time again when both of them would put the girls to bed together, telling stories that ended up in a pillow fight? Who was she kidding? It had been a long time since that had happened. It was usually her putting the girls to bed on her own. There was no point being sentimental for a time that was long gone. She needed to deal with reality now, a reality from which there was no escaping.

Eileen walked into the kitchen and sat down in the silence of the room. She reached into her bag and pulled out her phone and rang Joan. They spent almost an hour talking about the events of that evening until Eileen felt too tired to discuss it anymore.

"Frank, you're not going to believe it, but that was Eileen on the phone," Joan said. Joan rushed into the kitchen, her cheeks pink with colour.

"*Jaysus*, that's hard to believe alright," Frank said as he cleaned his accordion on the kitchen table.

"It's not funny. Do you have to do that on the kitchen table?" Joan asked, faced with the mess he had created.

"Look, newspaper underneath it. You won't even know it was there," Frank said as he vigorously rubbed the instrument with a cloth. "Now, what's going on with your friend, Eileen? I thought she had the life of Reilly."

"Far from it," Joan said and immediately regretted telling him about Eileen's wonderful life and husband. Joan sat down at the table, her shoulder twitching furiously.

"Her husband's having an affair and she's just found out. And there's more. Only a couple of days ago she was here, and she told me..." Joan paused before whispering, "in confidence, I don't know if I should say anything."

"Have it your way, love, but I can't help if you don't tell me."

"Don't tell anyone, but her husband has awful money problems and she was assaulted," Joan blurted out.

"*What? Did her husband attack her?*" Frank said in shock, and immediately stopped what he was doing.

"No, for *God's sake*. Are you listening to me, Frank?" Joan asked impatiently.

"I'm listenin' to every word. Now, will you slow down and tell me properly. I'll put on the kettle and you can tell me the whole story."

Joan nodded and went to find her mother's china in the press. Distracted by Eileen's news, she stumbled on the mat and came very close to sending her treasured cups and saucers flying. Joan let out a scream as Frank steadied her and gently took them off her. "Sit down, love. I'll make the tea," Frank instructed and steered her towards the chair.

They both breathed a sigh of relief that a near-catastrophe had been averted. Frank returned to the kettle and made a strong pot of tea. When they were both sitting with a cup in hand, he started again.

"Now, will you tell me properly what's goin' on?" Frank asked.

Joan proceeded to tell Frank about Eileen's long litany of disasters.

"God almighty, the poor woman. Can we do *anything*?" Frank asked.

"She was talking like a robot, Frank, like she was reading the weather forecast. I don't think it's really hit her, you know? I mean she only found out about the affair this evening," Joan said. Joan sniffled and blew her nose.

"*Jaysus*, I never heard the like. And they're solicitors aren't they? A right crowd from the sounds of it," Frank said and shook his head like he had had a lucky escape.

"Where is she now?" Frank asked.

"At home. She won't let him back in the house tonight. She's going away for a few days on her own at the weekend," Joan said in a low voice.

"Do you want to call over and see her? I'll drive. You're in no fit state, love," Frank said.

"No, she said she wants to be on her own tonight. You should've heard her Frank. She was all business, talking about moving out and renting a house. I'm going to meet her on Saturday. I think she's going to leave him. Oh God, poor Eileen," Joan said, and her tears dropped into her cup of tea.

"*Jaysus,* that's a bit sudden, isn't it? Well, maybe it's not if he's been at it for a year. Christ almighty, shouldn't he be the one movin' out if he did the dirt?" Frank asked.

"I know. Still, I'm telling you there was no talking to her. She asked if we knew anyone renting."

"Sure, how would we know anyone *renting a house*? You couldn't find a house for love or money these days. Aren't they only saying it on the news every day? If that was me, I'd be givin' him the boot out the door," Frank bellowed.

"Well you're not her, Frank, but if you ever did something like that, I'd definitely throw you out," Joan declared.

Frank smiled, knowing that would be the last thing she would do. "What sort of a man is he, to go off with a woman much younger than him when he has a beautiful wife and two young daughters at home?" Frank said.

Frank was instantly reminded of his own near-miss with Kate from the factory a few years back. He had been flutered drunk, which wasn't his style, but they had just been made redundant. Still there was no excuse. Nothing had happened and he had made a quick escape. It sounded like Eileen's husband hadn't copped himself on, and for a year at that. That was no mistake.

"Well, she's better off without him from the sounds of it. A lovely woman like her will have no problem meetin' someone else. *Jaysus*, he must have been out of his mind, unless she's a *total psychopath*?"

"That's an awful thing to say, Frank," Joan interjected. "We have to try and help her. Eileen doesn't sound like she has anyone else. Oh Frank, isn't life so unfair?" Joan asked. Frank squeezed Joan's hand.

"Well that's for sure, Joan, but sure who ever said life was fair?"

Eileen sat at the kitchen table making a list of everything she needed to do. With the girls in bed and the house to herself, she knew she needed to make a plan. She scribbled *Clare - Job* on the paper and prayed that her meeting would go well tomorrow. Eileen saw the irony in applying to work in a law firm that specialised in family law at the same time that her own family was falling apart. Maybe the gods were looking down on her after all.

Rent house was next on the list and the most urgent. She had just hung up the phone to Joan and she thanked her lucky stars for her friend. Fragile as she was, Joan was kind and Eileen didn't have a lot of that in her life right now. Eileen didn't hold out much hope on her knowing anyone renting a house, but it was worth a try. Joan had been close to tears when she broke the news to her. However, Eileen bit her lip, determined not to join her. Eileen would save her tears for the times she will now lie alone in bed. Eileen looked at her phone and saw the string of texts that Dave had been sending all night. She switched it off and was determined to pull the landline out of the wall if Dave dared to call.

Eileen added *hotel* to her list and went online to book somewhere for the weekend. She found a room quite easily but paid over the odds for it. Eileen felt like retching at the thought of Dave wining and dining Julie in hotels around the country. She had considered upgrading to a suite, considering all the money he had squandered but decided against it. If Eileen really wanted to stoop to his level, she would be picking up some young buck while she was at it. All she would have to do is click her fingers.

She hadn't thought about Fran Daly in a few hours, but with the way she felt right then, she could have marched straight down to the Garda station and reported him.

****

Delighted with Franks' invitation to dinner, Séamus walked the short journey to their house, armed with a bottle of wine and a bunch of flowers for Joan. He almost collided with Johnny as he marched out the front gate fizzing with high octane energy. Séamus recognised the angry 'I don't give a shit about the world' expression that Séamus had worn himself when he was younger.

"Hey there, Johnny," Seamus said and slapped Johnny's back.

"Hi, Séamus," Johnny replied, nervously looking at his feet.

Séamus couldn't help noticing a bounce in the young boy's step like a champion boxer before stepping in the ring.

"Are you heading out for the evening?" Séamus asked.

"Yeah. That was class by the way, on Wednesday night," Johnny mumbled.

"Thanks. Remember, I'm around if you want to experiment a bit, try out a few instruments," Séamus said.

"*Really?* I've only ever messed around on the drums, years ago," Johnny said and looked at Séamus. A smile spread across Johnny's face.

"Well, it's never too late to learn. Trust me. I was older than you are when I first picked up the fiddle," Séamus said.

"*You were?*"

"As I said, it's never too late. Call up to Tigh Neachtain some Wednesday and we'll have a right chat," Seamus said and shook Johnny's hand.

Séamus stood for a short while to watch the troubled teenager strut up the road. There was no doubt in his mind that Johnny was up to something. He could smell it off him. Please God Johnny would take him up on his offer before he found himself in any serious bother.

Séamus rang the bell and was still thinking about Johnny when the door opened.

"Séamus, come in. It's great to see you," Frank said, delighted to see his friend.

Joan had insisted Frank make an extra special effort. Joan had laid his good white shirt on the bed along with a beige pair of trousers. Frank shifted uncomfortably on the doorstep as the starched collar irritated his neck.

"You're looking swell, Frank," Séamus said, taking in Frank's jaunty appearance.

"And you're not lookin' too bad yourself, for a yank and all," Frank said and laughed before leading Séamus into the living room.

The fire was lit and Séamus looked around the cosy room. It brought back memories of his own humble beginnings in a house with very little money, but a lot of love.

"Is this the famous Abbie?" Séamus asked.

Séamus' face lit up when he saw Abbie sprawled on the couch with her leg stretched out on a cushion. Her green eyes shone as Séamus handed her a gift of a ukulele.

"Oh, thank you. *Wow*, I've always wanted one. My friend Saoirse has a ukulele," Abbie said in delight.

"Well, I hear you can teach yourself to play these days courtesy of YouTube, not like in our day, isn't that right, Frank?"

Having no children of his own, Séamus never tired of seeing a child's face light up with happiness over the simplest of things.

"You can say that for sure, Séamus. I've never even seen Youtunes."

"YouTube, Dad," Abbie said and giggled.

Joan rushed in from the kitchen hearing all the commotion. "Mam, look what Séamus gave me," Abbie said, lifting up the ukulele.

"Oh, that's very generous, Séamus. There was no need."

Séamus handed Joan the wine and flowers as he greeted her with a peck on the cheek. Joan couldn't hide her delight and blushed.

"You're a real show-stopper tonight, Joan," Séamus complimented her, noticing that she looked a lot more laid back than in the pub on Wednesday night. Séamus thought that Joan must have taken a leaf out of Mary's book as he took in the floaty shirt that was covered in colourful flowers and her faded jeans.

"Oh, this old thing, but thank you," Joan said.

Joan was glad of the Xanax she had taken earlier. Between Eileen's news and the dinner tonight, Joan felt that she couldn't have coped otherwise. Just then, Cyril breezed in, hoping to make a quick exit out the front door.

"Séamus, this is Cyril, the real gaffer in the family. Isn't that right, son?" Frank remarked. Cyril made a face when he heard the word gaffer.

"Are you off to a weddin'?" Frank jested, examining his clean cut and well-dressed son. A set of overalls for the garage was normally his preferred item of clothing.

"Nowhere special. Just meeting a couple of friends," Cyril said. He smiled at Séamus and went to shake his hand.

"Nice to meet you, Cyril. You've the look of a man on a date I'd say," Séamus said and immediately regretted having said it when he saw the look on Cyril's face.

"A date!" Frank said and laughed. "I think our Cyril's idea of a date is having his head under the bonnet of a car with Bill our local mechanic. Isn't that right son?"

Cyril blushed and made his excuses. He had no intention of hanging around for an interrogation in case his loved-up demeanour might give the game away. Cyril wasn't yet ready to share the magical Linda with anyone. Séamus looked at him apologetically for nearly letting the cat out of the bag. Séamus knew only too well the look of a man in love. As Cyril made his escape, Mary arrived at the front door.

A vibrant apparition, Séamus did a double take as he took her in. Mary had a beautiful green silk shawl draped around her shoulders and her hair was held in place with clips that were decorated with sparkling butterflies. Mary didn't want to look like she had made too great an effort and had dithered for some time in front of the mirror earlier as she decided what to do with her hair.

"Well, aren't you a sight for sore eyes," Frank said, breaking the silence.

"Mary's joining us for dinner, or should I say has cooked the dinner. We'd be lost without her and all the work she does around the house," Frank said. Joan shot Frank a filthy look.

"That's awesome. What a nice surprise," Séamus said and tried to keep the excitement out of his voice. "You've a busy house, Frank. I haven't seen as much coming and going except at one of my concerts," Séamus said and laughed.

"This is something else, Mary," Frank announced when they were all sitting down at the table. Joan elbowed him, but he looked away. "What do think, Séamus?" Frank asked.

"All I can say is you better not expect me to return the favour," Séamus said and smiled at Mary as he picked up his napkin. "Where did you learn to cook like this?" he asked.

"Aw, stop. I'm sure you're well able to cook. What did you do all those years in America?" Mary asked.

Mary had noticed the sulky look on Joan's face and deliberately changed the focus of the conversation.

"Well, I did a bit, but just simple food like steak and fries, nothing like this," Séamus declared, helping himself to more of her beef stew.

"Nothin' wrong with a good steak, Séamus," Frank said through a mouthful of food.

"What was it like over there, *really*?" Mary asked, curious to learn more about this mysterious man.

"What was it like? It's hard to describe in a few words. It's big, that's for sure. We're a drop in the ocean on our little island in comparison."

Séamus had only been too happy to lose himself in the city of New York after the claustrophobia of growing up in Ireland.

"Did it feel like home at all?" Frank asked, trying to imagine what living the American dream must be like.

"It did, but only after about 10 years," Séamus admitted.

Séamus looked faraway as he remembered the lost years, those years when he had done his best to kick off the shackles of home.

"That can't have been easy," Mary said and looked at him sympathetically.

"It wasn't, but you know I think it made me in the end. I loved their positivity and their can-do attitude. I can tell you that I wouldn't have been successful if I had stayed here, that's for sure. I couldn't take any more of the garbage we were being fed back then in Ireland," Séamus said.

There was silence as they all contemplated his words. Each of them wondered about the path their life might have taken if they had left Irish shores and ventured into unknown terrain.

Séamus noticed the impact of his words among his table mates.

"Fuck the begrudgers! Pardon my French. That was my attitude back then, I've let all that anger go. It mightn't look like it, but this is the new improved version of Séamus Feeney," he said.

"*Jaysus*, you hid it well back then," Frank jested. He couldn't believe the transformation in his old friend, a friend who had struggled to find his way in the world when he was young.

"That's the problem, Frank. We're masters at hiding what's really going on. I did a lot of therapy over there and it changed my life. Now, enough of me…" he said at the very point in the conversation that Joan and Mary hung on his every word.

"What about you, Mary? What do you like to do?" Séamus asked.

"Me? Oh, I don't know. Simple things… my garden, cooking, this gang now and Boots my cat," Mary said.

Mary gave Frank a warning look when she spotted the mischievous glint in his eye. Mary was well used to the cat comments.

"Don't say anything, Frank, or I'll clatter you…" Mary said.

"My lips are sealed. You see, Séamus. It's the women here in Ireland who really rule the roost. Isn't that so, Joan?" Frank remarked and nudged Joan after noticing how quite she was.

"What?" Joan asked and looked up at him through bleary eyes. The heady combination of wine and the Xanax had taken effect.

"I said you're the boss, love. You're the boss of me," Frank said. Frank reached over, took her hand and smiled.

"Love's young dream, you two. You don't know how good you have it. It's a tough world out there for us single folk. Mary and I know all about that, don't we?" Séamus remarked and winked at Mary.

"Speak for yourself," Mary said with a glint in her eye. "I was made an offer by Paddy in the bar the other night."

"I've no doubt you were. You better add singing to your list of talents, Mary. It's a shame not to share such a beautiful voice. By the way, folks, Mary's coming down to sing a few songs tomorrow night in Tigh Neachtain. We're having a fundraiser for a children's charity. You might join us," Séamus announced.

"We'll see. We might just put the feet up and leave you two young ones to live it up," Frank said, watching the banter with interest.

Frank glanced over at Joan, who was now on the verge of dozing off.

"I think it's time for a cup of tea. Séamus, why don't you and Mary head into the fire? We'll follow you in," Frank said.

Mary stood up and started to clear the dishes.

"Leave those, Mary. You've done enough. Joan and I will look after them," Frank said and waved them out of the room. Joan stirred at the mention of her name.

"Yes, yes," Joan said.

"Are you alright, love? Have a cup of coffee, will you? You'll thank me tomorrow," Frank said.

Joan gripped the sink as she poured herself a glass of water. "*Of course*, I'm alright, Frank. *Don't be fussing*. I'm just a bit tired that's all," Joan snapped. She rubbed her eyes and let out a yawn.

"Well, if you're alright, did you see how those two are gettin' on like a house on fire? I've a sixth sense about these things, Joan," Frank said and made a strong mug of coffee and handed it to Joan.

Joan took a large mouthful and felt the caffeine kickstart her system.

"Oh, I almost forgot. I should say something to them about Eileen. You know about her looking for a house to rent," Joan said as she drained the mug.

"I don't know, love. She mightn't appreciate you blabbin' her business to every Tom, Dick and Harry."

"*They're not* every Tom, Dick and Harry *for God's sake.* You never know, they might know someone who can help," Joan said.

Frank wondered how a musician who had only returned home after years living abroad and a woman who had lived like a hermit for the last twenty years could be of any help to her friend Eileen, but he thought better of saying it.

When they were settled in front of the fire with mugs of tea, Joan picked her moment when Frank had gone up to check on Abbie.

"Seeing as you're both here I wanted to ask you something," Joan said, looking at them with a serious expression on her face.

"Is everything okay?" Mary asked.

"It's not me. It's a friend. You know the friend I mentioned during the week. She's going through a rough time and is looking for a place to rent with her two daughters. You know how hard it is these days, what with all the homeless and all, but she is pretty desperate. I just thought you might know of somebody or could ask around," Joan asked.

"Surely, they're not being *turfed out on the street already? Those bankers have a lot to answer for, putting profit before people at every turn*," Mary said, indignantly.

"Well, not exactly…" Joan said and hesitated, trying to calculate how much to say.

"What about *that husband* of hers? Or *is he the cause* of all her problems?" Mary asked.

"Surely the banks give you a bit of warning. They can't just evict her from her house," Séamus added.

"I can't really go into it. Since you don't know her, I'll just say that she needs some time away from her husband. He, he…" Joan's said, her voice now cracking.

"*What is it*, Joan? You're among friends, you know that," Mary said.

"Oh, I shouldn't say anything. Frank will be annoyed with me, please say you won't tell a soul?"

"I don't know if I can be of any help, Joan, I'm only back a wet week, but please don't upset yourself. Tell us whatever feels right and trust that neither of us will breathe a word," Séamus said calmly, and he looked over at Mary who nodded in agreement.

"She's just found out that on top of *everything else* her husband is having an affair. *Can you believe it?*" Joan asked. She brushed away the tears.

"*What?*" Mary asked in disbelief.

Mary had pushed the image of Dave Danaher with another woman to the back of her mind, thinking she might have misconstrued what she saw.

"Pardon me, but am I missing something? *Surely*, he should be the one to leave," Séamus remarked and leaned forward in his chair, trying to understand.

"I don't know all the details to be honest. She just told me that she's looking for somewhere to stay for a while," Joan said.

Just then, Frank walked into the room and with a quick glance at Joan's tear-streaked face, he sighed and sat down, putting his arm protectively around her. A smile crept across Frank's face as he sat with Joan. Very few people knew the darkness she had struggled with all her life, but Frank did.

"I wouldn't know anyone renting a house, Joan. I hardly meet a soul as it is. To be honest, it isn't a big surprise to me that he's having an affair," Mary said.

They all turned to Mary, Mary who supposedly lived like a hermit. The room went silent.

"What do you mean?" Joan gasped.

Mary took a deep breath and proceeded to tell them about the scene she had witnessed on Monday evening. She was in no doubt it was Dave Danaher as he had marched right past her, his face boiling with anger.

"*Jaysus,* Mary. You're a *right turn up* for the books," Frank said more impressed by Mary with each passing day.

"I didn't say anything, Joan, because I couldn't be one hundred percent sure of what was going on. It was dark and… I'm not one for sticking my nose in someone else's business," Mary said and looked at Joan, hoping she wouldn't be annoyed.

"You did the right thing, Mary, as far as I can see. Too many people spend their days stickin' their nose in things that have nothin' to do with them," Frank butted in, directing his words at Joan before she had a chance to open her mouth and disagree.

"God help her. Tom knew her father-in-law well. He was a tough businessman, but he had integrity, unlike that son," Mary said, fuming.

Joan shivered. Eileen's story was a stark reminder that marriage didn't protect you from the prospect of infidelity and heartache. Now, here it was almost on her doorstep.

"He's a bastard, that's what he is," Joan said and almost spat out the words. Frank patted her on the arm.

"We're not *all* like that love, isn't that so Séamus?" Frank remarked.

Seamus nodded and smiled.

"But how do I help her? She's going away on her own this weekend," Joan said. "She's staying in a hotel and leaving him with the two girls, *but she can't stay in a hotel forever.*"

"I think I might have an idea," Mary said softly. "You know I'm in the house on my own. It's not as big as their house, I'm sure, still there are three bedrooms and they've been empty for well on fifteen years," Mary said. "Your friend can come and stay with me for a short while, for a few weeks anyway until she figures out what to do. That's if she wants to."

The words were hardly out of her mouth before she had time to think it through properly, but once she said them, she knew it was the right thing to do.

"Are you sure about that, Mary? You'll have no peace. *Mark my words*," Frank said.

"Frank, I've had enough peace and quiet to last me a lifetime. It'd do me good to have a bit of young blood around the place. I'm a changed woman since I started coming here," Mary declared confidently.

"Oh, Mary, that's a great idea!" Joan exclaimed, and almost jumped out of the chair to hug her.

"I think you should take the night to think about it. You don't know what you're letting yourself in for," Frank said and wondered how much wine Mary drank.

Mary, however, had the assured look of a woman who wouldn't change her mind. Séamus, who hadn't said much during the exchange, looked at her admiringly. Séamus had a sneaking suspicion that the subject of their discussion and the woman he had chatted to yesterday was one and the same. Galway was indeed a small place. There was no chance in hell of that happening in New York.

SEVENTEEN

Cyril's mouth dropped open when Linda greeted him at the door. She looked like she was just fresh out of the shower and the heady smell of her apple shampoo filled the air. Linda's hair was damp and piled in a knot on the top of her head. She wore a long grey cardigan that was belted tightly and only further emphasised her tiny waist. Cyril thought Linda looked almost saintly as he took in her alabaster skin and perfect features. However, the glint in her eyes gave the game away. The last word anyone would use to describe Linda was saintly.

"Well, don't just stand there gawping, handsome, come on in," Linda said and pulled Cyril into the house before he could find his words. Linda had invited Cyril over with reassurances that her parents were out and wouldn't be back until late. Cyril didn't feel remotely ready to be introduced to them as her boyfriend when he was only coming to terms with the fact himself.

"I hope I'm not too early," Cyril said, peering around almost expecting one of her parents to jump out of the shadows.

Linda's house was a beautiful, old period home set in its own well-tended grounds on the edge of the city. Cyril inhaled deeply as he took in the expansive hallway and the chandeliers that hung precariously above his head.

"Not at all. We have the place to ourselves, except for Fi," Linda said, and pointed towards the left-hand side of the living room. "She won't bother us though," Linda said, whispering. "Fi, this is my friend, Cyril," Linda announced.

Linda pushed Cyril into the room in front of her sister. He didn't feel very enthusiastic about meeting her after what Linda had told him. Fi was much the same age as Abbie, but she didn't sound anything like his charming little sister. Fi reluctantly tore her attention away from her tablet and practically scowled at Cyril. She looked like a smaller, angrier version of Linda with the same trademark red hair, but without the dazzling looks. Cyril knew he shouldn't compare them, but the big puss on her face certainly didn't do her any favours.

"Hi, how are you?" Cyril asked, brightly.

"Hi," Fi muttered and then turned back to her screen.

"Come on," Linda said and directed her eyes up to heaven. "We'll leave her to it. I'm starving and I've a pizza in the oven," she said.

Linda led Cyril down the hall, opening a door into the largest kitchen he had ever seen in his life. He gasped at the expansive room that looked out onto a garden of even more gigantic proportions. Linda opened the oven and took out the pizza, placing it on the island in the centre of the room. Cyril watched her and shivered involuntarily as he tried to process the wealth of her family. It definitely didn't look like DoneDeal had been involved in the furnishing of this house.

"I'm telling you, these are the most amazing pizzas ever. Mum buys them in a local deli. I bet you wouldn't find better in Italy. I'll see soon enough anyway. We're going to Rome during the Christmas holidays," Linda said as she sliced the pizza, oblivious to Cyril's stunned expression.

All Cyril could think of was the selection of Dominos pizzas that were stacked in their freezer at home and only taken out as a major treat. He dreaded to think what Linda might make of his own pokey home and the kitchen that was probably the size of their bathroom. Linda didn't sound like she had any great interest in the material aspects of life, but that's a lot easier when you were surrounded by the best of everything.

"It's pretty fantastic," Cyril agreed as he bit into the luscious pizza. Tomato sauce dribbled down his chin.

"I told you so. Now, when we're finished, I need your help with something," Linda said as she started on her second slice.

"What is it?" Cyril asked and looked up from his plate.

"I want to put a portfolio together, you know of all the clothes I've designed, and I need you to be my photographer. You can be my business partner if you like. When I'm famous you'll be glad you met me," Linda announced as she reached across flirtatiously and wiped the sauce from his face. Cyril blushed and felt an ache of desire, which he had never experienced before.

"*Photographer?*" Cyril stuttered, "I don't know *anything* about taking photographs. *I've hardly ever* used a camera, not even on my phone."

"It's a doddle. I'll show you. I can't do it on my own. Please, I want to put them on Instagram and Facebook. My eventual plan is to have a website, but this will do for now," Linda said, and her eyes were shining as she gushed about her plans.

Cyril noticed that they were darker and now looked like the green of the sea on a stormy day, he hoped not a premonition of any trouble on the horizon.

"You've it all worked out, haven't you?" Cyril said and grinned at her as she finished off the last of the pizza.

"Yes, I do. You need a plan. Things don't just happen by themselves you know," Linda said emphatically.

"I suppose they don't," Cyril said, feeling out of his depth.

"Dad taught me that," Linda said. "You met him in the garage. He has his own business. He's a designer, you know, ads and stuff. Maybe he could help you when you have your own garage… to come up with a clever name. He's won lots of awards."

"*My own garage?* At this stage, I'd just be glad to work for Bill," Cyril said, regretting his lacklustre words once they were out of his mouth.

Cyril's parents hadn't exactly instilled any entrepreneurial notions in him. His Dad had been a factory worker for many years, like his own father before him, so the idea of being your own boss was an alien concept in their family.

"Yeah, but down the road. If you don't think about it, it'll never happen," Linda said forcefully. Linda then stood up to clear away the plates.

"I guess, but that's a while away yet," Cyril said.

Cyril imagined Linda tiring of his laid-back nature fairly quickly as she set her sights on taking over the world.

"There's no time like the present. Now, let's take some photos," Linda said, placing her hands on her hips.

"Okay, I'll do my best," Cyril said, trying to muster some enthusiasm.

"That's the spirit. They'll be amazing, I know they will. Now, come on."

Cyril followed Linda out of the kitchen and up the wide staircase towards her bedroom.

"Are you sure your parents are okay with this?" Cyril asked nervously.

"They're fine. Take a chill pill, Cyril," Linda said.

Linda stepped inside her room, walked over to the desk and turned on her laptop. Cyril surveyed the room, taking in what looked like a mosquito net around a large double bed that was piled high with teddies. Colourful was what came to mind as his senses were assaulted by the bright red furnishings, colourful art on the wall and Linda's signature apple scent that pervaded the room.

Linda handed Cyril the camera and without being in any way self-conscious, Linda slipped off her clothes and reached into the wardrobe for the first of her creations. Cyril practically fell against the door as he watched her, feeling powerless to avert his gaze. His eyes travelled over every inch of Linda's muscular body, hungry to memorise every square inch of it. Although Cyril had seen naked women online, this was the first time he had seen one in the flesh, and she was standing grinning at him only a few feet away. Cyril was struck by Linda's confidence and how comfortable she was in her own skin. For sure, Linda was nothing like the woman who had reared him, or indeed any other woman he knew.

Linda pulled on this new creation and sashayed across the room. Cyril felt giddy as he watched her hips sway with every step. His appreciation made itself known through the growing bulge in the front of his trousers and looking down, Cyril was mortified. He pulled his shirt out in an effort to disguise his excitement and as he did so, Linda gave him a knowing wink.

Cyril spent the next couple of hours clicking as Linda strutted and changed outfits until there were none left.

"That's it," Linda declared, looking into the wardrobe. "Now, let's see my works of art," she said excitedly.

Linda grabbed the camera off Cyril, eager to transfer the results to her laptop.

"I can't wait to see them," Linda shrieked.

"Come on. I'm the photographer. Let me do it," Cyril said and feeling frisky, he grabbed the camera off her.

"Stop Cyril, I'm doing it." Linda feigned annoyance and put her arms around him from behind, took the camera from his hands and then held it above her head.

"Okay, okay, have it your way," Cyril laughed and sat down on the edge of the bed as he struggled to calm himself down.

"Oh, look. They're fantastic. I love them," Linda gushed.

Cyril watched as Linda sat cross legged at the desk, nibbling on her nails as she scrolled down through the photos. He looked around the room, determined to memorise every detail of this magical moment.

"You look fantastic," Cyril said.

"I do, don't I?" Linda remarked. "*Done*," she announced and hit the return button to post them online.

"I think I love you more than I ever did before," Linda said.

Linda turned around, and before Cyril knew what was happening, Linda stood up and reached her hand inside his shirt. Linda then took his hand and pushed Cyril down on his back. Cyril felt every nerve ending in his body tingle and gulped.

"Take it easy, Linda. Your sister is downstairs," Cyril said, breathing heavily.

Although Cyril had kissed girls before that was as far as it had gone. He was both eager and nervous at the same time. There was a flood of emotions and thoughts streaming through his body and mind.

"Don't mind her. She won't be budging any time soon. She's addicted to that thing," Linda said and sat on top of Cyril, pinning him to the bed.

Linda pulled her dress over her head, much to Cyril's delight. Cyril felt he couldn't contain himself for much longer but wanted more than anything for this experience to continue. As Linda opened the buttons on his jeans, Cyril began to shake.

"What are you doing?" Cyril said but desperately wanted Linda to continue.

Linda opened his jeans and pulled them down, and Cyril willingly obliged. Linda flung the jeans across the room.

"I haven't done it before, have you?" Linda whispered in Cyril's ear.

"No, well not exactly…" Cyril stuttered.

Linda reached forward and nuzzled Cyril's neck. Cyril couldn't help a snort of nervous laughter escaping.

"Oh, you like that do you?" Linda said and opening his shirt, she continued to kiss every inch of his chest, just stopping at the top of his underwear. Cyril moaned, willing her to go on.

"You're not as innocent as I thought, Cyril Hughes," Linda teased.

"You're no angel yourself, but I'm not complaining," Cyril gasped breathlessly.

"I can see that. Well, there's a first time for everything and we like each other, don't we?" Linda said.

Linda put her hand down his boxers and despite the fear of being caught, Cyril didn't want her to stop. Linda was gorgeous and she wanted him. There could be a lot worse ways to lose your virginity than with a beautiful girl, who seemed to have the hots for you.

"Slow down, Linda. *Are you sure?*" Cyril asked, his father's voice ringing in his ears. "The woman has to be sure," Cyril said.

Linda ignored him and pulled her hair loose and it now fanned across Cyril's face.

"We don't have much time. My parents will be home soon," Linda whispered in Cyril's ear. At the word parents, Cyril came to his senses.

"*Jesus*, Linda, when are they due back?" Cyril croaked.

"Not for ages, they're never home before eleven," Linda said and stopped as if she had suddenly realised something.

"What time is it? What time is it Cyril?" Linda said, frantically.

"It's quarter to, why?" Cyril asked, looking at his watch.

"*Get up. Get dressed.* Quickly! I forgot they said they'd be back early tonight. Did you hear a car?" Linda asked and pushed him off the bed. Cyril landed awkwardly on the floor with a loud thump.

"No, I don't know. *For fecks sake*, Linda," Cyril snapped.

Cyril struggled to his feet and looked around the room for his jeans.

A knock sounded on the bedroom door.

"Fi, *is that you?*" Linda asked. "I'll be down in a minute. Just finishing up on my laptop," Linda called out as she threw on her dressing gown.

"It's Mum. Fi said you had a friend visiting, a boy. What are you doing in your room, Linda?" her mother asked from the opposite side of the door.

Cyril tried to think of a faintly plausible excuse for standing almost buck naked in their daughter's bedroom but came up empty.

"Quick, quick," Linda hissed. "Under the bed."

Cyril spotted his jeans in the corner and grabbed them. He pulled them on as Linda gestured at him to hide.

"I was just changing, Mum. Give me a minute," Linda waited until Cyril was safely under the bed before opening the door.

Cyril could feel his heart thumping so loudly in his chest that he was sure Linda's mother would hear it.

"*What's going on, Linda? Who said anything* about bringing a boy home when we're not in the house, *and to your bedroom!*" Linda's mother barked, looking past Linda and scanning the room.

"*How many times do we have to have this conversation?* If it wasn't for Fiona, *we'd never know* what you are up to half the time."

Cyril cowered under the bed, afraid to breathe. He didn't want to think what Linda's mother might do to him if she found him. Cyril had no idea what she looked like, but he imagined a huge sumo wrestler type woman who would floor him in a second.

"Jesus Christ!" Cyril yelled inside his head.

"He's gone home Mum, relax. He's just a friend and he was helping me out on my laptop. *Look*," Linda said, and she pointed to all the pictures that were displayed on screen.

Cyril listened in amazement to Linda talking to her mother as if butter wouldn't melt in her mouth.

"Well, *that's not what Fiona said. She said he was still here. I mean it Linda, I've had enough of your lies and it stops now*," Linda's mother snapped.

"Give it a rest, Mum. There's nothing going on. You need to chill a bit," Linda replied.

"*How dare you?*"

Cyril heard a loud slap. There was silence and then the sound of Linda softly crying. Cyril felt every muscle in his body tense with revulsion and he put his hand over his mouth to quieten a yell.

"I'm sorry, love. Look what you made me do. Why do you have to drive me to this every time?" Linda's mother asked in a soft voice.

"Leave me alone, Mum. There is no one here," Linda said, sobbing and sat down on the side of the bed.

"Let me see. Did I hurt you?" Her mother asked and moved towards her, but Linda pushed her away.

"*Please* leave me alone. I'm okay. I just want to go to bed," Linda said.

"Is everything okay up there?" Linda's father called up from downstairs.

"Please, Linda," Linda's mother quietly begged, and she locked eyes with her daughter. Linda looked at her mother and felt her anger dissolve as she saw her mother tremble at the prospect of her grubby little secret being discovered. Linda knew that her mother would never forgive her if she betrayed her.

"It's fine, Dad," Linda called out. "Isn't it, Mum?"

"Yes, everything's fine, Seán. I'll be down in a minute," her mother answered.

Cyril knew that it wasn't the first time this had happened, and that Linda's father had no idea at all.

"Please leave me alone," Linda whimpered.

"I'm so sorry, darling. Please don't say anything to your father, I didn't mean it. I love you."

Cyril heard the door click but was afraid to move. He was sickened by what he had heard. There was no sound from Linda, so after a minute Cyril crept out from under the bed. Linda was stretched out on her bed, her arms behind her head. Cyril rubbed his eyes finding it hard to compute what was going on.

"Linda, are you okay? Did she *hit you*?" Cyril asked.

Linda stood up, locked the door and sat back on the bed.

"Yes, I'm okay. She just has a bit of a temper," Linda said.

"*What? Do you hear* yourself? It's not *okay!*" Cyril insisted. Linda started crying. "Does your father know?"

"Of course not. I couldn't tell him. It would ruin everything, and they would blame me," Linda said.

"You're not to blame. *Don't be crazy*. You need to say something to him. It's not on," Cyril said and moved to give her a hug, but Linda pulled away.

"Look, you better go, Cyril. There's a tree outside my window. It's safe. You can leave by the side gate. Nobody will see you. I've used it myself plenty of times," Linda said. Cyril looked at Linda.

"Go on. Don't worry about me. I can look after myself. I always have," Linda insisted.

Cyril opened his mouth to speak but heard footsteps on the landing, so he opened the window and climbed out.

Cyril ran down the road and passed the park. He saw Johnny hanging around a bush with Jack at the edge of the park but kept going. His mind and emotions raced, and he needed space to work out all that happened.

"So, you finally decided to turn up. I thought I'd have to go looking for you," Brian McCabe said, walking towards them with his backup in tow.

Brian always had a ballsy attitude when he wasn't alone.

Johnny smirked at him as he sat on the wall swinging his legs. Jack sat expressionless beside him. He had his hand on his pocket, eager to make the payoff and be out of the park before dark.

"Look, we're here now, and we have your money. Can we just do this?" Jack asked and reached for the envelope, struggling to keep his voice steady.

"I like your style, Jack. The pity muttonhead beside you isn't as cooperative," Brian McCabe sneered.

Johnny clenched his fists, itching to wipe the smile off McCabe's face.

"*Cool it*," Jack whispered to Johnny, feeling the adrenaline releasing from his friend's every pore.

"I'm surprised your Mammy let you out tonight, Johnny. It must be well past your bedtime," Brian McCabe said, delighting in taunting him.

"*Fuck off*, McCabe," Johnny retorted. "At least my mother isn't a whore. What's that like having a mother for a whore and some perv for a father?" Johnny asked. His eyes flashed angrily, and his fists clenched.

"*You bastard! Who do you think you are*, you jumped up *piece of shit?*"

McCabe made a move towards Johnny, but Johnny jumped off the wall, dying for any excuse to throw a punch. As he did, Brian McCabe caught him on the side of the jaw with his fist and Johnny stumbled back against the wall. A few more punches landed on him before he had time to catch his balance.

"Leave him alone will you, *for fucks sake*. Just take your money and go!" Jack shouted and leaning forward to jump off the wall, he was caught in the crossfire. Receiving a sharp elbow in the face, Jack fell backwards landing on the side of the road. The fight was forgotten as Jack lay on the ground motionless.

"*Jack. Jesus, Jack are you okay?*" Johnny shouted, and staggered to a stand.

"*Get up*, Jack. Stop messing! Johnny shouted, but there was no response. He jumped over the wall and shook Jack's limp body. "Look *what you fuckers did*. Call an ambulance, someone call an ambulance!" Johnny yelled. Brian McCabe stood rooted to the spot and then gathering his wits about him, beckoned his cronies and made a run for it. Brian McCabe had no intention of taking the rap. Johnny fumbled with his phone as an older man walked by with a dog and stopped.

"Hey there, son. What's going on?" he asked.

Taking one look at Jack lying on the ground the man reacted quickly, pulled out his phone and called 999.

"I don't think he's breathing," Johnny said, trembling. "*Jack, Jack*, can you hear me? *Please*, wake up," Johnny called.

"Take it easy, lad. The ambulance is on the way. He might just be knocked out," the man said and knelt down and gently moved Johnny to one side. "Let me have a look," he said and leaned over and checked Jack out. "It's okay, he's breathing, and he has a pulse but it's weak. I don't see any sign of blood or any major cuts on his head, but it's hard to tell in the dark," the man said. He pulled off his jacket and put it over Jack.

"Where's the ambulance, *for fuck's sake?*" Johnny cried and stood up, frantically scanning the road.

"It's my fault! I caused this mess. *Jesus, Jack,* I'm sorry, I'm *so* sorry," Johnny said and was still apologising profusely when the ambulance pulled up minutes later.

"We'll take it from here, son," the crew said and moved swiftly, putting Jack on a stretcher and whisking him away to the hospital.

Johnny didn't remember handing his phone to the man, his father arriving or being driven to the hospital where they sat for hours waiting to hear the fate of his friend Jack.

Séamus and Mary had insisted on staying with Joan until word came from the hospital. Finally, at midnight the landline in the hall rang and Joan ran out to answer it.

"Frank, is that you? I thought you'd never call. *How is he?*" Joan asked frantically.

"Relax, love. The poor fella has a concussion, a broken arm, cracked ribs, and a lot of bruising, but the doctors say he'll be grand. I can tell you his poor parents were out of their minds. Can you imagine it?"

"Oh, poor Jack. And *Johnny?*" Joan asked hesitantly. Joan was almost afraid to find out what he had been up to now.

"There's devil a bit wrong with him, other than the cat has cut his tongue. I suppose he's in shock. *Jaysus,* I can't believe it. I'm back in the hospital again. Go on to bed, love. We won't be long. I'll talk to you in the mornin'."

"But *what were they doing,* Frank? I don't understand," Joan asked, but Frank had already hung up.

Joan put down the phone and blessed herself before going back in to share the good news.

"Thank you, God. Thank you, God for saving Jack," Joan said.

Despite her issues with the church, Joan was quick to turn to religion when the proverbial shit hit the fan.

"What's the news?" Mary jumped to her feet when Joan came in the door and was relieved to see a more relaxed expression on Joan's face.

"Jack will be fine, thank God. He has a broken arm and cracked ribs, but he's okay."

Joan sank into the armchair, sighing deeply as the worry of the last few hours subsided.

"What happened?" Mary asked.

"I don't know, Mary. Frank just hung up on me. I was mid-sentence and then, click…"

"I'm sure it's crazy up there. You know what the hospital is like. That's great news. At least the young lad's okay and Johnny too."

Mary looked at Séamus for support.

"Absolutely. As long as they're both okay, isn't that the main thing?" Séamus concurred and looked at his watch.

"Now, with that good news, I think I better make tracks. It's nearly midnight. Mary, can I walk you down?" Séamus asked and stood up. Mary smiled warmly at him and nodded.

"Try and sleep, Joan, and I'll check in with you tomorrow," Mary said. She picked up her bag and moved towards the door.

"Sorry, where are my manners?" Joan asked and walked them out to the front door.

"Thank you for a wonderful evening… I mean… except for that poor lad, Jack, but thank God they're both okay," Séamus said and leaned forward and kissed Joan on the cheek.

"Thank you both for staying with me. I'd have gone out of my mind here on my own," Joan said and turned to Mary. "And thanks so much for helping Eileen out. I can't wait to tell her tomorrow."

Joan and Mary hugged warmly and as Joan stood and watched Mary and Seamus walk down the path, she couldn't help thinking that Frank might just have been right about the two of them. She saw an easiness between the pair, an easiness that's usually the reserve of couples who have been together forever.

"God, that was some evening wasn't it?" Séamus said as they strolled down the road.

"You can say that for sure. I do love them, dearly, but there's never a dull moment in that house," Mary confessed.

They continued walking in silence, a silence that was punctuated only by the distant sound of raised voices. Their attention drifted to the other side of the river where an assortment of bars and restaurants eagerly catered to the locals who were out in force to let their hair down at the end of another week.

"Mary, tell me if I'm interfering, but are you sure about your offer, you know with that woman, Eileen? I mean it's very generous, but it'll be a big ask. It's not too late to change your mind. Anyone would understand," Séamus said.

His words jerked Mary back to the present. She came to a standstill and looked up at this tall, thoughtful man.

"You know, I thought about that. To be honest, if anyone had asked me a few weeks ago, there wouldn't be a chance in hell I'd have said yes," Mary admitted.

"So, what's changed?" Séamus asked.

Mary hesitated and pulled her shawl tighter around her against the cool night air.

"I didn't have a very happy childhood. You see, my father was a gambler. He spent every penny we had and when he lost, which was more often than not, my mother took the brunt of his frustration. I saw her being battered and beaten for years. I never did anything, because I was afraid he would turn on me. I know it's an awful thing to say, but it was the best day of my life, the day he died," Mary confided.

Mary was surprised at how easily she had opened up, and they both stood in silence for a few seconds before Séamus spoke.

"That must have been very difficult," Séamus said.

"I know that now, but back then I blamed myself… I could easily have ended up with a husband like my father, but thankfully I met Tom. He saved me I can tell you. There was no one you could talk to back then and my mother just wanted to forget. We never spoke about him ever again. You know what my mother said to me on her deathbed? I'm sorry, Mary. I should have left your father years ago, but I wasn't brave enough."

Mary's voice shook as she remembered sitting beside her mother before she took her last breath.

"She blamed herself you see, but back then there was nowhere for us to go. We had no money. It's not like now," Mary tried to explain.

"Well, she sounds like a very strong woman."

"She was. She was a wonderful mother. Eileen is being brave and doing what a lot of women wouldn't do… like my mother. I want to help her. It'll help me," Mary said, feeling the truth of her words.

Joan reluctantly left Frank with monosyllabic Johnny late the following morning and drove to meet Eileen at the hotel. Joan nervously pushed her hair behind her ears as she came through the double doors. She looked around for Eileen and spotted her sitting in a corner of the lobby.

"Hi, Joan. Thanks so much for coming," Eileen said.

Eileen put down her newspaper and stood up to greet Joan with a warm hug. Eileen wore a long, white linen shirt over a pair of leggings and Joan thought she looked more like a woman on a yoga retreat than facing a number of life crises all at once. "Hi, Eileen," Joan said, relaxing at the warm reception.

"Sit down, sit down. I'm telling you I've really needed these couple of days," Eileen gushed effusively.

"You look amazing, Eileen," Joan said, "and so calm."

"If you saw me yesterday, you wouldn't be saying that. I still don't know what upsets me the most, the affair, the money and then there's Fran Dempsey. Would you believe I almost forgot about him with everything else that has happened?" Eileen remarked and could feel her stomach tighten at the mere mention of his name.

"I really can't believe that your husband would have an affair. I mean being married to you of all people. It makes no sense," Joan admitted.

"Well, thank you I guess," Eileen said.

"Do you know who she is?" Joan asked.

"I finally wormed it out of him, a girl in the office. Of course, she's young and blonde. It's just so predictable," Eileen fumed, brushing her hair out of her eyes. "Would you believe he denied it outright until he knew that there was no point? That asshole Fran Daly hinted at it and then… well let's just say I found out and he had to admit it. Maybe I should be thanking Fran Daly after all, despite everything?"

"Don't say that, Eileen. He's a pervert. God, I'd be locked up at this stage if that happened to me," Joan said, and her shoulder started twitching again at the mere thought of it.

"Well, it's only beginning really, so don't hold your breath. I've to find somewhere to stay, tell the girls and start a new job. And on top of that, we have to sell the house. We're broke. So, a lot more can go wrong yet…" Eileen's voice trailed off as her words began to drain her of all energy.

"You have a new job? That's good news," Joan chirped.

"A silver lining to the episode with Fran Daly. It's a great practice. Would you believe, they specialise in family law? Maybe the gods were looking down on me after all and knew I'd need some help on that front," Eileen said.

"Do you mind me asking, Eileen? Why are you so definite about moving out of the house? Shouldn't *he* be the one to go?" Joan asked, strengthened by Séamus' words.

"I know, it sounds mad, considering he is the one who did the dirt, but I can't stay there Joan. That's the bottom line. I never liked the house and we're selling it anyway, but most of all…" Eileen said and hesitated. "I don't want to be the one left behind," Eileen said and paused as her voice cracked.

Eileen could feel the tears starting again. She brushed them away, frustrated with herself.

"Oh, Eileen, *I'm so sorry*. I didn't mean to upset you. It must be so hard. I really can't imagine it," Joan said, and reached over on the couch and hugged her.

The gesture of affection was almost too much for Eileen to bear and she gently untangled herself from Joan's embrace, wiping away her tears.

"Look, it is what it is. I *have* to be the one to leave. I just have to. I've no idea where I'm going to go, but I can't stay there," Eileen said.

"Well, I might have a solution for you," Joan said, eager to help. "I hope you don't mind, but after you called and said that you were looking, I mentioned it to Mary, you remember me talking about her?"

"The whole town probably knows already, Joan, so one more person isn't going to make any difference. Does she know of a place to rent?" Eileen perked up.

"Well, not exactly. She's living on her own, just down the road from us and she has lots of space. Mary said you can stay with her, at least until you find your own place. It would be perfect for you, Eileen. You're in town, near everything and I have to say, she's actually very nice," Joan explained.

"Stay with *her? Are you serious*, Joan? Does she know about the girls?"

"Yes, I told her all that. To be honest, I think she's a bit lonely. Mary's great with Abbie... Mary's offering you a place to live, Eileen," Joan emphasised, having expected Eileen to jump at the offer.

"That's a very generous offer. I didn't mean to sound ungrateful. It's just a surprise, that's all. But it's a good one. Yes, it's a very good one," Eileen said and sat back on the couch to let Joan's words sink in.

Eileen would obviously have to meet Mary and see that the place was suitable, but Eileen calculated that this could be the answer to one of her problems and a fairly urgent one at that. It did sound ideal, right beside the girl's school and her work.

"I know I gave out about her, Eileen, but I didn't really know her. To be honest I feel awful about it now. I think you would like each other, really I do," Joan encouraged.

"It all sounds almost too good to be true, but I'm telling you. Thanks so much, Joan, and yes I am interested," Eileen said. "I'd have to pay Mary something of course. Could I meet her tomorrow? I'm staying here tonight, and I told Dave I'd meet him at home tomorrow evening. It would be good to know what I'm doing when I speak to him."

There was an urgency to her words as she saw a plan taking shape. Eileen sat forward on the couch, her eyes darting around as she processed what this new possibility could mean for her and the girls.

"Of course, I'll call her when I go home. Are you sure, Eileen, that it's… you know… over? Is there any chance you'll go back to him?" Joan asked, not wanting to overstep.

"Am I sure? No," Eileen said. "Either way, I can't pretend like nothing has happened. How can I stay in the house with him and play happy families? I need some time apart to figure out what I want."

"Of course, you do," Joan said and placed her hand on Eileen's.

Joan's eyes misted and she smiled at Eileen, marvelling at her strength in the face of such upheaval in her life.

"I don't think I'd ever be brave enough to leave Frank even if he did have an affair. I'm too long with him now. I wouldn't know how to survive on my own," Joan admitted.

Joan knew it was true. However mismatched they might appear to an outsider, their love for each other went deep and they were now like a comfortable old pair of shoes that you would never give up.

"Trust me, you would. You survived before you met him, didn't you? You are stronger than you think and here you are now, helping me no end," Eileen said with conviction.

As Joan absorbed her words, her eyes filled up at the very idea of being described as strong.

"I'll call Mary when I'm home, Eileen, and I'm sure tomorrow will be no problem," Joan said and stood up to go.

Joan felt anxious to see Johnny. Joan had seen Johnny angry, sulky, excited even over the years, but she couldn't remember ever seeing him so vacant and lifeless. She shivered as she remembered the dead look in his eyes when she had left the house earlier.

"Sorry, but I better go, Eileen. I won't go into it, but we had a bit of bother with Johnny last night. It's okay, but I told Frank I wouldn't be too long," Joan said.

"Of course. Thanks a million. I hope Johnny's alright," Eileen said and embraced Joan.

"Oh, Johnny's fine, it's the other boy that I'm worried about," Joan said.

"I can't believe I might actually have a new home and it's all because of you. Thank you, Joan," Eileen said, holding on for a little longer than was necessary.

Every fibre of Eileen's being hungered to be wrapped safely in someone else's arms, to be told that everything would be okay. As they separated, Eileen thought of Dave. She couldn't remember the last time they had shown each other any real affection. A sure sign that what had happened was just the inevitable.

EIGHTEEN

"Come on, son, sit down with me for a minute," Frank said.

Frank decided to bite the bullet and try to figure out what had happened the night before. Johnny's demeanour told them there was a possibility of finally hearing the truth from him.

"I don't want to talk about it, Dad," Johnny muttered as he made a cup of tea. The thought of talking about it was like jumping into the abyss without a safety net. Johnny had no idea where it might lead.

"*Come on*. You'll feel better if you get it off your chest," Frank said.

Frank stood behind Johnny and gently steered him towards the kitchen table and on to a chair. Ken's words were ringing in Frank's ears again.

"I've nothing to say. *Can't you give it a rest?*" Johnny snapped.

Johnny wrapped his hands around his mug of tea and sat staring into space. Frank scanned his face with the concern of a father desperately wishing to help his son. It was like the light had gone out in Johnny's eyes tonight and Frank was concerned that Johnny would walk the same path as Joan. Frank would have given anything to see Johnny's eyes flash with anger as he made his usual derisory remark, but he had no idea what to do with this silent, vacant boy sitting in front of him. Frank remembered Ken telling him to ask questions, listen and not judge or try to fix.

"Can you just tell me what happened? I won't bite your head off," Frank said. "It must've been some shock to see Jack just lyin' there. He's goin' to be okay, you know that don't you?" Frank reassured Johnny.

With no response from Johnny, Frank's primal instincts were to shout at Johnny but instead, he took a deep breath, determined not to go down that cul de sac.

"It was an accident, Johnny. You know that don't you?"

Frank waited for a reaction. The silence as he waited was heavy with tension, but to Frank's surprise, Johnny spoke.

"It was *all* my fault," Johnny mumbled, looking at his feet. "What'd you say son?" Frank asked and leaned across the table.

"It was my fault," Johnny repeated louder.

Frank noticed his shoulders tremble as he said the words out loud. Frank flinched. He couldn't remember the last time he had seen Johnny cry. Being his father's son, Johnny was more inclined to shout and lash out than give into tears. This was a whole new ball game now.

"What do you mean?" Frank asked gently.

"I'm such a loser. A *fucking loser!*" Johnny swore at the top of his voice and Frank glanced towards the door.

Frank was glad that Abbie was up in her room and he hoped she would stay there.

"Stop it with that talk!" Frank said loudly. "*Do you hear me?*"

"It's true. I'd be better off…" Johnny said and withdrew.

Frank didn't need him to finish. It was obvious where his train of thought was leading.

"I mean it, Johnny. You're no more a loser than the rest of us, *do you hear me?*" Frank spluttered. "Now, just tell me what happened. I'm all ears."

"If I tell you, you'll hate me," Johnny said and looked up at Frank as tears streamed down his face.

"I'm sorry to disappoint you, Johnny, but nothing you say or do could make me hate you. It's part of the programming when you're a parent. I could never hate my son," Frank said, resisting the urge to stand up and hug him.

"I've done plenty of things I'm not proud of, we all have. You talk and I'll even keep me big trap shut for a change. How's that for a deal?" Frank asked.

When his tears subsided, Johnny took a deep breath.

"The reason we were in the park is because we owed McCabe money. Remember, I told you? Jack wangled the money from Liam and we were going to pay him off… Jack asked me to stay cool…" Johnny said, and his voice faltered.

"So, what happened?"

"I shot my mouth off, *that's what happened,*" Johnny argued.

"What do you mean?"

"I ended up in a fight with McCabe. He was rising me, *the bastard*, and I took the bait. Jack happened to be in the way and…"

"It sounds like an accident," Frank interjected.

"It was *my fault*, Dad! If I had kept *my bloody mouth shut, none of this would have happened.* We'd have walked away from there and had nothing to do with McCabe again. I'm *such a fucking idiot!*" Johnny yelled.

Frank listened for a little longer until there were no more words from Johnny.

"I've an idea what the money was for, but I'd prefer if you told me. I won't give out, I just want to know."

"I think you do know. We smoke the odd joint and we bought it off McCabe, but never again."

"Never again you're smoking it or never again with McCabe?" Frank asked, hoping it was the former.

"*Very funny*, Dad," Johnny said, trying not to laugh. Johnny returned his gaze to the floor.

"For Chrissakes! I'm not a fool. Sure, you could knock a horse with the smell in the house sometimes," Frank said, deliberately keeping his voice light despite the alarm bells that were going off in his head. Frank paused, reminding himself to tread carefully. For the first time, Johnny was really opening up to him and he didn't want to mess it up.

"All I'm sayin' is that you're a lot smarter than I ever was. Don't let it go to waste. *Please, son.* Don't throw in the towel before you've even started out," Frank said and searched Johnny's face to see if he had reached him at all.

"You don't understand, Dad. I'm useless and I'm sick of my life. I hate everything, Dad, *everything.* All anyone talks about is money, university, careers. I don't want anything to do with it, *nothing.*"

Johnny's voice broke and Frank felt sick to the pit of his stomach.

"*Jaysus.* I'd no idea it was that bad. I'm sorry, son, so sorry."

"And what's with Mam?" Johnny whispered.

"What do you mean?"

"She's like a fucking yo-yo. She can hardly look at me most of the time," Johnny said, and the hurt inside him erupted like a volcano.

"Christ almighty, how can you say that? Your Mam loves you very much. *We both* love you very much."

"Yeah, right," Johnny said, brushing the remark aside.

Frank looked out the window and thought about how to explain it. He inhaled deeply. Frank had always known this day might come, but Joan had begged him not to say anything to Johnny, falsely believing that telling him about the depths of her darkness would only alienate him further.

"Your mother had that post-natal depression after you were born," Frank blurted out. "It had nothing to do with you and it isn't your fault. It just happens. We just about managed to keep the show on the road then," Frank continued.

"*What?*" Johnny cried.

"Maybe we should have said something before now, but we, I wasn't able to talk about it. Your mother wanted to, but I thought it was better to just let sleeping dogs lie. If there's anyone to blame it's me, not her," Frank confessed.

"We did our best, son, but we made a lot of mistakes," Frank said and shook his head.

"Most of the time I come home from school and she's in bed or out of it on pills. *Do you know what that's like?*" Johnny cried. "I thought it was me. I thought I had done something wrong. How could you not say anything?" Johnny asked, now enraged.

"I'm so sorry, Johnny. She does her best. We both do and have always done. Maybe that's not good enough, but it's the truth. I suppose we hoped things would improve on their own."

Frank heard himself and realised how feeble his explanation sounded. There was no point telling Johnny that they had many an argument as they tried to figure out what to do and many a sleepless night of worry. So many 'if only's played in Frank's head. Hindsight was a great thing and Frank would do anything to turn back the clock right now and do it all differently.

Johnny looked at his Dad, trying hard to understand. He took in his Dad's pained expression and watched him wring his hands.

"Dad, I… I was only a kid, you know. I was only a kid. I'd come home from school and she was away with the fairies. All I wanted was my mother… I still want her," Johnny whispered, slumping in his seat.

"I know," Frank said. "I really am sorry. I know things aren't perfect. I'll try harder and your mother will too. Is there anythin' that I can do right now? Do you want to go to the hospital to see Jack?"

"Maybe later," Johnny said.

They sat in silence and Frank stole a glance at Johnny. He felt a wave of protectiveness as he looked at his youngest son. Johnny was right, Frank thought. He was only a kid back then and it wasn't right that any boy should have to suffer so much when so young. Johnny listened to his Dad's carefully chosen words and he couldn't deny that he was trying to make amends. Johnny heard the pain in his father's voice and realised that it hadn't been easy for him either.

"What are you going to do about the drugs, Johnny?" Frank asked but Johnny didn't respond. "Johnny?" Frank asked. Johnny shrugged his shoulders.

"Would you like to talk to someone, like a professional… I've a friend. His name's Ken… I think he's working with talking and that kind of thing," Frank said and leaned closer. Johnny shrugged his shoulders. "Will ya talk to him, Johnny? I don't have to know anything about it," Frank said and hoped and prayed that Johnny would say yes. Johnny nodded.

"Okay, so. I'll talk to him and see if he could talk to you. Good lad, Johnny." A wave of relief flooded Frank as he sensed they were making some progress.

"I'm proud of you son," Frank said seriously.

"*Proud?*" Johnny exclaimed.

"Yes, you make me very proud," Frank added with a smile.

Johnny swallowed hard as he listened to his Dad's heartfelt words.

"Johnny?"

"Yeah."

"Please tell me that you won't … you know… you can always talk to me," Frank said. Johnny nodded.

"Come here, son" Frank said.

Frank stood up and pulled Johnny into a bear hug. He had no more words left. Johnny was stiff in his arms, but eventually he softened and rested his head on his father's shoulder. All the fight had gone out of him for one day.

"It will be okay, Johnny. I promise, it will all be okay."

Frank looked up and saw Joan standing in the doorway. Joan felt like an intruder on the scene. She was overcome by the sight of her angry boy with his head lying on Frank's shoulder. He had a childlike expression on his face and Joan was reminded of how he used to climb up on her knee when he was little, burrowing in for a cuddle.

Frank looked up and smiled. His eyes told her that there was nothing to worry about. Then Johnny lifted his head and turned to look at his mother. Joan instinctively held out her arms to him and silently Johnny moved towards her. When they finally hugged, it was like the years of pain and anger were being washed away as they clung on to each other for dear life.

"I'm sorry, I'm sorry for everything. I love you, Johnny, so so much. I always have," Joan whispered.

The strength of this woman grew with every interaction Joan had that day. It seemed that others started to recognise this in Joan and none as much as Eileen. It was Joan's strength that carried Eileen through the next few hours and checking out of the hotel didn't seem as daunting.

"I'd like to check out please," Eileen said, standing at the reception counter.

"Absolutely, Ms Murphy. I hope you enjoyed your stay," the receptionist said. Eileen flinched at the words, realising that she would have to become used to the sound of her maiden name again. "I did, thank you. It was just what I needed," Eileen said, taking out her credit card to pay. She glanced in the mirror behind reception and was relieved to see a more rested face looking back at her than when she had arrived on Friday night.

"We look forward to seeing you back here again whenever you need us," the receptionist said and handed Eileen back her card.

"I look forward to it," Eileen said, hearing her phone buzz in her pocket. She reached for it as she picked up her bag and walked towards the entrance of the hotel.

"*Bloody hell,*" Eileen remarked. Eileen, wondering what Dave wanted, discovered that it was a message to say that Dave had started cooking the dinner for everyone.

Eileen sent Dave a message back that she would be home at six o'clock and then buried her phone in her bag, as far away from her reach as possible.

Eileen climbed into her car and threw her overnight bag on the passenger seat beside her. An overwhelming sense of loneliness swept over her. Eileen gripped the steering wheel like it was an anchor that would steady her and after a few minutes, the feeling subsided. Eileen drove straight to the beach for some much-needed fresh air.

It was almost empty when Eileen pulled up at the promenade. The day was grey and windy which might have put others off, but pulling on her runners and fleece, Eileen welcomed the bracing sea air on her face and in her hair. Eileen grabbed a blanket from the boot of the car and strolled the length of the beach. She found a sheltered spot beside a rock and lay down on the blanket and closed her eyes.

Like many couples, Eileen had never entertained the possibility of flying solo again. Yet, here she was. A whole new life lay in front of her, where going out to dinner or the cinema would take a bit of planning rather than just giving the person on the couch a nudge. It had been many years since she had to go looking for a companion for holidays, meals, for anything really.

The crashing waves jolted Eileen and her thoughts turned to Joan and how she had really come through for her.

"Shit," she cried, remembering Joan's earlier text message.

Eileen was meant to meet Mary at four thirty and it was now four fifteen. Eileen quickly gathered up the blanket and jogged back to the car. Despite everything, Eileen couldn't help feeling a bit hopeful at the thought of going on a new adventure.

Eileen stopped outside Mary's address at exactly half four. Hopping out of the car, she took in her surroundings with nervous enthusiasm. Mary's house overlooked the river and from there it was a five-minute walk into town. Eileen stood outside the brightly painted red door and cleared her throat before reaching for the shiny knocker. Joan had painted a picture of an eccentric looking, large woman in her seventies but when the door opened, Eileen was met by a fairy godmother type figure – a soft-featured woman with warm, smiling eyes, dusting flour from her hands and apron.

"Oh, hello, you must be Eileen. Sorry, I did a bit of baking and lost track of the time. Come in, come in," Mary said nervously.

She recognised Eileen instantly as the woman from the newspaper and the supermarket, but it was another thing meeting her in person. Mary had spent Saturday tidying up around the house and was grateful she had decided to declutter the previous weekend. The compact house had once been an orderly home for a family of seven, but it had drifted into a more relaxed set-up, with only one inhabitant free to spread herself out and no one to pass comment.

"Thank you. Eileen, isn't it? It's lovely to meet you," Mary said and led Eileen down the hall.

Mary opened the door to a bright kitchen that was a far sight smaller than the huge catering-sized, monochrome kitchen in their own mansion, but it was much more welcoming in Eileen's mind. The little room contained an eclectic mishmash of items that reflected the owner's personality. Little potted plants and herbs were dotted around the room, an old kitchen dresser stood in the corner filled with an assortment of colourful trinkets and ornaments, and a beautiful turquoise reclining armchair had pride of place facing the double doors out to the garden. Perched on top of this armchair was a large ginger cat, fast asleep.

Mary pulled out a chair for Eileen to sit on and then busied herself making a pot of tea. Eileen took off her jacket and sat down, glad of the time to gather herself.

"I just want to say how grateful I am for your offer. I couldn't believe it when Joan told me. I'm not sure how much you know," Eileen said. "I'm going through a difficult period at the moment," she said and placed the cup back down on the saucer.

"I just found out that my husband is having an affair and has been for the last year. Um… we're practically bankrupt and I've had to move job. Everything's up in a heap right now," Eileen said.

"Would you like a slice of cake?" Mary said, placing a slice of madeira cake onto a plate for Eileen.

"Thank you," Eileen said. "I just can't stay in the house any longer. We have to sell it, so it wouldn't be long before I'd have to move anyway. I've two young girls," Eileen added.

"I heard," Mary remarked and sat down with her slice of cake.

"I'd totally understand if you changed your mind," Eileen said.

Eileen still couldn't believe that this woman who had only met her today was being so generous.

"Eileen," Mary said softly. "It's okay. There's nothing at all to worry about on my account. You don't have to explain yourself or tell me anything unless you want to. I'm very happy to help you. I'll show you around after you've had your cake and if you're happy with the house, then we'll set a few ground rules to make sure everything runs smoothly," Mary said and cut into her cake with the fork.

"We won't be under your feet for too long, and I just want to make it clear that I'll be paying you rent," Eileen said. "It will keep everything above board, so we both know where we stand."

Mary nodded and smiled warmly.

"I suppose your right," Mary said.

"Would you believe the new firm I'll be working in specialises in family law? Isn't that ironic?" Eileen remarked.

"Life does have a funny way of surprising us, doesn't it?" Mary said. "It's not all bad." Mary's thoughts drifted to Séamus and she couldn't stop a smile spreading across her face. "Now, why don't I show you around the house? You'll want to see if it suits you."

Eileen stood up to follow Mary.

"I'm sure you're used to a lot more space, but we raised five children here, would you believe that? Times were different then," Mary explained.

Mary led the way upstairs. She opened the first bedroom that her daughters Bernice and Janet had shared many moons ago.

"It's not exactly the height of fashion nowadays," Mary said, referring to the pink floral wallpaper and pale pink carpet, "but my two girls loved it."

Beside each bed was a little wooden locker and the compact room had a view out to a back garden that was even more impressive than the front. The second room was almost a replica of the first, except for the furnishings that were more neutral.

"My eldest, Maggie, slept here and insisted on decorating it more to her own taste as she grew older. Hence the no-pink rule," Mary said and laughed.

"This is just perfect, Mary. Really it is. I don't know what to say."

Eileen followed Mary downstairs and into the cosy little living room that had an open fire and soft, well-worn furniture.

"Now, there's one more room that I think might just suit your two girls," Mary said and she showed Eileen into a small room off the kitchen.

"This used to be a bedroom and then a spare room, but there's a couch and TV, so they're welcome to use it for their toys," Mary suggested.

"This is great. I really don't want to be an intrusion, so we can happily use it as our living room."

"Don't worry about that. We'll figure it out as we go along. How's that for a plan, Eileen?"

Mary touched Eileen's arm lightly in a gesture of reassurance that relaxed Eileen.

"Can I ask you a question? Feel free to tell me to mind my own business," Mary said.

"Go ahead," Eileen replied.

"Have you told your family, your parents, I mean? Couldn't they be a support to you? You're going through a difficult time and maybe they can help in some way," Mary said softly.

"You haven't met my parents," Eileen said and rolled her eyes. "My mother never thought Dave was good enough for me, so I really don't want to see her 'I told you so' face… Dad, well, he's a different story. He'll try to fix everything. I'll tell them, but I just haven't had the energy to do it. It's all been a bit sudden, you know."

Eileen looked at Mary, hoping she would understand.

"Of course," Mary said. "I'm being an awful busybody, but you know, they might surprise you." Mary wanted to say to Eileen that every parent only wanted to see their children happy but decided she had said enough for now. As they came back into the kitchen, Boots woke up, stretched and purred, and they both laughed.

"Maybe you're right, but I'm not ready just yet," Eileen said, reaching for her coat and bag.

"One step at a time, as they say," Mary said softly.

"Is it okay if I come back to you during the week?" Eileen said as they walked to the front door.

"You call me when you're ready. I'm not going anywhere," Mary said and after waving Eileen off she closed the door and went back to the kitchen.

Mary sat down in her armchair, and Boots on cue hopped up on her lap and purred, letting her know that he approved.

"Can you believe it, Boots?"

Mary had been very tempted to tell Eileen that she knew exactly what her girls were like. The younger one hyper and relentlessly bombarding her mother with requests for sweets as they waited in line at the cashier, the older girl more laid back, quietly taking everything in.

"She's definitely an open book. I wasn't expecting that," Mary said and stroked Boot's coat.

Boots showed his appreciation by drifting off to sleep again and gently snored.

NINETEEN

"Mum, you're home. I missed you so much," Amy called, barrelling down the hall at full speed, almost knocking Eileen off balance as she stood at the front door.

Eileen felt a lump in her throat as she whisked her little girl into her arms and held her close.

"I missed you so much as well, darling. I hope you were good for Daddy. Did he spoil you rotten?" Eileen asked and squeezed her even tighter. "Go on, you can tell me," Eileen said and tickled Amy until she collapsed on the floor in a fit of giggles.

"That's a secret," Amy shrieked as she escaped and ran down the hall to announce her mother's arrival home.

Despite Eileen's current disillusionment with men, she didn't want her daughters becoming man-haters or starting off their lives full of mistrust. However, this wasn't easy when all she wanted to do was to throttle the man in the kitchen. Eileen dropped her bags at the foot of the stairs and followed Amy down the hall. Stopping at the living room door, she found Sophie engrossed in a TV programme.

"Hi, darling," Eileen said, and Sophie just about glanced up.

"Hi, Mum," Sophie replied.

Hearing a lot of clattering and banging coming from the kitchen, Eileen guessed that Dave was trying to do his best Gordon Ramsay impression. Desperate times called for desperate measures.

"It's way too late for that sunshine," she muttered under her breath as she followed the sounds into the kitchen.

"Daddy, Mum's home, Mum's back," Amy said, tugging at Dave's shirt.

"Oh, hi. I just made dinner," Dave said timidly and wiped his forehead.

"It won't take long. It's nothing fancy, just Spaghetti Bolognese. I hope that's okay. Why don't you sit down and have a glass of wine?"

Dave chattered nervously as he moved around the kitchen like a Duracell bunny on speed.

"I'm going to unpack. I'll be down in a few minutes," Eileen said casually and left them both in the kitchen.

There was only so far she could go with the happy families' pretence.

Eileen wanted to scream at him and tell him that the last thing on earth she wanted to do was sit and have a glass of wine with a man who had betrayed her with another woman. Eileen wanted to kick him out the door and lock it behind him. Eileen unpacked her bags, changed into an old tracksuit and T-shirt and lay on the bed. Eileen reassured herself that she and Dave would talk that night. Dave had pursued her, like he had pursued a lot of things in his life, but he had also bored of a lot of things in his life. Dave had always been a thrill seeker and it was his single-minded and driven approach that had attracted her at first. Still, he was never satisfied. Dave always wanted more. Eileen should have known that he would tire of her like he tired of many things, quickly replacing them, like their old house, his new car, friends and on and on it went.

"Mum, dinner's ready," Amy called from downstairs.

Eileen summoned the energy to drag herself off the bed. She inspected her reflection in the mirror, pinching her cheeks to add a bit of colour and she pulled her hair back in a ponytail. Finding her slippers under the bed, Eileen pulled them on and trudged downstairs to give an Oscar-winning performance.

"So, what did you do this weekend?" Eileen asked brightly.

The girls were sitting in their usual places, totally unaware that anything had changed. She looked at them as they laughed and bickered like any normal Sunday evening dinner. Joining them, she watched Dave almost hyperventilating as he tried to serve up dinner, before dropping into the seat opposite her.

"We went to a movie, Mum, and Daddy let us have popcorn and then we went to visit Nono," Amy said.

Nono was the name they gave Dave's mother. She had outright refused to be called any version of Grandma or Granny. Her name was Noreen, but Nono was what the girls had christened her.

"Really?" Eileen asked surprised.

Dave must have been really struggling if he had brought them to visit his mother. After all, she wasn't the most child-friendly adult and usually complained of a headache or needing to lie down within half an hour of being in their company.

"Yes, she was dying to see them," Dave said, avoiding eye contact. "It was lovely to see her girls, wasn't it?" Dave added, looking to them for a bit of moral support.

"She had a headache and we had to leave after an hour," Sophie whispered.

The family didn't dawdle over dinner as they usually did and the girls, itching to go back to their own worlds, pleaded to have dessert watching TV.

"Okay, but bed in half an hour okay. No arguments," Eileen warned them, but they were already gone.

Eileen stood up from the table and prepared two bowls of ice cream.

"Eileen, I'm so sorry, I really am. I realise what a mess I've made of things," Dave said, interrupting Eileen's train of thought.

"Stop, Dave. Not now. We agreed. When the girls are in bed we can talk," Eileen said.

"I know, but I just wanted you to know how sorry I am and…"

Eileen could feel every muscle in her body tighten. She turned to him, gripping the tub of ice cream so tightly that it hurt. "Dave, I'm warning you, *leave it.* No apology will change what you did, and you need to understand that. Now, I'm going to join the girls and I trust you can clean up the dishes," Eileen said.

Eileen poured herself a large glass of wine and disappeared, leaving Dave sitting at the table. Dave buried his head in his hands in despair. Eileen hadn't softened one bit, but surely Eileen wasn't going to throw away fourteen years of marriage over one mistake. After some time, Dave stood up to clear away the dishes. He decided to do his best to show Eileen that he meant what he said, and so he washed the pots and pans and cleaned the kitchen from top to toe. Dave would do whatever it took to win Eileen back. As soon as the girls had gone to bed and Dave heard Eileen walk into the living room, he decided to approach her.

"Close the door after you, Dave. I don't want the girls hearing us," Eileen said sharply.

Dave shut the door with a hangdog look on his face and went to sit down beside Eileen on the couch. Glancing down at the glass of wine that trembled in her hands, Eileen reached forward and placed it safely on the coffee table.

"I just wanted to let you know my plans," Eileen said. Her voice was clipped, and she stared past him out the window.

"I've had time to think and I've made some decisions that you need to know about."

"What do you mean decisions?" Dave asked nervously. He sat forward on his seat.

"Well, you hardly think we can stay living as we are."

"I don't understand," Dave said.

"We need to put the house on the market as soon as possible. In the meantime, while that is going through, I've found a place for myself and the girls and it's ideal. It's in town and close to the girls' school and my new job."

The words struck Dave like a thunderbolt and from that point onwards, he could barely hear Eileen's words.

"Obviously, you can see them whenever you like, I'll never deny you that, and they can come here and stay with you at the weekend, if you plan to stay here…"

Dave pulled himself back into the present moment on hearing Eileen speak about visitation rights.

"Stop, Jesus Christ! *What are you talking about Eileen?*" Dave asked, absolutely gutted by her words.

"What am I talking about? Do I really have to spell it out for you? You decided that you didn't want this family when you went and had an affair. *What did you think was going to happen?* That I wouldn't find out and you could have your cake and eat it? Well, you can't, and I *will not* degrade myself any more by staying in this house with you. It's over Dave, do you hear me?"

As Eileen said the word 'over' she turned and faced Dave and held his gaze without blinking. Dave gulped as he absorbed the gravity of her words, words he had never imagined hearing from his wife.

"*Over*? You can't mean that? After fourteen years of marriage?" Dave pleaded.

Eileen realised that she did really mean her words. This is what she wanted. Dave's face paled and Eileen thought he might faint or throw up.

"*Please, Eileen. Please*, just give it some time. I know I did something awful but it's the first and only time, and it will never happen again. I promise you that. I made a mistake, I know a big one but surely in a marriage we are allowed one mistake, one stupid, stupid mistake," Dave cried.

"But it wasn't just one mistake, Dave, was it? A mistake is forgetting to put out the bins, forgetting a birthday or anniversary. You don't see another woman behind your wife's back for a year and call it a mistake. *That's a bloody insult to me.* There was no mistake in what you did. It was a deliberate act," Eileen said firmly.

"It was a mistake, Eileen, the biggest one I've ever made," Dave whispered and hung his head.

"Seriously, where did you think this would end up? I guess you weren't thinking, or at least you weren't thinking with your head."

Eileen stood up, feeling the need to create some space between them. Couples sat beside each other when they felt emotionally close, when they wanted to be within arm's reach of the other, but this wasn't who they were anymore. Eileen walked over to the armchair that faced the couch and sat down across from Dave.

Dave clutched his stomach like he had taken a punch to the gut. The prospect of everything falling apart had not seemed real until now. Eileen had always adored him, always forgiven him. He had always been able to count on that. However, this time, Eileen had a steely look in her eyes and even the timbre of her voice had indicated that this was the end.

Eileen looked at Dave and was amazed that she felt nothing. His movie star charisma had dissolved right in front of her eyes. All she could see now was a man who had so little respect for her that he actually thought Eileen would just roll over and forget that he had betrayed her.

"Look, we have the girls to think about. I don't want it to be any more difficult than it already is, Dave. But we have to talk to them.

I don't have much work on this week, so I'm going to start preparing for our move. We need to talk to them, and I think it should be tomorrow," Eileen said.

"Tomorrow? So soon?" were the only words that Dave could scrabble together. His life was unravelling before his eyes and he was powerless to stop it.

"We can tell them we are selling the house and that while we find a new home, they are going to stay with me," Eileen said.

Dave tried to process the information but struggled with every word that dropped from Eileen's mouth. He hadn't counted on her being so strong and determined. Dave had expected anger, hysterics and tears, but this was a whole other ball game.

"The girls will see you all the time. They have to be our number one, Dave," Eileen said.

Eileen reached forward and took a drink from her wine. She looked down at her hands and realised that she had been clenching them so tightly she had almost cut off the circulation on her wedding ring finger.

"Please, can't we all just stay in the house, for a while at least and try and work through this, for the girls' sake at least. *I'm begging you* not to give up on us so quickly. I'll do whatever it takes, *anything.* I just can't lose you, I can't lose you all," Dave cried.

"I'm sorry, but my decision is final. Look, I don't know where this is all going to lead, Dave, but I need this time away from you. You owe me that. We won't decide anything beyond selling the house. Is that fair enough?" Eileen said.

Eileen noticed the slightest flicker of hope in Dave's eyes, eyes that used to stop her in her tracks they were so magnetic. However, today Eileen didn't feel anything. Dave ran his hands through his sandy hair and cleared his throat before speaking.

"Okay. We'll talk to them tomorrow evening. I will do whatever it takes to win you back, Eileen. I promise… *anything,*" Dave said.

****

At the arranged time on Sunday evening, Cyril sat on the weather-beaten bench by the sea, anxiously awaiting Linda's arrival. Cyril couldn't believe Linda had agreed to meet him. It had taken a stream of messages, but Linda had eventually caved in. Cyril had been careful not to refer to the events of Friday night as he knew she would just pull away. Knowing Linda wasn't one for punctuality, Cyril used the time to rehearse what he wanted to say, letting the gentle lapping of the waves calm his nerves.

Cyril thought about the advice he had received from Séamus. He had poured out his worries to him when he had bumped into him on the street. Séamus' words still rang in his ears and sent a chill down his spine. Séamus had told him that abuse always thrived when there was a conspiracy of silence.

From the corner of his eye, Cyril saw Linda approaching in the distance. Linda was hard to miss with her flaming red hair. Yet, it was only the tip of the iceberg when it came to her fiery personality, he was fast learning.

"Hey, you can't see enough of me, can you?" Linda asked and plonked herself down on the bench beside him. Linda brushed her hair off her face. No one would ever suspect she was a victim of abuse.

"Hi. You look great."

"Thanks. You do too," Linda said and smiled.

"You won't believe the drama in my house when I arrived home on Friday," Cyril said lightly.

Cyril proceeded to fill Linda in on the events in Johnny's life in a desperate attempt to delay raising the uncomfortable subject of her mother.

"*Jeez. That's mad.* And you think *I'm crazy*," Linda said, nudging Cyril playfully.

They sat side by side looking at the sea twinkling in the evening sunlight. There wasn't a soul in sight as Cyril reached over and took her hand.

"I'm glad you came, Linda. I like you a lot, you know," Cyril said as he looked out to sea. "I wanted to talk to you. Please just hear me out."

"Well, here I am. Spit it out why don't you, Cyril," Linda said with an edge to her voice.

"Please, don't be angry, but I want to talk to you about what happened with your mother. It is not nothing, so don't say it is. It's wrong, do you hear me?"

"I know you mean well, but *please* lay off. It has nothing to do with you. My mother loves me, she just has a temper. Lots of people have tempers. It's not the end of the world," Linda said as she idly peeled the paint off the bench.

"Can you hear yourself, Linda? Your mother hits you and you say it's nothing. I know you're probably afraid, but she needs help, she will thank you for it in the long run. I know she will."

"You must be joking. You want me to report *my mother*?" Linda shrieked as she catapulted off the bench. "I don't see you reporting any of your family and from what you've told me they sound as mad as a bag of cats."

Linda paced up and down in front of Cyril, furiously biting on her lip. Cyril flinched at her words. It wasn't like her to be so bitchy.

"*Please*, sit down Linda," Cyril said.

"I'm sorry, I know that was mean, but *I* don't meddle in your family's business, *so please* don't meddle in mine," Linda argued.

"Okay, just relax, would you," Cyril said, seeing the splotches of red on her face and neck.

Linda stopped pacing and sat down closer to Cyril this time.

"Please drop it. I can't see you again if you're going to be like a dog with a bone. We could have a lot of fun together you know," Linda said and smiled at him flirtatiously.

"God you're infuriating, you really are…" Cyril said.

Before Cyril could say anything more, Linda kissed him, and he was putty in her hands.

****

Johnny had finally been persuaded to visit Jack on Sunday afternoon. He had nervously chewed his nails to the quick for the whole journey as his thoughts ricocheted from Jack to his mother's revelations only yesterday. There was nothing like raw emotion to break down barriers. Left alone in the kitchen, Joan had opened up to him about her depression, her pain at failing him, her guilt at not being there for him. Johnny had just listened, not knowing what to make of all this attention from his mother.

"Here we are," Frank announced as he pulled up outside the hospital.

"I'm going in on my own," Johnny insisted when Frank went to hop out of the car.

"Sure, son. I'll hang on here then and catch the rest of the match," Frank said. Frank turned on the radio and leaned back against the headrest. "Jaysus, I think I overdid it on that trifle your mother made, if that's what it was. A strange concoction all the same, wasn't it?" Frank asked, rubbing his stomach.

Johnny stared at his feet trying to muster up the courage to move. He felt torn between making sure Jack was okay and the fear that Jack might be angry and reject him. Johnny's head told him to cop on and make a move, but his feet felt like they were glued to the floor.

"Are you alright there, son?" Frank asked.

Frank nudged Johnny.

"*Yes, I'm going,*" Johnny snapped and willed himself out of the car.

Frank watched Johnny trudge into the hospital with his head down.

Jack's parents had told them the room number, so Johnny walked straight to the lift and up to the second floor where he stood at the open door and looked at his friend. His eyes were closed, and Johnny took a moment to survey the damage. Jack's arm was in a cast and there was a big swollen mound in place of his left eye. Johnny was sorely tempted to turn on his heels and run. As he shuffled nervously Jack stirred and opened his eyes.

"So, you decided to show your face. I thought you'd left the country," Jack jested and flashed a lopsided smile that gave him a sinister look, courtesy of the swelling on his face.

Johnny trudged into the room and planted himself on the chair beside the bed.

"How are you feeling?" Johnny asked with his downcast eyes.

"I don't feel as bad as I look if that's any consolation," Jack said and shoved himself up in the bed and flinched with the pain.

"I'm sorry, Jack. I know I was a total gobshite, as usual. I thought you were… you know… I didn't know what happened," Johnny said.

"*Dead? Thanks a lot*, mate. I'm not as soft as *that*, you know. You're an idiot, *you know that?* It wasn't your fault. It was McCabe who landed a punch on me not you."

Johnny looked up.

"Are you sure? I thought I knocked you off the wall," Johnny said.

"Nope, it was McCabe. He landed one right here," Jack said and pointed at his eye. Johnny looked at the balloon of flesh in its place.

"But if I hadn't started things with him, you wouldn't be here. I'm a *fuckin' waste of space*."

"*Jesus*, you've your moments, but take it easy. *It's all cool*, man."

"Did your parents ask what happened?" Johnny asked.

"I just said a few of us were messing around when I fell off the wall. They bought it. Just hold it together, will you? I'll be fine," Jack said and then motioned Johnny to the jug of water that was on his locker.

Johnny obediently stood up and poured his friend a glass and handed it to him. After taking a long drink, Jack lay back against his pillow.

"You know what, you should take your man Séamus up on his offer. Both of us should. We could form a band. What about that? When we need a break from our high-pressured jobs running our own restaurant," Jack said and laughed. He then groaned and held his ribs. "You gotta cool it though. You're like a *bloody time bomb* most of the time," Jack said.

"I know. I've just been pissed off with everything to be honest." Johnny felt close to tears and dropped his head.

"You need to deal with it, *seriously*. When you're running your own business, you'll have plenty of opportunities to explode," Jack said. "Jesus, my ribs hurt like hell when I talk. You better make a move before the folks arrive. I'll see you when I'm home," Jack said.

Johnny stood up and as he walked back to the car, he felt relief wash over him. He had a chance now for a fresh start and he wanted to take it.

At home in Johnny's house, so much had changed for Joan. Yesterday's breakthrough with Johnny had been everything Joan could have hoped for and more. Joan felt like she was two stone lighter as she started to shed the guilt and sorrow that had plagued her for years. There was a long way to go yet, but it could be a new beginning for both of them.

"It's been some few weeks, hasn't it? Just one thing after another,"

Joan chattered away as she poured the tea. "We'd have been lost without you, Mary."

"It's me who should be thanking you. I feel like a new woman these days. Between you and now Eileen," Mary said, beaming. "And Séamus," Joan added.

"Aw, would you go away? He's a lovely man, but that's all it is," Mary said and served the carrot cake.

"How did it go with Eileen? She's so nice, isn't she?"

"She called me this morning actually. They're moving in on Thursday," Mary said and sat down. "Eileen was so polite. She's sure been through the wars… I'm surprised she hasn't reported that horrible man," she said.

"I think she's still in shock to be honest," Joan said, passing the milk to Mary.

"God help her. She can't let him away with it though. Nothing will ever change if people don't speak up," Mary declared. "I mean it, Joan. All this talk of gender equality and women are still afraid to open their mouths. If a woman like Eileen is too scared to stand up to that sort of abuse, I'm telling you, there's no hope for the rest of us," Mary angered. Joan nodded.

"We'll have to meet up, the three of us, when she's settled in. What do you think?" Joan asked.

"I'll tell you what. I've an even better idea. It's actually my birthday at the weekend and I'm going to be, well, would you believe it, I'll be seventy," Mary said. "I want to invite you all over on Saturday. Nothing fancy, just a bit of food and drink. I thought it would be a nice way to welcome Eileen and her daughters to the neighbourhood?"

"That's a wonderful idea. Will Séamus be joining us?"

"Well, I'll have to ask him. *Now, don't start getting ideas, Joan*," Mary warned.

"I wouldn't," Joan said with a glint in her eye.

I'm glad I've met him now. He's a gentle old soul. I enjoy his company and he seems to like mine. That's all there is to it," Mary said.

"He's mad about you. The way he looks at you with those big blue eyes of his. Oh, wouldn't it be lovely if you married and we could all go to the wedding?" Joan said dreamily.

"Good God, don't let him hear you say that," Mary shrieked, almost spilling her tea.

"It's nice to dream," Joan remarked and smiled.

"So, are you okay with Saturday then?" Mary asked.

Just then the door opened, and Abbie burst in with Frank following behind her.

"Mam, I can go back to school next week. I'll see my friends again," Abbie said excitedly as she hopped around the kitchen.

"Oh, that's great, love, come here and give me a hug," Joan said and pulled Abbie close.

This news was hard for Mary to hear and the disappointment was etched in her face, now that she realised her lifeline was being wrenched from her.

"Mam, stop will you. I'm not a baby," Abbie said, rubbing her cheek.

"I'll really miss you, Mary," Abbie said.

"Oh…" Mary said.

In that moment, Frank walked through the door.

"I swear to God, I have a path worn up to that madhouse, so I have," Frank said and sighed. "Is Johnny back yet?" he asked. Frank suddenly noticed the sombre mood in the room. "What's wrong?"

"I'll leave… I won't bother you," Mary said, standing up to leave.

"Sit down, Mary. I hope you're not leavin' on my account," Frank said.

"Are you leaving, Mary?" Joan said, pining for her already.

Frank pulled up a chair at the kitchen table.

"*Sit down*, Mary," Frank insisted, and Mary sat back down.

"Did you not ask her, love? Sitting here drinking tea and you didn't think to mention it?"

"I…" Joan said, uncertain of what Frank meant.

"Mary, we'd like you to stay on a couple of days a week and do a bit of cleaning and cooking," Frank said.

Mary was sure her heart did a somersault in her chest and it was all she could do not to jump out of the chair. Mary couldn't imagine a life that didn't have the lively Hughes family in it. She looked around the table and grinned from ear to ear, trying to contain her excitement.

"I'd be delighted. To be honest, I felt a bit sad at the idea of it all coming to an end, even though I'm happy you're feeling better, Abbie."

"There's nothing comin' to an end. Would you relax, Mary?" Frank said, reaching across the table for a slice of Mary's carrot cake.

"I would miss you all, you know, I really would. I'm sure I'll have my hands full with three new people in the house, but I don't want to be on top of them all the time either."

"We have a deal then," Frank said and bit into the cake.

"And Mary's invited us to a party in her house on Saturday. It's her birthday and we're all invited. Séamus is coming too," Joan said, struggling to keep the excitement out of her voice.

"That's mighty, so it is." Frank nodded and a conspiratorial smile passed between Joan and Frank.

TWENTY

"I'll pick you up after school and we'll go to Mary's house, okay," Eileen said, facing Amy and Sophie in the backseat of the car. Eileen spoke with a steadiness that belied how she felt.

"Okay, Mum. See you later," Sophie said.

Sophie grabbed her heavy backpack and hopped out of the car, giving Eileen a supportive smile before she closed the door. Amy was another story. Ever since she and Dave had sat them both down to tell them about the move she had fluctuated between stony silence and melodrama. It didn't matter how much reassuring they did, Amy found it exceptionally difficult to cope with this news and struggled to feel safe in a world that was now uncertain and tumultuous. Dave had told Amy that it would be an adventure for them all, but Amy wasn't the type of child that embraced adventure very well.

Eileen tried to make small talk on the way to Amy's school, but Amy just looked out the window with a scowl on her face. She felt completely powerless and expressed herself in the only way a child knew how.

"We'll have your favourite dinner tonight, Amy, pizza. How about that?" Eileen said, but Amy didn't respond. "*Amy please*, what's wrong?"

"I'll miss, Dad," Amy finally said with tears in her eyes. "*It's not fair.*"

"I know, love, but you'll see him all the time, probably more than you did before. You know Daddy's very busy at work, but now he's going to make a special effort to see you more. Isn't he taking both of you out for the day on Saturday for Sophie's birthday?" Eileen gushed while glancing back at Amy in the rearview mirror.

Amy looked out the car window as she tried to suppress a little smile.

"Here we are," Eileen said and pulled up at the gate of the school.

"We'll go for a hot chocolate after school. How about that?" Eileen asked.

Amy nodded happily and hopped out of the car without a word to Eileen. Amy trudged slowly through the yard with her head bowed. As Eileen sat in the car watching Amy, guilt overwhelmed her at the thought of uprooting them from their home. Eileen slowly drove on and gave Amy a quick smile when she looked over her shoulder to her mother.

A few minutes later, Eileen pulled into the driveway of their home and realised that it would be one of her last times to do so. The 'For Sale' sign had been erected the day before and it definitely marked the end of an era in their lives. She stepped out of the car and paused at the front gate, remembering the first day they had moved in. Dave had insisted on carrying her over the threshold, though she had been heavily pregnant with Sophie. He had almost put his back out, but nothing could have dimmed their happiness back then. They were living the dream. Life couldn't be any better in their eyes.

Eileen opened the front door and was overwhelmed with a sense of loss. Gripped by a wave of nausea, Eileen ran to the downstairs bathroom just in time to empty the contents of her stomach down the toilet. Retching until there was nothing left, she collapsed on the floor and cried a primal sound that tore through her body. Eileen didn't feel the cold of the marble floor as she sat there. She slowly struggled to her feet and inspected her reflection in the mirror. Dried rivers of eye makeup streaked her face and Eileen was wet with perspiration. Eileen turned on the tap, noticing the tremor in her hands and splashed cold water on her face.

"You've got this," Eileen said, drying her face with a towel . "You've got this," she repeated, looking at her pale reflection in the mirror.

Eileen spent the rest of that morning packing suitcases and at half past twelve, she left the house without a backward glance and drove straight to Mary's, taking a deep breath before hopping out of the car.

There was no one to carry her over the threshold this time, but that hadn't been an insurance policy that everything would work out, she reminded herself. Eileen took the suitcases out of the car, located the key under one of the multitude of pots outside the front door and let herself into their new home for now. Eileen threw her coat over the banisters, and slowly climbed the stairs with a heavy suitcase in each hand.

Opening the door of the girls' new bedroom, Eileen startled at the sight of soft toys left on each bed and the selection of books Mary had added to the bookcase. Eileen dropped the suitcases and walked across the hallway to her own room. There she saw the lavender candle on the bedside locker and a herbal tincture in a bottle that Mary had labelled 'Relaxation blend'. Eileen felt like crying. Mary had also folded a fluffy blanket at the end of the bed. Eileen was very tempted to just curl up on the bed and forget her problems. Just then, Eileen's phone rang.

"What now?" Eileen cried.

She sank on to the bed and checked her phone. It was her mother who hadn't responded so well to the news when Eileen had told her. As expected, she had called Dave all the names under the sun and reminded Eileen that she had always thought him untrustworthy. Eileen hesitated, then grimaced and picked it up.

"Hi, Mum," Eileen said, putting on her brightest voice.

"Are you still going through with this madness, Eileen?" her mother asked in a sharp tone.

"I've just finished the move, Mum, if that's what you're referring to," Eileen said, picking at the candle wax.

"*Of course, that's what I'm referring to*," her mother angered. "He should be *out on the street*, Eileen."

"*Mum, please*, leave it. I've made my decision and it's final," Eileen said, rolling her eyes.

"I always knew there was something very shifty about him. Didn't I try to tell you only the other day? Your father saw him in the pub, looking way too cosy with a young blonde girl. He didn't see your father, but he was up to no good. I'd say he has never been up to any good, if you want my tuppence worth."

Eileen had forgotten that piece of information. She must have tuned her mother out as she did during a lot of their conversations.

"Please, Mum, that's enough. Everything is sorted. I don't want you doing or saying anything to Dave and the same goes for Dad.

We're keeping it civil. Now, I've to go and pick up the girls from school," Eileen said.

Eileen cut her mother off and hung up the phone, desperately trying to save herself from falling apart. Her mother always had the ability to knock the stuffing out of Eileen with just a few words. Eileen was in no doubt that it wouldn't be long either before her father was on the phone.

"He'll have sourced the best divorce lawyers in the country," Eileen said, looking down at the phone.

Eileen thought about all the next few months would entail and vowed to content herself with whatever was her due from the sale of the house, if anything, and she would use this towards a new home for herself and the girls. Eileen grabbed her keys and left Mary's house.

****

"*Well, hello*, you must be Amy, am I right?" Mary asked, having instantly recognised the little girl when she arrived home later that evening.

Mary noticed how much quieter Amy was now than the hyper little girl she had seen in the supermarket. She cowered behind Eileen in the kitchen and when she peaked her head out, Mary resisted the urge to burst out laughing at the sight of the ring of dark chocolate around her mouth.

"Hi," Amy said politely.

"I'm Sophie," the older sister said, and Sophie stood up from the kitchen table and put out her hand to greet Mary. "Your house is very nice. Thanks, and I love our room."

Sophie put her hand out and took Amy's and then smiled as she disappeared into the newly adopted living room with her sister.

"I hope you don't mind, Mary, but I gave them dinner earlier. I've saved some pizza and garlic bread for us if you'll join me? It's nothing fancy," Eileen said and grabbed the oven gloves and stooped down to take the food out of the oven.

Eileen closed the kitchen door and poured them both a glass of wine as they sat down at the table.

"At last," Eileen said and sighed, taking a mouthful of wine.
"How did it go today?" Mary asked, seeing the exhaustion written all over Eileen's face.

"As well as it could under the circumstances, I suppose. I'm a bit worried about Amy. She's been mopey all week since we told her." Eileen played with her food not feeling remotely hungry.
"She'll be fine, Eileen. Children are very resilient. Just give it a bit of time."
"Do you think so?" Eileen asked.

"*Absolutely*. I think it would be a lot worse for them if you stayed and were miserable. If you can find a way to be happy, trust me they will be happy," Mary said, taking a bite out of her pizza.

"I made a mess of things with my own children, but I'm thinking of writing to them," Mary said, staring out the window.

Eileen looked at her, taking in her warm grey eyes, softly lined face and the most beautiful head of silver hair that fell to her shoulders.

"For what it's worth, I think they're very lucky to have you," Eileen said.
"Eileen, when you're my age, you realise that all the grudges you hold only harm yourself. I'm the one who has missed out on seeing my grandchildren grow up. I've missed christenings, birthdays and all the milestones," Mary said, and the immensity of her words hit her. The truth was that she had missed out on all these events, events that should have been cherished occasions in any grandmother's life. Mary looked at Eileen and imagined being her age again, a young mother, full of hope for her growing children, excited to watch them gain independence and make their own way in the world. Mary might have made some mistakes, but she decided there and then that she would do everything in her power to turn over a new leaf with her estranged children.

****

On Thursday night, Cyril decided to bite the bullet and tell his parents about Linda. They were insisting that he go to some party in Mary's house on Saturday, and he had no interest in hanging out with his parent's friends on his own. He looked over at them from the armchair, his long legs reaching under the coffee table. They were lost to the TV and Abbie was propped up between them, half dozing on Frank's shoulder.

"Can I bring someone with me to this party?" Cyril asked casually.

Frank and Joan looked up at him as if he had just announced he wanted to join the priesthood.

"Bring someone?" they both said at the same time.

"Yes, a friend, a girl actually," Cyril said.

As good-looking and charming as their son was, Frank and Joan had never known Cyril to show any interest in girls before today.

"Oh, right, a girl is it?" Frank said and winked at Joan. "Is she a girlfriend by any chance?"

"*Stop it*, Frank. Let him talk," Joan said and faced Cyril.

"Oh, that's lovely, Cyril, if you want to bring a girlfriend. Who is she? Do we know her?" Joan asked, excited at the thought of introducing her at the party.

"*Jesus.* Take it easy both of you. I don't know what she is exactly. We've just been hanging out together. She's actually going to be a designer. She's really good," Cyril said proudly.

"A designer, is it? Oh, you have it bad, son," Frank said.

"What's her name?" Joan asked.

"Linda, Linda McDermott. I think you might know her mother Lorna," Cyril said and looked at Joan for some piece of information she could provide. "I'm only asking her if you stop with the twenty questions, *okay?*"

"Don't worry, we'll be on our best behaviour, won't we?" Frank said and looked at Joan.

Joan looked downcast. The penny had just dropped. Linda's mother was that awful snob Lorna who never even gave her the time of day. The one who wouldn't look twice at her at the school gates. Oh God, she had been part of that WhatsApp group. Of all the families to be involved with, Cyril had to pick the McDermotts. Joan was close to saying something but bit her lip.

"Joan? We'll make her feel welcome, won't we?" Frank asked.

Cyril and Frank were both looking at her waiting for a response. "Yes, of course. We'll make her feel very welcome," Joan said with a tight smile on her face.

****

The day of the party dawned bright and sunny.

"This is so nice, Eileen. I've never been here before," Joan gushed, looking around.

They had been shown to a window seat in one of the hippest new coffee shops in town.

"It is, isn't it?" Eileen agreed as she gave her order to the waiter.

They had spent the morning having their hair and makeup done for the party. Then, they had hit every boutique in town where Eileen was on first name terms with the owners, and Joan had been persuaded to splurge on a new dress. Mary had practically pushed Eileen out the door that morning, insisting that she would achieve more on her own and not to come back until the late afternoon.

Eileen looked up at Joan and hardly recognised the woman sitting across the table from her.

"You look great, Joan. I don't think you know how pretty you are," Eileen said.

The expert application of makeup had transformed Joan's fine features and her blonde hair had been blow dried until it hung like a curtain of gold around her face.

"Thanks, but I think it's the makeup," Joan said, her cheeks pink from the compliment.

"Not at all. You look better than a lot of women twenty years younger, I can tell you. We both look good and why shouldn't we? And aren't we doing it for ourselves, more importantly? To the future Joan," Eileen said and lifted her glass of water in a toast to whatever lay ahead. Taking a sip out of it, Eileen placed the glass back on the table and smiled as she breathed in the contented hum of her surroundings. Eileen vowed to spend more time with Joan and with Mary. They were real friends, friends that she could rely on.

"I don't mean to put a damper on things, but can I ask you something, Eileen? Do you know Lorna McDermott?" Joan asked.

"Aw, Joan, please don't go down that road again. That message is forgotten. She's a bitch if that's what you mean, and she's not worth wasting any energy on. We're meant to be having fun today, not worrying about some gossipy woman who has nothing better to do with her time," Eileen retorted.

Eileen looked at her nails and was not remotely interested in hearing about the life and times of Lorna McDermott.

"It's not that, well not really. It's just that Cyril just announced he has a girlfriend."

"*A girlfriend?* That's good news, isn't it?"

"Well yes, until he told us who she is," Joan said.

"What do you mean?"

"She's Lorna's daughter. Her name is Linda McDermott and he's bringing her to the party," Joan explained, the colour rising in her face.

"So what? That doesn't mean she's anything like her, Joan. It doesn't mean you have to meet Lorna. They're not exactly getting married, are they?" Eileen said, taking a bite of her sandwich.

"No, but what if they do? Can you imagine us both at the wedding? I'd die, I really would. She has never even spoken two words to me in all the years doing the school pickup. She looks at me like I'm a piece of dirt on her shoe."

"Well, why do you care so much about what Lorna McDermott thinks then? She's not exactly Mother Teresa," Eileen remarked.

"You're right," Joan said and tried to let go of the worst-case scenarios roaming around her mind.

"You know that her main criteria for friendship is the size of your bank account and your status around town? She probably won't give me the time of day now that Dave and I are splitting up. Actually, that's a bit of a bonus now that I think of it. She's not a woman you want to emulate, trust me. I'd take you ten times over as a friend, Joan," Eileen said. "Now, please let's drop the subject of Lorna McDermott."

"Okay, I promise. No more talk of Lorna McDermott. We're out to enjoy ourselves," Joan agreed, flicking back her hair as she took in the compliment.

Eileen looked around and her eyes stopped at a table across the room where two women were having lunch together.

"Is everything okay?" Joan asked, following Eileen's gaze.

"You're not going to believe this."

"What?"

"There are two women sitting across the room," Eileen said. She paused and took a drink of water. "One of them is Julie Mahon. Do you know who that is?" Eileen said, and felt her temperature rising.

"No, should I?"

"She's the woman, or should I say *girl,* that Dave has been having an affair with for the last year. Jesus Christ, *of all the places in town,* she would have to choose to have lunch here with her mother. Look at her smiling away as if butter wouldn't melt in her mouth," Eileen angered.

"Oh, no. What do you want to do? Do you want to leave?"

"*Absolutely not. Why should I leave?* I don't think she has noticed me. She worked in Clancy's a long time ago," Eileen said. Eileen looked at Joan but couldn't help it and looked back at the table.

"She knows me, and she still saw nothing wrong with carrying on with my husband? I know he's as much to blame but seriously, some women…"

"Oh, I had no idea. Is she the blonde girl in the corner?" Joan asked and looked over, but Eileen tapped her on the arm.

"Don't look, Joan. I don't want her seeing me. They just came in a few minutes ago… I wonder what her mother would make of her having an affair with a married man?" Eileen heard herself speak but felt like she was talking about someone else. The word 'affair' was not a word that Eileen Danaher had ever entertained using when describing the state of her marriage.

"You're not going to do anything that you might regret, Eileen? Look we're nearly finished. Will we just pay the bill and leave?" Joan fretted. She didn't like scenes.

"Okay, maybe you're right. I'll settle up and then we'll make a move," Eileen said and dropped her napkin on the table and stood up.

Joan watched Eileen pay the bill and almost jumped out of her seat when she saw her walk towards the two women's table with a smile plastered on her face.

"Julie, is it? You worked in Clancy's a few years back," Eileen said.

The young woman looked up from her conversation and the colour drained from her face. Eileen noticed that she was very conservatively dressed, no doubt for the benefit of her mother who had no idea what her daughter had been up to.

"I'm Eileen Danaher, Dave's wife? I thought that might jog your memory. Is this your mother?"

The older elegant lady nodded and said hello while Julie looked like she might throw up.

"Well hello, Mrs Mahon. Lovely to meet you. Your daughter used to work in the same office as me. She's now working in the same building as my husband. You know him, Julie, don't you?"

Julie's mouth moved but no words came out.

"Are you okay, Julie? You seem very pale," Julie's mother said and took her hand across the table.

"Yes, you don't look very well, Julie. Are you okay?" Eileen asked smugly.

"I'm fine, it must be the heat in here. I'm okay," Julie said, stumbling over her words. "Yes, I do remember you, Eileen, of course. Clancy's was a very nice place to work. It's good to see you," Julie said and forced a stiff smile, praying that Eileen would go away.

"I'm afraid it's not as nice a place as you think, Julie. I've just left there myself because of a very difficult, or should I say inappropriate client. Imagine an older man making advances towards me and he a married man. It's disgusting. Of course, I showed him where to go. Totally inappropriate as I said. I'm a married woman and he is a married man. Awful behaviour, isn't it? I couldn't tolerate it," Eileen said.

Julie's mother answered, as Julie was lost for words.

"Oh, that's a disgrace. Some people have no morals it seems these days. I'm very sorry to hear that, Mrs Danaher," Julie's mother tut-

tutted.

"That's very kind of you, but I don't know if I'll be Mrs Danaher for much longer. You see my husband has been having an affair with a young woman in his office, would you believe that? I just found out and seemingly it has been going on for a year. I'm sorry now for telling you all of this, but I just thought you might be interested," Eileen glared at Julie.

"I've left him, for your information. I just thought you'd like to know."

Julie's mother looked at her daughter and then back at Eileen with a confused look on her face. Eileen wasn't sure if the penny had dropped, so she decided to make it very clear. Julie's mother was unfortunately going to be collateral damage.

"Oh, sorry, your mother doesn't know, Julie, does she?" Eileen asked.

Julie looked at Eileen, her eyes pleading with her not to say anything. Eileen enjoyed watching her wriggle in discomfort.

"What's going on, Julie? Am I missing something here?" her mother asked.

"Yes, Julie, what is going on? Well, I can fill you in Mrs Mahon in as much as I know. It seems that my husband has been having an affair and it is with none other than your daughter. That's correct, isn't it, Julie? My husband finally admitted it to me last week. They've been carrying on for a year, *a year mind you and not a bother to either of them that he had a wife and two young girls at home*. Well, as far as I'm concerned, Julie, he is all yours," Eileen announced.

"*What? Julie? Please* say this isn't true," Julie's mother said and waited anxiously for Julie to make a denial.

"*Please,* Mum, not here, not now, people are looking," Julie whimpered.

She looked around at the customers who were enjoying a lot more entertainment than they had bargained on for a weekend lunch.

"I'm sure you've a lot to discuss. It was lovely to meet you, Mrs Mahon, I'm sorry for dragging you into this mess, but I'm afraid it was unavoidable. Julie, just one word of warning. Men who do this once have a habit of repeating themselves. So, one day I'm sure you'll have the pleasure of being in my position. We'll see how you like it then. *Goodbye*," Eileen said and marched back to Joan who had been watching the spectacle in awe.

"Come on," Eileen said, and she grabbed her bag and walked out of the coffee shop.

"Oh my God, Eileen. I had no idea," Joan said as she rushed to catch up with her.

"Trust me, Joan, I had no idea either. I really was just going to pay the bill, and something came over me. I had to say something. Just the thought of this girl who has destroyed my marriage sitting there happily with her mother as if butter wouldn't melt. I know it takes two, and Dave is the married party, but she knew what she walked into."

Eileen took large strides up the street, walking more determinedly with each step.

"I *do* feel sorry for her mother. I didn't want to upset her, but what could I do?" Eileen said. She stopped and searched Joan's face for understanding.

"You were amazing," Joan said full of admiration.

"Let's go and have a real drink before we head home. I need it after that. Come on."

Eileen grabbed Joan by the arm as they went in search of the nearest pub and far away from the coffee shop.

Later that afternoon, Cyril anxiously waited for Linda to arrive. He couldn't believe that she had agreed to come to the party with him and now that she had, he was consumed with all that could go wrong when they arrived. He paced up and down outside the park, clutching his stomach. It did somersaults every time he thought of Linda meeting his parents. Cyril decided that it was definitely not the time to tell them about her mother's violent outburst.

Cyril groaned while remembering his conversation with Séamus. He better not go blabbing, but Cyril had the feeling he was a discrete sort of character. Thankfully he didn't touch the booze anymore, because Cyril thought that would surely set his tongue wagging. Cyril rehearsed suitable conversation topics for his parents just as Linda strolled up the road. He looked at her and thought his heart might stop as he took in the vision in front of him.

Linda wore a long sea-green dress that to all intents and purposes could have been a nightdress. Combined with her flaming red hair tumbling down her back, she would easily pass for a mermaid that had just emerged from the sea.

"Cat caught your tongue?" Linda asked.

"You look… Wow, you look amazing," Cyril stuttered.

"You don't think it's too much, do you?" Linda asked.

"*No way*. Come on. Let's go," Cyril said and grabbed her arm before his nerves took over. He knew that if he thought about it for too long, he might freeze and call the whole thing off.

"Dad can be a bit, you know, he's a bit of a messer, so don't mind him, okay," Cyril said as they walked towards his house.

"*Relax*, will you? I don't bite, you know," Linda said and laughed.

"I know, I'm talking about him," Cyril said as he stopped outside their house.

"So, this is where you live. It's so cute. I love it," Linda said, looking at the two-up two-down little house with frilly white net curtains adorning each window.

"It has way more character than our concrete block. You're so lucky," Linda said.

Cyril looked at her, wondering if she meant to slag him, but he could see by her eyes that she meant every word.

"Aw, come on Linda, you practically live in a *mansion* compared to our little house," he said.

"This looks like a proper home to me. It has way more character than our house."

Linda marched up the path to the front door and Cyril ran to catch up before she had a chance to knock on the door. Scrambling for his keys, he almost fell in the door in his hurry to make an entrance first and to assess the lay of the land.

"Well, who do we have here?" Frank asked. He turned from admiring himself in the hall mirror and pushed past Cyril.

"*Jesus, Dad, take it easy, would you?*" Cyril remarked, stumbling against the hall table.

Linda stuck out her hand to Frank.

"Lovely to meet you, Mr Hughes. Cyril has told me all about you."

"Has he now?" Frank said and squinted at Cyril. Frank gave Linda a firm handshake.

"Don't worry. All good of course," Linda said and giggled.

"Well, either way, I'm delighted to meet you, Linda. Come in for a minute before we head," Frank said and ushered her down the hall to the kitchen.

"Are you not a bit OTT?" Cyril asked and looked his father up and down.

His dark hair was lathered with Brylcreem to cast it back from his face and he sported a pinstriped suit with a bright red shirt and black tie.

"And what's wrong with dressing up for a party? You need to make a bit of an effort, isn't that right, Linda?" Frank said and turned and slicked his hair back.

"I think you look fantastic, Mr Hughes. I love the suit. You could teach my fuddy-duddy father a thing about fashion," Linda said and realised straight away that Frank was a man of style and personality.

"Now, do you hear that son? I must say, I like your girlfriend already," Frank said. Cyril blushed at the word girlfriend.

"Why don't you leave us alone to have a chat while you go up and change?" Frank said, sitting down at the table.

"Change?" Cyril looked down at his jeans and T-shirt and then at Frank and Linda.

"Jaysus, will you at least put on a shirt, and make it sharpish," Frank said and pushed him out the door.

"He spends too long under the bonnet of a car, I'm afraid," Frank said. "So, you're the lady that has him in great form these days."

"Oh, I don't know about that. He's such a gentleman, Mr Hughes," Linda said, flicking her hair back.

"Well, our Cyril has never given us a day's trouble, thanks be to God. He tells me you're going to be a designer, is that right?" Frank asked.

"Yes, I actually am a designer. I made this dress myself, my own design," Linda replied.

"By God, *did you?* I know nothin' about fashion, but that's a beautiful dress, so it is."

"I plan to have my own business one day and Cyril will have his own garage. We're both going to be very successful. I'm sure of it," Linda said with a steely look of determination on her face.

Frank couldn't help thinking that this girl might just be the one to light a fire under his eldest son.

"Jaysus, I hope you're right. You might have to give himself a kick up the arse, mind. Our Cyril is the best in the world, but if he was any more laid-back, he'd be dead," Frank said. He crossed his arms and sat back in the chair.

"You need a calm head for business, Mr Hughes, my father told me that and Cyril is definitely as cool as a cucumber, not like me. I'm the more creative type. So, we're a good match," Linda said with a glint in her eyes.

"Well, speakin' of laid-back," Frank said and glanced at the clock on the wall, "we'd better make a move, or we'll be late."

Frank went out to the bottom of the stairs and let out a roar.

"Cyril, come on, will you? It's nearly five."

"I'm awful sorry Joan's not here to meet you," Frank said, coming back into the kitchen.

"She went out to lunch and I haven't seen her since. It's not like her, mind you," Frank said and scratched his head.

"I'll meet her at the party, won't I?" Linda said. She stood up and straightened her dress.

"I hope you will, unless she has finally done a bunk on me after all these years," Frank jested. "I think I hear him, Linda. Come on. We'll make a move," Frank said, ushering her out of the kitchen.

Cyril met them at the bottom of the stairs, wearing a denim shirt and grey jeans. He ran his hands through his blonde floppy hair as it fell into his eyes.

"*Woohoo*, very handsome. Isn't he Mr Hughes?"

"A chip off the old block if I say so myself, hey son," Frank remarked and nudged him.

"Where's Mam? I hope she went easy on the booze or we'll be carrying her home," Cyril said, having been mortified after the fiasco of the Christmas drinks party.

"*Stop it*, would you? Don't mind him, Linda. Joan hardly touches a drop, only on a special occasion. I'm going to give Mary a call just in case she's down there," Frank said and picked up the phone before shouting up the stairs again. "Johnny, Abbie, we're going in a few minutes, so be ready."

"Mary, is Joan there? Grand. We're on our way," Frank said and hung up.

TWENTY ONE

"You're welcome to him, Julie," Eileen announced as she raised her glass, drained it and banged it down on the bar.

"We better go, or we'll be late," Joan said, checking her watch.

Two brandies combined with the adrenaline rush of their eventful lunch, and Eileen was feeling invincible.

"Okay, take it easy. We've loads of time."

"We don't. It's after four and everyone's arriving at five," Joan fretted as she hopped up from the bar stool and did a little dance on the spot.

"God, is that the time? I better not give Dave any opportunity to question my mothering skills," Eileen said and grimaced.

Eileen reached for her shopping bags and stood up. Coming out of the dark pub into the sunlight of the afternoon, they both squinted and burst out laughing.

"At the rate things are going, Joan, we'll probably bump into Lorna McDermott. I can just see the look on her face, Ms Goody Two Shoes."

"Oh, don't say that," Joan said, linking Eileen as she tried to steady herself.

They headed downtown towards the bridge that would take them to Mary's house, giggling as they tried to dodge all the weekend shoppers.

"God, we're some pair. You know what, I'd bet anything that her nibs was straight on to Dave moaning about his wife making a scene. He better not be at the house when we get back. I'm not in the mood for him," Eileen said, marching down the street.

"*Wait up*," Joan called.

She stumbled on a loose cobble stone as she tried to keep up with Eileen's long strides. Grabbing hold of a nearby lamp post, Joan saved herself two grazed knees.

"Sorry," Eileen said and slowed down. She fumbled in her bag as she tried to locate her phone.

"Jesus, *this bloody bag*. I can't find *anything* in it. I'll look for it once we're home," Eileen said.

"I really enjoyed this afternoon… I mean apart from the coffee shop… that was awful, but you know what I mean, sorry," Joan gushed as they continued walking.

"It was fun. To be honest, it felt good to let Julie have it. I'm done with being a doormat, especially with other women," Eileen said. Joan was tempted to say that the last thing Eileen could be described as was a doormat.

"Great, no sign of a car. Looks like we're in the clear," Eileen said and pushed open the front gate. "Best behaviour now, Joan. God, we're like a pair of teenagers," Eileen said as she put her key in the door and Joan jigged on the steps beside her.

"I need to use the bathroom," Joan said.

"Top of the stairs," Eileen pointed and hung her coat on the banisters.

"Thanks."

Mary opened the kitchen door just as Eileen was checking herself in the mirror.

"Did you have a good time? It sounds like it from the racket," Mary said and laughed.

"We did. Sorry we're a bit late," Eileen said.

"No need to apologise. You just missed Dave. He wanted to talk to you."

"*What?*" Eileen asked.

"I told him you had an appointment in town. I didn't think you'd want to see him today?"

"Definitely not. Not after the lunch we had," Eileen whispered, and she walked into the kitchen.

"Did something happen?"

"You could say that. Are the girls okay?"

"Of course, they are," Mary said. She pointed towards their adopted playroom where loud squeals of laughter emanated from behind the closed door. "They had a good time Eileen, don't be worrying. Their Dad even came in and set up some computer game he bought Sophie."

"*What*, he came in? I'm sorry that he barged into your house, Mary. He had no business doing that," Eileen fumed. "What sort of a mood was he in, by the way?"

"To be honest, Eileen, I've never met the man in my life so I've no idea about his moods. He was very polite, but he did seem a bit preoccupied. He wanted to know when you would be back," Mary said.

"I'm sorry to drag you into the middle of this. I really am. He shouldn't be traipsing through your house. I'll have a word with him," Eileen said.

"There is no need to apologise, Eileen. He was totally courteous and as long as things stay like that, I'm happy. I draw the line at any scenes or shouting in the house, so if there's peace you won't hear a word from me. Now, let's enjoy the evening," Mary said.

They were interrupted by the phone and Mary went to pick up her mobile as Joan arrived into the kitchen.

"Hello, there's nothing to worry about, Frank. Yes, she's here and looking…" Mary said, looked at Joan and almost did a double take, "fabulous… Talk to you later. Bye." Mary hung up the phone.

Joan blushed at another compliment.

"Is it okay if I change here, Mary?" Joan asked, holding up her bulging shopping bags. "We had a busy day."

"Of course. That must have been *some lunch* from the looks of it. I'd say there were a few tipples involved," Mary said and laughed.

"Only a couple. They were medicinal. Isn't that right?" Eileen asked and Joan nodded. Joan's body shook with laughter.

"Now, I'm going to catch up with the girls," Eileen said and followed the noise into the playroom.

"Use my room, Joan. It's at the end of the landing, facing you," Mary said. They were interrupted by the shrill ring of the doorbell. "That couldn't be Séamus. It's too early," Mary said.

"Do you want me to answer it?" Joan asked.

"No, it's fine. How do I look?" Mary asked and patted down her hair.

"You look lovely," Joan said. "He obviously can't wait to see the birthday girl."

"Aw, stop it would you? He's a gentleman and gentlemen arrive on time, or early it seems," Mary said.

Mary waved Joan away and hurried to open the front door. Séamus stood on the doorstep with a wide grin on his face and before Mary had time to say anything, he thrust an envelope into her hands.

"Happy Birthday, Mary."

"Oh, thank you, Séamus. Come on in. I'll open it later if you don't mind, when things have calmed down a bit," Mary said and gestured towards the noise coming from the back of the house.

"Hi, Séamus," Joan said and darted past him and up the stairs with her shopping bags.

"Oh, hi Joan."

Joan found Mary's room at the end of the hall and pushing the door open, she almost felt like an intruder as she entered her private space. Joan's senses were assaulted by a room that looked and smelled alive. Joan's eyes were straight away drawn to a colourful tapestry hanging on the wall above Mary's bed. Joan was transfixed by it. She moved closer, unable to resist the vibrant creation. Inspecting it closely, Joan was amazed by its intricacy and the innumerable threads that weaved in and out, colliding with each other, separating, all of them ultimately on their own path, but also part of something bigger that they were unaware of. Joan struggled to decipher the image and slowly moved away from it. With each step Joan took, the picture started to come into focus and when she stood with her back to the opposite wall, Joan saw the image of a beautiful oak tree. There was a small inscription at the bottom of the tapestry and Joan moved closer again to read it.

"The Tree of Life. We are all one," Joan read.

Joan shivered as the words resonated deeply. She knew it was no accident that on this very day she was standing in Mary O'Sullivan's bedroom, looking at the tapestry on the wall, a tapestry that only existed because of the presence of each individual thread.

Joan realised she was one of those threads as were each of the guests who mingled easily together downstairs. They all made up the tapestry of her life. Joan wasn't alone. She had never really been alone. On hearing her name being called, Joan reluctantly dragged herself away from the image and quickly emptied out her shopping bags.

"Coming!" Joan called.

Joan slipped on the pale pink dress, embroidered with small flowers that perfectly complemented her blonde hair. Then she stepped into the strappy sandals that were higher than anything she had ever worn. Emboldened by the earlier couple of brandies, she looked in the mirror, then glancing back at the tapestry, Joan smiled and with a renewed sense of purpose, she left the room. Judging by the noise downstairs, the party was in full swing and it wasn't long before Joan recognised Frank's bellowing voice coming from the kitchen.

"Well, aren't you the picture?" Séamus said as Joan slipped into the small kitchen that was now bursting at the seams.

"Thanks," Joan said meekly.

She was almost immune to all the compliments and the noise. Joan looked around the room and felt giddy as she took in the colourful scene. Eileen was helping Mary put the finishing touches to a table that was laden down with food. Frank was deep in conversation with a striking looking red head. Johnny sat quietly at the kitchen table sipping on a coke, and there were shrieks of laughter coming from the playroom. It was as if a dark cloud had lifted and Joan saw them clearly for the very first time.

"Are you okay, Joan?" Séamus asked.

"Yes, yes, it's lovely to see everyone together, isn't it?"

"It is. It sure is," Séamus said.

"You know, you and Mary would make a great couple," Joan announced confidently.

Even though it was Frank's bright idea to introduce them, Joan had rewritten history in her head, so that she was now the instigator of the romance.

"Heck, you're the right matchmaker," Séamus remarked and laughed, but he couldn't have agreed with her more. "You look a million dollars, Joan. Frank's a lucky man."

"Well, *look who it is?* You're lookin' gorgeous, love. You look like a film star. Don't you be gettin' any ideas, Séamus. She's mine," Frank said and joined them.

"And if it isn't Don Corleone himself," Séamus responded.

"I'm afraid I'm feeling very underdressed," Séamus said and looked around the room.

He wore his signature brown cords and a denim shirt, but he had added a touch of colour with a red silk scarf that hung loosely around his neck. Mary thought it gave him a touch of panache. She found it hard to take her eyes off Séamus. It didn't matter what he wore, to her Seamus always stood out in a crowd.

"Mary, you look awesome," Séamus said, moving towards her.

He hadn't looked at her properly until now and he loved that she had left her hair loose which, combined with her colourful wardrobe, gave her an easy-going, bohemian look. Then out of the corner of his eye, Séamus thought he spotted a familiar face, a face that he had never imagined he would ever see again. He had his suspicions after Friday night, but he still did a double take when they locked eyes. They were both transported back to that day by the river.

Eileen, also having had her suspicions from conversations with Mary had time to prepare herself and held out her hand to Séamus. "Séamus, isn't it?" Eileen asked. "This man was my saviour last week. He was a very good Samaritan and came to my aid when I badly needed it. I never thought I'd have a chance to thank you again in person," Eileen said. Séamus took her outstretched hand.

"It's lovely to see you again too. I'm so glad that you seem to be doing so well."

Eileen looked a far cry from the heartbroken woman he remembered only a few days earlier.

"How in the name of God do you two know each other?" Frank asked, moving towards them.

"It's a long story and a chance meeting," Séamus said. "Isn't that right, Eileen?" he asked, and Eileen nodded.

"Mam, you haven't met Linda. Linda, Mam," Cyril said and clenched his jaw, hoping Joan would keep it together.

Frank stayed close, ready to give her a nudge if she didn't.

"Hello, Linda, lovely to meet you. That's a beautiful dress you're wearing," Joan said.

"It's lovely to meet you too, Mrs Hughes. Cyril has told me all about you and can't stop singing your praises," Linda said, and Joan looked at Cyril who winked at her.

Trust her eldest son to be as full of charm as ever. Linda did seem like a nice girl though, not at all like her mother Lorna, and she definitely looked nothing like her.

"Come on, everyone. Time for food. Please take a plate and help yourself," Mary said and pointed at the feast on the table. "We'll eat in the front room."

Although it was a bit cramped, they all took turns to fill their plates from the buffet and then squeezed around the dining table in Mary's front room. It was a wedding present that had served more as a filing cabinet of sorts for many years, and she couldn't remember when she had last set the table for a get-together.

"Look at the candles, Mum," Sophie said, her eyes twinkling with delight.

"You're some woman for one woman, Mary, that's for sure," Frank said.

Frank then proceeded to direct the seating arrangements. Séamus was seated next to Johnny, Joan was kept well away from Linda and the two birthday girls were seated at each end of the table. The wine flowed for those partaking and to anyone who might have eavesdropped on the occasion, they looked like any extended family that had been recently reunited. Mary looked around the table and delighted at the sight of a full house.

"How's your friend doing? I hear he'll be right as rain in no time," Séamus said to Johnny.

"He's okay, I think. He'll be home in a few days," Johnny mumbled flicking his hair out of his face.

"That's swell."

"I'd a lucky break," Johnny said.

"And why would you say that? It wasn't your fault he fell," Séamus said.

"Maybe not, but I didn't help things," Johnny said glumly.

"Well if that's the case, you're getting a second chance, so you better make the most of it. I've been there. Trust me, if I managed to turn things around you can too. Do you hear me?"

Johnny stirred in his seat as he felt a faint glimmer of hope.

"Why don't you call over to me one of the days? We'll have a chat. No pressure, but I'm telling you, we all have a talent for something. If I figured it out, anyone can."

Frank looked down the table, relieved to see Johnny talking. If anyone could reach Johnny, he thought Séamus could.

"I will. Thanks, Séamus," Johnny said.

Cyril watched Linda closely, hoping that she was enjoying herself.
"So, what do you think? Do you like them?" Cyril asked.

"They're a blast, Cyril. Why didn't you tell me your family were so much fun?"

"*Fun?* I'd *never* have used the word fun to describe them, crazy maybe but fun, never."

"You're hilarious," Linda said and squeezed his knee under the table.

"It's great we live so close now," Abbie said to Sophie who was in her element at the top of the table.

"Wouldn't it be great if you lived here forever? We could see each other all the time."

"I know, but I think we're moving back in with my Dad once we find a new house. I hope so anyway… but I think there is something more going on," Sophie said.

"A toast to the birthday girls!" Frank announced.

Frank stood up to do the honours. They all raised their glasses and then Eileen slipped out to the kitchen and with the help of Cyril, reappeared with candles lighting on two birthday cakes. The two recipients might have been about sixty years apart in age, but tonight age didn't come into it.

"Make a wish, ladies," Frank said.

Sophie closed her eyes and fervently wished for her family to be together again. Mary looked around the table and wished that all these wonderful people would continue to be a part of her life, and Mary and Sophie blew out the candles.

As slices of cake did the rounds and everyone cheered, they were interrupted by the sound of the doorbell ringing persistently.

"Who could that be at this hour? I never have any visitors," Mary said, startled.

"Do you want me to answer it?" Eileen asked and jumped up.

Eileen had a foreboding feeling that it was for her and exchanging glances with Mary, they both came to the same conclusion. Eileen went out to the hall, closing the living room door behind her.

"Come on, Frank. Visitors always have to do a party piece in this house," Mary said, hoping to drown out any conversation at the door.

Eileen took a quick glance in the mirror, rubbed her teeth to remove any stain of red wine, took a deep breath and then opened the door.

"What are you doing here?" Eileen asked, prompted by Dave's red, angry face staring back at her.

"I've been ringing that doorbell *for ages. What the hell is going on inside?*"

Eileen quickly closed the front door behind her and nudged Dave away from the house and out onto the street.

"What's going on, Dave? You've had the girls with you all day and we're just having a little party. I'm entitled to celebrate my daughter's birthday too, you know. Do you want to go and upset them, today of all days?" Eileen said, struggling to keep her voice calm.

"No, of course I don't, but I've been trying to contact you all afternoon and left you messages. If you weren't going to return them, I had no choice but to call."

"*What could be so urgent?*" Eileen asked.

"Aw, come on, get a grip. Lunch today? *Totally humiliating Julie and her mother in public?* I mean, Eileen, you of all people, what possessed you? What good could it do?" Dave angered.

Eileen grabbed his arm and pulled him further down the road out of earshot of the house.

"Will you *keep your voice down for God's sake? Do you want everyone to hear you?*"

"You must be joking. That didn't seem to bother you when you made a fool of yourself in public today, embarrassing an older woman who has *nothing to do with this, as well as making a spectacle of yourself. I thought we were going to do this respectfully*," Dave said.

"*Respectfully?* You're one to talk," Eileen said sharply. She felt a ferocious rush of anger that was fuelled by the alcohol she had drank earlier.

"You have a nerve, Dave. I'm out having lunch with a friend and in comes your *dolly bird*, smiling away with her mother, as if she is as pure as the driven snow. *Do you know how humiliating that was? Do you?* No of course, you don't, you asshole."

"I'm sorry. It's just that she was calling me all afternoon. She was in a state. I was afraid the girls might guess that something was going on," Dave tried to explain.

"You know, I actually had been thinking that for the sake of the girls I should give it another chance, but tonight you have helped me finally see the light," Eileen said.

"Please, Eileen," Dave begged.

"I've a party to go back to," Eileen said and walked away from Dave without once looking back.

Eventually hearing Dave's footsteps recede down the road in the opposite direction, Eileen stopped and sat on the steps of a nearby house. Without the fight, there was only the large black chasm of grief that engulfed her again. They should have been celebrating Sophie's birthday together. Realising she had secretly harboured hopes that they might actually come through this, Eileen now knew it was over. There was probably no going back.

****

"I'll give you a hand with the dishes," Séamus said and was on his feet when he saw Mary heading for the kitchen.

"I'll make sure you're not disturbed," Frank said and winked as Séamus passed him on the way out the door.

Séamus went into the kitchen and started filling the dishwasher as Mary piled up the plates beside him.

"I'm forgetting my manners. I haven't even opened your card yet. Sorry, there's just been so much going on," Mary said and reached for the envelope that she had placed on the windowsill.

Mary eagerly tore off the wrapping paper. Séamus watched her and his face creased with a smile as he saw her reaction.

"Oh, that's *so* generous. Thank you, Séamus. I love it. It's just what I need to get back to my singing, though God knows how I'll find time with all these new people in my life."

"It's just when you mentioned Sean Nós singing, I thought of my friend, Padraig Ó Riain. He's a great teacher."

"I love it, Séamus, really."

Without thinking, Mary put her arms around him and gave him a warm hug.

"Sorry, I didn't mean to… I mean, I shouldn't have," Mary said, realising it was the first time they had embraced.

"Don't be silly. It's me who should be thanking you… I wanted to ask you…" Séamus said and paused.

"Yes, go on," Mary urged.

"You know I've been on vacation since I came home," Séamus said.

"Yes."

"Well, it has been the best break I've ever had…" Séamus said shyly. "To be honest, I've settled back so well that I'm not sure I want to do a lot more touring, but there is a gig I've committed to in the new year, around Europe for a few weeks."

"Okay," Mary said, unsure what would be said next.

"It could be fun, you know, seeing lots of cities. There'll be plenty of time off," Séamus said and hesitated.

"And?" Mary asked.

"Will you come with me?"

"Yes, *of course I'll come*," Mary said before he had the words out.

"*You will?* You'll come with me on the tour. *Seriously?*"

"Didn't I say I would? I haven't been outside the country in years and I can't think of a nicer travelling companion," Mary said.

Séamus gently held her and they kissed.

Frank kept an eye on the door and wouldn't let anyone step outside the living room, not even for a toilet break.

"Frank, I'm worried about Eileen. She's been gone for ages. I think it was her husband at the door. Do you think I should go after her?" Joan asked, lifting the curtain.

"Aw, Joan. Stop with the Peeping Tom act. Will you give them a bit of privacy and come back to the party?" Frank asked and pulled Joan away from the window.

"You don't understand, Frank. Something happened at lunch today. Look, trust me, I know what I'm doing," Joan said and grabbed her jacket.

"I'm just sayin'. You know what you're like when you've had a few drinks," Frank said, following her out to the hall.

"Would you *stop fussing*, Frank? I only had one glass of wine with the meal. *I'm not a drunk*, you know. Now, *I need to go and check on my friend*," Joan said and opened the door.

"*Who are you* and *what* did you do with my wife?" Frank asked, stupefied as he watched her walking down the path.

Joan looked up and down the road but couldn't see Eileen anywhere. She had almost expected to hear a full-scale argument, but the only sound was the soothing clink of boats on the river across the road. She walked briskly in the direction of town, not sure why she had chosen this direction, when she spotted a person sitting by the water, sobbing her eyes out.

"Eileen, is that you? What is it? Did something happen?" Joan asked and sat down beside her. "What happened? It was Dave, wasn't it?"

"Yes. It's over, Joan. It's really over. I know I've said this already, but it's really sunk in tonight."

"I'm sorry. I truly am," Joan said, not knowing what else to say.

"I'm not. Do you know why he was here? Because of his precious Julie. He wasn't concerned about me. *Poor Julie* was upset, and her mother was. That's what he came here to tell me. I'm supposed to be his wife and he's more concerned about *that trollop*."

"Well, I suppose, at least now you know. It might help you to move on. You deserve so much better than him," Joan said and squeezed her hand.

"I know, but it still hurts. I've been with him for fifteen years, almost half my life. All of our dreams are smashed to pieces. I know he's an asshole, but we had good times and the girls. Now, I've to start all over again… on my own."

"Please, don't say that. Didn't you see everyone at the party tonight? The last thing you are is alone," Joan said.

For the first time in her life, Joan knew she actually meant it when she said those words.

"I'll be back in a minute," Cyril said, spotting his Dad in the hall.

Linda and Johnny hardly noticed him leave. Johnny hung on every word from Linda's mouth. She had been regaling them both with plans for her business.

"Dad, can I've a word?" Cyril asked and glanced back to the living room. Linda was so engrossed in her conversation with Johnny, he doubted she had even noticed he wasn't there.

"Is it about Linda? I can tell you for nothin', you have my blessing and your mother's," Frank said and slapped Cyril on the back. "I'll have to start practising my speech."

"*Stop it, Dad, I'm being serious*. Promise me you won't say anything. Linda won't speak to me again if she knows I've told you," Cyril said.

Cyril looked into the living room again to make sure Linda couldn't hear them.

"*Jaysus,* well we can't have that. What is it?" Frank asked and pulled him away from the door.

"Well, I was over in Linda's house last Friday night and her parents were out. We weren't doing anything, just on the laptop in her room. Anyways, her mother knocked on the door when they got home and I had to hide," Cyril confided.

"Right," Frank said, trying to appear non-judgemental.

"Then… her Mam came into the room and… I heard her hit Linda. She slapped her across the face, Dad, and it's not the first time. Linda won't talk about it. I don't know what to do, but I can't just pretend like nothing happened," Cyril's words tumbled out.

"*Chrissakes.* You're havin' me on. *Her mother hits her? Jaysus*, that's not on *at all.* I'll talk to her or better still, I'll get the authorities on it," Frank said.

"*No, Dad. Please* don't say anything. I've tried to bring it up, but she said she'll finish with me if I don't let it go. I was going to talk to her father. He comes in the garage, but Séamus said I shouldn't," Cyril said.

"*Séamus* knows?" Frank remarked a bit taken aback.

"*I had to tell someone.* You and Mam had all that drama with Jack going on and the hospital. I just bumped into Séamus on the street, that's all. *Please* don't say anything to her tonight. *Do you hear me?* It'll be over between us if you do," Cyril pleaded.

"You have my word, but we have to do somethin'. A *bloody disgrace* it is. Her mother will not get away with this, no siree. She will not get away with this."

Joan opened the front door and seeing the living room door shut, she beckoned Eileen that the coast was clear.

"Come down to the kitchen when you're ready. We'll have a drink before going back to the others.

"Thanks, you're a lifesaver, Joan," Eileen said and tiptoed up the stairs to freshen up.

When Eileen was out of earshot, Joan went into the living room and waved at Frank to come out to the hall.

"What's with *all* the cloak and dagger? You're turnin' into a right Ms Marple, so you are. It's very sexy you know," Frank said and grabbed Joan round the waist.

"Will you stop it, Frank. It's not funny," Joan said and pushed him away.

"*Eileen's* a bit upset. She's gone upstairs, but will you give us a few minutes alone in the kitchen when she comes down? We'll have a drink with Mary and then we'll come in and join you. Okay?"

"I think there's someone in there with…" Frank said.

"I don't have time now, Frank" Joan said and walked down the hall.

"I was only goin' to say that Séamus was havin' a moment with…" Suddenly, Joan startled when she found Séamus and Mary embracing by the sink.

"Oh, I'm so sorry…" Joan stuttered and backed out of the room.

"Not at all. I was on my way back in anyways," Séamus said, seeing the worried look on Joan's face.

Séamus gave Mary a wink before he left the room. Nothing could dim his happiness at that moment.

"What's going on, Joan? You look like you've seen a ghost," Mary said.

"Before Eileen comes back down," Joan said and glanced furtively out into the hall before closing the door. "I just want to tell you she's had a rough day and that was Dave at the door. They had an awful fight and she was very upset. I think everything has finally hit her and it's hit her hard. I thought the three of us might have a drink together in here, you know, give her a bit of time to recover. You'll know what to say, Mary, I'm no good at things like this," Joan said and collapsed on a chair.

"I'd say you're doing just fine. You're way too hard on yourself," Mary said.

Mary walked over to the cabinet and paused at her best crystal glasses that were saved for special occasions.

"Yes, you're right. It's time we girls finally had a drink together," Mary said.

Mary reached up and took the glasses from the shelf. She dusted them with a tea towel and poured three generous glasses of sherry as they waited for Eileen to come back downstairs.

"Sorry for lowering the tone, but I had to change out of those clothes and have a shower. I'm feeling a bit better now," Eileen said, entering the kitchen.

"Thanks, Joan," Eileen said, and sat down.

Eileen had scrubbed her face clean and her rosy complexion was like that of a teenager. She was wearing a tracksuit and had swapped her high heels for a comfortable pair of slippers.

"How are you doing, Eileen? It seems like you've had some day. I'm sure Joan said this to you already, but you're not alone. You have us. Isn't that right, Joan?" Mary asked. Joan nodded.

"I don't know what I'd have done if you weren't here. I'm so grateful I met you both, I really am," Eileen said and smiled at the two women who sat on either side of her.

Tears filled Joan's eyes again, but they were happy tears, borne out of the warmth of friendship.

"I'm the one who should be grateful. Look at me, an old woman of seventy and I have two young and beautiful women as my friends… I've some exciting news to share with you," Mary said.

"You're getting married?" Joan asked with delight. This caused Eileen to laugh.

"*Not that again.* No, I'm not getting married, but I'm going on a trip in the new year," Mary said.

"With Séamus!" Eileen and Joan shouted in unison. They were both delighted to see Mary so happy. Considering what they knew about her lonely existence for the last number of years, they thought it high time that she had some fun in her life.

"Yes. He's asked me to go with him on a tour he's doing in Europe in February. Just for a few weeks or maybe a month. *Isn't that exciting?* I said yes, just in case you're wondering," Mary said and crossed her arms proudly.

"That's amazing, Mary. You deserve it, you know. It's about time you enjoyed yourself," Joan gushed.

"And if it suits you, Eileen, you could look after the house for me while I'm gone. You'll still be here then, won't you? There's no rush on you getting another place for a while," Mary said.

"Thanks. That would be fantastic. Good for you… You know he was my knight in shining armour the day I found out about Dave," Eileen said and smiled broadly.

"Plenty more fish in the sea for you, I've no doubt," Mary said and patted Eileen's arm.

"I don't want to see another man for as long as I live. No offence ladies, Frank and Séamus are great, but I'm done with them."

"Aw, go away outta that. All you need is some time to regroup and you'll be back on the horse again," Mary said. Eileen and Joan laughed.

"Don't laugh. I'm right. And you know you could start getting some clients while you're here, put up a few notices around town," Mary said.

"Good idea, but…"

"But *what?*" Mary asked.

"There is something else I have to do first," Eileen said and looked around before continuing.

"I'm reporting Fran Daly. It's not going to be easy, but I can't in all good conscience do nothing. It's going to be tough, but I *have* to start as I mean to go on," Eileen said.

"Good for you. We'll help in any way we can," Mary said. "And you, Joan. Any plans? You're a natural with people, you know. You've just needed a bit of confidence. Look at how you've helped us all these last few weeks," Mary said.

"Oh, I don't know about that," Joan said. "I think I might go back to my counsellor and I really want to get off these tablets. I'm sick of them, even if I have to have a fight with my doctor," Joan said.

Joan looked down, feeling embarrassed at the admission.

"Sounds like you should change doctor while you're at it," Eileen said.

"Maybe, you're right. Things are going a bit better with Johnny too, so I'm going to work on that," Joan said.

"That's the attitude. It looks like we three are only getting started," Mary said and raised her glass for a toast, and they clinked glasses again.

"Did anything catch your eye in my room, by any chance?" Mary asked, noticing the new light in Joan's eyes.

"That sounds very mysterious altogether," Eileen said and laughed.

"Actually, yes. That tapestry above your bed? It's… it's so beautiful, so true, isn't it?" Joan remarked.

"It is, Joan. Do you know that it was given to me by an old friend after Tom died? She's dead now too, unfortunately. She brought it back from India for me. Cait Malone…" Mary said and sighed.

"She was a great friend, she really was," Mary said.

"I'm intrigued. What's so special about it?" Eileen asked.

"You just have to see it, Eileen. It's stunning," Joan said.

"I'll give you Cait's take on it. I can't do justice to her explanation, but I'll do my best," Mary said.

"We're all ears, Mary," Eileen said and sat up in the chair.

"Well, the old Indian lady who sold it to Cait told her that the tapestry basically summed up life. Each of us is a single thread in the tapestry. As we move through life, like the thread in the tapestry, we touch other people and they touch us and so it continues," Mary said and left her glass down on the table.

"All of us are part of something bigger. If we don't live our lives fully, we deprive others of what we have to contribute, you know, of having an impact on them and them on us. Each of us is needed to make the tapestry complete. It's a beautiful message," Mary said.

The three women went quiet as they each contemplated the message of the tapestry for their own lives. Then they smiled at each other and nodded in agreement. In only a short couple of weeks, they had already had a profound impact on each other. None of them had seen that coming.

Just then the door opened, and Abbie burst in on top of them.

"This is like the best party *ever*. Thanks, Mary," Abbie said, beaming, and they all laughed.

"What's so funny?" Abbie asked, leaning into Mary who put her arm around her.

"Life, dear Abbie," Mary said.

"What do you mean?" Abbie asked.

"I mean that I'd be lost without you all. You're a great gift to me and have brought me back to life," Mary remarked.

"I think we'd all be lost without each other, don't you?" Eileen added.

The room went silent and Joan's thoughts went again to the tapestry in Mary's bedroom.

"I'm glad then that I fell down the stairs," Abbie said with conviction.

The four generations of women laughed, and the happy sound of life reverberated throughout the house.